Reginald Hill

Reginald Hill is a native of Cumbria and a former resident of Yorkshire, the setting for his outstanding crime novels, featuring Dalziel and Pascoe, 'the best detective duo on the scene bar none' (*Daily Telegraph*). His writing career began with the publication of *A Clubbable Woman* (1970), which introduced Chief Superintendent Andy Dalziel and DS Peter Pascoe. Their subsequent appearances have confirmed Hill's position as 'the best living male crime writer in the English-speaking world' (*Independent*) and won numerous awards, including the Crime Writers' Association Cartier Diamond Dagger for his lifetime contribution to the genre.

The Dalziel and Pascoe novels have now been adapted into a hugely successful BBC television series, starring Warren Clarke and Colin Buchanan.

Visit www.AuthorTracker.co.uk
for exclusive information on Reginald Hill

By the same author

REGINALD HILL

A CURE FOR ALL
DISEASES

A NOVEL
in six volumes

HARPER

Harper
An imprint of HarperCollins*Publishers*
77–85 Fulham Palace Road,
Hammersmith, London W6 8JB

www.harpercollins.co.uk

This paperback edition 2009

First published in Great Britain
by HarperCollins*Publishers* 2008

A catalogue record for this book is
available from the British Library

ISBN-13: 978-0-00-725269-5

Set in Meridien by Palimpsest Book Production Ltd
Grangemouth, Stirlingshire

Printed and bound in Great Britain by
Clays Ltd, St Ives plc

Mixed Sources
Product group from well-managed
forests and other controlled sources
www.fsc.org   Cert no. SW-COC-1806
© 1996 Forest Stewardship Council

To Janeites everywhere

and in particular to those who ten years ago in San Francisco made me so very welcome at the Jane Austen Society of North America's AGM, of which the theme was *Sanditon – a new direction?*, and during which the seeds of this present novel were sown. I hope that my fellow Janeites will approve the direction in which I have moved her unfinished story; or, if they hesitate approval, that they will perhaps recall the advice printed on a sweat shirt presented to me (with what pertinence I never quite grasped) after my talk to the AGM

– run mad as often as you chuse, but do not faint –

and at least agree that though in places I may have run a little mad, so far I have not fainted!

The Sea air & Sea Bathing together were nearly
infallible, one or the other of them being a match
for every Disorder, of the Stomach, the Lungs or the
Blood; They were anti-spasmodic, anti-pulmonary,
anti-sceptic, anti-bilious & anti-rheumatic.
Nobody could catch cold by the Sea, Nobody
wanted appetite by the Sea, Nobody wanted
Spirits, Nobody wanted strength. – They were
healing, softening, relaxing – fortifying & bracing
– seemingly just as was wanted – sometimes one,
sometimes the other.

Jane Austen, *Sanditon*

Then Sir Bedivere cried: Ah my lord Arthur, what
shall become of me, now ye go from me and leave
me here alone among mine enemies? Comfort
thyself, said the king, and do as well as thou
mayst, for in me is no trust to trust in; for I will
into the vale of Avilion to heal me of my grievous
wound: and if thou hear never more of me, pray
for my soul.

Sir Thomas Malory, *Le Morte d'Arthur*

We all labour against our own cure, for death is
the cure of all diseases.

Sir Thomas Browne, *Religio Medici*

Volume the First

Every Neighbourhood should have a great Lady.

1

FROM: charley@whiffle.com
TO: cassie@natterjack.com
SUBJECT: cracked jugs – daft buggers – & tank traps

Hi Cass!

Hows things in darkest Africa? Wierd & wonderful – I bet – but not so w&w as what weve got here at Willingden Farm. Go on – guess! OK – give up?

House-guests!

& I dont mean awful Uncle Ernie on one of his famous surprise visits. These are *strangers!*

What happened – at last after our awful wet summer Augusts turned hot – not African hot but pretty steamy by Yorkshire standards. Dad & George were working up in Mill Meadow. Mum asked if Id take them a jug of lemon barley – said it would please dad if I *showed willing.* Weve been in armed truce since I made it clear my plans hadnt changed – ie do a postgrad thesis instead of getting a paid job – or better still – a wellpaid husband – & *settling down!* But no reason not to *show willing* – plus it gave me an excuse to drive the quad – so off I went.

Forgot the mugs – but dad didnt say anything – just drank straight out of the jug like he preferred it – so maybe mum was right & he was pleased. In fact we were having a pleasant chat when suddenly old Fang let out a

3

growl. Lost half his teeth & cant keep up with the sheep any more – but still manages a grand growl. Dad looked round to see what had woken him – & his face went into Headbanger configuration.

– whats yon daft bugger playing at? – he demanded.

Youll recall that in dads demography anyone living outside Willingden parish is a *daft bugger* till proved innocent. In this case I half agreed with him.

The DB in question was driving his car fast up the lane alongside Mill Meadow. How he got through the gate I dont know. The HB had to take his chain & lock off after the Ramblers took him to court last year – but hes fixed a catch like one of them old metal puzzles we used to play with as kids. Maybe the DB just got lucky – he thought!

He was driving one of these new hybrid 4x4s – you know – conscience without inconvenience! – & when he saw how good the surface was – (*tractor tyres dont grow on trees!* – remember?) – he mustve thought – great! – now for a bit of safe off-roading.

What he didnt reckon on was what George calls *dads tank trap* – the drainage ditch where the lane bends beyond the top gate & steepens up to the mill ruin.

New tourist map came out last year – with *water mill* marked – no mention of *ruin*. Result – a lot of DBs decided this meant Heritage Centre – guided tours & cream teas! After losing out to the Ramblers – dad was forced to accept 'bearded wierdies' trekking across his empire – but the sight of cars crawling up his lane drove him crazy. So one day he got to work with the digger – & when hed finished – the drainage ditch extended across the lane – a muddy hollow a hippo could wallow in – the *tank trap!*

Most drivers flee at the sight of it – but this DB obviously thought his hybrid could ford rivers & climb Alps – & just kept going.

4

Bad decision.

For 30 secs the wheels sent out glutinous brown jets –
like a cow with colic – then the car slipped slowly sideways – finishing at 45 degrees – driver side down.

– now hell expect us to pull him out – said the HB with
some satisfaction.

Moment later the passenger door was flung back. First
thing out was a floppy brimmed sun hat – sort posh lady
gardeners wear in the old Miss Marple movies. Beneath it
was a woman who started to drag herself out – followed
by a scream from below – suggesting shed stood on
some bit of the driver not meant to be stood on.

She looked around in search of help – & there we
were – me – dad – George – & Fang – staring back at
her from 50 yds.

– help! – she called – please – can you help me? –

George & me looked at the HB – G because he knows
his place – me because I was curious what hed do.

If it had been a man I doubt hed have moved – not
without serious negotiation. But this was a woman doing
what women ought to do – calling for male assistance.

– reckon wed best take a look – he said – *we*
meaning him & George – of course.

He drained the lemon barley – thrust the jug into my
hands like I was a docile milkmaid – & set off towards the
accident – G close behind – even old Fang got to go.

I dropped the jug on to the grass. Sods Law – hit a
stone & cracked. – O shit! – I said. It was that old
earthenware one thats been around forever. I knew the
HB would reckon bringing out the lemon barley in
anything else would be like serving communion wine
from a jam jar. O well – from now on hell have to make
do with a plastic bottle!

I set off after them. This was the first mildly interesting

thing to happen since I came home – & I wasnt going to miss it.

Woman was thin & wispy – bonnet askew – big straw shoulder bag round her neck like a horses feed sack. She looked so worried I thought the driver must be seriously injured – but now I know its just a couple of notches up from her normal expression of unfocused anxiety. Another thing I noticed – words sprayed on the car door – pro job – elegant cursive script –

Sandytown – Home of the Healthy Holiday.

She was saying – please can you get my husband out? I think hes hurt himself –

– no – Im fine – came a mans voice – really – just a sprain – nothing in the world to worry about dear – *aargh*! –

As he spoke his head had appeared at his wifes waist level. Gingery hair – soft brown eyes in a narrow mobile face – not bad looking even with a bloodied nose & a footprint across his left cheek – mid to late 30s. He was trying a social smile – till presumably he put more weight on his ankle than it could take.

George jumped up on the side of the vehicle – hooked his hands under the womans armpits – & swung her clear of the muddy sump into dads arms. At 18 – G makes Arnie Schwarzenegger look like a hobbit! On our skiing trip last December – (yeah that one – when I hooked up with lousy Liam) – I could have rented G out to my mates by the hour. In fact – if you count free rounds of *gluhwein* as rental – thats exactly what I did!

The injured man came next & the HB passed the woman on to me – looking relieved to be rid of her. Thought of making some crack about him preferring men – he still thinks gays should be treated surgically – but decided not time or place.

6

– youre so kind – many thanks – Ill be fine in a minute
– Mary my dear are you all right? – burbled the man.

She said – Oh yes. But your nose dear – its
bleeding –

– its nothing – must have banged the wheel when we
stopped – he said – rubbing at a mark across his bridge.

Looked very like a footprint to me. I gave him a plus
for diplomacy. Made a change from dads Old Testament
determination to track all bad shit back to females.

The DB now decided to introduce himself. Unfortunately
this involved twisting out of the HBs grip to offer his hand
with the inevitable result to his ankle.

– Tom Parker – he said – my wife Mary – *aargh!* –

Another plus – in dads eyes anyway. Had to be
English – first thing they taught us in psych school was
only the English risk pain for the sake of politeness.

– let me have a look – I said – set him down there
dad –

Dad obeyed. Must be a first!

– my daughters had St John Ambulance training – he
said proudly. Touched me for a moment to hear him bragging about me – then he spoilt it by dragging you into it!

– when she wanted to go to college – he went on – I
told her she ought to sign up for training as a nurse like
her sister Cassie – but of course it was like banging my
head against a brick wall –

1st time the famous phrase had cropped up in a week.
Found Id been missing it!

I said – ignore my father. When he dies were going to
build him a headstone out of cracked bricks. Now lets get
that shoe off while we can –

The DB winced as I removed his shoe & sock – then
regarded his enlarged ankle with a kind of complacent
pride. I was about to offer my not very expert opinion

when he forestalled me – addressing his wife – something like this.

– look Mary – some typical subcutaneous swelling – the beginnings of what will doubtless be an extensive ecchymosis – tarsal movement restricted but still possible with moderate to acute pain – a strain I would say – certainly no worse than a sprain. Thank heaven I have always mended quickly. What a laugh they will have at home when they ask how I hurt myself – & we tell them I did it looking for a healer! –

This odd bit of self-diagnosis – with its odder conclusion – confirmed dads suspicion he was dealing with a particularly daft DB – & he burst out – what the hell were you playing at? This is a country lane not a public race track! –

Parker replied – youre right of course. But I didnt anticipate even someone as unworldly as a healer would let his driveway fall into such bad repair –

– its worse than bad – its dangerous! – chimed in his wife – The man should be taken to court for letting it get into that condition. How does he expect people to get anywhere near his house? –

& George put his large foot in it by saying with a grin – aye – theres not many get past dads tank trap –

The woman looked at him suspiciously – while dad gave him one of his shut-your-gob glares – then changed the subject by demanding – house? – What house? –

– Mr Godleys house. There – said Parker.

He pointed up the hillside towards the ruins. From below – the alders in full leaf – that one bit of wall still standing does look like there might be a whole building behind.

– you mean the old mill? Well you could have saved yourself the bother – declared dad – Nowt to be seen up

8

there – all the machinery were taken out twenty years ago
– you can see some of it along at the Dales Museum – if
youve got time to waste. As for the building – roofs fallen
in & most of the walls. Id have knocked the rest down
years back only some daft bugger got a conservation
order put on it –

– but that cant be right – protested the man – darling
pass me the magazine –

The woman dived into her bag & produced a copy of
Mid-Yorkshire Life. It was folded open at a short peice entitled 'Healing Hands' – with a pic of a slightly embarrassed
bearded guy holding up what were presumably the hands in
question. His name – thisll make you laugh – was Gordon
Godley!

– look – said Mr Parker triumphantly – its got the
address quite clearly here. *The Old Mill – Willingdene.*
Seeing the village signposted as we drove back from
Harrogate – a sadly unproductive visit – once it may have
been a serious spa town but now it has given itself over
almost completely to commerce & frivolity – I naturally
diverted & enquired of a young lad the way to the Old Mill.
He gave me most precise directions which brought me
here. Are you now telling me that is not the Old Mill? –

Im giving you Tom Parker verbatim – else youd miss
the flavour. Its like listening to an old fashioned book come
to life!

Dad smiled. You know how much he enjoys putting *daft
buggers* right.

– it were once a mill right enough – & its certainly old.
But theres not been anybody living there for half a century
or more & Ill tell you why. This here is Willing*den* – just
the one *e*. Willing*dene* is way up at the northern end of
the dale –

If hed been a footie player – hed have set off running

9

round the meadow – whirling his shirt over his head! He just loves winning – no matter who gets beaten. Remember those games of snap we used to play?

Mr Parker seemed more cast down by this news than by his sprained ankle.

– Im sorry my dear – he said to his wife – I should have taken more notice –

Taking all the blame on himself again – even though she was the one with the mag article. Nice – I thought. His reward was her continued terrier like support.

– it makes no difference – she said – this is marked on the map as a public right of way & someone ought to keep it in a proper condition –

– Charley – said dad quickly – whats the verdict on that ankle? –

I couldnt see any point in disagreeing with the patient.

– I think Mr Parkers right & its just a sprain – I said – a cold compress will help & he certainly shouldnt put any wieght on it –

How was that Nurse Heywood?

– right – said dad – Charley bring the quad – lets get Mr & Mrs Parker down to the house – make them a bit more comfortable. George – you stop here & get the car pulled out of that mud. Clean it up & check for damage. Ill get on my mobile – tell your mother to put the kettle on – Im sure these good people are ready for a nice cup of tea –

I caught his eye & let my jaw drop in mock astonishment at this transformation from dedicated xenophobe to Good Samaritan.

He actually blushed! Then he gave me a sheepish grin that invited my complicity.

I grinned back & headed off towards the quad.

Hes not such a bad old sod really – is he? As long as

he gets his own way. Bit like you! All right – & like me too. The fruit doesnt fall far from the tree. But you led the way. If you hadnt stood up to him & gone off to nurse – I doubt Id have had the nerve to hold out to go to uni & do psychology – & now after 3 years – whenever he gets close to driving me mad – I try to think of him as a case study!

But Ive still not told you how the Parkers came to be house-guests.

Thing was – when G pulled their car out of the tank trap – he found it wouldnt steer properly. Winstons garage said they could fix it – but theyd have to send away for a part. Tomorrow – they said – but knowing Winstons Im not holding my breath.

When Parker heard this he said – thats fine. No problem whatsoever. Perhaps – Mr Heywood – you could give me the number of the inn I saw in the village? – It looked a comfortable sort of place for us to rest in till the cars ready –

I could see the thoughts running through dads head like hed got a display screen on his brow. Being the most litigious man in the county – in Parkers place hed have been thinking compensation soon as his car hit the tank trap. Locally his views on *daft buggers* are well known – & he even boasts about his various stratagems for discouraging them. But these days – with tourism rated higher than farming in the rural economy – not everyone approves of him – & the enthusiastic gossips of the Nags Head bar would leave the Parkers in no doubt who to blame for their 'accident'!

So I wasnt too surprised when I heard him say – Nags Head? – aye – its well enough. But the floors are uneven – stairs narrow – not at all what a man in your state needs. No – youd best stay here. Ill get George to bring your bags up from the car –

11

The Parkers were overcome by dads generosity. So was mum – with amazement! – but she quickly recovered – & I gave dad a big wink – & got one back!

So there you are. We have house-guests – & its time to go down & have supper with them. Ill keep you posted on how the HB bears up under the strain.

Take care – dont catch anything I wouldnt catch – & if you fall in love with a big handsome black man – e me a pic of you & him – & Ill stick it in dads prayer book so hell see it for the first time at church on Sunday morning!

Lots & lots of love

Charley X

2

FROM: charley@whiffle.com
TO: cassie@natterjack.com
SUBJECT: sex – Sandytown – & psychology

Omigod Cass! I must be psychic! OK – you say hes not
black – but teaky bronze. Same difference – & is that all
over? I mean *all* all over? & hes a doc too – just like in
mums Mills & Boon stories! Means youll probably have
trouble with some slinkily gorgeous lady medic – wholl
manage to get you blamed when she accidentally offs a
patient – but dont worry – itll all come right in the end!

I definitely want a pic. Cross my heart I wont stick it in
dads prayer book – not till you give the word! But can I tell
mum? Shes desperate for grand-kids. Adam & Kylie show
no sign of producing – even if they did Oz is a hell of long
way off – can you imagine getting the HB on a plane to fly
twelve thousand miles? Rod spends most of his time at
sea – & we know what sailors are! She was desolate
when I got back early from my camping trip with Liam &
Sam & Dot – & told her it was all off – irreconcilable differences – which is what us psychs say to our mums when
we catch ex-partner Liam banging ex-best-mate Dot up
against a pine tree. So – unless you settle down & start
calving – I think she may strap me to my bed – & get to
work with an AI straw!

Your news makes my stuff about the Parkers seem v dull – but you say youre interested so here goes with the next instalment.

As house-guests go – they havent! Winstons – as forecast – got *let down by their suppliers* – again! So 1 nights turned into 3. But its been OK. I like Mary Parker a lot. Doesnt say much around her husband – except in agreement with him – or defence of him! But – get her to herself & shes great.

Tom Parkers v different – thinks silence is for the grave & the living have a duty to resist!

His favourite topic – unless checked his *only* topic – is Sandytown – as advertised on the side of his car!

Remember Sandytown? I think that was the last Heywood family outing. Me 9 or 10 – you 13 – sea cold & grey – sand gritty – wind so strong it blew our wind-breaks away – & Sandytown itself seemed to be shut! To cap it all – on the way back – George was sick – & that set me off – & soon we were all at it! Dad sang all the way home! After 3 years doing psychology I reckon I know why. He clearly saw the whole trip as a successful experiment in aversion therapy!

So when Tom Parker started rattling on about Sandytown at supper that first night – I didnt dare catch Georges eye.

Ill give it you verbatim again – really – this is how he talks!

– Sandytown! – he said – Beautiful Sandytown – the most lustrous pearl in the long necklace of the Yorkshire coast! You see Charlotte – (fixing his eye on me – I think hes decided Im the intellectual epicentre of the Heywood family – or maybe he just likes my boobs!) – a new age of the English holiday is dawning. Compared with it – the old age – which died with the onset of cheap Mediterranean packages – will seem but a trial run. Two practical reasons for the change – global warming & global terrorism! We travel in fear & we travel in discomfort. We have our personal belongings – & indeed our persons – searched by hard-faced – & hard-fingered – strangers. We are prodded into line by armed police. We are forced to eat with implements which – lacking the rigidity necessary to be a threat to soft human flesh – cannot begin to cope with airline food. Nor can we feel safe on arrival. Tourists are everywhere regarded as a soft terrorist target – while global warming – exacerbated by the soaring emission levels of flight – has led to a dramatic increase in the incidence of natural disasters – floods – drought – hurricanes – earthquakes – tsunamis – etc –

By now dad was regarding him with gobsmacked amazement – mum with polite interest – his wife with fond admiration – & the twins were choking back their giggles.

To me it was clear that Parker was reciting some kind of sales pitch – one made so often the record would run to its end unless interrupted.

So when he paused for breath I got in quick with – Why were you looking for a healer Tom? –

– a very perceptive question Charlotte – he replied smiling at me – to which my answer is – health! Let me explain. We live in a sick world – a world suffering from some deep-rooted wasting disease – of which terrorism & warming are but symptoms. To cure the whole we must start with the smallest part – the individual! The English seaside holiday originated in a search for recreation in the strictest sense. Pure ozone-enriched air to cleanse the lungs – surging salty water to refresh the skin & stimulate the circulation – peace & quiet to restore the troubled spirit –

15

Seeing he was getting back into his groove – I cut in again – Sounds to me like a healers the last thing you need! –

– A good point! – he cried with delight. (Its a great technique this – being delighted with everything anyone says!) – To understand the healer it is of course necessary to understand the history. Some 2 years ago – when Mid-Yorkshire Council began discussion of their Eastern Region Development Plan – naturally Lady Denham & myself took a keen interest in their proposals for the Sandytown area . . .

– whos Lady Denham? – I asked – reducing him to amazed silence – & dad – always glad to know something I dont – chipped in – This the Denhams of Denham Park?

– you know the family? – said Tom – delighted.

– know of them – grunted dad – & little good – bad landowners – worse landlords – thought theyd gone to the wall long since –

– in a sense they have – agreed Parker – but Lady Denham – now alas a widow for a second time – only bears the name through marriage. Her 2nd incidentally. Before that she was Mrs Hollis – & before *that* Miss Daphne Brereton – only daughter of the Breretons of Brereton Manor – Sandytowns premier family – well to do – highly respected. Money calls to money – place to place – that is my experience – though I do not suggest that love was absent when she caught the eye of Howard Hollis –

– Hollis? – Dad interrupted – Hog Hollis? – him as got et by his own pigs? –

I saw the twins perk up. Anything grisly really turns them on!

– indeed – there was a tragic accident – said Tom – You knew Mr Hollis? –

16

– met him a couple of times – said dad unenthusiastically
– folk reckoned he kept his pigs in the sea his meat were
so salty & watery! Made a fortune but he were a right
miserable sod – only time he ever smiled was for yon
photo on them Hollis's Ham freezer packs you see all over
the supermarkets – & that were probably wind! –

I caught mums eye & we shared a moment of speculation about when dad had last been inside a supermarket!

Tom said – he was certainly a man who – despite his
great success – remained true to his roots. Perhaps it
was the contrast offered by the more refined manners of
Sir Henry Denham that made the widow look favourably
upon his advances. Alas – fate is not sentimental – &
within all too short a time Sir Henry was also brought
low –

– et by the pigs too? – chimed in David hopefully.

Dad gave him a glower. He can say what he wants but
he expects his kids to observe the conventions.

– a riding accident – said Tom – & while Daphne
Breretons first marriage certainly left her with even more
wealth than she brought to it – from her second – it is
general knowledge – she derived little more than the
respect due to an ancient name –

Pause for applause. Instead – Mary P gave a little
gasp – maybe a repressed sneeze – echoed by dads
openly incredulous snort.

Parker – unperturbed – went on – She & I – as
principal landowners in the area – had already been
planning to put Sandytown on the map long before the
MYCC proposals. She had led the way by being instrumental in bringing the Avalon Foundation to Sandytown. You
have heard of Avalon – of course? –

This time me & dad both nodded. Hardly need to tell
you what dad said!

– oh aye – we know all about the Avalon. When I read in the papers – a few years back – the Yanks were building a fancy clinic out on the coast – I said to our Cass – that ud be a grand place for you to work – them Yanks know how to pay nurses & you could get home in an hour – but it were like –

– banging my head against a brick wall! – chorused the twins – then collapsed in giggles.

Dad gave them a glower – & Tom Parker went rattling on.

– Lady Denham & I – in our private discussions – had pre-empted the Councils conclusion that Sandytown was perfectly placed to take advantage of the changes in recreational climate – both meteorologically & intellectually speaking – & formed a loose alliance – & put 1 or 2 projects in train. But now we approached the Councils Development Officer – who was rapidly persuaded by our projections of the increase in local employment – & of tourism – plus our plans for a measure of affordable housing – to join with us in the formation of the Sandytown Development Consortium – a true partnership between the public & private sectors – underpinned – through the good offices of my brother Sidney – by significant investment institutions in the City –

He paused – momentarily lost in the forests of his own verbosity – & his wife came in with a prompt – The Avalon dear – & the healer –

Indeed! – he resumed – the Avalon. The siting of such a famous centre of medical care & recuperation on our doorstep seemed to me a hint almost divine. At the centre of our Development Plan is the conversion of Brereton Manor – Lady Ds childhood home – into a 5 star luxury hotel & recreational health centre. All the conventional attractions – golf – tennis – horseriding – swimming –

18

beauty treatments – saunas – gymnasia – & so on – will be on offer here – & available to all visitors to our town – not just those who can afford the Manors necessarily high prices. However – to place us firmly in the new niche market where Sandytown – I forecast – will rapidly dominate – we are offering a range of complementary therapies for those who find that conventional medicine does not answer their needs –

He paused – for breath not applause – then pressed on – alternative medicine is – you will agree – another great 21st century growth area. We already have several practitioners in residence – an acupuncturist – a reflexologist – a homeopath – a Third Thought counsellor – but spiritual healers are harder to come by. I was hoping to talk to Mr Godley – the gentleman at Willingdene – with a veiw to persuading him to be – as it were – a visiting consultant –

By now dad had heard enough – indeed too much!
– healers! – he snorted – Load of mumbo-jumbo. Me – Id rather be treated by my vet – even though the bugger charges a fortune –

– then perhaps you should read this article – suggested Parker who seems quite unoffendable – it claims that Mr Godley has had some astonishing results with animals –

A sharp glance from mum made dad choke back his suggestion what Tom could do with the article – but David burst out – Charley thinks its all a load of bollocks too! –

– David! – said mum sternly – Language! –

– but its true – the little gobshite defended himself – You do think its all *rubbish* – dont you Charley? You were telling us you were going to write a composition about it –

Parker looked at me quizzically – & I said – Ignore him. His ears are bigger than his brain. What he misheard

19

is that Im proposing to do a thesis on the psychology of alternative therapy. The medical establishment says its mostly nonsense – the practitioners point to what they claim are well documented successes. Im not interested in joining in the debate – but in looking at a variety of these therapies – & seeing if I can find any common psychological elements in their practise & their results –

Good – eh? Should be. Parkers not the only one who has a selling line off pat!

Across the table I could see the Headbangers eyes starting to roll & Id hardly finished before he broke out – There you have it Mr Parker. My clever daughters already spent three years with her nose in a pile of musty books – learning a lot of nowt about a lot of nowt just to get some letters after her name – & now she wants to spend another God knows how long doing much the same just to get some more. She can go on till shes got the whole damn alphabet – but wheres it going to lead? thats what Id like to know. Ive tried talking sense into her but its like –

Here he glared at the twins – daring them to finish his sentence again. I think David would have – but Freddie kicked him under the table. Bet she wants to wheedle some more spending money out of him for her school trip this autumn! Since G & me went skiing – she thinks shes owed a month in a 5 star in Miami!

Tom Parker endeared himself to me by saying – But that is marvellous Charlotte – understanding the mind is the first step to restoring the body – we need more young people like you to put this sick world of ours to rights! –

See – you dont have to go shogging off to Africa to be a saint!

Later – as Mary helped Tom limp from the room – he said to mum – A delicious meal Amy – best Ive had –

outside of Sandytown – & Mary added – Yes – thank you both for your kindness. Youve got a lovely family Amy –

Well you know how much dad loves to hear mum being praised – so he hardly moaned at all about our guests when theyd gone upstairs – though I thought hed explode when we heard next morning the car wouldnt be ready for at least 3 days!

I did my bit – keeping them from getting under his feet. No problem – like I say – I really got to like them – & they seemed to like me too. Tom showed real interest in my thesis proposal – & today he said – Charlotte – (they both call me Charlotte – which is nice) – you know we intend calling on Mr Godley the healer on our way home – why dont you come with us? You could talk to him about his patients – for your thesis –

I said – but youd be well on your way home by the time you got to Willingdene & you wouldnt want to turn round & come all the way back here –

& Mary said – actually we did wonder if youd like to come all the way to Sandytown & spend a few days with us at Kyoto House –

I said – Kyoto? – thinking Id misheard.

Tom said – yes – perhaps I was hasty – the Kyoto Protocol has proved pretty toothless hasnt it? If Id waited I think Al Gore House might have been more appropriate –

Mary didnt look as if she agreed – but she nodded vigorously as Tom went on – please come – you could meet our other therapists – give us the benefit of your take on our great experiment – & most importantly – wed get more of your company! –

Well its always nice to be wanted – even so Id probably have said thanks but no thanks – only dad had come into the room at some point – & suddenly he spoke in that Wiz of Oz voice he uses when hes really laying down the law.

21

– nay – he declared – shes not been back home 2 minutes – shell not want to be gallivanting off afore shes needed her sheets changed –

Maybe I should have been touched at his desire to keep me close. All I actually felt was the usual irritation that – even at 22 – he still wanted to treat me like a kid.

I said – no reflection on your own personal hygiene dad – but Ive changed my sheets at least twice since I came home. Now getting back to the matter in hand – thank you very much Tom & Mary for your kind invitation. Id be really delighted to accept –

So there you have it. Heres me – a rational being – with a degree certifying Ive spent 3 years studying what makes people tick – & what do I end up doing?

Going to visit a place Ive no reason to like – in the company of people I hardly know – just to prove Im not a kid anymore!

Now thats *really* mature – eh?

Watch this space for my next exciting adventure in darkest Mid-Yorkshire.

& I look forward to some truly madly steamy revelations from darkest Africa!

Lots of love

Charley xx

Ho'd on. How the fuck do I know this bloody thing's working?

HELLO! HELLO! DALZIEL SPEAKING! LOOK ON MY WORKS, YOU MUGWUMPS, AND DESPAIR!

Now, let the dog see the rabbit . . . I'll try pressing this, like the bishop said to

Christ, do I really sound like that? No wonder the buggers jump!

So it works. So what? Hears everything I say and plays it back word for fucking word. What's so clever about that? Old Auntie Mildred could do exactly the same – plus good advice! So that's you christened, right? Mildred!

But listen, Mildred, you start telling me to wear my woolly vest and it's straight out of the window for you!

Yon Festerwhanger were right, but. Nice bit of kit this.

Jesus, Andy, listen to yourself! Nice bit of kit! You be careful, lad, else you'll end up like all these kids with their p-pods, walking around with idiot grins on their faces and their heads nodding like them daffs in the poem.

Keep a record of little thoughts you might lose, Fester said, and mebbe some big questions you normally don't have time to ask yourself.

Right, Dalziel, sod the little thoughts, let's start with the biggest question of them all.

How the fuck did I end up here in Sandytown talking to meself like the village loony?

Let's try and build it up bit by bit like Ed Wield 'ud build up a case file.

Back to the big bang in Mill Street that set it all rolling.

That were the Bank Holiday, end of May.

Don't recall much of June, mebbe 'cos I spent most of it in a coma.

Good thing about a coma, they told me, was it gave my cracked bones time to start mending. Bad thing was it didn't do much for my muscle tone.

Never knew I had muscle tone before.

Found out the hard way.

First time I tried getting out of bed by myself, I fell over.

Let a week go by, then tried again. But this time I made sure there was a nice fat nurse to fall on to.

Third time I took three steps towards the door and fell into Pete Pascoe's arms.

'Where are you going?' he asks.

'Home,' sez I. 'Soon as I bloody well can.'

'How do you propose doing that?' sez he in that prissy voice he puts on.

'I'll bloody well walk if I have to,' sez I.

He let go of me and stepped back.

I fell over.

I lay there and looked up at him with pride.

When I first met him he were a detective

constable, soft as shit and so wet behind the ears you could have used him to clean windows.

Now he were my DCI, and he were hard enough to let me fall and leave me lying.

He'd come a long way and ought to go a lot further.

'OK, clever clogs,' I sez. 'You've made your point. Now get me back into bed.'

Soon it were getting on for August, and I were still the only one talking about going home. Cap made encouraging remarks, but changed the subject when we got on to dates. I thought, sod this for a lark, they can't keep me here when I want to be off!

I said as much to Pete and the bugger sent in the heavy squad.

His missus, Ellie.

From the first time I met her, I saw she were already hard enough to let me fall and leave me lying. In fact back in them early days I reckon she'd have been happy to give me a helping push.

She said, 'I hear you're talking of discharging yourself, Andy. So who's going to look after you when you get home?'

'I'll look after myself. Always have done,' I said.

She sighed. Women have two kinds of sighs. Long-suffering and ooh-I'm-really-enjoying-that. Lot of men never learn the difference.

She said, 'Andy, you got blown up in a terrorist explosion, you suffered multiple injuries, you lay in a coma for weeks . . .'

'Aye, and most of the time since I came out of it I've spent on this bloody bed,' I said. 'So where's the difference?'

'Don't exaggerate,' she said. 'You're on a carefully

25

planned course of supervised physiotherapy. They say you're doing well, but it will be ages before you can look after yourself.'

'So I'll get help from Social Services. That's why I pay my bloody taxes, isn't it?'

'How long do you think that'll last?' she asked.

'Till I get fed up wi' them? Couple of weeks mebbe. By then I should be fine.'

'I meant, till they get fed up of you! Who'll look after you then?'

I said, 'I've got friends.'

'Arse-licking friends maybe,' she said. 'But arse-wiping ones are a bit thinner on the ground.'

Sometimes she takes my breath away! Mebbe I were taking too much credit for putting the steel into Pascoe's backbone. Should have known that all them years the bugger were getting home tuition!

'For you mebbe,' I said. 'Treat folk right and they'll treat you right, that's my motto. There'll be folk queuing up to give me a hand.'

'Takes two to make a queue,' she said. 'You're talking about Cap, aren't you?'

Of course I were talking about Cap. Cap Marvell. My girlfriend . . . partner . . . bint . . . tottie . . . none of them fits. Or all of them. Cap bloody marvellous in my book, 'cos that's what she's been.

'So I mean Cap. She won't let me down. She'll be there when I need her.'

I let it out a bit pathetic. Could see I were getting nowhere slogging it out punch for punch, but even the really hard ones are often suckers for a bit of pathos. Vulnerability they call it. Make 'em feel you need help. Stood me in good stead many a time back in my Jack-the-ladding days.

26

Didn't take long to realize it weren't going to get me anywhere now.

'Boo hoo,' said Ellie. 'You've been together a good few years now, you and Cap. But you never set up shop together, you've both kept your own places. Why's that?'

She knew bloody well why it was. We've got our own lives, our own interests, our own timetables. There's stuff in my pack I don't want her getting touched by. And there's definitely stuff in hers I don't want to know about. Every time there's an animal rights raid, I find myself checking her alibi! But the real big thing is lots of little things, like the way we feel about muddy boots, setting tables, using cutlery, eating pickles straight out of the jar, watching rugby on the telly, playing music dead loud, what kind of music we want to play dead loud, and so bloody on.

I said, 'An emergency's different.'

'So this is an emergency now? Right. Whose place will you set up the emergency centre at? Your house or Cap's flat? And how long will you indenture Cap as your body servant before you set her free?'

'Don't go metaphysical on me, luv,' I said. 'What's that mean?'

'You're not thick, Andy, so don't pretend to be,' she said. 'Cap's life has been on hold since you got blown up. You know she's got a very full independent existence – that's one of the reasons you've never shacked up together, right? She's not one of those ground-you-walk-on worshippers that only live for their man.'

'I know what she is a bloody sight better than thee, Ellie Pascoe!' I declared, getting angry. 'And I know she'd be ready and willing to put in a bit of time taking care of me if that's what I need!'

'Of course she would,' said Ellie with that smug look they get when they've made you lose your rag. 'Question is, Andy. Do you really want her to?'

No answer to that, at least not one I wanted to give her the satisfaction of hearing. And I didn't say much either when she started talking about the Cedars out at Filey, the convalescent home provided by our Welfare Association for old, mad, blind and generally knackered cops. Alcatraz, we call it, 'cos the only way out is in a box.

What I did say, all grumpy, was, 'Were it Cap that put you up to this then?'

She grabbed hold of a bedpan and said, 'That's the daftest thing I've ever heard you say, Andy Dalziel. And if you let out so much as a hint to Cap what I've been talking to you about, I'll stick this thing so far up your behind, they'll need a tow truck to haul it out! You just lie here and think about what I've said.'

'Yes, miss,' I said meekly. 'Tha knows, lass, Pete Pascoe's a very lucky man.'

'You think so?' she said, looking a bit embarrassed.

'Aye,' I said. 'It's not every husband's got a big strapping wife he can send up on the roof if ever a tile comes off in a high wind.'

She laughed out loud. That's one of the things I like about Ellie Pascoe. No girlish giggles there. She enjoys a real good laugh.

'You old sod,' she said. 'I'm off now. I've got my own life too. Peter sends his love. Says to tell you that he's got things running so smooth down at the Factory that he can't understand how they ever managed with you. Take care now.'

She bent over me and kissed me. Bright, brave, and bonny. Pete Pascoe really was a lucky man.

And she's got lovely knockers.

Any road, I did think about what she'd said and a couple of days later when I were talking to Cap, I said I were thinking of going to the Cedars.

She said, 'But you hate that place. You once went to visit someone there and you said it was like a temperance hotel without the wild parties.'

That's the trouble with words, they come back to haunt you.

'Mebbe that's what I need now,' I lied. 'Couple of weeks' peace and quiet and a breath of sea air. Me mind's made up.'

I should have known, men make up their minds like they make up their beds – if there's a woman around she'll pull all the bedding off and start again.

Next time she came she had a bunch of brochures.

She said, 'I've been thinking about what you said, Andy, and I reckon you're right about the sea air. But I don't think the Cedars is the place for you. You'd be surrounded by other cops there with nothing to do but talk about crooks and cases and getting back on the job. No, this is the place for you. The Avalon.'

'You mean that Yankee clinic place?' I said, glancing at the brochures.

'The Avalon Foundation is originally American, yes, but it's been so successful it now has clinics worldwide. There's one in Australia, one in Switzerland . . .'

'I'm not going to Switzerland,' I said. 'All them cuckoo clocks, I'd never sleep.'

'Of course you're not. You are going to the one in Sandytown, where as well as the clinic and its

29

attendant nursing home, there's an old house that's been converted into a convalescent home. My old headmistress, Kitty Bagnold, you may recall, is seeing out her days in the nursing home. I visit her from time to time, so it will be very convenient for me to have both my broken eggs in one basket.'

That were the clincher, of course, her managing to make it sound like I'd be doing her a favour by coming here. I asked who'd be paying. She said my insurance would cover most of it and in any case hadn't I always said that if you ended up with life left over at the end of your money, the state would take care of you, but if you ended up with money left over at the end of your life, you were an idiot!

There's them bloody haunting words again!

Any road, I blustered a bit for the show of things but soon caved in. When I told Ellie Pascoe I thought she'd have been dead chuffed, but she seemed right disappointed I weren't going to the Cedars. Even when I assured her I wouldn't let Cap be out of pocket here, she still didn't seem too pleased.

Women, eh? You can fuck 'em but you can't fathom them.

But Cap were happy and that meant I felt pretty pleased with myself when a couple of weeks later she drove me here to Sandytown.

I soon stopped being pleased, but. Cap had hardly set off back to the car park to drive home afore it was being made clear to me that the Avalon weren't like a 5-star hotel with the guests' wishes being law.

'Convalescence is a carefully monitored progression from illness to complete health,' explained the matron. (Name of Sheldon – calls herself Chief Nurse, but with tits a randy vicar could rest a bible on while he preached the gospel according to St Dick, she were a shoo-in for the role of matron in one of them Carry On movies!)

'Oh aye,' I said, taking the piss. 'And visiting hours from three to quarter past every third Sunday!'

'Ha ha,' she said. 'In fact no visitors at all to start with until we've had time to observe you and assess your needs and draw up your personal programme – diet sheet, exercise schedule, medication plan, therapy timetable – that sort of thing.'

'Bloody hell,' I said. 'Schedules, timetables – makes me feel like a railway train.'

She smiled – I've seen more convincing smiles in a massage parlour – and said, 'Indeed. And our aim is to get you puffing out of the station as quickly as possible.'

I could see she liked her little joke. But I didn't argue. I just wanted to sleep!

That were a couple of days ago. Spent most of the time since then sleeping 'cos every time I woke up there were some bugger ready to pinch and prod and poke things into me. Assessment they call it. More like harassment to me!

Third day, matron appeared all coy and girlish, straightened my sheets, plumped my pillows and said, 'Big day, today, Mr Dalziel. Dr Feldenhammer himself is coming to see you.'

And that's when I first set eyes on Lester Feldenhammer, head quack at the Avalon. I could tell he were a Yank soon as he opened his gob. Not the accent but the teeth! It were like looking down an old-fashioned bog, all vitreous china gleaming white. Bet he gargles with Harpic twice a day.

'Mr Dalziel,' he said. 'Welcome to the Avalon, sir.

Your fame has preceded you. I'm honoured to shake the hand of a man who got injured in the front line of the great fight against terrorism.'

I thought he were taking the piss, but when I looked at him I could see he were sincere. They're the worst kind. Never trust a man who believes his own crap.

I thought, I'll have to watch this one.

He shook my hand like he wanted to make sure it were properly attached and he said, 'I'm Lester Feldenhammer, Director of the Avalon, also Head of Clinical Psychology. I think we've just about got your programme sorted, but the greatest aid to speedy recovery must come from within. I've taken the liberty of putting a little self-help book I've written in your bedside locker. It may help you to a fuller understanding of what's happening to you here.'

'Gideon Bible usually does the trick,' I said.

'We like to think of them as complementary,' he said. 'I'm really looking forward to monitoring your progress, Mr Dalziel. On matters physiological you will, of course, have access to our specialized medical staff. On all other matters, I'm your man. Anything you want to know, you have only to ask.'

'Is that right?' I said. 'So what's for dinner?'

He decided this were a joke and laughed like an accordion.

'I can see we're going to get on famously,' he said. 'Now, there's something I'd like you to do for me.'

He pulled out this little shiny metal thing.

'I'm not swallowing that,' I said. 'And if tha's thinking of getting it into me by some other route, tha'd best think again.'

This time, mebbe because it were a joke, he didn't laugh.

'It's a digital recorder,' he said. 'State of the art, practically works itself. What I'd like you to do, Mr Dalziel, is keep a sort of audio-diary. Make a record of your feelings, your experiences, anything that comes into your mind.'

'You mean, you want me to start talking to myself?' I said. 'Like the nutters do?'

'No, no,' he said. 'Not to yourself. Just talk as if you're speaking to someone who knows absolutely nothing about you.'

'Like you, for instance?' I said.

He gave me a smile I could've played 'Chopsticks' on and said, 'I do in fact know a little about you. And I shouldn't like you to think you're addressing me specifically. In fact, let me assure you, Mr Dalziel, I shall never listen to any part of it without your permission.'

'So if you're not going to hear it, what's the point?' I asked.

'The point is you saying things, not me hearing them,' he said. 'You can keep a record of all those interesting little thoughts we so easily lose track of. Also you can ask yourself some of the really Big Questions. Think of it as part journal, part self-interrogation. I'm sure a man with your skills will be able to detect truth through no matter how cunningly woven a web of evasion and deceit. Will you do that for me?'

I said, 'Mebbe. But if I don't get some grub soon, I may just swallow it anyway.'

He went off, laughing. And that's how I come to be lying here, talking to myself like a loony. Took another couple of days afore I dug Fester's little toy out. Man in bed's got to play with something. Nowt else to do. Newspapers these days aren't fit to wrap chips in. Telly's worse, and they don't feed me enough grub to enjoy a good crap!

Can't even do a runner. First, I've got no clothes. Spoke to Cap on the phone and she says she'll bring me some soon as they let her visit me. Second, got to face it, my leg's getting there, but I'm not back to running mode yet. I dumped them poncy elbow crutches they gave me at the hospital and got Cap to buy me a stout walking stick. I'm OK for short bursts, but after a couple of minutes, I'm ready for a sit-down.

Got to keep reminding myself, there's a world out there, a real world with people in it, and pubs, and it's likely full of scrotes pissing themselves laughing 'cos I'm stuck in here, talking to a machine.

Let them laugh.

I'll be back.

Sure as eggs.

4

FROM: charley@whiffle.com
TO: cassie@natterjack.com
SUBJECT: an exciting journey!

Hi!

Nothing from you – maybe your teaky bronzy doc is keeping you busy – nudge nudge.

Ive made it to Sandytown – just finished unpacking in Kyoto House – built on a cliff top to catch all them healthy breezes – very eco-friendly – solar panels – wind driven generator – etc etc. Lovely room – looking out over the North Sea – all blue & sparkly just now – but I hope we get a storm before I go. Funny that – only other time I was here I prayed for warm sunshine – this time I want thunder & lightning!

The journey first – we stopped off at Willingdene as planned – to meet Gordon Godley – the healer.

I quite liked him – nutty as a fruit-cake – but sort of nice with it.

Hard to say how old – 45? – 55? – not helped by a mad black beard threaded with silver – like a bramble bush on an autumn morning – but v young v gentle grey eyes – a nose like a flying buttress in a dolls cathedral & a lovely smile. I could see the unclaimed treasures of the area queuing up to have his hands laid on their aching joints.

Dont think he took to me though. Tom didnt help — introducing me with a version of my thesis proposal that made me sound like the witch-finder general — out on the rampage! Mr Godley wouldnt meet my eye — answered my questions with monosyllabic grunts — so I soon gave up.

However — he listened to Toms pitch with great courtesy — tho I got the impression — using my finely honed analytical powers — that in fact he already knew a lot more about the Sandytown project than he was letting on. In the end — to shut him up I think! — he accepted Toms invite to make a visit to see if he felt called to bring *his ministry* there — Toms dead keen to get him on board for what he calls the Festival of Health — scheduled for Bank Holiday weekend — Ill be long gone — thank heaven! —

Finally — at Marys request — Gord laid his healing hands on the sprained ankle.

As we left Tom claimed his injury was much improved.

— I felt a warmth — he asserted — A definite warmth as from a powerful sun-lamp —

Back in the car — out of earshot of Mr Godley — I observed that — in veiw of the nature of the injury — I would have been more impressed if hed felt a definite coldness.

He turned in his seat — hed wanted me to sit in the front — but I insisted he needed the space because of his ankle — & gave me a delighted smile & said — see Mary how good Charlotte will be for us. Scientific objectivity — thats what we want. No chance of charlatanism ruining the good name of Sandytown with her keen eye upon us! —

Im not sure what lasting effect the healers hands might have on the sprained ankle — but one thing I feel certain of — Tom Parkers optimism is incurable!

Mary drove well & very carefully. If shed been at the

wheel I doubt theyd have ended in the tank trap. On the other hand I couldnt regret that they had. My acceptance of their invitation might have been made in pique – but now I found I was really looking forward to the visit. Dont know if Ill get much useful thesis fodder out of it – after my start with Godly Gordon I guess Ill need to brush up my interviewing techniques – but being cast in the role of detached scientific observer tickled my fancy.

Like a camera – I will record – & not judge.

Or maybe Ill judge just a little! I am after all Steve Heywoods daughter.

Difference being – Ill keep my judgments to myself!

& you – of course!

Short break there.

Eldest kid – Minnie (= little Mary) – burst in to say lunch would be ready in 20 mins – & see if Id got everything I needed. Gave the impression shed been sent – but I suspect it was mainly her own idea – to check out the new fish! She talked non-stop – while her eyes gobbled everything up – especially my laptop. Shes 9 going on 90 – reminds me of me at that age. Havent been bothering much with security – but now I may reactivate my password!

Got rid of her – by main force! – after a couple of minutes – so now I can get to the really exciting bit of the journey here – so pay attention!

Even at Marys steady pace it wasnt a long drive – but long enough for me to learn a little more about the Parkers. Old Yorkshire family – made their money in building – Tom trained as an architect – offices in Scarborough but siezed the opportunity offered by mod tech to work from home – 4 kids – Minnie 9 – Paul 8 – Lucy 6 – Lewis 5 – apples of his eye – Marys too – but Tom comes first. I get the

37

impression she doesnt like letting him take off alone – not cos she dont trust him sexually – but cos she worries what scrapes his enthusiasm might get him into! Like driving into the tank trap – I suppose!

He talked – with great affection – of his financier brother Sidney – younger – & invalid sister Diana – older. Without saying much – Mary gave the impression she has a few reservations about Sid in the City – & a whole bucketful about sister Di!

More to Mary than meets the eye. When Tom started rattling on about Kyoto House – inviting her agreement that it was in every way superior to the old Parker family home theyd swapped it for – she replied dutifully – I suppose youre right dear – but the old place did have such a pleasant garden – & so sheltered –

– yes – thats it entirely – he declared – as if shed confirmed everything hed said – It was indeed sheltered – from the benefits of the sea breeze – & sheltered from the veiw too – no outlook save for fields & trees! Now – from Kyoto up on North Cliff – on a clear day you can see halfway across to Holland – & when Im working out ideas for the Development Scheme I dont need to sit at my drawing board – I just go into my garden & look down & there it all is at my feet – as it were! –

– did you design Kyoto yourself? – I asked.

– naturally! – marvellous feeling – not having anyone looking over your shoulder at the drawing board – do you follow? The opportunity afforded me by the Consortium – of getting involved in planning & building on a large scale – was not the least of its attractions. Its going to be something new – I promise you – nothing piecemeal or accidental – every step carefully thought out – every detail pertinent & planned! – & a carbon footprint no bigger than a cats! –

The quality of light ahead was now giving promise of the sea. Against the intense blue sky I could see the rather sinister silhouette of a large house – more than a house – a mansion – with enough towers & turrets to give the impression it had had youthful ambitions to grow into a castle!

– Denham Park – said Tom.

– where Lady Denham lives? – I guessed.

– oh no. She lives at Sandytown Hall – he replied – which her first husband – Hollis – acquired – along with the Lordship of the Sandytown Hundreds – an ancient traditional rank – acquired by purchase – unlike her subsequent title –

It sounded to me like shed got that by purchase too – & I think I detected a little twitch from Mary. Us psychologists are v sensitive to twitches!

– the Denham property – Tom went on – & the baronetcy of course – went to her nephew-in-law – Edward –

Here our conversation was interrupted – wed been driving with the sun-roof open – to get the full benefit of the invigorating Sandytown air I presume – & suddenly – in an instant – the car filled with the most disgusting smell imaginable.

Pig shit! – on a huge scale – it made our slurry lagoon seem like a rose-bowl!

Mary hit the button to close the sun-roof – apologizing profusely.

– the Hollis pig farm – she said – except calling it a farm is an insult to real farmers! –

– now now my dear – said Tom mildly – its a natural smell – & nothing natural is harmful to man –

– nothing natural about the way they keep those poor animals – said Mary.

– intensive farming is the price we pay for not wanting to pay the price we would have to pay without it – said Tom – & its very rare that the wind is in a quarter which wafts the aroma into Sandytown –

– indeed no! – said Mary – which is why Daphne Brereton spent most of her time at her first husbands house – even after shed married her second! –

Yes – I know – mysterious! – but all will be explained later. Meanwhile we drove for a mile or more alongside a high wired fence through which I could see rows & rows of concrete buildings with all the charm of a concentration camp. Finally we reached the main entrance to the site – with a huge double gate – & a sign reading **HOLLIS'S HAM – the Taste of Yorkshire** – except that someone had been at work with a spray can – & it now read – **the Taste of Death.**

There was a man up a ladder with a bucket & scrubbing brush. He paused in his work as we passed & gave a wave. Tom wound down the window & called – Morning Ollie! More trouble, eh? – but Mary didnt slow down enough to give the man time to reply – & Tom closed the window again but not before wed got another near fatal dose of the porky pong!

A few minutes later Mary signalled to turn seawards as we approached a sign saying Sandytown via North Cliff.

Tom said – my dear – why dont you takes us round by South Cliff – & through the town – so Charlotte can give us her reactions – first impressions are so important –

Obediently Mary switched off the signal & drove on.

I didnt correct Tom about first impressions. Diplomatically I hadnt mentioned the famous excursion. Now I began to see for myself what Tom – of course – had already told me – that Sandytown – originally just a fishing village – is situated in a broad bay between two lofty headlands – North Cliff & South Cliff.

A loop of road runs down from North Cliff – through the village – then up to the coastal road again – via South Cliff.

Got that? – or do you need a diagram! –

As we approached the South Cliff turn off – I could see the headland here was dominated by a complex of buildings. One of them looked like an old mansion house – green with ivy – with a long extension – in keeping but definitely recent. A couple of hundred yards away was a modern two storeyed building – the stonework brilliant white – broad reflective glass windows catching the drift of small white clouds across the bright blue sky. Alongside that – a long single storeyed building – in the same style.

We turned off the coast road – but before we began the descent proper – at Toms request Mary pulled in by a gilded entrance gate – set in a dense thorn boundary hedge – bit like the entrance to heaven in that Pilgrims Progress you got for a Sunday School prize – remember? – we used to tear pages out to roll our ciggies!

A large elegantly designed sign board was inscribed *Welcome to THE AVALON FOUNDATION*. There was a small gatehouse from which a man emerged – his face breaking into a smile when he recognized the car.

– Morning Mrs Parker – Mr Parker – he called.

– Morning Stan – replied Parker – How are things? Family well? –

– Yes thank you – all middling well. Yourself? –

– in the pink Stan – said Parker – which was either a bit of an exaggeration – or Mr Godleys healing hands really had done the business.

As they talked – I studied a site diagram beneath the welcome sign. It indicated that the main two storeyed

41

modern block was the Avalon Clinic – the long single storey was the Avalon Nursing Home – & the old house was the Avalon Convalescent Home.

A phone attached to the gate-mans belt bleeped. He excused himself & turned away to answer it.

I said to Tom – how do the locals like having the clinic on thier doorstep? –

– some initial unease – lots of loose talk about lunatics & lepers – Tom replied – country folk are ready to believe the worst of strangers – but they also have an innate trust in authority. Round here that means Lady D & – to a lesser extent – myself. Once we showed the way – they followed – & suspicion has long been replaced by pride –

– the jobs & the extra income helped – observed Mary dryly.

The gate-man was saying into his phone – no definitely not – nobody in the last hour – yes – Ill keep an eye out – dont imagine hell go far dressed like that! –

He switched off – turned back to the car & said – sorry Mr Parker – one of our convies has gone walkabout – elderly gent – might be a bit confused – Id best bring his photo up on the computer. See you soon I hope –

– you too Stan – said Parker.

Mary set the car forward. Ahead the road began its descent to the village.

– *Convies*? – I said – thinking *convicts!*

– what? – Oh thats what the staff call those staying at the convalescent home. Patients at the clinic are *clinnies* – & residents of the nursing home are *rezzies.* What *they* call the staff I dont know – *Mary – take care!* –

Mary Parker – as I have said – drove very carefully – & shed stayed in low gear for the descent – so we werent doing much more than twenty miles an hour when she slammed the brakes on.

All the same – the sudden stop threw me forward – & I was glad for once Id obeyed the law & fastened my rear seat belt.

As they say – it all happened so quickly – but I still had time to glimpse a man rolling down the embankment rising steeply on the left to the Clinics boundary hedge.

Then he bounced into the road & vanished under our wheels.

Everything stood still. The car – time – our hearts. We were all convinced wed run him over. But surely there would have been a bump? – I told myself.

Then there was one. Or at least the car shuddered.

For a moment this felt like a delayed confirmation of our worst fears.

But that didnt make sense. You cant run over someone after youve stopped!

Even as I reached this logical conclusion – a broad-domed almost bald head began to rise like a full moon over the horizon of the bonnet – & I realized that the shudder had been caused by the man gripping the front of the car to pull himself up.

He leaned on the bonnet. Heavily. There was enough of him to suggest that – if there had been a bump – it would have been a big one!

He stared at us unblinkingly – out of the kind of face movie animators dream up for ogres.

His mouth twisted in a snarl – & he spoke.

It took a moment to register that in fact the snarl was a smile – & the words he spoke werent a threat – but a greeting.

He said – how do folks – what fettle? –

Now he moved round the side of the car. He walked slowly – like a bear that would have preferred to be on all fours – rather than upright. He gave Tom & Mary – still

43

paralysed by the shock – a friendly nod in passing. Then he took hold of the rear door – & pulled it open – & looked in at me.

– how do lass – he said – heading for the village? –

I nodded – not trusting myself to speak.

– grand – he said – room for a little un? –

& – without waiting for an answer – he pulled himself in alongside me.

Up to this point – Id thought he was wearing a garishly striped summer shirt & a casual woollen jacket – but now I saw him clearly – & I thought – oh shit!

He was dressed in pyjamas & a dressing gown. On his left foot was a leather slipper. His right foot was bare. There were leaves clinging to him & thorns sticking into him. His face bled through a few light scratches.

But looking at him more closely – as I had no choice but to do – I realized hed suffered more physical damage than could be explained merely by pushing through a hedge – & rolling down the bank into the road.

There was a lot of him – but a kind of pallor & the looseness of the skin on that broad face suggested that there used to be a lot more. Your nurses eye would prob-ably have done a full diagnosis in half a sec – but even I could see enough to work out hed recently been very ill.

An escaped loony – I thought! Then I recalled the gate-mans phone call. This had to be the *convie* whod gone missing – a bit of a relief – though not much!

He said – youll know me again luv –

I realized Id been staring.

I said – yes – sorry – hello – Im Charlotte Heywood –

Automatically I offered my hand. Good manners never hurt anyone – remember dad drumming that into us? Then hed head out across the fields – to chase some *daft bugger* off his land – with his shot gun!

44

The escaped convie took it – & held it in a surprisingly gentle grip.

– glad to meet you – he said – Andy Deal –

– Tom Parker. My wife Mary – said Tom – are you all right? –

– grand – he replied – nifty bit of driving that luv. Lot of women I know would have run me over – while they were still looking for the brake –

Somehow it came out as a genuine compliment.

Mary – reassured – gave him a smile & started the car again.

I realized the man was still holding my hand. He peered into my face & said – Heywood – thas not one of Stompy Heywoods brood out at Willingden – are you? –

– Steve Heywoods my father – I said – but Ive never heard him called Stompy –

– thats likely cos tha never got in his way at the bottom of a loose scrum. Aye – I thought I could see a likeness –

Being told I resembled dad wasnt the biggest compliment Id ever had! I dont – do I? Answer yes – & Ill publish details of your steamy affair all over the internet!

I snatched my hand free – & gave him a glower – & he grinned as if this confirmed his identification.

Ahead of us a banner stretched high across the road – & inscribed *Welcome to Sandytown – Home of the Healthy Holiday* – told us we were now entering the village. Except it wasnt a village – more a small town. Usually when you go back to places you recall as a kid – everything seems to have *shrunk* – could impress you with the physiological explanation for this phenomenon – but I wont! Sandytown was different – very much bigger than I recalled – looking prosperous too – our route took us past several shops – a small supermarket doing good business – an art & craft gallery – a working pottery – a jolly café – a Thai takeaway – & a sea food restaurant called Mobys!

The cobbled streets were clean & litter-free – the buildings freshly painted & well kept. Distantly I could see bathers sporting in the dark blue waves of the sea – & holidaymakers taking thier ease in deck chairs set on the golden sand. Posters everywhere showing an outline map of Yorkshire – with a big cross on the coast – & the legend – SANDYTOWN IS OUR TOWN – LETS PUT IT ON THE MAP! – while across the main street hung a banner reading FESTIVAL OF HEALTH – August Bank Holiday.

Maybe the Headbanger didnt bring us here at all – but found some run-down shanty town to put us off family trips forever!

Tom Parker – clearly delighted at these signs of activity – gave a running commentary on each individual attraction – & occasionally leant out of the open window to greet pedestrians – as Mary drove us slowly along.

– right luv – this ull do me – said Mr Deal suddenly.

I looked out & saw an old freshly whitewashed building displaying a sign which read *The Hope & Anchor – licensee A. Hollis*. One of the pig family? – I wondered. Mary pulled in. Deal leaned forward & said – Thanks for the lift luv. Sorry if I scared you back there. Lost me footing. Lost me bloody slipper too. Not to worry. I dont doubt Prince bloody Charming ull come looking for me. Tom – tha seems to be a local lad in good standing. I daresay tha gets on well with them up at the Avalon? –

– yes indeed – said Tom – I know Dr Feldenhammer very well – often visit –

Wrong answer – I thought. You cant survive as a student for 3 years without getting a nose for a touch!

– grand. Thing is – Im staying up there for a couple of

46

nights – & I seem to have come out without me wallet. So if you could sub me a fiver – better still 10 – Ill leave it with old Fester for you to collect next time you call in – right? –

It would have taken a lot harder man than Tom Parker to refuse.

The money was passed over – 20 in the end I noticed – & Mr Deal got out.

He turned & said – thanks for the lift – missus – & for the loan – Tom –

For the first time Tom Parker got a real look at him – full length – standing by the open door – in his pyjamas – with one bare foot. It was clearly a shock – & I think that inside he was bidding a fond farewell to his 20 quid – but he still managed that beaming smile as he said – our pleasure – our very great pleasure – goodbye –

Now the man turned his gaze on me.

– bye luv – he said – remember me to your dad –

– bye Mr Deal – I said.

He moistened his lips & leaned forward. For a dreadful second I thought he was going to kiss me!

– *Dee Ell* – he said very distinctly – get that straight – else thall niver go to heaven. *Dee Ell*. Cheers –

He turned & limped into the pub.

– oh dear – said Tom – I doubt if theyll serve him – looking like that –

I said – would you refuse to serve him Tom? –

He glanced round at me – then he smiled.

– you know – I dont believe I would! – he said – but the further adventures of Mr *Dee Ell* are no concern of ours! Mary – drive on. Lets get home & see the children! –

Which is what we did.

Minnie has just burst in again to tell me lunch is ready – knocking at doors must come late on the Parker curriculum! Better go. Watch this space for more exciting news from sunny Sandytown!

& dont forget that pic!

Love

Charley xx

5

There! What do you think of that, Mildred?

I did it!

Jumped the gun, surprised myself even, and now I'm in disgrace, quacks tut-tutting and feeding me pills, matron's bosom heaving like Moby Dick in a hurricane, Cap on the phone, spitting blood, and calling me a stupid infantile prat, and saying the only clothes she'll be bringing me's a change of nappies!

But it were worth it.

I think.

Cant say its done me a lot of good, but. To tell truth, I'm feeling a lot worse now than when I arrived here!

And I can't even take credit for putting together a cunning plan.

In fact there were no plan at all.

Today the weather were so nice, they suggested I had my lunch outside. The grub's pretty good, all fresh local stuff nicely cooked, but they don't exactly pile your plate up. When I asked if I could have a pint of ale to wash it down, the lass serving me said, 'Couple of days, maybe, Mr Dalziel. You're still on assessment. No alcohol till your diet sheet's been finalized, that's the rule.'

She smiled as she said it, a real smile, nowt made up about it. I smiled back. Weren't her fault, and she was a nice lass with a lovely bum which I admired as she walked away. But it did piss me off a bit, specially as I looked around the terrace where I was sitting and saw half a dozen old farts at another table supping vino and wearing real clothes, like they were on holiday on the Costa Saga.

But sod it, I thought. No reason not being dressed for dinner should stop me taking a stroll around to explore the place. They've started me on physio with Tony down in this little gym. Queer as a clockwork orange, but he knows his stuff, and though I'm still a long way off Olympic qualifying, I'm feeling a lot lisher than when I came.

I checked there were no one looking, then stood up and went down the steps from the terrace with a lot of care. Didn't fancy breaking me other leg!

Once on the lawn, I just meant to have a bit of a wander, but I'm still best in a straight line and as I'd got up a fair head of speed, I just kept going with the house at my back till I found myself ploughing through some shrubbery.

Here I stopped and checked back. The house were out of sight. That would get the buggers worrying, I thought. Bit childish, mebbe. But if they're going to treat me like a kid, I might as well enjoy myself like one!

So on I went till finally I came up against the boundary hedge. Thick and thorny. Good for keeping intruders out. And prisoners in!

I wandered along it for a while. I were beginning to feel knackered now and I was just thinking of setting off back when I spotted this gap.

Not a gap really. Just the point where two sections of hedge met but without getting all inter-twined.

I heard a car go by on the road. The road that led into Sandytown.

The road to freedom.

I felt sudden urge to take a look at it.

And why not? I thought. I'm not a prisoner! And my dressing gown's one of the thick old tweedy kind, none of them flimsy cotton kimonos or whatever they call them.

So I took a bit of a run, or mebbe a slow trot's nearer the mark, and got my shoulder into the breach.

Before my spot of bother I'd have walked through here, no trouble. But it turned out to be narrower than it looked and for a moment I thought mebbe I was going to get stuck and end up shouting for help.

Didn't fancy that, so I gave one last heave and burst through on to the roadside verge.

Except it weren't the kind of verge I expected, nice and flat and grassy. Instead it were a steep bank that fell away to the tarmac about twenty feet below.

No way of stopping. All I could do was try to remember all I'd learnt about falling, and curl up tight and try to roll. It were sod's law that there should be a car coming down the hill exactly at that moment. I had time to think, whatever hitting the tarmac don't break the collision will take care of!

Then I was under the front wheels and waiting for the pain.

When it didn't come, or at least not so much as you get shaving with a lady's razor, I slowly got up.

No sudden agony, no broken bones. I'd lost a slipper and my stick, but I were alive and didn't feel much worse than I'd felt thirty seconds earlier.

51

If we look closely we can see God's purpose in everything, my old mate Father Joe Kerrigan once told me.

I looked closely.

Here was a road leading down to Sandytown which had to have a pub, and I was leaning up against a car.

Joe were right. Suddenly I saw God's purpose!

They were nice folk in the car. Real friendly. I sat in the back with this lass. Could have been thirteen, could have been thirty, hard to tell these days. Turned out I knew her dad. Played rugger against him way back when I were turning out for MY Police. He were a farmer and used to play like he were ploughing a clarty field. Couldn't see much point to having players behind the scrum. Reckoned all they were good for was wearing tutus and running up and down the touchline, screaming, Don't touch me, you brute! We had a lot in common, me and Stompy.

They dropped me at this pub. The Hope and Anchor. I didn't have any money with me. Likely I could have talked the landlord into giving me tick, but this guy Tom in the car volunteered to sub me twenty quid, so no need to turn on the charm. I went into the pub. The main bar were full of trippers eating sarnies and chicken tikka and such. On the other side of the entrance passage were a snug, half a dozen tables, only one of 'em occupied by a couple of old boys supping pints. I went in there, put the twenty on the bar, and said, 'Pint of tha best, landlord.'

Don't expect he gets many customers in their sleeping kit, but to give him his due, he never hesitated. Not for a second. Drew me a pint, set it down.

I took the glass, put it to my lips, and drank.
Didn't mean to be a hog but somehow when I set it
down, it were empty.

'You'll need another then,' he said with a friendly
smile.

I was really warming to this man.

'Aye, and I'll have a scotch to keep it company,' I
said. 'And a packet of pork scratchings.'

I nodded at the old boys who nodded back as I
took my drinks over to a table in a shady corner.
When a landlord treats me right, I try not to offend
his customers.

I nibbled my scratchings, sipped my scotch,
gulped my beer, and took in my surroundings. Nice
room, lots of oak panelling, no telly or muzak, bright
poster above the bar advertising some Festival of
Health over the Bank Holiday. With medicine like
this, I thought, it couldn't fail! And for perhaps the
first time since that bloody house in Mill Street blew
up, I felt perfectly happy.

It didn't last long. Rarely does. According to
Father Joe, that's 'cos God likes to keep us on the
jump.

Certainly kept me on the jump here.

Hardly had time to savour the moment when the
bar-room door opened and a man in a wheelchair
came rolling through.

He halted just inside the door in the one shaft of
sunlight coming through the window. His head were
shaven so smooth the light bounced off it, giving him
a kind of halo. His gaze ran round the room till it
landed on me.

Perhaps there was summat in the Sandytown air
that stopped people showing surprise. The landlord

had kept a perfectly straight face when a slightly bleeding man wearing jim-jams and one slipper came into his pub.

Now the wheelchair man went one better. His face actually lit up with pleasure at the sight of me, as though I owed him money and we'd arranged to meet and settle up.

'Mr Dalziel!' he exclaimed, driving the wheelchair towards me. 'Of all the gin joints in all the world, you had to walk into mine! How very nice to see you again.'

I did a double take. Couldn't believe my eyes. Or mebbe I didn't want to believe them.

'Bloody hell,' I said. 'It's Franny Roote. I thought you must be dead!'

6

Had a little sleep there. Bloody pills!

Where was I?

Oh aye. Franny Roote.

First time we met were at this college Ellie Pascoe used to work at not far up the coast from here. They'd found the old principal's body buried under a memorial statue. Roote were President of the Students Union. Bags of personality. Made a big impression on everybody. Made a specially big one on me by cracking a bottle of scotch over my head. Insult to injury, it were my own bottle.

He got banged up – not for attacking me but for being involved in the principal's death. When he came out a few years back, he showed up again in Mid-Yorkshire, doing postgrad research at the University. Then his supervisor got murdered. So did a few other people.

Folk were always dropping dead round Roote.

Pete Pascoe were convinced he was involved, in fact he got a bit obsessed about it. But he never got close to pinning owt on him. Then Roote started writing him letters from all over the place. Funny bloody things they were, dead friendly on the surface, saying how he really admired Pete. But they really began to freak the poor lad out.

But finally, big twist, what happens is Pascoe's lass Rosie gets taken as a hostage by a bunch of scrotes Roote had known in the nick. Roote manages to get her out, but only at the expense of getting a load of buckshot in his back. Looked a goner. But he hung on. Got transferred to some specialist spinal injury unit down south. Pascoe kept in close touch. Practically took control of his insurance and compensation claims. Felt he owed him, specially after all the nasty thoughts he'd had about him.

Me, I were real grateful too. Rosie's a grand kid, got the best of both her mum and dad in her. But just 'cos I were grateful didn't make me elect him St Franny!

Pete gave us bulletins. Quadriplegia seemed likely to start with, so when it finally came down to paraplegia, Pascoe acted like he'd won the lottery. Bothered me a bit. I told him, be grateful, OK, but that don't mean feeling responsible for the sod for the rest of your life. Pascoe slammed off out after I said that and I heard no more about Roote for six months or more. That's a long sulk in my book so finally I mentioned him myself.

Turned out the reason Pascoe said nowt was 'cos he'd nowt to say. He'd lost touch. Seems that when the medics decided they'd done all that could be done for Roote, he just vanished. Pascoe had traced him as far as Heathrow where he'd got on a plane to Switzerland. We knew he'd been there before. That's where some of the funny letters had come from. This time no letters, not even a postcard. Best guess was, being Roote, he weren't settling for a life viewed from belly level, he were going to spend some of that compensation dosh looking for a cure.

Would have been easy enough for us to get a fix on him. Even in our borderless Europe, a foreigner in wheelchair tends to leave a trail. But I reckon Ellie said to Pete that if Roote didn't want to keep in touch, that was his choice.

Now here he was, large as life, back on my patch – all right, on the very fringe of it – and I didn't know a thing about it.

I didn't like that. OK, I'd spent a bit of time in a coma recently, but that's no reason not to know what's going off.

He manoeuvred his chair alongside me and said, 'I read about your bit of trouble and I'm so pleased to see reports of your recovery haven't been exaggerated. Though tell me, is the bare foot part of a new therapy? Or have you finally joined the Masons?'

That was Roote. Misses nowt and likes to think he's a comic.

I said, 'You're looking well yourself, lad.'

In fact he was. If anything he looked a lot younger than last time I'd seen him – not counting straight after getting shot, of course. The landlord came over to our table and set a glass of something purple with bubbles in front of him. Mebbe it were the elixir of life. If any bugger found it, it would be Roote.

He said, 'Thanks, Alan. And thank you too, Mr Dalziel. Yes, I feel extremely well. So what brings you to sunny Sandytown? No, don't tell me. Let me guess. I'd say you're down here to convalesce at the Avalon. You must have arrived fairly recently, they are still completing their preliminary assessment, which you, growing impatient, have opted to pre-empt by making your own way to this excellent establishment.'

Told you he were a clever bastard.

I said, 'If we'd caught you younger we might have made a detective out of you, Roote. But I'm not complaining we caught you later and made a convict out of you instead.'

'Still as direct as ever, I see,' he said, smiling. 'Any minute now you'll be asking what I myself am doing here.'

'No need to waste my breath,' I said.

'Meaning of course you're just as capable as me at working things out,' he said.

Like a lot of folk who love playing games, Roote always reckoned other folk were playing them too. Don't mind a game myself, long as I'm making the rules.

I said, 'No. Meaning I'd not believe a bloody word you said! But I can work out you've been here long enough for our landlord to know you drink parrot piss.'

'Cranberry juice actually,' he said. 'Full of vitamins, you really ought to try it.'

'Mebbe after morris dancing and incest,' I said. 'As for your reasons for being here, I'm not interested. Unless they're criminal, which wouldn't surprise me.'

'Oh dear. Still the old mistrust.'

'Nay, just the old realism,' I said.

Then I went on 'cos I'd never said it direct and it needed saying, 'Listen, lad, I'll be forever grateful for what you did for little Rosie Pascoe. Thought you should know that. Won't make me turn a blind eye to serious crime, mind, but any time you feel like parking your chair on a double yellow line in Mid-Yorks, be my guest.'

His eyes filled. Don't know how he does that trick, but the bugger's got it off pat.

'I think that's the nicest thing you've ever said to me, Mr Dalziel. And how is the girl? Must be growing up now. And dear Mr Pascoe and his lovely wife, how are they?'

'All well. He were a bit upset losing contact with you. What happened there?'

He sipped his drink. I had to look away. If the buggers can ban smoking, I reckon at least they should put up screens for folk wanting to drink stuff that colour.

Then he said, 'I was deeply touched by Mr Pascoe's concern for me. He's a man I admire greatly. I would love to be able to think of him as my friend. Perhaps it was because of this that, as I gradually improved, I began to worry in case the gratitude he felt should become a burden. It's all too easy for gratitude to turn into resentment, isn't it? Mr Pascoe is a man of intense feeling. Sometimes perhaps over intense. It was a hard decision, but I felt it might be best if I cooled things between us, so when I concluded that medical wisdom as it stood in the UK had done everything possible for me and decided to head abroad in search of other treatments, it seemed a good opportunity. I'm sorry if that sounds too altruistic for your view of me, Mr Dalziel, but it's the truth.'

I found I believed him.

I said, 'I reckon you got things right for once.'

The bar door opened and a young woman came in, laden with carrier bags. She were tall and skinny as a bow string. Slim they likely call it in the women's mags, or slender or willowy, some such bollocks, but it's all skinny to me. I like a lass with a bit of something to get a hold of. Mind you, beggars can't always be choosers and I've known a lot of bow strings that had plenty of twang in them, but on the whole I've always steered clear of the lean and hungry ones. Not that this lass weren't bad looking in a hollow cheek modelly sort of way, with wavy brown hair, a good full mouth, a determined little chin, and soft blue eyes that fastened on Roote.

She said, 'Franny, hi.'

'Clara,' said Roote. 'Hi! Come and meet my old friend, Andrew Dalziel. Mr Dalziel, this is Clara Brereton.'

She came towards us. She were a lovely mover even with the bags. Fair do's, probably being skinny helps here, though my Cap doesn't get many complaints on the dance floor.

She said, 'Nice to meet you, Mr Dalziel,' like she knew how to spell it. And she was another who didn't blink when she spotted how I were dressed.

I said, 'Likewise, lass.'

'Why don't you join us?' said Roote giving her the full smarmy charmy treatment.

She sat down, saying, 'Just till Auntie comes. Teddy's taking us to lunch at Moby's. He's supposed to be meeting us here.'

She looked relieved to set the bags down.

I said, 'They don't deliver round here then?' just to make conversation.

Roote chipped in,'Indeed they do, but there's a small charge, and why pay that when you've got your own personal service?'

They smiled at each other. Something going on here? I wondered. With Roote, owt's possible. A gent would likely have made an excuse and left them to get on with it, but gents don't find themselves sitting in public bars in their dressing gowns. Any road, I wanted to see how Roote would play it. But there weren't time to make his play.

The door opened again and another woman entered, this one a bit more to my taste. The way her gaze fixed on Clara and Roote, I guessed straight off this were the aunt. She were knocking on, sixties bumping seventy, but well preserved, and built like a buffalo, with an eye to match. If there weren't enough meat on young Clara to make a Christmas starter, there were plenty here for a main course with something left over for Boxing Day. Not bad looking for an old 'un, but in a very different way from her niece. No smooth pallor here but weathered oak. Only thing in common were the determined chin which age had carved on her face into a bit of an ice-breaker. This was a woman used to getting her own way.

She said, 'There you are, Clara. You've got the shopping? Good. No sign of Teddy? No matter, so long as he turns up in time to pay the bill. Time for a quick one here I think. Alan!'

The landlord was ahead of the game again. There was already a G and T on the bar and an orange juice. No prizes for working out whose was which.

'Good day, Lady D,' said Roote. 'I hope you are keeping well.'

'I am always well, Franny. I firmly believe most ailments are the invention of the medical profession to extort money from fools.'

She brayed a laugh like it never struck her some poor sod in a wheelchair might not find this all that funny. Roote just grinned and said, 'If Tom Parker wants a living testimony to the health-giving properties of Sandytown, he need look no further than you.'

She preened herself and said, 'Kind of you to say so, Franny. It's true I have been blessed with a strong and lasting constitution. In fact I do believe I never saw the face of a doctor in all my life on my own account, but only on the two unhappy occasions when I was told of the death of a husband.'

Roote looked solemn for a moment, then said slyly, 'But surely, Lady D, you have seen the face of Dr Feldenhammer, very much on your own account, and on occasions not so unhappy?'

She laughed archly, like a cracked hurdy-gurdy playing 'The Rustle of Spring', and I reckon if she'd had a fan, she'd have rapped his knuckles with it as she said, 'You naughty boy, that tongue of yours will get you into trouble one day.'

'Then I shall call on you for a character reference,' said Roote. 'Can I introduce my old friend Andrew Dalziel?'

I'd seen those buffalo eyes taking me in during all this by-play and I don't think she much liked the look of me or mebbe it was just my outfit.

I said, 'How do, missus?' and in return she gave me a nod that would likely have broken my nose if she'd been close up, then turned to hoist herself on to a bar stool, showing off a pair of haunches a man would be proud to have the tattooing of. The landlord put her drink before her and she leaned forward to engage him in a low-voiced conversation.

The lass gave Roote's hand a quick sympathetic squeeze, then went to the bar to join her aunt.

I took a drink of me ale. Didn't taste as good as before. Nowt wrong with the beer, but. It were me.

Should have stopped with the first and certainly skipped the scotch. I definitely weren't feeling up to snuff. Mebbe that was what made me say, all surly, 'You'll not get anywhere there, lad. Rich aunts look after dependent nieces.'

One thing for Roote, he may play games but he doesn't play silly games, like pretending not to understand.

'Dependent nieces have wills of their own,' he said giving me a stage wink.

'Aye, and so have rich aunts, and they make bloody sure anyone gets cut out of them who doesn't toe the line,' I said. 'Any road, it could be a long wait if she's as fit as she looks.'

'Oh yes. Dear Lady Denham is nothing if not healthy. And wealthy, of course,' he murmured.

'And wise?' I said.

'In making and keeping hold of money, very wise indeed,' he said.

'Why am I not surprised?' I said. 'And I bet you know how much she's kept hold of, to the last decimal place.'

He grinned and said, 'You are forgetting, I suspect, that thanks to dear Peter Pascoe's aid and acumen, I am now a man of moderately independent means, even without the income I generate by my writing. If such a one as I could have any interest in the fair Clara, it would only be centred on her pilgrim soul.'

When an ex-con starts talking about pilgrim souls, I know he's talking crap, but I knew Roote weren't lying about the money. Pete had felt so grateful and guilty, he'd moved heaven and earth to make sure Roote got top compensation from Criminal Injuries, plus the leisure complex where he got shot had had a Personal Injury clause in their insurance which a smart brief persuaded a judge covered Roote's case. Best of all, Roote had just got back from the States on the day he got shot and when Pete were sorting out his stuff, he realized his travel insurance didn't expire till midnight. The buggers wriggled and wiggled like they always do, but in the end the same brief who'd done the leisure complex got them to cough up for total disability. When eventually it turned out Roote was going to be able to manage a wheelchair, this got considerably pared down, but it still amounted to a hefty chunk of money.

I said, 'Independent means ain't the same as independence.'

I were just talking about money but soon as I said it, I saw it could be taken as a crack about his legs. Me and buffalo woman had a lot in common. But I knew better than to say sorry and get the piss taken out of me, so I went on quick, 'So what's this writing that's making your fortune? You're not Lord Archer in disguise, are you?'

'Happily not,' he said. 'Nor did I mention a fortune. It's academic stuff mainly, so it pays peanuts when it pays at all. I managed to finish my PhD thesis during my convalescence. Yes, strictly speaking it's Dr Roote now, but no need to be embarrassed – I don't use the title. Strangers find it confusing and keep telling me about their back pain. Now I am completing Sam Johnson's critical biography of Thomas Lovell Beddoes. You recall dear Sam, my old supervisor, who was so foully murdered before he could finish his masterwork?'

'Aye, I remember the case,' I said. 'So you're

getting paid in advance for writing this Bed-loving fellow's life?'

'I fear not,' he said. 'Though my publishers in California, the Santa Apollonia University Press, have made a substantial research grant available to me. There are however profitable spin-offs in the form of articles and interviews and seminars. In addition I have a small retainer fee for my work as a consultant for Third Thought.'

Why was he so keen to impress me with his ability to earn an honest living, if you can call all this airy-fairy arty-farty stuff honest?

'Third Thought?' I said. 'You mean that dotty cult thing the lentil and sandals brigade are into?'

'How well you grasp the essence of things, Mr Dalziel! What more is necessary to say? Though the movement's founder, Frère Jacques, has written a couple of hefty tomes to bring out the fine detail.'

Always a sarky bugger!

He rattled on about how this Jakes fellow had nearly died and realized he weren't ready for it, so he'd started his movement to help folk get used to the idea afore it were staring them in the face, so to speak.

'A Hospice of the Mind, he calls it,' said Roote. 'My own initial connection with Third Thought was, I freely confess, based purely on self-interest. Then I had my own close encounter, and as I struggled to come to terms with my lot, my mind turned more and more frequently to Frère Jacques's teachings, and I renewed my connection, but this time with genuine fervour. Eventually Jacques invited me to become a paid acolyte.'

He glanced at me sort of assessingly then leaned

forward and said in a low voice, 'It occurs to me, Mr Dalziel, that after your own recent trauma, you yourself might be seeking a new philosophy of being . . .'

The bugger were trying to convert me!

I said, 'If tha's thinking of sending me a bill for this chat, lad, I'd advise thee to have third thoughts about it.'

He laughed so loud the two women at the bar glanced our way, the old bird with a disapproving glower. Probably thought I'd just told a mucky joke.

Roote settled down after a bit, supped his parrot piss, then said, 'So how are you getting back up to the Home?'

'On my own two feet if I have to,' I answered. 'If you're thinking of offering me a lift, I warn you, I'm not sitting on thy knee!'

He grinned and said, 'I'll be delighted to take you back in my car, though I suspect it may not be necessary.'

'Why's that?'

He glanced at his watch. It looked expensive.

'I suspect that within a few more minutes someone from the Avalon staff is going to arrive. They'll order a drink, glance round, look surprised to see you, have a quick chat, finish their drink, head for the door, then as an afterthought say, "Would you care for a lift, Mr Dalziel, or are you sorted?"'

'What makes you think that?'

'Because not long after you arrived, Alan will have made a call to the Avalon in case they haven't noticed one of their convies has gone missing. And he's probably just been reassuring Lady Denham that she needn't worry about you frightening off the more

66

sensitive customers all afternoon as you'll be out of here in ten minutes tops.'

'Why'd she be worried about that?' I asked.

'Because she owns the Hope and Anchor,' he said. 'In fact, dear Lady Denham owns a great deal of real estate in and around Sandytown. I told you she was wealthy as well as healthy. Moby's, however, where they are going to lunch, belongs to her dear friend Mr Parker. She enjoys the food there but never goes unless someone else is paying, in this case her nephew, Teddy Denham, who can ill afford it.'

'For someone not interested in money, you've got a sharp eye for how other folk spend it,' I said.

He said, 'Only because as a disciple of Third Thought, I have a deep interest in the human condition. Doesn't Paul tells us that the love of money is the root of all evil?'

'Paul?' I said. 'Thought that were one of Ringo's. No, sorry, bit further back. Adam Faith, right?'

Not often you can shut Roote up, but that did it.

The women finished their drinks and slipped off their stools, the lass like a snowflake, the old lady like an avalanche.

Clara gave a shy little wave as her aunt said, 'Alan, perhaps my scatterbrained nephew has gone straight to Moby's. If he does turn up here, tell him that's where we will be. And don't forget to get payment for our drinks. A gentleman does not invite guests and expect them to pay for themselves. Talking of money, these ideas you have about modernizing the cellar, I think we really need to do an in-depth costing. I need quotations, not estimates. If I have time I'll drop in later to take a closer look.'

The landlord bowed his head deferentially, or

mebbe he were worried in case his expression showed this weren't the best news he'd had today!

'Of course, Lady Denham,' he said.

Now she glanced our way and said, 'Toodle-pip, Franny. Don't forget you're lunching with me this week.'

'Engraved on my heart, Lady D,' said Roote.

Her gaze shifted to me and she ducked her head and gave a little snort like she were wondering whether to charge but headed for the door instead.

I muttered, 'Will that be lobster at Moby's?'

'Alas, no. Belly pork at Sandytown Hall, I fear,' said Roote with a little shudder.

Afore I could ask what he meant, the door opened as the women approached and a Yankee voice gushed, 'Daphne, Clara, how nice. How are you, dear ladies?'

Toilet tooth Festerwhanger.

Well, at least they really had sent Prince bloody Charming not some snotty-nosed orderly to round me up. Always supposing that's why he'd come. I could see Roote thought it was. He gave me one of them little looks. Quizzical I think they call 'em. Like Pascoe sometimes. Mebbe him and Roote had more in common than I realized.

Stepping into the bar, Festerwhanger flashed the young lass a spotlight smile, then got folded into buffalo woman's arms. It were like watching one of them Cumberland wrestlers tekking hold, except they don't clamp their gobs on to their opponent's face and give his tonsils a tongue massage. I saw now what Roote's little insinuation were all about.

Eventually he broke loose, staggering a bit like a diver who'd come up too quick. But to give him his

due, he made a quick recovery, and soon him and
Lady D were chatting away – him all Yankee charm
and her sort of girlishly flirtatious – like an elephant
dancing in that old Disney cartoon. I almost felt
sorry for old Fester. Got the feeling she could chew
him up and spit him out all over his consulting room
couch. Finally she gave him a farewell kiss which
made the first one seem like a rehearsal and set off
again but stopped dead in her tracks as the door
opened to admit another man.

Different this time, but. No gush and hugs. In fact if
I can read a face, there's neither of them would have
lost sleep if t'other had dropped dead on the spot!

The new guy had halted right in the doorway so
she couldn't get by.

'If you don't mind,' she said, haughty as a
duchess talking to a gamekeeper she don't fancy
shagging.

He didn't move. He looked about ninety and I've
seen healthier looking faces at an exhumation. His
eyes were deep sunk, his few bits of hair clung to his
pate like mould on an old plum, and he had a beard
like a wildlife sanctuary. Despite the heat, he were
wearing a mucky old donkey jacket, an old-fashioned
striped shirt without a collar and the kind of baggy
pants farmworkers used to tie up with string, only no
self-respecting rat would have cared to run up these.

Suddenly I didn't feel so badly dressed.

Still he didn't move or speak. Then the landlord
said warningly, 'Hen.'

Now he smiled. Bare gums mainly, and the few
teeth you could see through the foliage were greeny
yallery shading to black at the roots. I half expected
Festerwhanger to faint.

Then he stepped to one side and did a piss-taking bow and said, 'So sorry, Your Ladyship. Didn't see you there. So sorry. Would hate to get in Your Ladyship's way.'

'You won't,' she said. And went sweeping past him, young Clara in pursuit looking a bit embarrassed.

The old boy kicked the door shut behind them. The landlord said, 'Watch it, Hen. It's me as is responsible for fixtures and fittings. Your usual, Dr Feldenhammer?'

The Yank who'd been watching the incident with interest nodded. His usual was a short. Dark amber, enough ice to sink the *Titanic*. Jack Daniel's mebbe. At least it weren't purple. Festerwhanger sipped it, then turned and leaned against the bar. His face split into that toothy grin as he acted like he'd just noticed us.

'Well hello there, Franny,' he called. 'And Mr Dalziel too. Glad to see you're getting around, sir. You're looking well.'

Roote gave my thigh a told-you-so jab under the table. I'd have given him a let's-wait-and-see kick back, only with him not having any feeling in his legs, it didn't seem worth the effort.

'Aye, I'm not so bad,' I lied. Truth was, I felt distinctly woozy. The ancient geezer had got himself a pint without opening his mouth or handing over money, so far as I could see. Another time I'd have been interested to find out what had just gone off here, but at the moment, I didn't give a toss.

'Good. And you, Franny, how are you? Coming to Tom's meeting on Friday, I hope?'

'Of course. Exciting times, Lester. Won't you join us?'

Franny and Lester. Like an old music hall act.

Roote had really got his useless legs under the table round here. Sounded like his social calendar were pretty full too.

'Thanks but I mustn't stay,' said the Yank. 'Just came out to drop an express packet into the post office. My niece's birthday back home. Almost forgot, which would have been a capital offence. Felt I'd earned a quick one, but I need to be back up at the clinic pretty well straightaway.'

I weren't so ill I didn't notice there were too much bloody detail. Think a shrink would know summat like that. Plus, most country post offices I'd come across shut up at midday on a Saturday.

The door opened again. This were getting like a French farce. New arrival were a well set-up young fellow, one of them craggy faces that has five o'clock shadow at half past one. Looked like he reckoned the world owed him a living and the women in it owed him a shagging.

He said, 'Alan, any sign of my aunt?'

'Been and gone. Says she'll see you in Moby's.'

'Oh dear. Bit pissed off, is she? That will mean the lobster thermidor, I fear. But then she was never going to choose the monk fish pâté, was she?'

He made a wry sort of face to show he was joking, only he wasn't.

Now he let himself take in the others in the bar. Worzel Gummidge he ignored, me and Roote he shot a cocky grin at and said, 'Ah Franny, nursy taking you for a stroll?', then he did a double take as if he'd just noticed Fester and cried, 'Is that you, Dr Feldenhammer? Didn't recognize you in a sitting position, sir. I hope I find you well. Mustn't keep auntie waiting.'

71

Then he left, whistling raucously.

I saw Festerwhanger flush the colour of old port. Either he were seriously narked or he was going to have a seizure.

He downed the rest of his drink like he needed it, ice cubes clanging against his snowy teeth hard enough to dislodge a polar bear, slid off his stool, gave the landlord a curt nod, and marched through the door.

I said to Roote, 'Got that wrong, didn't you, lad?'

He said, 'I just think the game changed, but never fear, he'll remember. That tune Teddy Denham was whistling, I'm trying to recall what it is. I've got it on the tip of my tongue.'

Meaning he hadn't the faintest idea but would be glad to know what caused the Yank doctor to lose his cool. Didn't miss much, our Franny.

'Sorry, no idea,' I said. Which was a lie. I'd recognized the notes of a little ditty I've heard belted out at the back of rugby coaches more times than I care to remember.

Don't expect Roote spent much time in rugby coaches, and I didn't see any reason why I should enlighten him.

Roote were giving me one of his looks which said he knew I were holding out on him. Then his expression turned to I-told-you-so! as the door opened again and Fester stuck his head back in.

'It just occurred to me, Mr Dalziel – would you like a lift back up to the Home? Or do you have transport arranged?'

I suppose I could've told him I preferred to walk. Or that Roote were giving me a lift. But sod that. Only a fool turns down what he wants out of pride,

72

and what I really wanted now were to crash out in my pit.

'Nay,' I said. 'That 'ud be grand.'

I looked at my beer glass. It were half full. I realized I didn't want it.

Only a fool sups what he don't want out of pride.

But I could feel Roote watching me, and this time pride won.

I drained the glass, set it down, and hauled myself out of my chair.

'Thanks, mate,' I said to the landlord. 'Good pint that.'

'Thank you, sir. Hope we see you again soon,' he said.

'Never fret, I'll be back.'

Roote caught my arm and said in a low voice, 'Mr Dalziel, just one thing. About Mr Pascoe, I'll leave it up to you.'

Whether I told him or not, he meant.

I gave him a nod and left.

I wouldn't trust Roote as far as I could throw him, which, the way I were feeling just then, was about half a yard. But credit where due, I couldn't fault him over how he'd dealt with Pete.

Which don't stop me wondering now they've finally got me tucked up in bed and talking to myself under the sheet, if one of the reasons Franny Roote took off abroad with no forwarding address was 'cos he didn't want Pete Pascoe feeling responsible for him, then why when he came back to England did he opt to settle here in Mid-Yorkshire? OK it's right on the fringes of our patch, but it's still our patch!

Can't get that tune buffalo woman's nephew were whistling out of my mind. How did the words go?

Let's see . . . summat about an Indian maid . . . aye, that's it!

> *There once was an Indian maid,*
> *and she was sore afraid*
> *that some buckaroo would stick it up her flue*
> *as she lay in the shade.*

And so on. Gets dirtier. Not the kind of thing I'd expect Fester to choose for his *Desert Island Discs*. And why should it bother him so much?

Questions, questions, lots and lots of sodding questions hopping madly round my mind to that jaunty little tune. But it's always the same one leading the dance.

What the fuck is Roote really up to here in Sandytown?

Never fear, one way or another, I'll find out afore I go!

But all I want to do now is sleep.

So it's goodnight from you, Mildred, and it's goodnight from

7

FROM: charley@whiffle.com
TO: cassie@natterjack.com
SUBJECT: Min of Information!

Hi Cass!

Thanks for pic. He is truly gorgeous! I want one of my own. Does he have a brother? Nice smile. Whats he got to smile about – I wonder?!!

Back to dull old Sandytown! After lunch yesterday Tom excused himself – to catch up with all the stuff that had piled up in his absence – & Min – whos clearly decided to make me her own! – asked me if Id like to go swimming with her. I thought she was being kind – & meant the sea – & said yes please – but it turned out she meant the swimming pool at this 5 star hotel Tom told us about – the Brereton Manor. Seems the Parkers have membership of the Health & Leisure Club – natch – but the kids arent allowed in without a responsible adult – so Min the minx had elected me! Mary tried to rescue me – but I said – no problem – & off we went.

Minnie led me over the road – & through a gate – then across a golf course that looked to be in the final stages of construction.

– Should have been finished for Easter – Min told me proprietorially.

Serious money being spent here – I thought – confirmed when we reached Brereton Manor. Must have been a grand old house – now much modified & extended – all the eco friendly – carbon unfriendly – stuff theyve got at Kyoto – but tastefully blended in – the kind of detail that costs a fortune. Presumably the idea is youve been invited to a 1920s weekend house party – rather than asked to cough up a small fortune for b & b! Not many people around. Still bedding in. Official opening is not for a fortnight – Bank Holiday weekend – when Tom launches the Festival of Health – which I shant be around to enjoy – thank heaven!

This info again supplied Min!

She sailed in thru the front door like a grand duchess – & the receptionist greeted her with a big *Hi Minnie!* & gave me a smile too.

Everyone else we met en route to pool seemed to know Minnie. Swish pool – long way from Olympic – but big enough if you like that sort of thing. I did 10 or so lengths – very boring – specially as I had to stop from time to time to admire Minnies breast stroke – or back stroke – or diving. At 9 you need a lot of admiration! After – we sat in some very comfortable chairs in the café area – & had a coke – talked. Or rather – I listened! Didnt mind. I was getting interested in what made Sandytown tick – you know me – never happy till Ive got the inside of things outside! – & nothing that goes on round here seems to escape Mins sharp little eyes & ears! By the time shed done – I was thinking of her as my personal Min of Information!

The original house – as I knew – belonged to the well-heeled Breretons – the famous Lady Denhams family – but became superfluous to requirements when she married even better-heeled Hog Hollis – local lad made good –

who built up his pig farm into Hollis's Ham – the Taste of Yorkshire – & ended up master of just about everything he surveyed – Lord of the Sandytown Hundred – at Sandytown Hall.

He died – fattening the pigs who helped fatten him – (I had to practically kick Minnie onward from all the gory details – mostly imagined I guess – of the poor sods death!) – leaving his wife even richer than hed found her – & eventually she remarried – Sir Henry Denham – & Denham Park became her official address – though – probably not caring for the pig pong but reluctant to do anything that might interfere with her pig profits – she spent a great deal of her time at the Hall.

When Sir Harry in his turn died – (dont know what she does to the poor sods!) – she returned permanently to Sandytown Hall – refusing the chance to move back to her childhood home – Brereton Manor – when her ancient father finally died – because – according to Minnie – the Hall was a more prestigious address – & the Manor had certain inconveniences of access – & had fallen into such a dilapidated condition it would cost a fortune to put right.

– daddy owns nearly all the land all around – explained Minnie – where the new entrance drive is – & where theyre building the golf course. I think it was Uncle Sids idea that they should work together & turn the manor into a posh hotel. Uncle Sid knows all about money – which is why Lady D listens to him – mum says –

– thats nice – I said – so your uncle is a sort of financial adviser to the Consortium – right? –

– I think so – she said uncertainly. Then she grinned & went on – Uncle Sid says Lady Denhams tight as a ducks arse – & thats water tight – watching me closely to see how I reacted.

I just laughed – you cant be Stompy Heywoods

77

daughter without hearing far worse expressions than that!
– which emboldened her to say – me & Uncle Sid call her
Lady B – not Lady D.

– B for Brereton? – I guessed.

– no – B for Big Bum – she screeched.

I was beginning to feel intrigued by this Sidney
Parker – who chose to talk to his niece like she was an
intelligent human being rather than a backward dwarf –
which is how awful Uncle Ernie always spoke to me.
Min was vague about his actual job – & even from
Mary – *hes in banking* – was the best I could get –
which reminded me of dads response when Mrs
Duxberry boasted her moronic son was in banking – *oh
aye? – you mean – like Bonnie & Clyde?* –

Trying to work out the Parker family dynamic – OK – I
mean I was as nebby as usual! – I asked about the sister.
According to Min – Aunt Diana is really wierd – always
going on about being at deaths door – which used to
scare Min when she was little – thinking she meant the
attic door in their old family house – & that must be where
death lived! It was her Uncle Sid set her mind at rest – by
taking her up into the attic – & showing her the relics of
his childhood – & also by saying – dont worry about your
aunt little Min – when you yourself are finally laid to rest
– aged 150 or thereabouts – it will be Auntie Di who lays
flowers on your grave! –

Bit macabre comfort – I thought – but kids love
macabre & in Minnies eyes Uncle Sid is perfection itself!

Not sure if Mary would go as far as that. Tom vanished
after supper tonight – still catching up he said – & once
the kids had all been put to bed – in Mins case by main
force! – me & Mary had a large Baileys apiece – & got to
talking like old mates. I reckon shes been dying for
someone to confide in for years – someone outside the

78

family – & outside Sandytown. Like I said before – shes incredibly loyal – but I got a strong impression she secretly fears this Development Scheme will end in tears.

Shed confirmed what Min had told me – that it was Sid who got things started.

Sids always been good with figures & stuff – from an early age hes handled the Parker family finances – very successfully too – Mary admits. Good investments – steady returns – spotting which Lady D got in on the act – asking his advice – free to a friend of course – & so profitable that Sid soon became her blue-eyed blue-chip boy!

Anyway – Sid came up with this idea that the combination of the Brereton property & the Parker land & Toms architectural know-how could add up to a nice little earner. At least thats the way I guess he put it to Lady D. With Tom Im sure he painted things in more visionary terms – the greater good – benefit of the community – environmental concerns – etc – the kind of stuff Tom had been dabbling in all his life.

This was how the great Sandytown Development Consortium got into its stride – & since then – I gather – Sidney has acted not only as its financial consultant – but also as an umpire when Tom & Lady D dont see eye to eye. Lady D is far from persuaded that Toms preoccupation with complementary medicine & the environment is going to be a money spinner for the hotel. Upper class recreational pursuits – facials – manicures – massage – plus maybe the latest post Pilates exercise fad to work up an appetite for the gourmet grub – & thirst for the disgustingly expensive booze – thats what she sees bringing the stinking rich punters in. But Tom wont give ground here – insisting there has to be room for a full range of alternative

therapies – something in which his family have always had
a deep – in some cases – Mary hints & Min confirms –
an *obsessive* interest. Fortunately it seems Dr Feldenhammer
– boss man at the Avalon – after some initial doubts – has
been persuaded theres no harm in the clinic presenting a
united front with Tom re the complementary stuff.

– very enlightened of him – I said – surprised –
knowing most mainstream medics think its all a load of
crap – me too if Im honest – which Im not – around dear
Tom!

– yes – & the good thing – said Mary – is that it shuts
Daphne Brereton up a bit – her feeling about poor Lester
the way she does –

– eh? – I said – you dont mean . . .? –

– oh yes – shes got him in her sights – & wants him
in her bed – said Mary grimly – disgraceful – a woman of
her age –

Maybe this Sandytown air really does have something
special! – I thought.

Its clear Mary has mixed feelings about the relationship
between Tom & Lady D. Loyalty makes her stick up for
Tom all the time – but theres part of her that sees that its
Daphnes lust for profit thats going to keep the Consortium
solvent – rather than Toms idealism. When Big Bum –
funny how nicknames stick! – does let Tom have his way
– it usually means *him* paying more & *her* paying less –
so Tom looks like hes won a battle – but its cost him – &
Mary is always worried he might be overstretching himself.

Not that Tom seems to have a worry in the world! He
finally appeared – apologizing like mad for having
neglected me.

– tomorrow morning I should have caught up with
myself – he said – Ill take you on a tour of the town – on
foot! Best way to see a place & meet people!

– but your ankle dear – protested Mary.

– as good as new – he insisted – thanks to the first aid I received from our lovely talented guest – (thats me in case you havent twigged!) – not forgetting the healing touch of Mr Godley –

I left them arguing – or rather discussing – Tom doesnt have arguments!

Met Minnie coming out of bathroom – yawning histrionically! Wouldnt surprise me if shed been listening on Mary & me – & had to take cover when her father came out of his study – but I cant help liking her. Shed have followed me into my room – but I shut the door very firmly in her face. I can be tough too!

Nite nite sleep tite

Love

Charley xxx

8

FROM: charley@whiffle.com
TO: cassie@natterjack.com
SUBJECT: enter Big Bum!

Hi!

Decided to laze around this morning – guessing that any expedition with Tom would be energetic! Hed won the 'argument' about going on foot – but Mary insisted he took a stout walking stick – which seemed more likely to cause damage than prevent it – the way he flourished it as a handy pointer to interesting views as we made our way down the hill.

On our way up in the car – Tom had already pointed out to me the entrance drive to Sandytown Hall – home of Lady D. Admiring the view from Brereton Manor – Id glimpsed what had to be the tall chimneys of the Hall down towards the sea – rising above an extensive area of woodland – so her ladyships not overlooked by the hotel – or any other bit of quite a lot of modern development we passed on our way down the hill. Most of this seemed linked to the Development Scheme – executive dwellings – seeded – so Tom assured me – with affordable houses for local first-timers. I didnt need to guess which partner pushed for what!

We met quite a few people – car drivers stop to chat to

Tom! – & I was introduced as if I were the Development Schemes latest & greatest acquisition! Eventually – quite near the bottom of the hill where the old village proper begins – he halted outside a funny old house – very picturesque – built out of irregular lumps of sandstone – glowing in the morning sun – with a small old fashioned cottage garden – & a first floor wider than the ground floor – because it was built into the slope.

Reminded me of the gingerbread house in the fairy tale – so I wasnt surprised when Tom said – this is called Witch Cottage – because – according to tradition – its where Sandytowns last witch used to live. Now Miss Lee – our acupuncturist – lives there. I know youll want to meet her – Charlotte – because of your study –

Hed just lifted the brass knocker – & given the door a hearty rap – when this old Jeep came rattling up the road from the village. It looked like it had just completed a trek across the Kalahari – mud stained – lots of scratches & dents – & the nearside front bumper showed signs of recent violent contact with a tree!

Oh look – its Lady D – said Tom – come & meet her –

As we went back down the little path – 2 women got out. I knew which was Lady D straight off. Central casting – tweedy – sturdy – head thrust forward like shes eyeing up the opposition – if Id been a matador Id have headed for the barreras – good looker in her day probably – in a Fergie kind of way – nice healthy complexion – well weathered – the natural look – tho I spotted a touch of eye shadow & a smear of lipstick – so not without vanity – (I recalled what M said about her pursuing Dr Feldenhammer) – likes her own way – sharp – but maybe not so sharp as she likes to think.

& Minnie was right about her bum!

All that from a single glance! Arent you impressed?

The other woman was young − my age − bit older? − lovely slim figure − God − even when I did my anorexia thing I never got to look like that! − big boned us Heywoods − family gene thing − except this other woman − Clara Brereton her name is − turns out to be a relative of Lady Ds − so how come she doesnt look like a Hereford ready for market? In fact shes gorgeous − if you like your women fashionably *skinny* − which most men seem to − so − bringing my psychological objectivity to bear once more − I resolved to hate her!

Tom & Lady D greeted each other fondly − genuine on both sides from the look of it − tho I noticed she calls him Tom − while he only gets close enough to familiarity to call her Lady D − unlike Mary who refers to her − disapprovingly − as Daphne Brereton!

Credit due − the old bird did ask after Toms sprained ankle. He told her the story of how he got it − made it quite funny − & she brayed a laugh.

While this chitter chatter was going on I got a close up of the jeep − & I noticed someone had added to the general air of dereliction with a bit of graffiti − scrubbed off but not so efficiently I couldnt make out the letters P O L R & M U D R − which − I guessed from the gaps − added up to POLLUTER & MURDERER. Made me think of the sign outside the pig farm. Not only Mary who doesnt care for Lady D!

She was saying shed been going to call in at Kyoto House − Tom said lets go back there now & have some tea − she said no she couldnt possibly do that − Mary would have so much to do having just returned − he said Mary & the children would never forgive him if they discovered hed missed the chance of bringing Lady D home with him − she said it was flattering but she couldnt

possibly impose – & somewhere in the midst of all this Tom
& me had been translated into the back seat of the jeep.

As I got in I realized someone had answered Toms
knock at Witch Cottage – a stocky oriental looking woman
– who was watching us – inscrutably – like an extra in a
kung-fu movie. Tom – whod gone round to the other side
to get in – didnt notice her – but Lady D did – & she
called out – Good day to you – Miss Lee – I hope you –
& your ancestors – are well – which I took to be some
sort of Chinese greeting. For a moment the womans mask
slipped – & she looked daggers (or maybe – in view of
her profession – needles) – at her ladyship – then gave a
stiff little bow – & went back into the cottage.

Im getting the feeling that – living in Sandytown –
everyone is expected to know their place – which is –
Lady D on top – the rest below!

Lady D was still saying she wouldnt come in – as she
came in – & twenty minutes later was saying she definitely
wouldnt stay for tea – as the first cup was poured. Nice
technique – getting whatever you want without having to
be grateful for it.

But on the whole – I was more amused than alienated
by her on first meeting. Good-humoured – long as she
got her own way – showed a lot of interest in dad & the
farm – said shed heard that Heywood of Willingden knew
a bull calf from a bale of hay – treated the kids in the old
fashioned country way – gave them 50p apiece & then
ignored them.

Soon her & Tom got to talking about plans &
development & visitors & such. Big event next Sunday
– to celebrate progress & say thanks to those
concerned – is a party at Sandytown Hall – my ears
pricked when I heard them refer to it as a hog-roast –
remembering the nickname of Lady Ds 1st husband! –

but seems it just means theyre going to barbecue a pig. I got bored – & concentrated my clinical gaze on Clara – & tried to draw her out.

It was like trying to take a bone off old Fang – except she didnt growl.

Quiet as a nun – contained – gave nothing away – maybe shes got social problems – serve her right for being so good-looking! At least when time came to go – she offered to help with washing up the tea things – but Lady D was on her feet – & would brook no waiting. Whatever auntie wants – auntie gets!

I helped Mary clear up. Tom headed off to his study to work on his computer – declaring that Lady D was like Sandytown itself – a breath of fresh air – bringing new life to old ideas. Me – noting her cool reaction to some of his less commercial concerns – Id have said more like a breath of CO_2! But Toms enthusiasm is the kind that sees direct opposition as oblique encouragement!

Mary is much clearer-sighted. Over the washing up I asked about Clara – had she always lived with her aunt?

– oh no – said Mary – only for the last six months or so –

Didnt take much to get the whole story. Bit like a 19th century novel – in fact the whole place has that feel – slow paced & leisurely on the surface but all kinds of interesting plot stuff swirling around underneath!

Daphne Brereton – Lady D – wealthy by birth – & wealthier by her first marriage – is naturally the object of much interest – living – & even more – dead! The Great Philosophical Question occupying Sandytonians isnt the meaning of life – or even – can England ever win the World Cup again? – any world cup! – but – wholl inherit Lady Ds lolly?!

Mary has a nice narrative style – little overt malice

– but she purses her lips when certain subjects come up – & you get the message as well as the facts!

Not much chance of the money going to charity – it seems. Lady D feels the poor of the world probably deserve it – except for poor old horses – whose reward for having their spines bent by big bums like hers during their prime should be an old age of comfort & freedom! Used to be a very keen hunter herself – kept half a dozen top class horses – her one extravagance – Mary says. Gave them up after Sir Harrys accident – only keeping one old boy – Ginger – for looking down at the peasants from as she hacks around the countryside!

So – OXFAM – eat your heart out! Daphs stated belief is – money should stay in the family – but which family? – is the question.

Hot favourites for a long time were the Denhams – specifically a nephew who inherited the title & Denham Park when Lady Ds husband – Sir Harry – died. Nothing else – because there wasnt anything else – & even the house was a poisoned chalice – entailed so he couldnt sell it – & it would cost a fortune to get back to what it once was.

Love apart – Sir Harrys plan had been to repair the family mansion – & his own fortunes – by a 'good' marriage – told you it was like a 19th century novel! – but hed popped his clogs before any of his brides fortune could find its way into the Denham account.

According to Mary – Lady D had been heard to say – in confidential mood – that though shed got nothing but her title from the Denham marriage – on the other hand shed given nothing for it! Some dame – eh? Perhaps it was her sense of having lost nothing – plus of course it must give her a nice power charge – that made her play along when the new baronet – Sir Edward – & his sister

– Esther – started cosying up to her. Lady D loves having them dance attendance – drops them little tit-bits from time to time to keep them interested – took them on a skiing holiday last Christmas for instance. That made them think they were at the top of the inheritance list – so they must have got a nasty shock when shortly after they came back Lady D brought cousin Clara to live at the Hall! To compensate – maybe – she gave Sir Ed some kind of job in the Hollis pig empire – not his kind of thing at all – Mary implied – but hed had to take it – or risk losing his cosying-up access!

Seems first hubby – Hog Hollis – was built in the same mould – expecting relatives to put up with his bossy ways – & be grateful for whatever crumbs he dropped their way. Closest – in blood at least – was his half-brother – Harold – known as Hen – Hollis. Seems the pair never got on – & when they inherited Millstone – the family farm – rather than work together – Hog went with the pigs – & Hen with the poultry – hence their names – gerrit?!

Neck & neck at first – till Hen got hit hard by the salmonella scare way back. Needed cash badly – turned to Hog who was doing well – Hog offered a loan – but being *echt* Yorkshire – demanded Hens share of Millstone as security. When – despite the loan – the chicken business finally went bust – Hog gave Hen a job – in charge of quality control – in his pig business. But it was still family loyalty – Yorkshire style! Part of Hens salary came in the form of letting him continue to live at Millstone Farm – all of which now belonged to Hog!

Hog himself was now ensconced in Sandytown Hall – from which he wooed Daphne Brereton. They married – Hog continued to prosper – Hen & Lady D didnt get on – but both of them were used to not getting on with people so nothing strange there – then Hog died – & left nearly everything to his widow. His token acknowledgement of family ties was that he only left her Millstone in trust. The building & everything on the farm would revert to Hen – if he survived his sis-in-law.

Locally – says Mary – if you want to bet on Hen outliving Lady D you can get odds of 20 to 1! She enjoys vigorous good health – hes a hard drinker – & smoker – & 'choleric' – most of his choler being directed at his brothers relict – who is enjoying what he – & several other Hollises – thought should have come to the family.

Led by Hen – these disaffected Hollises raised objections to the will. Not all of them – some – like Alan Hollis who runs Lady Ds pub the Hope & Anchor – knew what side their bread was buttered on. The others got nowhere – Lady Ds smart London lawyer soon swatted off their flimsy legal objections. Lady D was ready to be patronizingly generous in victory – after all in their shoes shed have done exactly the same – but when she learned that Hen was trying a new tack – & circulating rumours that shed had a hand in her husbands death – she went bananas!

Daph & Hen had a violent – & public – row – which ended with Hen refusing to retract his insinuations. Maybe hed forgotten that Lady D was now his boss. If so he was quickly reminded when she fired him – & when he retaliated by saying he didnt fancy working for a fat old tart anyway – Daph really put the boot in by serving him notice to quit the Hollis farm – which she was legally entitled to do.

Happy families – eh? Makes our lot seem right cosy!

At least Hen has the satisfaction of knowing Daph has no way of stopping him getting Millstone back – if he outlives her. But the others – that is the Denhams – & cousin Clara – are going to have to sing her song for whatever supper she may leave them. Mary shows little sympathy for the bart & his sister – but she purses her lips on Claras behalf – implying her position in the household is less honoured guest than unpaid housekeeper & general factotum!

Made me feel guilty about bad-thinking her – Clara I mean – now I know shes a *poor relative* – probably shivering in an attic bedroom – & scrubbing floors & cleaning grates for her daily gruel – & brawn on Sundays!

– so Lady Denhams a bit tight with money? – I said – stopping short of Uncle Sidneys phrase.

– you could say that – said Mary.

– but she is throwing this big hog-roast party next Sunday – I said.

Mary did the pursed lip thing again. (I really must practice it! Might come in useful when patients ask my opinion about their amatory feelings towards their livestock!)

– the event is financed by the Consortium – she said – all Daphne Brereton is providing is the location. The Hope and Anchor – which she owns – is supplying the drink – & I gather shes even charging the Consortium for the Hollis pig – so – as usual – she will end up making a hefty profit! –

Interesting – eh?

Spent the evening playing snap with the Parker kids. Found it hard not to do a Headbanger & win all the time – so I rang home – just to remind myself what I was missing. Nice chat with mum – then dad came on. In a good mood – got the house the way he likes it again – no visitors – just him – mum – George plus the twins – & me where he likes me – at the end of a phone line – where were both at our best!

Told him about the escaped *convie* – Mr Deal – aka *Dee Ell* – who claimed to know him.

– big bugger? – he said – looks like his mam got put to stud with a prize bull? –

Got a way with words – our dad – but I had to admit he was on the ball here.

– aye – I remember him – Andy Dalziel – (He spelt it out) – hes a copper – dont know what he does to crooks – but he used to kick the shit out of us on rugby field –

– he remembered you fondly too – I said – called you Stompy –

– remembered that – did he? – said dad – sounding like he was touched – Not a bad sort – Dalziel – long as you dont cross him. Hard man to knock down – bet he dented Parkers car! – It were him that got blown up by them mad buggers earlier this year – you probably read about it – if you had time to look at a paper – between disco-dancing & getting drunk –

Interesting view of higher education – our dad!

– thats probably why hes at the convalescent home – I said.

– theyll have their hands full – he said – give him my best if you see him again –

I said I would – but not much chance – I think. Probably got him in a padded cell after his escape trick the other day!

So now to my lonely bed – thinking of you all tangled up with the bronze bonking machine! Just cos Ive given up men forever doesnt mean I cant enjoy them vicariously – so – give him one for me!

Lots of love

Charley XX

9

Morning, Mildred!

They've still got me banged up in bed, so I might as well talk to myself. At least I'll hear some sense!

No. Be fair. Like me old mam used to say, there's some folk you needn't be kind to, but you should always try to be fair with everyone.

I thought I'd wake up with the dawn the morning after the great escape and feel right as rain. Instead it were nigh on midday and I were busting for a piss, but when I slid out of bed, I almost fell over. Felt worse than I'd done in the Central.

Matron appeared like a flash – mebbe she's got me bugged!

'Mr Dalziel,' she said. 'You shouldn't be up!'

'Shouldn't I?' I said. 'It's either that or I'll be floating out of here on my mattress.'

She had the sense not to suggest I use one of them bottles, but slung my arm over her shoulders, grabbed me round the waist and together we staggered into the bathroom.

'There,' she said. 'I'll just tidy up your bed, then I'll be back for you.'

'Take your time,' I said. 'I'm going to.'

I left flushing the bog till after I'd got washed up so's she'd not have any advance warning and come rushing to help. Two quick steps from the bog to the doorway and I had to stop for a rest.

Matron were standing by my newly made bed, holding my recorder.

'Found this in your bed, Mr Dalziel,' she said.

'Oh aye. It's a sex aid,' I said.

'Really?' she said, holding it to her ear. 'What's it play? Beginner's instructions?'

Cheeky cow! But I had to laugh. And she grinned too, like she knew that my only interest in bed that moment was getting into it and going back to sleep.

I went forward at a stagger, grabbed the recorder off her and fell across the mattress. She tutted and pulled the duvet over me.

'I see you've got a visit scheduled tomorrow,' she said. 'Hope you can get down to your physio session in the morning or we may have to cancel it.'

But she was grinning as she said it.

Bit more to her than I reckoned. Could make summat of her yet! But need to be careful now she's set her sharp little eyes on this thing. Think I'll tuck it between my legs before I go to sleep. If anyone can get it out of there without me noticing, then I'm really knackered! But I'll need to find a better place to hide it permanent if I don't want them having a right giggle in the nurses' room. Old trick, wrap it in a plastic bag and stick it in the lav cistern. First place a cop 'ud look, but cops are one thing I don't need to worry about just now!

So, head down, and hope I can skip them funny dreams I keep on getting and work on a nice little fantasy about Cap instead. Roll on tomorrow. Couple of hours with Cap's all the physiotherapy I need!

10

OK, Mildred, I should have listened to you and put my woolly vest on!

Bad night. Didn't get my hoped-for fantasy about Cap but another bunch of them daft dreams about floating around and talking to God!

But my physio went well. Tony tutted a bit when he looked me over. But by the time he'd finished, I were feeling lish enough to reckon I could give Cap the welcome she deserved!

First, though, I had to put up with her giving me the bollocking she thought I deserved! Blabbermouth Festerwhanger must have really laid it on thick about how much damage I could have done to myself going over the wire.

I tried playing it down, doing the big bull thing, saying, 'Come here and I'll soon show thee how poorly I am!' Well, she came, and I showed her, and that's when I found out like mam used to say that my eyes were hungrier than my belly.

When I finally gave up, she said, 'That does it, Andy. From now on in, if they tell you to start the day with an ice bath, you bloody well take it! If I wanted a eunuch, I'd have looked in the Istanbul small ads.'

She's got a real lip on her, Cap.

She'd brought my civvies as promised and it were only by promising to be a good little patient and do what matron tells me that I stopped her from taking them back.

When I asked if she had any news from the Factory, she said nothing, except that Pete had told her everything was going fine and nobody was missing me. He'd asked her about visiting me. I told her no way, not till I were properly up and about. He'd seen me at the Central while I were still good for nowt. Next time he saw me, I wanted to be back to something like full steam, else he might start feeling sorry for me. I don't doubt the vultures are already circling over the Factory and if Pete comes back from a visit with a long face, they'll be flapping to land!

Cap said I were daft, I needed my friends. I said I knew what I needed better than her, and she rolled her eyes and said that what I clearly needed was another week in bed. And not long after she took off. Said she wanted to walk over to the nursing home and see her old headmistress who's on her last legs, it seems.

Her parting line was, 'Maybe that's where I should have put you, Andy.'

I saw her out. As I made my way back to my room, who should I see coming out of it but Franny Roote!

'What the hell are you doing?' I demanded.

'Looking for you, of course, Andy,' he said. 'A few of your fellow convies – sorry, convalescents – are interested in Third Thought, and after I finished with them, I asked Pet where I'd find you.'

'Pet?' I said.

'Nurse Sheldon. I'd have thought you'd have been on first-name terms by now, Andy.'

'Well, we're not. And neither are you and me,' I said grimly. 'Now bog off!'

I wasn't in the mood for chatting with Roote, not the way things had gone with Cap. Don't know who it was said that pleasures are always paid for, but the bugger got it right. My pleasure had been a couple of pints of ale, one of which I didn't really enjoy, and here I was, still paying for it.

Which reminds me. I owe yon fellow Parker twenty quid. Well, it will have to wait. I know its only tea time, but I need my beauty sleep!

11

FROM: charley@whiffle.com
TO: cassie@natterjack.com
SUBJECT: titled hunks & legless wonders

Hi!

No reply yet to mine of yesterday. Too busy? Doing what? – I ask myself.

Well – Im busy too – but its not going to stop me finding time to tell you all about it – which youd better read – therell be a test!

If theres anyone left in Sandytown that I havent met yet – anyone of importance I mean – they must be living in a cave! Late breakfast this morning – Tom & Mary said I should ignore all sounds of early reveille – their kids like kids everywhere want to sleep forever during term time but are up with the lark in the hols. Minnie – I suspect – must have got a death threat warning to keep her away from my door – but it worked – & I didnt come down till half ten!

Just enjoying a coffee with Mary – Tom I guess was out even earlier than the kids! – when the doorbell rang. Mary went to answer it – & came back with this *hunk* – in tight black motor cycle leathers – & you know what they can do for a guys figure.

Not that this one wouldnt have looked good in pinstripes.

6' 2" — handsome as hell — in that old fashioned Hollywood kind of way — before the new 3 day dead look came in — athletic build – wide shoulders – narrow hips – lovely bum – not *bronze* exactly – his face I mean – dont know about his bum – yet! – but a very even & natural looking light tan! OK – he clearly thinks hes Gods gift – but like the man said – when you got it – baby – flaunt it!

This was Teddy Denham – Sir Edward Denham no less – Lady Ds nephew-in-law – & one of her hopeful heirs! Having heard from Lady D that Tom was back – hed come straight round to say hello – & check on the now famous ankle.

Mary introduced us – & he said Lady D had mentioned me – with a bit of a grin to suggest I might be amused by the terms of the mention – & he shook my hand – with enough warmth to make it personal.

My gaze had been so fixed on him that I hardly noticed his companion – which was OK – as she made it pretty clear she didnt really think me worth noticing either!

This was his sister – Esther – beautifully turned out – beautiful too if shed give her face a chance. Thought she looked a bit familiar at first glance – but her first – & only – glance at me when introduced made me change my mind. Reminded me of dads comment about the vicars wife – *like shed bent to sniff a flower & found it were growing in a cow-pat!* If anyone had looked at me like that before I think Id have remembered.

She looked like her idea was to say hello–goodbye! – but *he* said yes hed love a coffee – & sat down beside me – & soon we were chatting away like wed known each other for ever. After ten minutes – Tom turned up. He & Teddy greeted each other like old mates – Esther gave him a condescending cold fish nod – which he took like it was a loving hug! Then Teddy asked after Toms ankle & got the full miracle recovery story.

– of course – declared Tom – I benefitted from instant & expert first aid from our dear friend Charlotte here – (this got me a *well arent you the talented one* grin from Teddy the bart) – but – Tom went on – I feel I must also give credit for the incredible speed of my recovery to Mr Gordon Godley of Willing*dene* – (he stressed the long e & smiled at me as if to say he was glad of the error that had led to me being here in Sandytown) – the famous healer whom I hope to entice to join our caring community –

As he spoke – he did a little jig to demonstrate his recovery. Esthers face had screwed up like a pigs bum at the mention of *healer* – & when she saw the jig I thought she might vomit in disgust. Fortunately for the high polished floorboards her mobile rang at that moment. She looked at the caller display – & her face rearranged itself so quick it might have been computer-enhanced.

– Aunt Daphne! – she trilled – how *are* you? –

She rose & moved away – not with the usual *sorries* most of us mutter when the mobile catches us in company – but more like shed have preferred the rest of us to move out of the room & leave her sitting!

But the change of expression revived my first impression – now I was really sure Id seen her before – or her twin! Remember – last December – the skiing in Switzerland near Davos – I gave you a *full* account about me & louse Liam – unlike the censored stuff youre giving me! Dad did his nut – till I assured him Id be back for Xmas – & it was costing hardly anything – travel by bus – hostel accommodation – bunk beds in dorms – which made him think – wrongly! – naughties would be out of the question. But it was George asking if he could come too that persuaded dad to cough up the readies. The HB thought George would be a chaperone – I thought hed just be a bit of a drag – but we were both wrong! In the end – like I told you – turned out he was getting as much action as I was!

Anyway – our *après-ski* consisted of a beer-swilling disco in the Bengel-bar – cross between Willingden Village Hall & the Black Hole of Calcutta – where all the impoverished young stuff went – & thats where Id seen the sour-puss look-alike – but not sour-puss – laughing like a drain – as she did high energy dirty dancing with this skinny blond guy – with hair down to his shoulders – & a soup strainer moustache. His name was Emil – second name Geiger-Counter according to George – but that was just his version of something like Kunzli-Geiger. How G knew him – I think they had a pee together – thats how guys bond – its in all the textbooks! – & next day hed met him on the piste & they had a bit of a race – which G lost. G was clearly impressed that a skinny fellow like Emil should be able to beat him at skiing – & – I suspect – tho he didnt spell this out – should have such a big whang! Must ask G when I ring home. *She* didnt have a name – just an initial – Ess – & one of my mates – watching the way they danced – christened them Ess & Em – which I had to explain to George – who thought it was the funniest wordplay since madam Im Adam – remember? – & rewarded my mate accordingly!

But still couldnt believe dirty dancing Ess & sour-puss Esther could be the same – though I recalled Mary had mentioned Lady D took the young Denhams on a ski holiday last Christmas. Shed stepped into the hallway – but her voice stayed at that upper-class level that assumes that servants – & others of that ilk – like me & the Parkers – are – or better had be – stone deaf. So we heard her quite clearly saying – no – not in the least inconvenient – no – a social call merely – in the circumstances you might call it a sick visit – an irksome duty – but a duty

100

nevertheless – as you of all people will understand – Aunt Daphne. Five minutes – scarcely that –

Tom meanwhile had asked Sir Teddy how work was going – & the bart pulled a face – & said – lets just say I hope Aunt Daph doesnt serve up pork for lunch – again! –

I said – do you have much actual contact with the pigs? –

– indeed – he said ruefully – from first squeak to final freeze-pack – I oversee quality control –

This was nepotism – Yorkshire style! – I thought.

Then Mary said – I wish theyd put someone in charge of odour control too –

Teddy smiled sadly – & said – you should try living out at Denham Park Mary –

From the doorway Esher said – Teddy – we have to go – Aunt Daphne has some family matter shed like to discuss with us –

Very peremptory – sweetness soured – light switched off – normal service resumed.

– whats the panic – Ess – said Teddy – glancing at his flashy Rolex – we arent due there for ninety minutes –

There! Hed called her Ess! Short for Esther – which is one of those names that really need shortening! It had to be her – tho the resemblance had faded as she was now back in sour-puss mode. But if – as I recall G saying – Emil was just a poor student – then that would explain why they were meeting in the Bengel-bar – where there was no chance of running into Lady D or her chums – who were probably drinking over at Klosters – with Big Ears & his tribe of Noddies.

– so why cant she just talk to us over lunch? – Teddy concluded.

– in front of Clara? – said Esther.

101

She spoke the name like it was a nasty taste.

– Claras family too – said Ted – winning a Heywood Brownie point.

– not *our* family – & besides the legless wonders going to be there too –

I saw Tom & Mary exchange disapproving glances – but neither spoke.

– is he? Whys that? – asked Teddy frowning.

– he seems to amuse her – & he doesnt eat much – look – Im off – you can follow whenever you find the strength to drag yourself away –

She nodded at the Parkers – didnt even glance at me – & span on her heel – very tall sharp heel it was – she knows how to dress – must run in the family – the bart looked a real dish in his leathers – & I could imagine him peeling them – James Bond-like – to reveal an . . . . . . immaculate dj! (Got you going there!)

Disappointingly – despite his protests – Teddy didnt have much trouble dragging himself away – tho he did gabble a rueful apology before heading after the Ice Queen.

As he left – Tom said to me – come on Charley – time to finish our tour –

When Tom decides something – its instant action! – & we were out of the house in time to see Esther climbing behind the wheel of a Range Rover – what else? – pretty ancient – but the landed gentry probably regard new RRs like new Barbours – as evidence of *arrivisme.* Ted – by contrast – was straddling a new looking Buell Lightning – in midnight black – with the words *Sexy Beast* scrawled across the tank in silver. Narcissism? I wondered. Or a gift from an admirer . . .?

As they processed at speed down the drive – I said – thought Mary said they were a bit strapped for cash – no wonder if they spend it on 7k mo-bikes! –

– as much as that? – said Tom – well – he really was lucky then – Ted didnt buy it – won it in a charity lottery – cast your bread upon waters – eh Charlotte? –

Lucky old Ted – I thought. No wonder he thinks the world owes him a living!

Walking down the hill – I wondered – dead casual – if there might not seem to be some conflict between Toms eco-enthusiasm & the bloody great carbon footprints the Denhams – young & old – seemed bent on planting all over the roads of Sandytown.

– just so! – cried Tom – as if delighted by some sharp & helpful *apercu* – this is how I see things too. Physician – heal thyself – then pass the cure on! To convert is better than to convict – to persuade than to prescribe. We all have our complementary roles – mine I see as a gatherer – bringing together the full spectrum of ability. It did not take long – dear Charlotte – to see how useful a talent like yours – to observe & analyse – would be to our little community –

It dawned on me then that in Toms eyes I was – like Gordon Godley – an opportunity not to be missed. The bugger was trying to recruit me!

But hes such a poppet I could only feel flattered!

As we once more approached Witch Cottage – recalling the small incident yesterday – I asked how Miss Lee – the acupuncturist – got on with Lady Denham. Tom – whos clearly into universal love – said – fine – fine – But hes also into transparent honesty – & he added – there has been a small contretemps – I believe – regarding the terms of Miss Lees tenancy – but Im confident a mutually satisfactory resolution has been reached –

I said – you mean Lady D owns Witch Cottage? –

– indeed – he said – & much more besides – the Breretons were substantial property owners in the town –

& Hog Hollis – Lady Ds first – rarely missed an opportunity to invest in bricks & mortar –

Id have liked to hear more – but realized I was only going to get a sanitized version of any unpleasantness from Tom – & made a note to bring the matter up with that young mistress of unsanitized versions – Minnie!

At the cottage – after a little delay – Miss Lee answered Toms knock. I was introduced – briefly. She did a little Chinese bob thing – like Pitti-Sing in the musical. She was wearing a sort of kimono – but close up her face looked a lot less oriental – more plastic than porcelain – & Id say the almond blossom complexion comes out of a jar. Her voice was pretty neutral – very precise – with the occasional Yorkshire vowel suggesting shed been around the county for some time.

She had a patient – she explained – but would join us shortly. We were standing in a narrow passage with a steep staircase up to the first floor – & 2 doors to the right – & another at the far end – open to reveal a kitchen. Miss Lee slipped through the first door – presumably not wanting us to see some poor devil stuck with needles like a hedgehog! – & Tom led me through the next door – clearly very much at home.

I found myself wondering – this alternative medicine thing – does he try them *all*?

We were in a crepuscular living room – small 16th cent windows in walls a yard thick – bit of a change from bamboo & rice paper – or is that Japan? Couple of pictures on the wall – prints of Chinese art – & a framed professional certificate – in Chinese characters. No – I havent taught myself Chinese – alongside it in the same frame was what I presumed was an English version – telling the world that Yan Lee had earned her qualifications – with distinction – at the Beijing Institute of Acupuncture

& Moxibustion! (You tell me – youre the familys medical expert!)

Tom settled into a dusty armchair – to read a dusty newspaper – & I wandered around – checking out the bookshelves. Us psychologists can tell a lot from bookshelves! Fiction mainly – chic-lit – historical romances – couple of classics looking like they were lifted from school. Non-fiction limited to royal reminiscences – & Delia – plus – which I almost missed – a very tatty paperback – *Teach Yourself Acupuncture*. Set book from the Beijing Institute maybe?

Miss Lee re-appeared as I was looking at it – so I quickly shoved it back into place – & hoped she hadnt noticed. Tom chit-chatted for a moment or two about local matters – then started talking about my thesis – making me sound like an FRS on a WHO funded research project! Miss Lee listened – then said – so you would like to talk to my patients to see if I really do them any good physically? I said – no – I would like to talk to those whose physical improvement is undeniable – with a view to understanding the mental processes involved. I have no interest in passing judgment on the status of acupuncture as medical therapy –

She gave me a little smile – like she didnt believe a word of it – & said – OK – Ill have a word with a couple of them – see what they think – & get back to you – now I must get back to work –

After that Tom whipped me round his aroma-therapist – middle aged Madonna lookalike – his reflexologist – like an undertakers receptionist – pallid complexion – black skirt & top – probably a Goth in her teens & couldnt yet afford to upgrade – his herbalist – funny little man with a young-old face – would have made a good Lord of the Rings elf. All happy to help me – after consulting patients first of course – Tom very persuasive – or – more likely – they see Toms enthusiasm for a complementary therapy centre at the Manor as their route to fame & fortune – so what he wants – he gets!

(Cynical? *Moi?* A lifelong beleiver its love makes the world go round? Love of *self* – or love of *money* – of course!)

Tried to see Toms homeopath but he was laid up with a bad cold.

– maybe hes treating himself for pneumonia – I said.

Tom thought this was very funny – once hed worked it out – & insisted on repeating it to everyone else we encountered – adding Wildean wit to my other talents. He was still chortling as he led me into the Hope & Anchor – the pub wed left Mr Deal heading for. Wouldnt have surprised me to find him still drinking there after what dad said about him – but no sign of him among the tourists eating bar snacks in the main bar – nor in the smaller room we turned into. No food here – just four or five men drinking pints – & one leaning on the bar – in close confab with the barman.

Tom introduced me to them. Barman was Alan Hollis – the landlord – & the other was Hollis too – Hen Hollis – the disaffected sibling – who was the 1st guy Id met clearly not a fan of Toms. Must see him as tarred beyond redemption with the Denham brush! Talking of tarred – this miserable old sod looked like hed not been near a bathtub since his 21st. If theres any family resemblance – Lady D must have been mighty releived when the pigs et hubby Number 1! Sorry. Shouldnt judge by appearances – specially in my line of work – but hes one of those long rangy guys – mean little eyes in a small narrow head – & a beard that made Mr Godleys look like it had been worked on by Errol Douglas – full of crumbs from the

crisps he was stuffing between his sharp yellow teeth. Like
a ferret on stilts – I thought – & he didnt like the look of
me either – glowering at me like I was the whore of
Babylon – I wish! – before he banged his glass on the
bar – & left.

Landlord Alan is v different – mid thirties – not bad
looking – easy to talk with – hard to believe hes related
to horrible Hen – no physical resemblance – hes one of
those steady calm-looking guys – the sort you want to see
slipping into the pilots seat when the aircrew all go down
with e-coli – while Hen looks like hes on friendly terms
with most known bacilli! But cant choose your relations –
can you? As we well know!

The seated drinkers were fine too. Tom introduced me
round – but I only really registered one of them – a man
in a wheelchair. Hes called Franny Roote – & Tom made
a big point of him being one of his alternative therapists.

Then Tom said – but shouldnt you be up at the Hall –
lunching with Lady D? –

Thats when it struck me with a shock – this was who
Esther Denham meant when she said *the legless wonder.*
What a cow!

– cant have a private life in Sandytown – said Franny
– quite right Tom – but not for another ten minutes or so
– & I much prefer the presence of new beauty to the
prospect of old pork –

Gave me a big grin as he spoke – big attractive grin –
so – telling myself Id better check if his kind of therapy
fitted into my research area – I plumped myself down next
to him – & we got talking – while Tom got deep into some
Consortium matter with a couple of the others.

Interesting guy – this Roote – something about him
thats different – & I dont just mean the wheelchair –
something about the way he looks at you – & the way he

talks. I found myself telling him all about me & my plans —
not just me either — but you & George & Adam & Rod &
the twins & mum & dad & the farm — OK — might be a
line — but made me feel he was really interested — gives
off a real sense of power — like theres nothing he cant do
— sexy too — though maybe being paralysed from the
waist down means there *is* something he cant do? — need
a bit of professional guidance here sis!

Youll be thinking I must be really frustrated — going on
about Teddy the hunky bart — & now Fran the dishy
paraplegic! Could be Toms right — & theres something in
the Sandytown sea breezes that gets the red corpuscles
bubbling — but I know that really my interest is purely
professional — Ive given men up — remember!

Finally I got him talking about himself — fascinating —
though as far as my research is concerned I soon realized
Franny doesnt fit in at all. His thing is 3rd Thought — have
you heard of it? I recall in my 1st year at uni going to a
talk given by a guy called Frere Jacques — in dads terms
very much a daft bugger! — who founded the movement.
Lots in it about modern living making us lose touch with
death — the need to establish a hospice of the mind — & a
lot of similar gobbledygook which us smart 1st year psych
students all rubbished like mad — but the guy himself was
gorgeous — had an aura — & a lovely ass. Frannys the
same — except his aura aint pure white like Frere Js —
more shot silk — changing & mysterious — & I didnt get
the chance to check out his ass! Anyway — thing is — with
3rd Thought theres no physical therapy involved — no
taking up your bed & walking — not surprising really — guy
in a wheelchair isnt likely to get far promising miracle
cures. So — nothing here for me — except — I really
enjoyed talking to him — & including him in my research
gives me a good excuse for doing it again! So we ended

by exchanging mobile nos & email addresses before he went off to Big Bums.

Anyway thats it for now. Spent the afternoon – after a sandwich in the pub – meeting the rest of the inhabitants of Sandytown – every single one of them it felt like! – then back here to Kyoto. Quiet night in – reading – & hammering the kids at snap! Make sure you answer this one sis. Dont see why you should get the details of my wild life in Sandytown while all I get from you is a pregnant (?) silence. So – no prevarications – I want dirt – I want dimensions!

Love

Charley xxx

12

FROM: charley@whiffle.com
TO: cassie@natterjack.com
SUBJECT: camomile tea!

Hi! Still no word. Working on the Headbanger principle that the only thing that travels faster than bad news is crap through a goose – Ive not started worrying – yet!

Here excitement piles on excitement – not sure if Ill be able to bear much more!

Thats called irony by the way – just in case youve completely forgotten everything Mr big-Dickenson at the comp taught you in English – though I dont suppose you heard much of what he said – above the roar of your randy hormones! .

First – Toms sister Diana turned up! None of the strong hints Id had about her oddness prepared me for the reality. Not bad looking – small & trim – full of words & fuller of energy – or so it seemed to me – though by her own – & Toms – account – she spends so much time lying at deaths door – she must be a real hindrance to his milkman!

Death must be on hold today – way she came bursting in at Kyoto like a small tornado.

– I am just arrived – she proclaimed – let me sit down – (which she did) – your raw sea air – a tonic I know for some – is too savage for my weak constitution. Where are the dear children − (jumping out of her chair) − I must see them at once − & this is Miss Heywood − I know you from Toms letters − my dear − its true Tom − a fine complexion − no trouble with *your* circulation − Tom − how is your ankle? − let me see − (here she knelt & pulled up her brothers trouser leg & folded down his sock) − looks fine to me − very little swelling − (not surprising as she was looking at the wrong ankle) − you say the Willingdene healer played a part? − an interesting acquisition − too late for me of course − years of misdiagnosis by incompetent MDs have put me beyond hope of healing − but I work tirelessly for others −

As I listened to Diana rattling on − I began to understand Toms preoccupation with alternative medicine. In his beloved sisters eyes − alternative was mainstream − she was into alternatives to the alternatives!

Finally Tom got a word in − asking where her luggage was − assuming she would be staying at Kyoto − causing Mary to wince before the polite smile formed − but relief was on its way.

− such was of course my intention − said Di − but as you know I have been ever industrious in singing the praises of Sandytown − Tom − & as you may have noticed − I have been instrumental in persuading a freind of mine − seeking a holiday destination for herself & her teenage neices − to choose Sandytown rather than one of the less salubrious resorts − so I thought I would drop in on her at Seaview Terrace to check that all was as perfect as I had promised −

− & was it? − asked Tom.

− alas no − she said − Unfortunately one of her neices had slipped while scrambling over some rocks on the shore − damaging her leg − not too seriously − but sufficient for her to wish to recuperate at home − &

111

naturally her sibling went with her. I found Sandy – that is my freind – Mrs Griffiths – undecided whether to follow their example – or stay on by herself. Seeing the danger that her early return might start a rumour that Sandytown beach was unsafe – whereas the truth is – as you know Tom – we have some of the least slippery rocks on the east coast – I immediately offered my services – both as co-tenant – & as a conduit into the best circles of the district – both of which offers Mrs Griffiths – that is – Sandy – was delighted to accept. Beleive me – only my sense of responsibility for the good name of Sandytown – & by implication of yourself – Tom – would make me inflict this disappointment on you & Mary –

She looked for applause – which Tom gave her – while Mary managed to murmur something about typical kindness – & all I could think was – unaccountable officiousness!

Tom – full of brotherly concern for her frail constitution – insisted on driving her back down to the Terrace – with me invited along too – I suspect in my capacity of St J Ambulance trained physician – in case the shock of the sea air brought on a seizure!

Sandy Griffiths – even though introduced as a 'vegan warrior'! – had no outward signs of the kind of dottiness I suspect must be a precondition of chumming up with Deaths Door Di. 40 something – strong handsome face – with a peculiarly disturbing stare – I thought she looked pretty good for someone who presumably existed on sprout fricassees & nut cutlets. She made us v welcome. Tea was produced – camomile for Diana – of course! – Typhoo for the rest of us – plus some v nice cream cakes – which Di thrust aside with shudder – declaring that one bite would be the death of her. All the more for me! I noticed that Sandy G had a nibble too – so not a total vegan! Nor – it seemed to me – a particularly close buddy of Dianas – which made me wonder how shed let herself be manoeuvred into having Di as her live-in guide. Tried some subtle probing – but Sandy G fixed me with her stare – so I backed off. Maybe being called Sandy makes her feel as proprietorial about Sandytown as Diana clearly does!

Tom clearly sees nothing but his sisters good points. He really is a sweetie. I find Im becoming as anxious as Mary that some people might be tempted to take advantage of his good-nature.

2 more excitements – then Im done. I dont want to risk over-stimulating you!

After we left the Terrace – driving back through the town – we saw Franny Roote hauling himself into his car. The ease with which he did it – reaching out to fold up his wheelchair & swing it into the back – suggested long practice – & my heart ached for him. OK – I know what youd say – all that stuff about handicapped people finding expressions of sympathy & offers of assistance patronizing – but I cant help it. Hes a young guy – & hes missing out on so much young guy stuff it breaks me up – so there!

Tom pulled alongside – & called – hello there Franny! – hows things –

– great – he said – giving me a big smile – & how are you – Charlotte?

– fine – I said – nice wheels.

Idiot thing to say – as it was a small boxy MPV – chosen – I guess – because the sliding doors made things easier.

– yes – he said – I dithered between this & the Porsche for a long time –

But he gave me a big grin – to show I hadnt really offended him.

Tom said – you wont forget the planning committee meeting at the Avalon on Friday –

113

– such excitements – said Fran – the committee on Friday – Lady Ds hog-roast on Sunday – then less than a week to recover before the Festival – be still my foolish heart! –

Tom – who doesnt do irony – said with concern – Fran – is there a problem? –

– no no – grinned Franny – of course Ill be there – Charlotte – will you be staying on for the Bank Holiday weekend & the great Festival of Health? –

– no – Im heading home this Saturday – I said.

Tom looked devastated – tho Id made it clear this was my plan – & Franny winked at me & said – then why not let Tom bring you along on Friday – not to the meeting – wouldnt wish that on my worst enemy – but Lester will be laying on some booze & snacks afterwards. Its the Festival action committee – so all us therapists will be there – great chance to pick their brains for your thesis – & Ill be first in the queue! –

Tom thought this was an excellent idea – & I was rather flattered by Frans keenness to see me again. (OK – I know – Im anybodys for a kind word!) Also I wouldnt mind seeing the inside of the Avalon – so I said – why not? – giving Franny my best smile.

– great – he said – look forward to seeing you then –

– me too – I said – meaning it.

Dont know whats happening to me! Maybe Sandytowns one of those magic places – like Brigadoon or Oz – that you stray into – then get taken over by.

Yes – thats it – definitely a magic place. But what colour magic Im not yet sure!

Write soon before I forget the real world out there!

Lots of love.

Charley xxxx

13

How do, Mildred!

Don't recall when I've slept for so long if you don't count being in a coma! Must have needed it 'cos when I woke up this morning I felt more like my old self than any time since I'd been here. Went for my physio session with Tony. Said he were pleased and suggested I finished with a massage. I said no thanks, thinking it were one thing doing knee bends with Tony on hand to steady me if I keeled over, quite another to be lying on my face with my bum in the air while he took a running jump at me!

Then this strapping blonde appeared, lovely smile, said her name was Stiggi and she was sure she could help me, wouldn't I change my mind? So I did.

It were grand, nice and relaxing. Too relaxing. Suddenly lying there face down with her straddling me back, I realized I were close to embarrassing myself, so when she tried to turn me over, I let on I'd dozed off. She wandered off to do something and I scrambled into my jim jams and dressing gown. Hadn't got dressed so fast since that time thirty odd years back when I were banging Sergeant Pocklington's missus and I heard his size fifteens coming up the stairs! All I need now is a bit more red meat on my plate and I'll soon be ready to make Cap eat her

Hang about. I'm coming . . . oh, its you.

Hi there, Mr Dalziel! How're you doing? Hearing good things about you so I thought I'd drop by to check you out for myself . . .

Oh aye? Well, take a look, lad. What you see is what you get, isn't that what them ET anoraks say?

IT I think you mean. Yes, they do, but it doesn't really apply in my line of business any more than I expect it does in yours. We both know there's no art to read the mind's construction in the face, right?

If you're trying to say you need to be a trick-cyclist to be a good cop, you've come to the wrong shop. I'm not saying it never comes in useful but I've got clever buggers working under me to do the fancy stuff. Me, its collars I'm interested in fingering not souls.

Souls? Interesting choice of word, Mr Dalziel.

Sorry. Limited vocabulary. Don't have the Latin so I've got to make what I do have go a long way.

I believe it. And it's a journey I'd like to make with you if you let me. To lay it on the line, Mr Dalziel, physically you seem to be back on stream after your little glitch. You're looking good . . .

I'd look a lot better if they stopped feeding me like a prize greyhound.

I'll have a word. But as I was saying, how fast you're recovering from the mental trauma of your experience, only you can say. I hope pretty soon you'll trust me enough to feel able to say it, but that's entirely up to you. How're you getting on with the audio-diary, by the way?

Eh? Oh that recorder thing. Sorry, went right out of my mind. Can't even recollect where I put the bloody thing.

That's OK. I'm sure it will turn up. So, before I go, anything I can do for you, apart from seeing you get more red meat on your plate?

One thing, there's a guy lives locally, name of Parker. Says he comes up here sometimes.

Tom Parker? Oh yes, I know Tom well. Important man round here. He's got big plans for Sandytown, him and his partner, Lady Denham.

Her in the pub? You're not saying he's shacked up with her? Nay, I met his missus, at least I assumed she were his missus . . .

No, sorry, I was using partner in its old pre-permissive sense. Their union has much to do with Mammon and nothing at all with Hymen.

No need to talk dirty. Any road, I owe him twenty quid. Mebbe if I gave it to you, you could pass it on?

Happily. But better still, I'm having a little get-together tomorrow lunchtime. Tom Parker has persuaded me that the Avalon ought to play a major role in this Festival of Health he's organizing to launch the hotel. We're meeting together, some of my staff and his alternative therapists, to make sure we all understand our roles. Afterwards there'll be drinks and snacks and there'll be a few other people there to help things swing along. I'd be delighted if you could join us, and if you did, then you could repay your own debt, couldn't you? I'm a great believer in a man repaying his own debts; that in some ways is what my work is all about. So, won't you come?

I'll think about it.

Excellent. Nice to talk with you, Mr Dalziel. About one o'clock. Petula will show you the way.

Handy little gadget this. Didn't realize I'd left it running when I shoved it in my pocket after

Festerwhanger tapped at the door. Its picked up every word him and me said.

Dead sensitive, like me!

Not that hiding it fooled old weasel-eyes. I reckon he'd been listening at the door for a couple of minutes afore he knocked. Played it back to be sure and there it was, red meat on my plate. Coincidence? Mebbe. But I'll take more care from now on. Simplest would be to toss the bloody thing into the sea. But, fair do's, it could be the bugger's on to something with this talking to myself thing. Admit it, Dalziel, your bollocks might be back to twitch mode, but you're still not right in your head, not while you keep having these funny dreams about talking to God!

Mebbe it's that post-menstrual traumatic sin thing they go on about these days. Likely there's a lot of it about in a place like this, so no wonder if I've caught a dose.

Any road, if yakking about it helps, nowt wrong with yakking. But I'm definitely not going to spill my guts to yon Yankee wanker!

Jesus, there it goes again. Knock knock knock. Who's there, in the name of Beelzebub? All right, I'm coming. There'd be less traffic living on Scotch Corner roundabout.

Oh, hello, matron.

Sorry to disturb you, Mr Dalziel, but Dr Feldenhammer said you were having some problem with your diet.

Only problem is seeing it, luv. I'm a growing lad. I need fettling.

I won't argue with you there. Can I be frank with you, Mr Dalziel?

Long as it don't involve dressing up in leather.

You have a large frame, and I can understand your desire to fill it again. But this might be a good time to take stock and ask yourself if you really want to put back on all the weight you lost during your recent unfortunate experience.

How do you know how much I weighed before?

We have your medical records. No one comes to the Avalon without a complete legend.

So I'm a legend, am I? I'll tell you what, luv. You fatten me up till I reach what you think is my legendary shape, then we'll see how we get on from there, OK?

That sounds reasonable. Now I gather I'm to escort you to Dr Feldenhammer's lunch meeting tomorrow.

If you're Petula, that's right, matron.

Yes, that is my name. My title incidentally isn't matron. I am Head of Nursing Care and usually I'm addressed as Mrs Sheldon.

But I bet you're undressed as Pet, right? Nay, don't look offended, not when you've got such a bonny smile. That's better. Let's start again. If we're going out together, I'm going to call you Pet. And if you're going to get me back to my proper shape, you can call me Adonis. But Andy will do if you're worried about folk talking.

Andy it is. Will you be up to walking to the clinic, Andy? Or shall I bring a chair for you?

Ee, I do love a cheeky woman. Now, if you'll excuse me, I fancy a shower. Don't suppose you'd like to come in with me? I've got these muscle pains when I try to scrub my back.

I'm sorry to hear that, Andy, but it would be more than my job's worth.

Oh, I think I could guarantee that, Pet.

Who's a big mouth then? One little twitch when the beautiful Stiggi's straddling your bum and you're making like Don Juan! And it were only a few days back you were thinking that lass would have made a good concentration camp warder! Funny how feeling better changes your view of folk. Reminds me of summat Pete Pascoe once said when I wanted to haul someone into the Factory for questioning. Let's start him off at home, he said. Once you feel like a prisoner, everyone looks like a guard.

Clever clogs were right, as per usual! I don't feel like a prisoner any more and I can see yon Pet's not a bad-looking woman, specially now I've got her to crack her face.

Time for that shower. What's that, Mildred? Better make it a cold one?

Just for that you're going back in the cistern!

Over and out!

14

FROM: charley@whiffle.com
TO: cassie@natterjack.com
SUBJECT: the hunk & his handle!

Hi!

Really pleased to hear from you – was getting worried – but not as worried as I would have been if Id known! No – nothing on the news here – small African hospital under mortar fire – no one dead – doesnt hit the headlines. Just as well maybe – for mum & dads sake I mean – saves a lot of brick walls from being banged!

Anyway – I feel real guilty – lounging around here – in what must be the safest healthiest place in the world – boring you with my rustic rollickings! But you say it helps keep you on an even keel knowing theres still places like sleepy little Sandytown in the world – so heres the next exciting episode!

Or rather the next several episodes – each centred on a man – just so you dont get the impression youve got exclusive rights!

First Teddy – the hunk with the handle – literally! – as I have seen – & you will hear!

Weather was so warm today – I thought Id head for the beach – see if it had improved since the famous trip! Tom was too busy to join me – thank heaven – I wanted to swim not talk – or rather listen! He said this was the day hed fixed for Mr Godley – the healer – to drive over & take a look at the set-up in Sandytown – & he hoped Id be back in time to meet him – as he knew how it would help with my study – which Im finally making a bit of progress with. Remembering how Godly Gordon took against me first time we met – I dont anticipate much encouragement there – but of course I said I hoped so too.

One other thing Tom said – rather awkwardly for him was – re the meeting at the Avalon – Charlotte – as it is mainly – nay solely – concerned with the alternative therapists – we – that is Lester Feldenhammer & myself – deemed it unnecessary to invite Lady Denham – so – should you chance into her company – it might be diplomatic not to say anything about it! –

Playing with fire there – Tom – I thought. But I was rather flattered to find myself part of a Sandytown conspiracy – so I said – no bother! – & my reward was that big boyish smile.

The kids were off doing their own thing somewhere – so I didnt have to offer to take them – which was a relief. My dip in the hotel pool had whetted my appetite for a real swim – not paddling around in the shallows – keeping an eye on young Parkers.

So off I went – cozzie on under a wrap – towel over my shoulder.

Only a fifteen minute walk down into the village – might take a bit longer coming back up the hill – I thought – but sufficient is the evil – remember?

Met quite a few people who said hello – more than Im likely to meet in Willingden – being Tom Parkers guest gets you on the social register big time!

The beach was pretty crowded. School hols – lots of

families – an ice cream van – a burger stall – deck chairs – all the usual stuff for screwing money out of people. I guessed the Hope & Anchor was doing pretty good business too. All in all – Sandytown looks like its booming. Good news for the Consortium – Tom delighted because the prosperity gets shared around – Lady D because she sees her investment paying out big.

Mary – in her oblique way – has made it quite clear that civic responsibility doesnt figure large in Lady Ds world view. Profits the thing. With her own family money – plus the Hollis fortune – she could lounge her life away in luxury. But a lots never enough for the rich. She wants – even more!

Sorry – boring!

But you can wake up now. Im getting close to the beach – & the hunk!

Like I say – it was crowded – so I wandered along to the furthest extreme of the bay – marked by a rocky outcrop running out into the sea from the foot of North Cliff. You could probably get round the end of this at low tide – but now – with the tide well up – tho retreating – it created a bit of a barrier – reinforced by a sign on a steel post driven into the rock which warned – NO PUBLIC ACCESS – PRIVATE BEACH.

This was just the kind of thing the HB would have erected! So naturally I went scrambling up there without a moments hesitation!

From the top of the outcrop – I found myself looking down on to another bay – much smaller than Sandytowns – but also a lot emptier. In fact there were only four people there – & I wasnt too surprised to see they were Lady Denham – Teddy & his sister – & Clara Brereton.

The younger ones were wearing swimming costumes – Clara a polka dot bikini – that showed her boobs & bum to advantage – slender she might be – but even malice couldnt call her skinny. Lovely pale skin – dont know what sunblock she uses but its worth every penny to keep that lovely pearly glow – probably bathes in asses milk every morning. Stopped feeling sorry for her – even if she does have to skivvy for Lady D!

Esther was in a black one piece – revealing she was no frump either – though while Claras charms – asses milk apart – look all natural – I guess Ests are the best money could buy.

Miaow!

Mind – I had to look at her twice – because – sitting at Lady Ds feet – looking up at the old bat – & listening to her with every sign of interest & pleasure – it was hard to recognize the sourpuss Id encountered the previous day – no – once again I was put in mind of the sweaty laughing girl Id seen at the Bengel-bar disco.

Her ladyship was – naturally – enthroned in a canvas directors chair – with the others – naturally – occupying rugs on the sand.

Teddy – yes Im getting to the *meat* of my tale – was sprawled alongside Clara – almost but not quite touching – looking up at her with what – even at a distance – I recognized as hot bedroom eyes. She was sitting on her haunches – holding her two yards of shapely leg close to her body – as if scared any relaxation would invite an immediate assault on her pudenda – though whether it was concern for her honour – or awareness of Lady Ds proximity – that kept her virtuous – I couldnt tell.

& Teddy the bart? Im happy to say – he isnt one of those prezzies where the wrapping promises more than the gift. Long – lean – as beautifully brown as Clara is gorgeously white – all of his contours muscle – enough

124

hair on his chest to be interesting but well this side of
apish – in short – or indeed at length – a dish.

I was going to beat a retreat – but drinking in Teddys
delights – objectively! – kept me there longer than I
meant – & suddenly Lady Ds beady eyes clocked me.

Theres someone there – she boomed – damn cheek!

They all looked – then Teddy rose to his feet – one
movement – like a panther – except they dont stand on
the hind legs – do they? – but you know what I mean! He
cried out – its Charley! – hey Charley – come on down
here & join us! –

Might have made an excuse & left – but I saw Sister
Esthers face congeal from dimpling attentiveness to pack-
ice mode – & that did it!

– Hi – I said – scrambling down – didnt mean to
intrude – but the beach back there is absolutely packed –

Bit of an exaggeration – but without thinking Id pushed
the right button for Lady D – to whom bodies on the
beach ultimately translates into boodle in the bank – &
she said – never mention it – my dear – any friend of
Toms is always welcome here –

Clara smiled up at me – while Esther gave me a twitch
of a nod – then – unfreezing her face – turned back to
Lady D & said – now auntie – you mustnt lose your
thread – not when you were telling me the fascinating
story of your plans for the estate –

I was trying to work out how to sit close to Teddy –
without drawing too much attention to the contrast
between my kitchen table legs – & Claras works of art –
when he solved the problem by saying – youve obviously
come to swim – ready for a dip now? – come on! –

He grabbed my hand & started leading me down the
beach.

I said – what about Clara? – & he said – oh shes all

125

right – needs to stick close in case auntie needs her back scratched – or something fetched from the Hall –

I glanced back – & up. The cliff rose steep & bare for about 80 feet – with a zig-zag path marked by a guard rail – & then for the next 40 or 50 feet the incline became easier – with lots of greenery now – till presumably it flattened into the grounds of the Hall. Quite a trip to send someone to fetch the hankie youd forgotten! Dont expect that would worry Lady D though – & to give her her due – it was quite a climb – up & down – for someone her age. Must be fit as a butchers dog – as the HB likes to say!

I said – must be nice to have your own private beach –

He said – strictly speaking its not aunties at all. Anything between the high tide & low tide marks belongs to the Crown – & the spring tides here reach several feet up the cliff – but it would take a bold trespasser to argue the point! –

I couldnt argue with this. We soon reached the edge of the water – where he paused – staring out to sea – & said something I didnt catch.

– sorry? – I said.

He spoke again – more clearly – but I still couldnt make any sense of it.

Seeing this he smiled – rather patronizingly I thought – & repeated the sounds.

– thalatta thalatta – he declaimed – (thats how its spelt – I checked it out on the Net) – the sea – the sea –

– no argument there – I said – its the sea – sure enough –

– its Greek – he said – tho I hadnt asked – its what the Greek army – in retreat from Marathon – all shouted in releif – when they breasted a hill – & saw the Aegean – which meant they were home – I know how they felt –

126

my own heart always swells when I glimpse our own dear North Sea –

I suppose he was trying to impress me with his classical learning – & his poetic sensibility – but I just felt he was trying a bit too hard – plus when I checked the word on the Internet – I also got the history – & the plonker didnt even have his facts right! Not Marathon – but some place called Cunaxa – & not the Aegean – but the Black Sea!

I said – OK – now weve established what it is – are we going to swim in it? –

He said – of course – & then – youre not going to believe this – he pushed his trunks down – & stepped out of them – so there I was – standing alongside this guy wearing nothing but his big nobbly Rolex – thats his watch I mean! – with his trio of womenfolk not thirty yards away.

I said – for Godsake! –

He said – dont be shocked – I always skinny-dip –

I said – Ive got 4 bros – plus I grew up on a farm – Im not shocked – but what about Lady D – & the others? –

He laughed & said – oh theyre used to it – auntie pretends to look the other way – but like many old country ladies she likes her meat well hung – & Ive often caught her taking a peek –

– through powerful binoculars you mean? – I said – sneering – quite unjustly! – hed have made a donkey envious! – then waded out till the water was deep enough to dive into.

He took his watch off – dropped it on his trunks – followed me in – came up alongside me – & stayed there – doing a pretty fair crawl – smiling at me from time to time – as if to say – dont worry – I wont sprint away & leave you – so youre quite safe –

Well – you know me – not the fastest thing on fins –
but can keep going forever.

There was a buoy – about 1/4 mile offshore – I fixed
my eyes on it – & got into my rhythm. He stuck with me
for a while – then dropped behind – & when I reached
the buoy it was 3 or 4 minutes before he joined me. He
tried a smile – but I could see he was knackered – & I
started to feel guilty. Just cos he had a lousy chat-up line
didnt mean he deserved to drown! & dragging that thing
along beneath him must have been like a plane trying to
take off with its flaps down!

We clung on to the buoy for a few minutes – then I
said – ready for home?

He nodded – & I set off back – breast stroke this time
– a lot slower – & it gave me room to keep an eye on
him.

By the time we reached the shallows – he was so
whacked – a little wave knocked him over when he tried
to stand up.

Big test time now – would he turn nasty – or could he
take it?

He collapsed on the sand. Wed come ashore about 30
feet from where wed left our gear.

He gasped – do me a favour – Charley – fetch my
trunks will you? – Id like to be buried decent – but not at
sea – please! –

So that was OK. Dont mind a prat – so long as he can
laugh at himself.

I fetched his watch & his trunks – he made himself
decent – then we sat on the sand together – warming
ourselves in the sun – till he got his breath back.

I said – do you ski as well as you swim? –

He said – better – youll be glad to hear – but I usually
keep my clothes on. Why? –

I said – I was out in Switzerland before Christmas –
near Davos – bunch of my mates from uni – thought I
saw your sister there – at a dance – but could be wrong.
Kind of place us poor students party at – not really her
thing – I shouldnt think –

He pulled a face & said – might well have been – Aunt
Daph had a rush of blood to the head – took me & Ess
on a skiing holiday last Christmas – near Davos –

That was generous of her – I said – where were you
staying? – Morasinis? – The Fluela? –

– O no – he laughed – dear aunties not that generous!
– we had a chalet – but in fairness it was very comfortably
appointed –

– so why would Esther be moving & grooving with the
plebs? – I pressed.

– why not? – he said in the casual tone the upper
classes use to disguise an evasion. – Could be there was
a ski instructor she fancied – holiday romance – no
strings – no harm – but wouldnt do for auntie –

I almost asked – whats it to do with her? – but I
didnt need to – being such a clever observer of human
behaviour! She who pays the piper calls the tune –
right? Lady D definitely would not care for the prospect
of any of her money – now or later – finding its way
into the pocket of a penniless foreigner. So if her
beloved neice wanted to stay in her good books & her
will – shed better pick her young men v carefully. The
HB feels much the same – so the way youre going – Ill
probably be getting your share!

I was also recalling that – according to George – Emil
was a student – not a ski instructor. Teddy – I thought –
either youre lying – or Ess lied to you –

I said – so Esther went slumming with us plebs – &
Lady D never found out –

He said – happily auntie had her own *affairs* to divert her –

The way he stressed *affairs* got me curious – but our interesting chat must have been observed – for now it was interrupted by a sergeant major bellow – Teddy! – what are you doing down there? – Time for lunch! –

The bart flinched – & made a face – but he still started to get to his feet.

Shes really got him at the end of a leash – I thought as we headed back to the group. Must be hard for both of them – having to be careful who they got the hots for – in case Lady D disapproved. Wonder how shed feel about me?

I was soon to find out!

The women were all on their feet. Clara was gathering up their stuff – bags – towels – Lady Ds folding chair – while Esther gazed out to sea like she was trying to freeze it over. Lady D greeted me with a stern look – then she said – Miss Heywood – if you could lend me your arm – too much sitting makes me stiff –

Not much sign of stiffness – the speed with which she walked me away from the others – but it quickly became clear what she wanted was a private chat.

– a word to the wise – she said – Teddy is a fine young man –

– yes – I noticed – I said.

That got me a sharp glance – then she went on – but alas – he may flatter to decieve –

– you mean hes not to be trusted with a girls affections! – I exclaimed – all shock horror.

– of course I dont mean that! – I am talking of his circumstances – she declared – He may look like a good catch – big mansion – expensive watch – but Denham Park is entailed – cannot be sold – & needs more spent on it in repairs than it would probably fetch anyway. As for the watch . . .

– yes – I noticed the Rolex – I said – all bright eyed – thinking no harm in letting the old cow peg me as a predatory fortune hunter – could lull her into a false sense of security if I decide to have me wicked way with the bart! – That must be worth 5 thou of anyones money! –

– yes indeed – she said triumphantly – mine! – it was Sir Harrys – my late husbands – Teddys uncle. I gave it to Teddy as a memento – there was nothing in the will – you understand – but I beleive Sir Harry would have wanted it – family meant much to him – & as Teddys circumstances have meant he has had to part with many Denham heirlooms – it is good he should retain at least one item – to remind him of dear Harry – & better days –

Meaning – I interpreted – that Teddy wouldnt dare flog it – cos shed be asking him the time whenever they met!

Well – I had news for her – Id wondered why the bart took off his Rolex before entering the water – those things are supposed to be still working when theyre dredged up from a ten year old shipwreck. So when I collected the guys trunks – I checked it out – & its definitely a Hong Kong job – 20 quid off a sampan – you could bend the expanding 'gold' bracelet with two fingers if you took a fancy to! I reckon Ted-on-the-rocks has flogged the original – & invested in a fake – to fool auntie. Could explain how come he could afford a Buell. That won-it-in-a-lottery story had sounded pretty feeble!

Good for him! – I thought – & I said to her – yes – I understand – & Im sure someone as attractive – & talented – as Teddy will have little difficulty in finding someone his equal in name – & his superior in income –

Nicely put – eh?

She nodded – & smiled – & said – Im so pleased we

understand each other – my dear – now I must toil up this path to lunch –

She let go of my arm – & Ess – whod been veiwing our tete-a-tete with great suspicion – went into ministering angel mode – leaping forward – presumably to ensure Lady Ds foot did not dash against a stone.

Her ladyship did not look at her – but gazed on me assessingly. I guessed she wanted to reward me for being a sensible peasant – possibly with an invite to lunch – which I wasnt crazy about – but might just accept – to put Esthers nose out of joint!

Then she said – in a very measured extremely condescending tone – Miss Heywood do tell Tom Parker to bring you to my hog-roast this Sunday –

Her hog-roast – which – according to Mary – the Consortium was paying for!

I resisted the temptation to do a curtsey – & said – that would be lovely – but Im probably going home on Saturday –

I expected her to react sort of amazed anyone could turn down a royal invite – instead she said – yes – of course – your family must miss you – family loyalties are so important. Come if you change your mind – meanwhile – do feel free to stay here as long as you like – & dont be afraid to come again – whenever the public beach is full –

There! In my place – or what?

I felt like kicking sand in her face.

Instead I said – very dignified – thank you – so kind – but I really ought to get back to my freinds – & off I stalked!

Id gone about a dozen yards when Teddy caught up with me.

– dont take any notice of the old bat – he said – she

132

cant help it – still thinks were living in the dark ages! –

Which might have impressed me with his independence – if he hadnt still been whispering – for fear of being overheard!

I said – better get back – else you might be sent to bed – without any lunch –

He grinned – hes got a great grin – & said – who cares about lunch – so long as the company in beds good? Look – Id like to see you again – soon –

I said – pushing it – is that an invitation to Denham Park then? – or do you need permission to invite someone to your own home? –

He winced – then said – of course not – though I warn you – the plumbings terrible! What Id really like is to give you a ride – on the Beast I mean. You could borrow Ests leathers. The trick is – to get the full experience – not to wear anything at all underneath! –

Who writes this guys scripts?!!

But – like a good thriller – it may be a load of crap – but you cant stop reading it!

I said – Ill think about it – & scrambled over the rocks – back to the main beach – even more crowded now than before. Suddenly the peace & friendliness of Kyoto House seemed very attractive.

So off I set to trudge back up the hill.

But my exciting adventures werent over yet!

However – youll have to wait for the next exciting episode – as I have to go & interview a woman who says that an infusion of whortleberries & a nettle oil massage have taken 20 years off her age.

You see – Im a working girl too!

Much love

Charley xxx

15

FROM: charley@whiffle.com
TO: cassie@natterjack.com
SUBJECT: sex on wheels!

Hi again!

Well that was fun! If the berries & nettles have made her 20 years younger – she must have been nigh on 100 before. Fits under my *grasping at straws* category. Ready to beleive anything except that youre going to die.

Back to the land of the living. Now where was I . . .? Oh yes. The foot of the hill.

The road up North Cliff seemed a lot steeper than when Id come down – & showing off to the bart had taken more out of me than I thought. By the time I reached Witch Cottage I was ready for a rest – so I sat on the little garden wall. There was an ancient motorbike plus sidecar parked outside. Some poor sod hoping to alleviate his saddle soreness by having needles stuck in his bum – I theorized.

I heard the door open behind me – & glanced round to see Yan Lee ushering a man out. He was wearing motor-bike leathers – & putting on a helmet – but the brambly beard was a dead giveaway. It was Gordon Godley – the healer from Willingdene. I remembered Tom saying hed agreed to come over – to check the set-up here in

Sandytown. Remembered too my sense he knew a lot more about the set-up here than hed let on.

& when I saw them exchange a hug & a kiss – not a one cheek peck either – but a full lip job – & I thought hello! – not so unworldly after all – bit of pillow talk going on here Id guess – wonder if theres a book on faith-healing in that *Teach Yourself* series!

When he clocked me sitting on the wall – he stopped dead in his tracks – like hed seen a rabid Doberman. Behind him Miss Lee gave me her little Oriental bob – went back inside – & closed the door – leaving him & me standing – facing each other – both stock still – like a pair of gunfighters in a spaghetti western – each waiting for the other to make a move. While his biking leathers didnt do for him what they did for the bart – they did have a juvenating effect – & I adjusted my estimate of his age down a few notches – more 45 than 55 –

He cracked first & finally started towards me like a man on his way to the gallows!

Funny – not nice having a really off-putting effect on somebody – not even somebody you dont care a toss about! Id have moved off without passing the time of day – but I felt I owed it to Tom to make it clear – in case Mr G hadnt grasped it on our previous meeting – that I wasnt a permanent blot on the village landscape. Wouldnt want it on my conscience that I was responsible for putting the Sandytonians out of reach of godly Gordons healing hands!

So I said brightly – hello – Mr Godley. Charlotte Heywood – remember? (Not that there was much doubt of that – the way he was looking at me!) – On your way to see Mr Parker – are you? Im staying with the family for a couple of days. Its lovely round here – isnt it? (Doing my best to give the place a puff!) – but I wont be sorry not to have to face this hill every day –

Even as I said it – I thought – oh no! – sounds like youre trying to hitch a ride!

Sure enough – what I could see of his face beneath the fungus turned colour a couple of times – like you when youre nerving yourself up to go in off the high board! – then he mumbled something about a lift.

My first instinct was to say – no way! –

Then I thought – dont be a prat – youve cut off your nose to spite your face once already by letting Lady Ds patronizing ungraciousness drive you off her empty beach – its stupid – & bloody difficult! – to cut off your nose again.

So – a moment later – I was sitting in the side-car – bouncing up the hill!

I couldnt help but contrast the Godley motorbike experience with what Teddy Denham had promised me on the pillion of the Beast. This was a bit like being dragged behind a tractor – in an old tin bath! At least it meant I didnt have to make small talk.

When we got to Kyoto I hopped out – said thanks – & dashed inside – yelling at Tom as I passed his work room – Mr Godleys here! –

When I got to my room – I met Minnie coming out. Said shed been looking for me – but I wasnt fooled. I remember when I was her age – I was always looking for a chance to get my sticky little fingers on your gear & make-up! I said I wanted to get out of my wet cozzie – & went in – thinking shed stay outside. But she followed me in – & sat on the bed watching as I towelled down – like she was a judge at a gymnastics floor exercise – so I said – OK how many points do I get? – & she said – quick as a flash – 7 for performance – 8 for interpretation –

Cheeky little cow – but you cant help but like her.

I took the chance to pump her for info about Miss Lee & Lady D – not that it took much pumping!

Seems Miss Lee got Witch Cottage on a long lease from Lady Ds land agent – whose arthritis shed fixed with a couple of judiciously placed pins. Then the great Consortium came into being – & it dawned on Lady D that funny old Witch Cottage – with its gingerbready appearance – & magical history – could be a real little money spinner when the tourists started pouring in. So she wanted it back. Only Miss Lee had a tenancy agreement – so – like the Chinese train passenger in that awful non-PC joke the HBs so fond of – she told Lady D – *you fuckoffee – me got 1st class ticket!*

Battle was joined – might v right – with Tom Parker trying to mediate. Then suddenly Miss Lee caved in – nobody knew why – big bribe was Mins best guess – & agreed to move out in the autumn – & relocate in new premises Tom had found for her.

Min had just finished her story & I was nearly dressed – when she heard the sound of an engine – & looking out of the open window she screamed – oh look – its Uncle Sid! – & shot past me through the door.

I went to the window & looked down.

There was this gorgeous deep red Maserati coupe bombing up the drive.

Minnie must have moved almost as fast – she came rushing out of the front door as the car came to a halt – & when the driver slid elegantly out of his seat – she flung herself into his arms. He lifted her high into the air & whirled her round. I got the impression as he spun that his gaze took me in – standing in my bra at the open window – so I backed away – & finished dressing. Modest – or what? But even that brief glimpse of him left me with the impression that – unlike hunky Ted the bart – Sidney was not someone to impress by flashing the flesh.

& why should I want to impress him? The car? OK,

maybe. What Id heard about him as a fast track finance wiz? No way! No — I think it was the fact that he looked as immaculate as his car when he got out of it — & he didnt show the least disinclination to being leapt upon & wrapped around by a 9 year old tomboy — who — I seem to recall — can be remarkably unhygienic creatures!

There you go — another sharp psychological assessment from your wise young sister.

Also — I admit — he did look quite dishy in a Hugh Grant kind of way.

I delayed long enough to let him get the family greetings over — then I went to make my entrance.

I was right. Seriously dishy — also seriously smooth — without being at all oleaginus — (dont know if thats how you spell it but its my favourite word this month!) Bit taller than Tom — same lively expressive face — the Parker soft brown eyes — hes one of those guys you know will always do the right thing — I dont mean morally — but like if your pants fell off on the dance floor — he would slip them into his pocket without missing a step! He was wearing a soft cream shirt under a linen suit that bore no signs of Minnies assault — & certainly hadnt come from M&S. On his feet he had soft leather sandals — no socks — & the sexiest toes imaginable! OK — maybe toes dont figure large in your erotic fantasies — but take it from me — Sids are the tops!

I was introduced with Toms usual hyperbole — which Sidney took in his stride. Unlike Ted the bart he made no particular effort to impress me — which impressed me!

Tom of course was pressing him to stay at Kyoto — & Mary backed up the invite — while Minnie was ready to go on her knees to persuade him.

But Sidney was adamant.

— Im booked in at the hotel — he said — the honeymoon suite! — No — Mary — I am not married — alas. I thought I might as well see what all those healthy honeymooners will be getting for their money –

The thought – need any help with your research Sid? – flitted across my mind.

Then our eyes met – & it was like he could read what I was thinking – & I felt myself blushing.

We sat on the terrace. Tom – inevitably – rhapsodized about the sea breezes – the pure air – the clarity that on a good day afforded a view all the way to Holland.

Sid said – I never quite understand – dear Tom – why you find the prospect of even a distant view of Holland so desirable –

As he spoke – he gave me a complicitous smile. I tried to feel defensive of Tom – but the bond of affection between them was so obvious that I realized this was only the kind of ribbing that goes on between – say – me & George – or you for that matter!

Anyway – he drew me into the conversation – effortlessly – made me one of the family – & – as youve probably gathered – though Im not a natural lover of smoothies – in a bottle or in the City – I soon found myself joining Minnie as a member of the Sid Parker fan club!

You must be thinking your little sis is seriously repressed. In Sandytown only 6 days – & already Ive let 3 men – Ted the hunk – Fran the wheelie – & Sid the smoothie – get my juices running!

Never fear. This is fantasy football. Lousy Liam has put me off forever! Im a career girl pure & simple. Recreational romping only!

So there we were – sitting & chatting – when I heard this odd noise – like a deer barking – & there – in the doorway – stood Godly Gordon – the hairy healer – coughing to attract attention!

In the excitement of seeing Sidney – Tom had forgotten all about him – & left him in his office! Tom of course was abject with apology – dragged him on to the terrace – made him sit down – & introduced him to Sidney in terms that made him sound a cross between Gandalf & Jesus. Smooth Sid was perfectly charming – of course – but I sensed the feeling – this is one bit of my dear bros plans for Sandytowns future that I need to keep out of any prospectus I prepare for my City chums!

Mr Godley was soon on his feet again – saying he needed to be on his way – & refusing all urgings to stay for lunch. Tom – dead keen to get him involved in the Festival of Healing – reminded him about the meeting at the Avalon.

– I think youll be really impressed by how open minded Dr Feldenhammer is – he said – this is a great opportunity for those of us who beleive in the road less travelled –

I saw Sidneys eyes glaze over in that expression us Heywoods know so well – the one we all wear when dad says something more than usually extreme in company – & family loyalty makes us keep our faces straight.

Mr G just looked uncertain & muttered something indeterminate – leaving Tom looking a bit downcast – but far too polite to press. I dont like seeing Tom disap-pointed – so when Sid said he couldnt stay for lunch either as he had to get down to the hotel to greet his guests – & we all went outside together – I went up to Mr G as he got on his bike – & said – I dont think I thanked you properly for the lift – it was great – I really didnt feel up to climbing the hill! –

He looked embarrassed – of course – but I think he was pleased – so I pressed on – saying – why dont you come to the meeting at the clinic? – no harm in looking the place over – is there? Usually costs a fortune to get in a place like that – be fun to see what they make of someone who wants to heal their patients without charging a penny!

He looked straight at me – a bit puzzled – like *fun* was a foreign word. Then he said – youll be there? –

Clearly he was worried in case I was going to be sitting in a corner – making sceptical noises – & notes for my thesis.

– perhaps for the refreshments afterwards – but definitely not at the meeting – I said – patting his gauntleted hand reassuringly.

Wow! Youd have thought Id zapped him with a cattle prodder!

He shot up out of his saddle – jerked his hand away from me so sharply he almost left his gauntlet – then said – Ill see –

& off he went – in a puff of blue smoke – definitely more Gandalf than Jesus!

Nobody else noticed – they were too busy saying cheerio to Sidney. I went to join them – & help prise Minnie loose from his car door.

His last words to me were more conventional – but hopeful too.

– I hope I see you again before you go – Miss Heywood –

I said – me too – & its Charley –

– & why not? – he said laughing – Bye! –

Minnie stood by my side – watching the Maz boom off down the drive.

– Isnt he great? – she said – eyes ashine – if he wasnt my uncle – Id marry him! –

Then she took my hand – & said – he liked you Charley. You could marry him & settle down in London – I could come & stay with you – all summer – & at Christmas! –

I said – is that all? – what dull Easters wed have –

She dug her nails into my palm – but not too hard – & said – but you do like him – dont you? –

– I like his car – I said.

This time her nails hurt – & I grabbed hold of her – & we had a wrestle – ending up rolling on the lawn – with Tom beaming down at us in delight – & Mary smiling too.

But Marys gaze kept straying to the end of the drive – & the road to the hotel – & with this wonderful power of mind-reading I seem to be developing – (perhaps I caught it from Mr Godley as I sat in the side-car!) – I guessed she was wondering whether it was some crisis of high finance that had brought Sidney to Sandytown.

Chatting to her later – I brought up the subject of Sidney – casually! Far too loyal to criticize – & she really likes him – but it soon came out – as Id guessed – that shes bothered that Tom relies on his brother so much – financially speaking – & she feels theres a lot more under that smooth surface than she understands.

Bit like Sandytown itself – I think. Dont know why – but Im getting the impression theres a lot more going on beneath its smooth surface than meets the eye!

OK – youre going to remind me of the time I decided the vicar had killed his wife – & buried her in Les Turpins coffin – cos Les was only seven stone when he died & the bearers staggered as they came into the church. Then the vics wife came back from visiting her sick sister in Beverley – & it turned out one of the bearers had taken badly at the last minute – & they had to get Iggy Earnshaw out of the bar to make up the numbers – & hed drunk seven pints already!

Cant win em all! But I was the one who spotted Mrs

Inlake – from the Post Office – was having it off with the oil tanker man – before anyone else!

So whats your next move – inspector? – you ask.

Who knows? I may be obliged to seduce Smoothie Sid to find out whats going on . . .

The things we psychologists do for our art.

You take care. Seriously. & for heavens sake – when your contracts up next month – come home! I know you – cos – except in the area of blood guts & bedpans – were so alike – & just as Im finding myself ingested by Sandytown – & starting to doubt if Ill ever be able to leave – so with you & your bomb-blasted mine-strewn disease-ridden chunk of Africa.

Difference is – nobodys trying to kill people in Sandytown!

Much love

Charley xxxx

PS When I rang home last night I got George – so I asked him if he remembered Ess & Em from our ski-trip. When he stopped laughing at his memory of the joke – he really should get out more! – he said yes he remembered Emil very well – in fact – gobsmacking coincidence! – hed seen him only a couple of days ago – here in Yorkshire! G was driving up to Newcastle to see some footie match – stopped for petrol near Scotch Corner & there ahead of him in the pay queue was Emil – unmistakable – same long blond hair & tash. G tapped him on the shoulder – when he got over his surprise at seeing G – they chatted for a while. Em said he was here on holiday – touring – & G scribbled down his name & address & said – why dont you call in at Willingden to see me? Then it was Ems turn to pay – & by the time G had paid – to his surprise Em was already getting into his car – & driving off. G thinks there was someone with him but didnt get a proper look.

G was a bit hurt – you know what hes like – thinks everyones as friendly as he is – but what I think is this – suppose Ess & Em are still an item – & hes come over to see her – but she wants to keep Big Bum sweet – so theyre still meeting on the quiet? Being seen by G not much of a risk – but not one Em cares to take.

Thats my theory anyway. OK – there she goes again – I hear you say – making up her fairy tales! But trust me – Im a psychiatrist! Love C x

16

FROM: charley@whiffle.com
TO: cassie@natterjack.com
SUBJECT: Viva Las Vegas!

Hi!

Yet another one hot off the press. When you lead an eventful life like mine – theres hardly time to breathe.

I slept on the barts invite – coincidentally having an embarrassingly raunchy dream – (details on application – in plain brown envelope!) – which had nothing at all to do with my decision to amaze everyone by getting up early – & asking Tom if I could borrow the car.

– to explore – I said.

– good idea – he enthused – tho you will be back for the Avalon lunch do? –

It had gone right out of my mind!

I said – look – Im sorry – of course youll need the car to get to your meeting –

& he said – no problem – Ill bike along the top road – it will do me good – after lunch – you can drive me back – so that I dont have to do myself any more good! –

He really is a lovely man.

I didnt mention Denham Park – cos I dont think Mary would have approved. In any case – I thought – I might change my mind.

145

Young Minnie volunteered to be my expedition guide —
naturally! — but I wasnt having that. Still didnt know if my
intentions were honourable — or what — but I certainly
didnt want my options closed down by having Min by my
side — taking notes!

She looked ready to argue her case — but Mary soon
shut her up — & I promised her Id take her for another
swim at the Manor before Uncle Sid goes home! Self-
interest — or what!

En route to Denham Park, it occurred to me — I was
being a bit arrogant thinking Teddy was going to sit around
all day on the off chance I showed. Thought of not finding
him home didnt bother me too much — but I didnt like the
idea of being told Id been stood up by his frozen faced
sister! So when I reached the Hollis's Ham site — I turned
in to check if the old RR — or the Sexy Beast — was in
the car park.

Didnt get far — there was a barrier across the
entrance & a little hut — presumably for the gatekeeper
— but no one in it. So I got out of the car — ducked
under the barrier — & began to walk towards this line of
vehicles I could see parked in front of the nearest
building. Id only gone a few yards when a voice called
out — hoy! — you! — stop right there! — & dont bloody
move! —

I looked round to see this heavyweight guy coming out
from behind a clump of gorse bushes — & heading
towards me at a lumbering trot. His hands were fiddling
with his fly — & I thought — oh God — Ive hit upon the
mad rapist of Sandytown — better run for it girl!

Then it dawned on me he wasnt pulling his zip down —
but up! Must have been having a pee. He still looked
pretty menacing — but us psychologists have got all kinds
of special stratagems for defusing menace.

I stared at him – & said – very Lady Bracknell – what kind of dog is it? –

– eh? – he said.

– this dog youre shouting at – what kind is it? – I said.

OK – this wasnt one of the special stratagems I learned – this was just me being pissed off at being yelled at like I was a criminal!

He caught on I was taking the piss – wasnt amused – but at least he was no longer Mad Rapist – more heavy duty Security Guard – as he said – oh yes – youll know all about the dogs – remember them from your last visit – do you? –

It struck me now where Id seen him before – hed been the guy up the ladder cleaning the sign the day of my arrival – the one Tom had greeted out of the window.

I said – its Ollie – isnt it? Perhaps you can tell me – Ollie – if Teddy Denham is on the site –

That stopped him in his tracks. As Freud says – getting them by the name is almost as good as getting them by the balls. He looked from me to the car on the far side of the barrier – then suddenly he turned from Security Guard to Mr Smilie – like the Good Witch of the North had waved her wand.

He said – you must be Miss Heywood – right? – her whos staying with Tom Parker – Miss Lee told me about thee – Im Ollie Hollis – would you like a cup of tea? –

It was recognizing Toms car that did it – of course. In Sandytown – if youre a chum of Toms – you have to be OK.

Two minutes later I was sitting in Ollies hut – drinking tea.

He was full of apology. Seems theyd had trouble with animal rights protesters – so anyone seen on the site without permission gets short shrift. The main attack –

147

Ollie explained – had happened a couple of years back – lots of damage done – pigs turned loose – lot of them never showed up again – & half the folk in this neck of the wood were eating pork till Christmas – he added with a big grin.

– so youre head of security? – I asked.

– I wish! – he said – could do with the salary! – No – Im just the gatekeeper –

– sorry – I said – I thought – being called Hollis yourself – youd likely be one of the family –

– oh aye – he said – Im a genuine Hollis – theres a few on us about – but Hog – he were my cousin – were tonly one as ever made it rich – & he werent the kind to spread it around! But shouldnt speak ill of the dead – & he always said as thered be a job for me – & he kept his word. Used to work with the pigs – but that didnt help my asthma – so Hog fixed me up here – but not security – just gatekeeper. Since them extremists started targeting us theres been a proper security guard with a couple of big German shepherds comes on at night –

Hence the confusion about dogs. The protesters had come back the night before I arrived in Sandytown – put a ladder up at the main gate – sprayed the sign – then climbed over.

– thats when they found out about the dogs – said Ollie gleefully – we got it on the security tape – you shouldve seen em run! – One on em made it OK – but one of the dogs got hold of tothers leg afore she managed to get over –

– she? – I said.

– Ay – they were wearing balaclavas – but you could tell the buggers were lasses – (an interesting concept – I thought) – by the way they ran – its the broad hips tha knows – thats what made me suspicious of you –

Ignoring the slander on my hips – I asked if theyd been caught. He said there was a car waiting for them – you could just glimpse it on the tape – & the unbitten one helped the bitten one into it – & it took off fast.

– Jug Whitby – thats Sergeant Whitby – our local cop – he said – is on the case – so I doubt well hear much more about it –

Self-interest made me ask about his connection with Miss Lee.

As Id guessed – its his asthma. Ollie was resigned to having to make do with the usual range of palliatives for the recurring attacks – until – at Toms suggestion – he consulted Miss Lee – whod needled his troubles away! Suspect hes her star patient – so natch shed mentioned my wish to chat about how people reacted to treatment.

I told him Id been looking for Teddy – & he said he hadnt been in today – & I said – sort of fishing – it didnt surprise me – Ted didnt give the impression of being a dedicated pig-man – which made him laugh. But he did say Ted does show up quite a lot – even if his main concern – not unnaturally – is to keep the pong down!

Ollie said he hardly noticed the smell now – though hed much rather the beasts were roaming loose – like when he was a lad – instead of being penned inside – never seeing light of day. Says Hog Hollis would have been happy to be a trad farmer if the government – the EU – & the supermarkets – hadnt forced him to become a millionaire!

I asked if Hog had really been et by his own pigs.

– oh yes – he said cheerfully – made a lot of folk smile that – specially when they were having their break-fast bacon – sort of poetic – bit like 'On Ilkla Moor Baht'at' –

– so what happened? – I asked.

149

– dont rightly know – must have been working late –
went to check something in one of the units – had a
stroke – or summat – collapsed in a feeding trough – owt
in theres grub for the porkers – & theyre used to getting
some pretty funny stuff to eat I tell you – so by time he
were found next day – he were well chewed over –

I finished my tea – & said Id best be on my way to
Denham Park.

He said – this were Denham land once tha knows.
Makes no odds – farmer or squire – once you start
selling rather than buying land – thats the beginning of the
end. But no need to tell you that – being a Heywood! –

The government could save millions on electronic
surveillance – if they just scattered a few hundred
Yorkshire tykes around the world!

I sniffed & said – the Denhams must have been
desperate to part with land so that Hog Hollis could build a
pig farm on their doorstep –

– nay – he said grinning – werent exactly like that.
Story is – way back when Daph Brereton were still Daph
Brereton – big mucker of Sir Harry Denham – him being
Master of the Hunt & her being such a keen rider – she
made him an offer for this bit of land – letting on she
were hoping to get planning permission for building houses
on it. Now Sir Harry had tried to get permission himself –
always strapped for cash the Denhams – & been turned
down – so he reckoned this were just some daft female
notion – & if she had spare cash to give away he might
as well take it – so he let her have the land – at top
agricultural price – even though it werent good for owt
but a bit of rough grazing – & thought hed done a smart
deal. Next thing he hears is that Daph & Hog has wed –
& Hogs planning to expand his pig farm on to his wifes
bit of land! –

– but wouldnt they need planning permission for that? – I asked.

– no problem – agricultural development – plus more pigs meant more jobs – & a bigger site meant more council tax – said Ollie – Also Hog were well in with the Planning chairman. So no bugger paid much attention when Sir Harry objected. Word is – he were threatening to take a horsewhip to Mrs Hollis next time she showed up at the hunt –

– instead – eventually he married her – I said – was that just to get her in whipping distance? –

– nay – thats another story altogether – he grinned – inviting me to prompt him for details. But time was moving on & Id had enough of talking about Lady D for one morning. More I heard about her – the less I liked her!

So I said I had to go but Id like to talk to him some time about his experience of Miss Lees 'cure' – & he said – Ill likely see you at the hog-roast? –

I said – doubt it – though Ive been invited – sort of. You too? –

– Im in charge of the roast – he said proudly.

– gosh – I said – sounding impressed – cos he clearly reckoned it was an important job – so what will you do – stick it on a spit – & turn a handle? –

– bit more to it than that – he said – Hog started it – after he made his pile – & bought the Hall & became Lord of the Hundred. Big annual event in the town – & I think it amused Hog to call it a hog-roast. Tried a spit at first – but that were hard work – with a full size porker – especially me with me asthma. So Hog got his brother Hen to build a proper bit of machinery. Always good with his hands was Hen – not so good with figures & poultry – but. Any road – I used to help Hen with the hog-roast gear right up to when Hog died. After that the annual

151

roast died too − & I were real surprised when I heard there was going to be another − & real chuffed when I got asked if Id check the equipment out & take charge −

− I thought Hen was the expert? −

− oh shed not ask Hen − he laughed − theyve not exchanged 2 civil words since he challenged Hogs will − any road − Ive been odd jobbing around the Hall for years − so I were on the spot − so to speak −

I said I looked forward to seeing him there − & took off to Denham Park.

Again − as on my first sighting − I was impressed by the magnificent situation of the house − perched high on its hill − grounds sweeping away eastward to the sea − & westward to the pig farm!

Up close it turned out to be even bigger than it looked on the horizon − but like an old movie star up close − the cracks showed. Past simple TLC − Id say − needs a complete makeover. Poor Teddy − cant sell it − & if he doesnt do something quick − I doubt if hell even be able to live in it!

Then I forgot all about him as I reached the front of the house.

The ancient RR was there − with alongside it a bright red Maserati coupe!

Sidney Parker was here!

Damn! I thought. Not that the prospect of seeing Sid again wasnt pleasant. But mightnt it give the wrong impression if he saw me dropping in on the hunky bart? − the wrong impression being we had something going.

In other words − yeah − I wanted to see them both − but not at the same time!

Thats the trouble with being a highly trained psychologist − youre always playing chess with other peoples thoughts!

I debated whether it might be best if I just headed off

out of here. Then I heard this throaty roar behind me – & when I turned & saw Teddys mo-bike – the Beast – heading up the drive – I thought Id got it wrong – & it must be Ess that Sid was visiting – which made me think – damn! – again.

Hard to please – aint I?!

However when the Beast halted alongside me – & the black leathered figure removed the silvery helmet – I saw it wasnt Ted – but Esther!

I found myself wondering if this was the spare set of leathers Ted had promised to loan me – & was the Ice Queen wearing anything underneath them?!

She said – Miss Heywood – this is a surprise – are you expected? –

Making it sound as likely as the Second Coming.

I said – Teddy did say drop in – but I see hes got company –

– yes – so it appears – she said – glancing at the Maz. Id have put money on her next move being to imply that – in the circs – a well brought up person would make an excuse – & be on her way. But she surprised me by smiling suddenly – not a five hundred watt freindly smile – & with no resemblance at all to the incandescence I remembered lighting up her face when she was dirty dancing with her Emil – but definitely a smile.

Sliding elegantly off the bike – she said – but you must come in now youre here – Im sure theyd both be delighted to see you –

Sudden rush of noblesse oblige to the head – or what?

Why not? I thought – could be fun to see smooth Sid alongside the hunky bart – so I could compare & contrast – & allocate points on the old Heywood girls scale – remember? Out of 10 for Wealth, Wheels & Social Skills & out of 20 for Sex Appeal!

To tell truth – dont think I had a choice of stay or go. Tho Ess didnt actually touch me – I found myself steered through the doorway into what would have made a lovely baronial hall – could imagine Fairbanks or Flynn fighting his way down – or up – the broad staircase in one of mums old favourites – but there were no suits of armour in the corners – no marble busts in the niches – no rich tapestries on the walls – in fact nothing at all except pale squares showing where pictures had once hung – all of which fitted what Id guessed from the fake Rolex business – that Teddy had been selling off the family goodies to keep body & soul together.

Ess flung open a couple of doors – giving me a brief glimpse into more rooms looking like theyd been stripped by marauding Vikings – & struck lucky on the third.

Nothing much in here either – except a few ancient chairs & a sofa – on which Teddy & Sidney were sitting – heads close – talking earnestly.

They looked toward us. Ted jumped to his feet – flushing as he recognized me – The invitation hed tossed my way had clearly gone right out of his head!

Sid – by contrast – gave me a lovely smile – like I was the best thing hed seen all day.

– Charlotte – he said – how nice to see you again – so soon –

– Youve met then – said Teddy – sounding – I hoped! – a bit jealous.

– Of course – when I called to pay my respects to Tom. Hi Esther. Just what our dull masculine deliberations could do with – two rays of feminine brightness –

OK – flowery froth – but hes got style enough to get away with it.

I grinned back like an idiot – & gave him a straight 10 for Social Skills! – (& it wasnt even his house!) – but at the same time I was wondering – what deliberations? – what are you two up to?

Ess had a look on her face that suggested she might have been wondering the same. All she said was – this is cosy – lets all sit down & have a cup of coffee – Im sure Miss Heywoods ready for one –

Something about the way she said that last phrase made me think she was taking the piss!

Ted said – oh sure – yes – fine –

Ive heard more enthusiasm from dad when mum asks him to chat to the WI about diversification!

I thought – to hell with this! Im not staying where Im not wanted. In any case – Ess will probably expect me to make the coffee!

I said – thanks but not for me – just dropped by to say hello – now I need to get back – promised Id pick up Tom to take him to the Avalon meeting –

Not so much a lie as an adjustment of the truth – Ive written essays on the distinction! Also – recalling Toms request that I didnt mention the meeting in front of Big Bum – I guessed the Denhams wouldnt know about it either.

OK – I should probably have kept quiet in front of them too – knowing the way they scratched if Lady D itched – but I couldnt resist giving Teddy a sharp prod to pay him back for forgetting me.

It worked like a dream.

Ted said – what meeting? –

I said – all surprise – sorry – was sure youd be going – its to tie up arrangements for the Festival of Health – you know – its marvellous of Dr Feldenhammer to be so receptive to new ideas – isnt it? –

Ess said – & what does it have to do with you exactly? –

I said – oh nothing – of course – Im just going for the
lunch party afterwards –

OK – I know – drinks & nibbles is hardly a lunch party
– but I was seriously pissed with the Denhams!

I headed back into the hall.

Ess followed me out. I thought she was going to see
me to the door – like a good hostess – but she just
started up the staircase.

– Ill see myself out then – I said.

She didnt even pause – let alone reply – I might as
well have been a parlour maid! – & I thought – Sod
this!

I trilled – by the way Esther – did Teddy tell you? – I
think we may have bumped into each other in Davos last
Christmas – at the Bengel-bar – you were dancing with a
good looking local boy – Emil I think his name was –
remember? –

Now she paused!

Gotcha! – I thought.

Dont know what shed have said – but before she could
speak – behind me – a telephone on a ledge beside the
door rang.

– get that – would you? – said Esther.

& I found myself getting it – just like a good little
parlour maid!

But blessed are the meek – for they shall get their own
back!

I said – hello – Denham Park –

Lady Ds unmistakable voice said – who is that? –

– its Charley Heywood – Lady Denham – I said –
looking up to see the Ice Queens reaction. Not much – but
I reckon I caught a flicker beneath that chilly surface.

I could almost hear Lady D choking back – what the
devil are you doing there? –

Instead she said – peremptorily – I would like to speak to my nephew –

If the Ice Queen hadnt been listening – I might have said – hes just getting dressed –

Instead I said – hes rather busy just now – a business meeting – with Sidney Parker –

That got a sharp intake of breath – which was then expelled – or rather exploded – very Lady Bracknell! – into – *a business meeting!* –

I began to feel sorry for Ted – not only caught entertaining a woman of ill repute – but also holding a secret meeting with Daphs financial advisor –

Ess was moving back down the stairs – but Ted came out of the drawing room before she could reach me. Feeling sorry for him didnt stop me holding out the phone – & saying – its your aunt –

He winced like the phone was hot – & I made a rapid exit – not bothering to glance up to see how far Esther had got.

As I reached the car – a voice called – Charley –

I turned – & my heart gave a little leap. Sid had come out to say cheerio.

He stood on the terrace – looking down at me – & smiling – & I started feeling guilty. It was one thing dropping Ted in it – but I had no reason for wanting to get Sid in Big Bums bad books.

– sorry youve got to dash away – he said – our business shouldnt take much longer. In fact – if – as I gather – thats dear Daphne on the phone – Im sure our meeting will be brought to a close with some expedition – so if you did have time to stay another few minutes – Id love a chance to talk with you –

Whatever was going on – Sid wasnt letting anything ruffle his smooth exterior!

I was tempted. But never show weakness – eh? – so I resisted – & said – no – Ive really got to go – but Im sure youll be coming over to Kyoto some time – wont you? – it would break Minnies heart if you didnt –

He fluttered his long silky eyelashes – could I get a transplant?!

– if the well being of a fair young maiden is in question – I must definitely come – though Hell should bar the way –

Like I said – takes real style to get away with that kind of schmalz!

We stood smiling at each other – his smile sort of sophisticated ironic – mine more idiot grin – & I thought – hes the one – definite!

Then Ted the Bart came out of the door on to the terrace – & stood alongside Sid – & suddenly I wasnt quite so sure. Hard to compare – but I did my best! Teds all macho hunkiness to Sids elegant smoothiness – depends whether your taste runs to chalk or cheese. On the beach I guess the bart would have edged it. 20 points to 19+ for sex appeal. Here it felt the other way round. & then there was the Maz. Definitely worth twice as much as the battered old Range Rover – or even the Beast.

Ted looked a lot less shell-shocked than I anticipated. In fact he looked rather pleased with himself. How had he survived? – I wondered.

Then the answer came to me – diversionary tactics! Before she could quiz him about this business meeting with Sid – hed told her that her toy-boy Feldenhammer was having a party at the Avalon that she wasnt invited to!

I thought – shit – should have kept your gob shut girl –

Ted said – sorry youve got to dash off Charley – well do that mo-bike ride another day eh? –

I thought – if you imagine Im going to risk getting frostbite in my crotch by putting it where the Ice Queens has been – youve got another think coming!

The withering look accompanying this thought was wasted however – as hed turned to Sid – put his arm round his shoulder – & drew him away.

But as they walked back into the house – Sid turned his head – & winked at me – tho the way he did it – so languid & sexy & full of promise – calling it a wink is like calling his Maz a jalopy!

I drove away very slowly – to sort out my thoughts – & pretty soon I reckoned Id cracked it! There was something going on here – & it was going on behind Lady Ds back. Had to do with money – Teddy desperately needed it – & it was Sids profession. Teds one remaining asset – far as I could tell – was Denham Park. He could do anything he liked with it – except sell it – wasnt that what Mary had told me? So what might he & Sid have been talking about? Turning it into another hotel in competition with the Brereton Manor? Possible – but you needed something else to hook in investors – some activity that had nothing to do with health & exercise & country recreation.

A gambling casino – I thought. Possible – except access wasnt great – & not even the sweet smell of money could mask the stench of the Hollis pigs. What about a retirement home? Do old folk lose their sense of smell Sis? But I couldnt see Ted & Ess as your jolly carers!

Whatever they were up to – clearly Lady D – & Tom too – werent in the loop.

Could see Sid might not mind pulling a fast one on Lady D – but I couldnt see him going behind his brothers back – just to make a quick buck.

Whatever the game was – Id given it away to Lady D

– with malice aforethought – but I resolved not to say anything to Tom – both for his sake – & also cos I didnt want to get any further up the noses of the 2 dishiest guys in town!

Now I decided to compensate for my bad behaviour by getting back to Kyoto in time to save Tom from the bicycle!

Neednt have bothered – Franny Roote had just turned up – & hed offered Tom a lift to the Avalon – so he told me to drive myself over for the lunch as planned. Tom was even more bubbly than usual – full of confidence his meeting was going to go well – & also chuffed cos hed rung Godly Gordon – & he was definitely going to attend!

I made some comment about his powers of persuasion – & I caught Franny grinning at me – as if he knew – which he couldnt – that Id put in my little twopennorth. I gave him the test. Wealth – 4 at most Id guess. Wheels – only 1 for his mini ambulance. Social Skills – this was hard – Im sure hed have no problem smoothing a girls path – dealing with all situations – keeping the talk bright & stimulating – but I get the feeling that from time to time hed enjoy dropping a handful of grit into the works! So 8 out of 10 there.

As for Sex Appeal – impossible to give points without more info. It could be like giving Sid 10 out of 10 for Wheels – then finding the Maz had no engine!

Hard – you say? Well – I remember who it was knocked 5 points off the vicars son after you found he had diabetes! The thought he might be pulling out his needle before he pulled out his dong – your words! – was a real downer!

Tom & Fran went off – leaving me with a good hour before I needed to make a move – so I thought Id bring you up to date.

Better dash now. Looking forward to seeing inside the

famous clinic. Got a feeling at some point – Big Bum may try to crash the party. If she does – I hope it doesnt come out who big mouth was!

Wont take Sherlock Holmes to guess that – I hear you say – not when your little sister has a mouth makes Julia Roberts look like shes whistling Dixie.

Youd better be careful – sis! When you come home with your bronze trophy doctor in tow – youre going to need all the friends you can find.

Love you

Charley xxxx

17

Well, Mildred, here I am, back from my first official outing, squatting on the khazi, and definitely not feeling like singing I could have danced all night!

First thought when I saw there were nowt but fizzy wine on offer was, mean bugger! Thought these Yanks always lashed out the hard liquor. My first guv'nor, old Wallie Tallentire, used to say, Bubbly's good for nowt but getting a girl's knickers round her ankles.

Certainly got my trousers round mine!

Talking of trousers, remember to thank Cap. When I pulled mine on for the first time since she brought them, I were surprised how well they fit. Then I checked and realized they were brand new and three sizes down from my old ones which would have hung around me legs like a mains'l in a dead calm. Bright lass! Dalziel, my man, you certainly know how to pick 'em!

So while I'm sitting here like patience on a fucking monument, I might as well make a note of Festerwhanger's little 'do' while it's still fresh. Always prided myself on not needing to be taking notes when I were running a case. If I can't remember it, it's not bloody worth remembering! Big boast. Let's put it to the test.

Yon clinic's a fancy place. Makes our old Central Hospital look like a heritage centre. Bet most of your common bugs and viruses turn tail and head back for town soon as they get a glimpse of what's waiting for them there. One look at the car park tells the story. There were enough high emission gear out there to punch its own small hole in the atmosphere. If the treatment fees match, then I reckon the patients will feel like they've paid for full privacy.

Pet led me to this lounge where there was a handful of people with glasses in their hand. I only recognized two of them. One was the landlord from the pub. He were talking to Stompy Heywood's lass that I'd sat next to when I broke out of the Avalon. I went up to them and said, 'How do, lass? How's thy dad?'

She looked puzzled for a moment then said, 'Oh, it's Mr Deal, isn't it? Didn't recognize you with your clothes on. You'll have met Alan Hollis from the Hope and Anchor.'

'Aye,' I said, laughing. I like a lass with a bit of spirit. 'Nice to see you again, Mr Hollis.'

The landlord said, 'You too, Mr Dalziel. You've not been back in.'

'Doctor's orders,' I said. 'But he's letting me off the hook today so I'll be down there shortly, you can bet on it.'

Pet came with a glass of fizz which I drank right off.

'Best get me another, luv,' I said. 'In fact why not bring a bottle over here so's to save you getting in a sweat running between me and the bar?'

She gave me a glower but she went off again.

I said to Hollis, 'Left your missus looking after the pub then?'

He said, 'I'm not married, Mr Dalziel. But I've got good staff. Just as well with the hog-roast on Sunday.'

I've noticed this before – folk out in the sticks always talk like everything happening locally's so important, complete strangers should know about it!

I said, 'What's that?'

'Don't you know?' he said, surprised. 'Lady Denham's big do at Sandytown Hall. Everyone will be there, everyone important that is. Sort of thank you from the Consortium to everyone who's helped in putting the town on the map. I'll be organizing the drinks, so the pub will have to look after itself.'

I thought, When buffalo woman snorts, every bugger jumps!

Pet came back with a bottle. I took it from her and filled all the glasses. Mine fullest 'cos I were catching up.

I said, 'Lady Denham sounds real important. She'll be in this meeting then?'

Pet and Hollis looked at each other, then Hollis said, 'No, I don't think so.'

I said, sort of poking around, 'Oh? Didn't strike me as the kind of lass you could keep away, her and Dr Feldenhammer being such good mates?'

Pet gave a kind of snort, and Hollis looked at the ground, and even young Heywood grinned. But before I could probe harder, the door opened and the folk from the meeting poured in. I saw Franny Roote in his chair. He gave me a wave, I gave him a glower. Then I spotted Parker so I excused myself, and went to pay my debts.

He were talking to a bearded guy in baggy pants and one of them fleecy jackets hikers wear. Either a tramp who'd strayed in off the road or an eccentric millionaire patient, I decided.

'How do, Mr Parker,' I said. 'Here's that twenty quid you were kind enough to loan me. Many thanks.'

He recognized me straight off, or mebbe Festerwhanger had warned him.

'Delighted I was able to help, Mr Dalziel,' he said, beaming at me. 'And how nice to meet you again.'

He sounded like he meant it, too, and not just because of the money.

'May I introduce you to Gordon Godley?' he said. 'Gordon, this is Mr Dalziel who's convalescing here at Avalon. Mr Godley's a healer whom I have persuaded to bring his ministry to Sandytown.'

Wrong twice. Neither a tramp nor a patient but one of the weirdoes Roote had been talking about!

I stuck my hand out. Godley didn't seem mad keen on taking it, and when he did it were barely a touch before he let go. Mebbe he were scared I were convalescing from summat contagious.

'Healer, eh?' I said. 'What's that about then? Charming warts in a moonlit churchyard or sticking lepers' noses back on?'

I were just being friendly, but I wished I'd not said it when he looked at me with his big grey eyes like a spaniel told he's not going walkies today. I were just going to pour a bit of oil when a voice behind me said, 'I'm sure Mr Godley could help you with your warts if they're bothering you, Mr Dalziel. Which part of your anatomy are they affecting?'

It were the Heywood lass, giving me the kind of look her dad used to give before clattering your goolies in a line-out. Godley, who was looking more

165

confused and unhappy than ever, mumbled something and moved off.

Heywood looked at me angrily and said, 'Now see what you've done. Tell me, were you always a bully or did you do a course on it at Hendon?'

I had to laugh. These kids. Know everything, understand nowt. But I liked her style.

Parker didn't seem to have noticed she were in a tizz.

Still smiling he said, 'I'm so glad Gordon decided to come to the meeting, Charlotte. He'll be such a valuable acquisition. All the other therapies are based on physical interactions. He provides a purely spiritual dimension. Charlotte, why don't you introduce Mr Dalziel to some of the others while I have a quiet word with Dr Feldenhammer?'

'Meeting must have gone well,' I said as he moved off. 'He seems happy.'

'Tom is always happy,' she said. 'He believes everything is for the best in the best of possible worlds. Pretty well the opposite of your world view, I'd guess, Mr Dalziel. Now, who'd you like to be rude to next?'

I got myself another drink, or rather another bottle as the first seemed to have emptied itself. Then Charley whipped me round some of the others – a chunky Chink lass who stuck needles into people; a herbalist you could have sprayed green and sold as a pixie in a garden centre; and a woman who looked like she'd been invited to a Halloween party and got her dates mixed. Didn't catch what she did, 'cos while we were shaking hands, I was hoping her black nails weren't painted with owt toxic. I began to wonder how come old Fester had got mixed up with this bunch of oddballs. If I'd found them setting up camp on my patch, I'd have escorted 'em politely to the Lancs border and pushed them across. They're more used to loonies over there.

When Charley finally introduced me to a woman she said was Parker's sister, I thought, thank Christ I'm back with the sane buggers. Some hope! Took all of ten seconds to realize she were dotty as a Frenchman's jock strap. Woman with her seemed OK, but. Name of Sandy something. Gave me an odd stare when Charley introduced us – or mebbe that's just how she always looks at big sexy men. I wish!

I'd got one thing right, though. Suddenly the door burst open and buffalo woman charged in.

'Lester,' she declaimed. 'I'm so sorry I'm late.'

Parker and Festerwhanger were in close confab over by the drinks table. I saw them look at each other, just a glance lasting a split second, but I'd put money on it each on 'em were thinking, You didn't tell me you'd invited her!

But Parker being a cock-eyed optimist and Festerwhanger being a smarmy Yank, neither of 'em had any bother turning on the full beam and coming forward to greet her.

'Lady D! Now we're complete!' declared Parker.

'Welcome, dear Daphne,' oozed Festerwhanger, offering one of them air kisses, but she moved her head at the last moment and caught him full on the lips so hard it probably bruised his gums.

The bodywork might be a bit rusty but the old internal combustion was still pounding away!

She weren't slow at lapping up the fizz either, I noted, getting through a couple of glasses at a rate of knots that made me feel like a Methodist and hitting the nibbles like she'd not et since Shrove Tuesday.

'Bet the mean old cow's brought a doggy bag,' muttered young Heywood.

I said, 'Being rude's OK behind people's backs then?'

'Just stating the facts,' she said pertly. 'Looks like maybe you're on the menu too.'

Didn't get her drift till I looked back to Lady D and there was the old bird wiggling her glass at me and giving me a turnip lantern smile.

What the fuck had I done to turn me from loony patient to dear old chum?

Mebbe it were friendship hour here in Sandytown, for suddenly the young guy I recalled whistling 'The Indian Maid' in the pub appeared and gave Heywood a smacking kiss. Opposite effect here. He was definitely aiming at the mouth but a nifty bit of head work diverted him to the cheekbone.

'Charley, here you are,' he said. 'What a joy to see you again.'

He sounded like an old-fashioned actor doing sincere. Good-looking young bloke, and he knew it. No harm in that. If you've got it, flaunt it, that's always been my motto.

Didn't look like it cut much ice with Heywood, but. She said, very accusing, 'You told your aunt about the meeting then?'

'Of course,' he said. 'But only in the fervent hope that she'd insist on coming, thus giving me another chance of seeing you.'

The lass rolled her eyes a bit, but I could tell she were pleased too. This young cock had learned what all successful young cocks soon work out, that you

168

don't need to worry about laying on the lard too thick with most women. Seeing what you're at makes them feel cleverer than you, which is what they all like to feel. But it takes a very clever one indeed not to let some of the lard stick!

She said, 'Mr Dalziel, this is Teddy Denham. Sir Edward, if you like titles.'

'Love 'em,' I said. 'Detective Superintendent Andy Dalziel.'

That froze his smile a second as we shook hands.

There'd been two others in the grand lady's train, a pair of lasses, one I didn't recognize and t'other the willowy niece, Clara, I'd met in the pub. Didn't surprise me to see Roote bearing down on her like the wolf on the fold. He came to a stop in front of her, reached out, grabbed a chair and pretty well forced her to sit down so's she were at his level. Didn't notice or mebbe didn't care that he were blocking the passage of t'other lass, who looked like she'd lunched on a radish salad and wished she hadn't. She could've walked round him but she didn't. She just got hold of the back of the wheelchair and twisted it out of her way, then wandered off to the window at the far end of the room, leaving Roote looking at the wall. Clara looked a bit pissed with the sour-faced woman but I could see Roote grinning as he manoeuvred himself back into position. Nowt I could teach that bugger about milking sympathy!

Alongside me, Teddy Denham was still laying it on with a trowel too, this time showing young Heywood how well read he were.

Looking round the room, he declared, 'This is precisely the kind of gathering Austen would have described so brilliantly, don't you think, Charley? Or perhaps you prefer the darker gaze of George Eliot?'

'I'm not sure,' she said.

'What about you, Mr Dalziel? *Aimez-vous* George Eliot?'

It was put-down-the-fat-plod time.

I said, 'Eh?'

'Do you like George Eliot?' he translated very slowly.

'Oh aye,' I said. 'He were my gran's favourite. Used to play "By the Silvery Moon" all the time. Excuse me.'

I gave Heywood a grin afore I moved off and she grinned back and gave me a big wink. Interesting lass. Not daft, just young. And won't be bad looking either when she lets herself grow into her body. Reminds me a bit of Cap.

In my experience buggers who want to be alone are either thinking of topping themselves or stealing the silver, so I joined the sour-faced woman by the window to find out which. She was staring across to the convalescent home. From this angle you couldn't see how it had been extended. Looking out to sea, with its tall chimneys and all that green ivy clinging to mellow red brick, it would have made a grand cover for an English Heritage magazine.

'Must have been a lovely place to live when it were a private house,' I said.

'Yes, it was,' she said softly. 'Very lovely. It used to belong to my family. A sort of dower house. My grandmother lived there. I always used to love staying with her . . .'

I could see her face in the pane and her expression

were sort of dreamy. Nice-looking lass. Then she clocked my reflection and suddenly it were back to radish time.

She turned to face me.

I said, 'Andy Dalziel,' and stuck out my hand.

Her hand shake were like one of them air-kisses. Made the healer's feel like an arm-wrestling session.

'Esther Denham,' she said.

'Oh aye. You related to Lady Denham then?'

Her face screwed up like she'd bit on a lettuce leaf and found a slug.

'By marriage,' she said, making it sound like an operation without anaesthetic.

Then Lady D's voice boomed, 'Esther, my dear, there you are. Come and keep me company. You too, Edward.'

It were like watching a kid who's just been told she can't have a sweetie realizing it's because she's being offered a tutti-frutti instead. As she turned from me, her face lit up like someone had triggered a security light.

'Coming!' she called gaily.

And she set off towards buffalo woman like a lost lamb to her yow.

I saw Sir Teddy had abandoned young Heywood just as quick and I went back to join her.

'The way yon pair jump, the old lass must really know where the bodies are buried,' I said.

'I think it's more where the money is banked,' she replied.

'Oh aye? Thought it 'ud be summat like that. They're brother and sister, right? And set on getting their share of the family fortune when auntie dies?'

'She's only an aunt by marriage, so I suppose it's

understandable they feel they've got to work at it,' she said.

'Sounds like you're on their side,' I said. 'Or is it just hunky Teddy's side?'

'No. I am being objective and analytical. I'm a psychologist.'

I had to laugh. Seen nowt, done nowt, and she were a psychologist!

'What's so funny?' she demanded, getting angry again.

I knew better than to tell her, so I said, 'I were just thinking, I bet old Stompy were chuffed to buggery when he found out he'd sired one of them.'

She gave me an old-fashioned look, then grinned.

'I see you knew my father quite well, Mr Dalziel,' she said.

'Well enough. How come Teddy's so hard up he needs to suck up to auntie?' I asked. 'His sister were saying the old house, and presumably all this land, used to belong to her family. Must have made a fortune when they sold it on to Avalon.'

'It did, but not for the Denhams, alas,' said a familiar voice.

I looked down to see Roote smiling up at me. The skinny lass had been sucked back into her aunt's orbit, or mebbe the sight of the young Denhams dancing attendance had made her decide she'd better keep her end up.

'Oh aye? Who then?' I said to him.

He smiled and lowered his voice so that I had to lower my head to hear him. The lass too. I got the impression she didn't want to miss owt.

'As I understand it,' he murmured, 'the story is that one result of the unfortunate if appropriate

172

demise of Hog Hollis was a rapprochement between his widow and Sir Harry Denham who had not been on the best of terms for some years. He held her responsible for sending the sweet odour of pigs wafting through his drawing-room window whenever he took afternoon tea.'

'This going to be a long tale?' I asked. 'If it is, I thought mebbe I'd go off somewhere quiet to read *War and Peace,* then come back for the climax.'

'Forgive me,' he said. 'I have fallen into rustic ways. Let me cut to the chase. Sir Harry, now close to insolvency, devised a cunning plan to solve both his financial and his olfactory problems at a stroke. He proposed to her. He was personable, reputedly virile – an important consideration for the dear lady – and of course he had what only money could buy, a title. This, I believe, was the clincher. She accepted.'

'Brings a tear to your eye, doesn't it?' said young Heywood.

I gave her a look. Don't care for cynicism in the young. If they don't have romantic delusions, what are old farts like me going to kick out of them?

Roote went rambling on. Cut to the chase, he'd said. More like verbal runs! Wieldy would have had it all spelt out, typed up, and on my desk half an hour back!

'As the wedding approached, he suggested that all that lacked to make them happy both was an odour-free threshold for him to carry her over. Now that Denham Park was to be her stately home too, perhaps the time had come to relocate the pig farm. She appeared to agree, only objecting that she would have to find a suitable site first. There was some spare capacity on the land belonging to Millstone Farm, the old Hollis farm, but she was reluctant to use that . . .'

'Knowing that if she snuffed it before her brother-in-law, the farm and everything on it would fall to Hen,' chipped in young Heywood.

Roote smiled appreciatively.

'Clearly psychology really is the listening profession,' he said. 'Yes, dear Lady D did not care for the thought of Hen benefiting more than he had to in the event of her death. She is, I believe, a very good hater. The upshot was she proposed to Sir Harry that this parcel of Denham land here on South Cliff would make an ideal site, well away from Denham Park, and too high above the town for any nuisance to be caused there. The old house could be adapted as an excellent administrative centre for the business.'

'If this is quick, I'm Speedy Gonzales,' I said.

'I've heard the rumours,' said Roote. 'Be patient, the end is near. Sir Harry was delighted, and even more so when she insisted on a proper business transaction, with Hollis's Ham Ltd formally purchasing the land. The deal was made, both deals, with the marriage top-billing in all the Yorkshire glossies. They went on a leisurely Caribbean cruise for their honeymoon, financed, local tradition says, by the money Hollis's Ham had paid for the South Cliff property. That must have made Sir Harry smile. His wife's money paying for their honeymoon, setting what he hoped would be the pattern for many years to come. Imagine his dismay when they returned some months later to discover the bulldozers had moved in here and with a true

174

American swiftness the Avalon Clinic was already beginning to rise.'

'You mean she'd got all this sorted afore they went off on honeymoon?' I said.

'Clearly so,' said Roote admiringly. 'Of course, after his initial shock, he must have consoled himself with the thought of the large profit made in the transaction. But I gather he was disappointed in this too. Victorian marital property laws had long since been repealed. The land had been signed over to Hollis's Ham, his wife's company, and all that he was going to get of her money was what she cared to allow him. He huffed and puffed but soon learned the lesson that huffing and puffing meant going to bed without any supper. No longer master in his own house, he was at least still Master of the Hunt until the government banned hunting with dogs. He is said to have roared, "Over my dead body!" On the first day of the season, he went out with the hounds and when they started a fox, he set out after them at a mad gallop, clipped the top of a wall, and ended in a ditch with a broken neck. He was, if nothing else, a man of his word.'

'And she walked away from the funeral with a title on her letterhead and the Avalon money in her purse,' said Heywood.

'So all this land and the old house used to belong to the Denhams,' I said. 'No wonder that poor lass Esther looks so pissed off.'

That got me a surprised glance from Heywood who said, 'Oh, she always looks like that, except when she's sucking up to Lady D.'

I said, 'Must be nice to have a smart understanding chap like Stompy for your dad so you don't have to go sucking up to any bugger.'

Roote laughed and said, 'Bravo, Andy. Your compassion does you credit.'

'It's got limits,' I said. 'So Lady Denham's got the chinks, and Sir Teddy and sis are sticking close as shit to a blanket in the hope some of it rolls their way when she topples off the twig?'

'I think that sums it up,' said Roote.

'Could be a long wait,' I said. 'The old bird looks good for another thirty years or more. And ain't she got blood relatives of her own, like yon skinny lass, Clara?'

'My, you really are a detective, Mr Dalziel,' said Heywood, recovering from my little put-down. 'That's right. Quite a lot, I gather. And, though most of them are very long shots indeed, there's a whole bunch of her first husband's relatives on the card.'

'Looks like I'm not the only detective,' I said. 'Only here two minutes and you've got all the local crack noted and analysed! So, rich old lady, lots of hopeful relations. Hope she locks her windows at night and doesn't go out in the dark.'

She said, 'Your line of work has clearly clouded your view of human nature.'

I said, 'You reckon? You did the Pollyanna psychology course, did you?'

She said a bit defiantly, 'I know it's a cliché, but I do think there's good in everybody if you look hard enough.'

'Me too,' I said. 'That's why I became a cop – so's I could spend my life turning up stones looking for it.'

I glanced down at Roote as I said this, but he just grinned back up at me like I'd offered him a compliment and said, 'Charley, dear, I wonder if I could trouble you to get me a glass of fruit juice.

Pomegranate if there is any, but the ubiquitous orange will do. And I see Andy's glass is empty . . .'

'Sure,' she said. 'Would you like it in an earthenware jug?'

'What's that about a jug?' I asked as she walked away.

'Ah, the sweet enigma of a woman's words,' he said. 'It is not for us to seek meaning. Andy, now we're alone, there's something I want to ask you.'

'Ask away,' I said. 'But tek note – just because I won't hit a man in a wheelchair doesn't make us first-name friends.'

'I'm sorry,' he said. 'Would you prefer the official title then? Lady D was certainly very impressed when I told her you were Head of Mid-Yorkshire CID.'

Now the change in buffalo woman's attitude was explained. She clearly enjoyed power, and anyone that smelt of it probably turned her on.

'Mr Dalziel will do,' I said.

'Oh, thank you kindly,' he simpered. I found myself liking the sour-puss lass who'd shoved him aside more and more.

'So what's it you want to ask?' I demanded.

He turned very serious and said, 'The thing is, I'm asking for a review of my case in the hope of getting the verdict overturned. I hoped you might support my appeal.'

Not many folk can gobsmack me, but somehow Roote's learned the trick.

'Eh?' I said.

'It's a question of getting into America for the publication of my Beddoes biography. The dean of St Poll University called in some favours to get me a special dispensation a couple of years back – but since 9/11 if you've got three penalty points on your driver's licence, they're reluctant to let you in, I need to be there, for interviews and signings. Keeping me out is a violation of my basic human right to make a living!'

Just then Heywood came back with a drinks tray. Just as well else I might have forgot me scruples and picked Roote up, wheelchair and all, and hoyed him through the window! Instead I downed my bubbles in one, then grabbed another glass, hers I suppose, and drank that too. I drew the line at Roote's juice. I weren't that far gone. Heywood didn't say owt, just buggered off back to the drinks table.

At last I could speak.

'You want me to support your appeal against a conviction which my evidence helped to get? A conviction that's only ever bothered me because I reckon the sentence should have been twice as long!'

'Exactly,' he said. 'You can see your support would really impress the court.'

I didn't know whether to laugh or cry.

I said, 'I need another drink.'

And I'd have gone after the lass only my legs didn't seem to want to work.

Roote reached up and got a hold of my arm.

'Really, you mustn't try so hard,' he said seriously.

'What the fuck are you on about?' I demanded.

He pulled me down so he was talking in a low voice right into my face.

'When you've been as close to death as we have,' he said, 'you don't just take a single step back to where you were, it's a long, long journey.'

'Thank you, Dr Roote,' I said. 'I were wondering

178

what I were doing in a conva-fucking-lescent home, and now you've spelt it out. I'm conva-fucking-lescing!'

'I'm not just talking physical here,' he said. 'It's a long way back to yourself. Mostly we do it by acting ourselves. We remember the way we were and we devote all our energy to trying to get back into the part, even if it involves drinking fifteen pints before breakfast. But it is just a part, Andy. Now's the time, while you're still relearning it, to pause and consider just who this being is that's doing the learning.'

My head were really spinning now. Didn't know whether it were from Festerwhanger's bubbles or Roote's babbles. Didn't care either. I pulled my arm free and came close to keeling over, except someone got a hold of my other arm and I heard Pet Sheldon say, 'Time to be on our way, I think, Andy.'

Places I normally drink, no bugger calls closing time on me. I forced the world back into focus. Distantly I saw buffalo woman beckoning me like I was a head waiter. I gave her a smile and a wave and said to Pet, 'You're right, luv. Take me to bed.'

The fresh sea air hit me like a flying fish and I leaned heavily on Pet as we tacked towards the old house. There were a din like the clatter of the weaving room in an old wool mill as an ancient motorbike and side-car went rattling by. The rider had his helmet and visor on, but I recognized Mr Godley's beard. Funny, it were likely the fresh air, but just the sight of him made me feel better.

'There goes the healer,' I said, managing to straighten up a bit. 'Old Festerwhanger takes him on, you could all be out of work.'

'I shan't hold my breath,' she said. 'It's nursing

gets sick people better, not dosing them with herbs, or sticking them with skewers.'

'Nay, lass, you shouldn't rush to mock what it says in the Bible,' I said.

'Laying on of hands and that stuff?' she said. 'We've moved on a bit since then, I hope. Just because that chap looks like Jesus doesn't mean he's going to raise you from the dead. So let's get you to your bed, shall we?'

'That's what I'm talking about, luv,' I said. 'Old Testament therapy. Like King David and Abishag the Shummanite. Any chance of fixing that for me?'

She knew her Bible 'cos that made her laugh.

'My old gran always used to say the devil could quote scripture,' she said. 'Now shut up or I'll drop you here on the drive and let Lady Denham run you over with that rust bucket of hers. She's a menace, that woman.'

She spoke so vehemently, I thought, there's a bit more than road rage here!

What's she done to rattle your cage? I wondered.

It took me another half-dozen paces to work it out. Back afore the big bang, I'd have seen it half an hour ago.

It's old Festerwhanger! Pet's got the hots for him too! It must really get up her nose, seeing the way he fawns on Lady D and she trets him like her personal property.

I said, slurring it a bit to encourage indiscretion, 'Time for her to marry again then. Tried it twice so she must have a taste for it.'

'Woman of her age should know better,' said Pet, very pursed-lips proper. 'Do you need to lean on me quite so much? A couple of glasses of wine and you're wobbling like a blancmange. I thought you detectives all had hollow legs.'

I straightened up a bit, but it were hard. Must be all that rubbish the quacks have been pumping into me. That's twice a couple of glasses have reached parts that it used to take fifteen pints to get close to.

Pet got me back in my room, laid me in my bed, laughed when I invited her to join me for a bit of Platonic dialogue, and buggered off. Soon as she'd gone I got up and checked my sunken treasure in the cistern. Half a bottle of malt and Mildred. Checked no bugger had been interfering with either and took a slug of the Caledonian cream.

Always reckoned that Dr Scotch was a cure for everything, but this time I'm having me doubts. That's why I'm sitting here on the bog, talking to Mildred. Good spot for meditation. Don't need one of them fancy computers if you've got a comfy bog – soon have this case sorted out.

What the fuck am I talking about!? What fucking case? Am I going doolally? Mebbe being off the job's giving me withdrawal symptoms, so everything starts looking like a case waiting to happen . . . victim set up . . . suspects in place . . . motives well established . . . great detective on the spot . . . all waiting for a writer to give them the nod . . .

For fuck's sake, you daft bugger, you've let yon scrote Roote get inside your mind! All that crap about relearning your part. And it's this place too. The Avalon. Sandytown. The sooner you get off this bog and into your bed, the better.

But I've definitely got this feeling something bad is coming . . . something very real . . .

Oh Jesus Christ! and here it is . . .!

18

Oh, Mildred, what have I done?

Woke up feeling great, sort of cleansed and purged. No wonder after what came out in the bathroom, and if any bugger don't believe me, I can play them the sound effects, courtesy of Mildred!

Better out than in, they say, and this morning I really did feel better. Put my dressing gown on and went and had breakfast on the terrace. Pet stopped to have a chat, told me I looked like Noël Coward, and we had a laugh together. Then I went back to my room and me and Mildred were just reviewing what I'd said and done at the party when there was a tap at the door. It were Pet, not smiling any more. She said, 'You have a visitor, Mr Dalziel' all formal, but afore I could ask her what was amiss, she was bundled aside by buffalo woman who said, 'Thank you, Nurse Sheldon, I won't keep you from your duties any more.' Then she came into the room and shut the door in Pet's face!

I thought, watch out, lad. Likely it's your lily-white body she's after, and you in your dressing gown! I made sure Mildred were switched on just in case it ever came to court!

Needn't have worried, it were my brains not my body she wanted! Or mebbe that should worry me more. I've listened to the recording half a dozen times, don't know whether to take it seriously or not. I mean, a lot of rich old biddies think someone's trying to kill them, don't they?

Any road, I think I reassured her. I were certainly glad to get shut of her. After she'd gone I didn't feel quite as bright as I'd done before so I stripped off and got into the shower. Ten minutes lightly boiled then thirty seconds quick freeze usually gets me fighting fit! The light boiling were working its magic and I were enjoying a bit of a sing-song, seeing how many verses of 'The Indian Maid' I could remember when the shower door opened behind me and I felt a pair of arms go round my waist and what felt like a pair of soft pumpkins press into my back.

I thought, 'Right first time, Dalziel! It really is your lily-white she's after. Prepare to repel boarders!'

I span round and put my hands up to the pumpkins to push her away. Plenty to push against, I tell you!

Then the steam cleared a bit, and I realized the pumpkins I had my hands on weren't Lady D's but Pet Sheldon's!

I said, 'What's going off, luv?'

She said, 'You said you were having trouble scrubbing your back, remember?'

I said, 'Then I'd best turn round, hadn't I?'

And she said, 'Oh no, I think I can reach from here.'

And somehow as we talked my push had turned into squeeze and she didn't need to reach all that far 'cos I found I were stretching to meet her.

Well, like I've heard a lot of the witnesses say, after that I don't remember much, it all happened so quickly. Seemed no time at all afore I found myself lying on my bed with Pet draped all over me, telling me how great it had been. Already I knew I weren't going to feel good about it, but hearing her piling on the praise eased the pain a lot, till I realized that, mixed up with stroking my ego, not to mention my undercarriage, she were slipping in a lot of questions about what Daph Denham had wanted with me. Even then I were so laid back in every sense, I got as far as having a laugh and saying the silly old biddy thought some bugger were trying to kill her afore it dawned on me that this bit of Q & A were likely the main aim of the exercise.

The thrust of her questions told me her main concern was old Fester. Didn't know how I felt about that, getting a shag from one woman so's she can pump me about another on behalf of the fellow she really fancies! In the end it made my head ache, but, being a man, a little thing like a headache didn't stop Pet's busy fingers from having a reviving effect.

Knew I had to make a decision. At the moment I reckoned that if ever I had to explain myself to Cap (which heaven forfend!), I could just about justify what happened in the shower by pleading surprise attack and long abstinence. This time I'd be going into it with my eyes wide open. So, tho the prospect of seconds weren't unattractive, I surprised myself and Pet by rolling off the bed and saying, 'Thanks for that, luv, but I can't lie around all day enjoying myself. Things to do.'

She didn't speak, just got dressed and let herself out, but I could see she were thinking maybe this hadn't been all that good an idea! That made two of us!

I felt like a drink and a bit of quiet to drink it in, so I got dressed, strolled down to the gatehouse and got Stan to call me a taxi. Told him to take me to the Hope and Anchor, but when we got down there it were all shut up. The taxi driver laughed when he saw my face and said, 'Where you from, mate? You don't look French. But you'll not find many pubs here open before ten in the morning.'

I said, 'It'll open for me!'

Didn't want to make a scene banging on the front door, so went round the back, where I found the supply hatch open and I could hear someone down in the cellar.

I hollered out, 'Hello, the house. That you down there, Alan?'

A moment later his face appeared below me and once again he proved he were my kind of landlord. Just like the first time I showed up, he expressed no surprise but shouted up, 'Come on down, Mr Dalziel. If you don't fancy the ramp, you'll find the back door's open.'

Time was I'd have just rolled straight down, but tempus fuckit, and I went in through the kitchen and down a flight of stairs so narrow and worn, the ramp might have been a better bet. And what I found there made me wish I'd not bothered!

That cellar were like something out of an old Hammer horror flick. Gloomy, cobwebby, full of black beetles and musty smells, and lit by a single bare bulb, it were the best advert for aluminium kegs and plastic pipes I've ever seen.

I said, 'Jesus, lad, they don't build 'em like this any more!'

He said, 'Aye, there's been a pub here since good

King Charles's golden days, and I don't reckon much has changed since then. I'm trying to persuade Lady D we need a bit of modernization.'

I looked at the racks the beer kegs were lined up on. Hearts of oak mebbe in the seventeenth century, they looked like hearts of wood-rot now, and the whole cockley edifice were propped up against the uneven unplastered wall with what looked like a pair of clothes poles.

I said, 'Bugger persuasion! Get Health and Safety in, they'll soon get her sorted. Looks to me like this lot could come tumbling down any time.'

'Likely you're right,' he said. 'But Her Ladyship don't take kindly to officials or any other bugger telling her what to do. Never fear, I'll get there eventually. Now let's head off upstairs and I'll get you that pint.'

Hadn't mentioned a pint, but like I say he's a pearl among landlords.

I supped my ale and he had a half to keep me company. I really weren't worried about what Daph had said to me, so it were more just to make conversation that I said, 'Lady D a nervous type, is she?'

'You're joking,' he said. 'Not a nerve in her body. When she were out with the hunt she were famous for taking hedges and walls a lot of the men balked at.'

'Gave it up, but, didn't she?'

'Aye, well, I suppose the sight of your husband with his head looking down his spine might seem like a bit of a warning. But it weren't nerves – she just enjoys life too much to want to leave it early.'

'So what's she like to work for then?' I asked.

'Easy enough, so long as you do things her way,'

he said. 'As you'll likely find out if you stay around long enough. Unless you go over to the other side.'

I thought he meant die, and I said, 'I don't look that bad, do I?'

He grinned and said, 'No, sorry! What I mean is, one way or another most folk in Sandytown are either working for Lady Denham or they're working for Tom Parker.'

I said, 'But they're on the same side, aren't they?'

He said, 'I think you'll find Tom's working for the town, but Daphne's only working for herself. Best not to get involved if you can avoid it. Get well soon, and leave! Now I'd best get back down to the spiders. If you fancy another one, draw it yourself, OK?'

A pearl among landlords, did I say? A prince, I meant!

Any road, Mildred, that's been the story of my day so far, that's how I've ended up here at ten of clock in the morning, talking to thee, with a pint in my belly, a shag on my conscience, and a tale of attempted murder on my mind.

What's the rest of the day got in store?

Nowt! Get well and leave, said Alan Hollis. That's beginning to sound like good advice. Don't get involved, Dalziel. Forget everything that happened this morning, Daph and Pet both. Pet's not going to blab. She may be willing to open her legs for Fester's sake, but she's not going to tell him that! As for Daph, likely she's just another dippy old woman. Best steer well clear. She ended by inviting me to this barbecue she's having tomorrow. Everyone's coming, she said. Well, not me! No, I've learned my lesson. Keep to yourself, eat your greens, do your physio, keep your flies buttoned tight, lock your door at night, and in another week you'll be fit enough to go home.

There you are, Mildred. No need to be ashamed of me.

I'm a changed man!

Now I think it's time for that second pint.

19

FROM: charley@whiffle.com
TO: cassie@natterjack.com
SUBJECT: bloody murder!

Cass – omigod I was so wrong – nobody kills anyone in Sandytown I said! Listen – dont come home – youre probably safer where you are – no thats stupid! – whats one death compared with what you see? – & why am I so excited? – not just horrified & scared – tho those too – but excited – do you feel like this sometimes? – or am I just wierd?

Sorry – Im babbling & you must be wondering about what? Here goes – what happened – in order – must have order – first rule of psychology my tutor said – be a still point in the midst of chaos – so – deep breath – Im a still point – here we go.

First – Im still here in Sandytown – why? – because Im an idiot – thats why!

After the do at the Avalon – I got to thinking – dont know why – that something was building up here – dont know what! – but woke up yesterday feeling – if I go home now it will be like leaving the cinema just as the orcs come marching out of the gates of Mordor! OK – thats exaggerating a bit – I thought! – but suddenly it seemed like Lady Ds hog-roast would be a climax I shouldnt miss.

189

For once I wish to hell Id been wrong!

So I asked the Parkers if I could stay another day. Youd have thought Id given them first prize in the lottery! Minnie flung her arms around me & gave me a kiss. I felt really good. So I rang home – the HB was furious – natch! – but mum was pleased – I think she suspects Ive met a *nice young man* – & with luck hell turn out a cross between her favourites Harrison Ford & Tom Hanks!

So I spent yesterday writing up what notes Id taken – but mainly just lazing around.

& today – the hog-roast!

Oh Jesus – that phrase – youll see!

Everyone was there – all the Parkers – natch – Di had brought Sandy G along – so at least old Deaths Door was keeping her promise of getting her the S-town social scene! Toms bunch of wierdos were there too – including Godly Gordon – folk from the Avalon – Feldenhammer – Miss Sheldon the chief nurse – plus a whole bunch of people I didnt know – at their centre a guy with a gold chain round his scraggy neck – probably local councillors enjoying a freebie – all the buggers are good for according to dad. Hunky bart & the Ice Queen were there – naturally. He looked like hed got out of the wrong side of someones bed – not mine! Having a row with his sister – caught my eye but just looked away when I tried a friendly wave. Sod you! I thought. Then – to my surprise – the IQ flashed me a big friendly smile – like she thought the wave was for her – or maybe she was just looking at someone important over my shoulder!

Lady D made a welcome speech – very gracious – thanked all the friends & supporters of the Consortium for all thier efforts to put Sandytown on the map – looked forward to everyone reaping the rewards – all the time contriving somehow to give the impression this was her

190

own personal party – apologized because thered been a hitch with the actual roasting bit – so no pork ready for another hour or so – but lots of other goodies – & buckets of booze – so enjoy!

The mob didnt need any encouragement! As freebies go – this was a good one. No expense spared. Top quality booze – no plonk – & acres of grub – china plates – real cutlery – nothing plastic – all laid out on tables on the lawn in front of the Hall. Id expected a hog-roast would mean roast pork or nothing – but not a bit of it. All tastes catered for.

There were half a dozen kids there – including Minnie & Paul – whod come prepared for a swim from the private beach. Not without an adult – Lady D insisted.

Couple of adults volunteered – including Miss Lee – her of the long needles! – & Teddy got in on the act – looking to win brownie points no doubt! He ushered the kids inside to get changed.

I went to take a look at the famous roasting machine – situated well away from the Hall – presumably for safetys sake – hidden by a heavy rhododendron shrubbery on the house side – & protected seaward from the prevailing east wind by a mixed copse of pine & beech.

Ollie Hollis was there – looking a bit chastened – ie like hed been rolled on by an angry elephant – which is probably what being told off by Lady D feels like! But when I spoke to him kindly – he was happy to show off his machinery.

The roasting device itself isnt a spit but an ovoid metal basket into which the pig is fitted & which then revolves slowly over a long trench filled with burning charcoal. Its worked by a fine geared weight driven device – bit like a grandfather clock – takes Ollie about ten minutes to get the weight to its apogee – but then it will turn the basket for the next forty five minutes without human aid. The whole thing is on big metal wheels – running on rails – starting in a wooden hut with a tin roof – where its kept out of the weather. The ground slopes down from the hut – so its easy to get the basket in position – & theres a winch inside so it can be hauled back up. Ollie didnt seem keen to let me take a look – maybe hes got a woman in there! I thought – & it was too hot to stand around the charcoal pit long – humid thundery weather – plenty of sunshine & blue sky but lots of big lurid clouds bubbling up eastward too – making me think I might get that big storm across the sea Id been hoping for – so I headed back to the lawn.

Got there just in time to see the beach party setting off – Ted looking v Greek Godish – all rippling brown muscle & curling black body hair (did the Gk gods have body hair?) & a pair of swimming trunks that left just enough to the imagination! I hoped hed have enough sense not to be tempted into skinny-dipping. One thing dropping your kegs in front of a mature young woman – thats me! – quite another in front of kids. These days youd get ten years – no questions asked.

Everyone was well scattered by now – some exploring the woodland walks – oldies on the lawn in garden chairs – councillors not straying far from the drinks table. Had a chat with Sandy G. Asked her how her neice was. Got that funny stare – then she said – oh shes fine – not sounding all that concerned. Maybe shed been glad to swap a pair of teens for Diana! No accounting for taste – as the HB likes to say.

Bumped into Esther – to my surprise I got another friendly smile – called me Charley – & insisted on making sure I got my bubbly topped up.

– Hello! – I thought. When the Ice Queen melts – get your flood defences up!

Had to admit though – when she turns on the charm – youve got to remind yourself what shes really like! & of course she looked drop dead gorgeous in a skimpy top & organdie skirt. Not for her the Clara pallid look. Long golden limbs with no suggestion that the tan stops anywhere!

Then she reverted to type when Franny rolled his chair toward us – turned on her heel – & made off into the shrubbery.

– sorry – said Franny – didnt mean to break up your tete-a-tete – you two seemed to be getting on rather well –

– dont worry – I said – probably a mistake anyway – maybe someone told her I once screwed a guy whod screwed a girl whod screwed Prince Harry –

That made him chortle so much he almost fell out of his chair.

Kept on glimpsing Godly Gordon out of the corner of my eye – watching me – but whenever I turned he looked away! Finally I decided to go & ask him if my slip was showing or something – just to see him blush when I said *slip!* – only now – of course – he wasnt watching me but standing a little way off – at the edge of the shrubbery between the main lawn & the hog-roast pit – having what looked like a furious row with Lady D – & I certainly wasnt going to get mixed up in that.

Soon it was clear the weather was definitely on the turn – wind getting up – clouds eating up the blue – hotter & more humid than ever. Mary – who had her two youngest in tow – began to get worried about Minnie & Paul on the beach. I said theyd be fine – Teddy was with them – but to set her mind at rest I offered to go & take a look.

At the top of the cliff path I met Esther again. She looked a bit dishevelled & overheated – not at all like an

Ice Queen – & this time I didnt think it was anything to do with me.

– Charley – she said – have you seen Teddy? –

– isnt he down on the beach? – I asked.

– no – Ive just looked there –

– shit! – the kids arent swimming by themselves – are they? –

– what? – no – theres someone with them – she said – tho I got the impression that they could have been carried off by a killer whale for all she cared!

She set off towards the lawn where everyone was heading towards the house – except for Franny – sitting there in his chair – a glass of bubbly in his hand – smiling at the great retreat. To my surprise Ess actually stopped & spoke to him.

I thought – the cow must be really keen to find Teddy if shes deigning to address the legless wonder!

I set off down the cliff path. Easy going at first – gentle descent along a track winding down through heather & clumps of rhododendrons – steepening eventually to a long ledge where there was a protective railing. One length of the wooden rail was tied to a metal upright with binder cord – & there was a handwritten notice saying – do not lean on the railing. Good job Mary didnt know about that! I thought.

It was here – I recalled from my visit to the beach – that the real exposure began – & a steep path zig-zagged down the cliff face – with a hand-rail all the way.

I paused on the ledge & looked down to the beach – I could make out figures in the deepening gloom – children & a couple of adults who seemed to be rounding them up. I was going to carry on my descent when I heard a noise – coming from behind me I thought – & I looked back along the ledge & saw there was a sort of little track winding off it – climbing back above the shrub & vegetation line. The noise came again – very faint in the rising wind – but to my famous little sharp ears it sounded human – so just in case Minnie had decided to do a bit of exploring I went to take a look.

The track led to a particularly thick clump of rhodies. I pulled a few branches aside – & found myself looking into a sort of cave – more of a deep overhang really – but rendered dark & shady by the thick foliage.

Then out over the sea a huge jag of lightning split the horizon – & in its brief light I saw two figures in there.

One I recognized instantly – though I could only see his back. Those muscular thighs & bulging calves were unmistakably the hunky barts. The noise was coming from him – a kind of rhythmic groaning. He was lying on top of the other figure – also face down. All I could see of her were the long white legs – sprawling wide – but that was enough. Lady D might think she could jerk Teddy & Clara around at will – but the fire in the blood had made short work of her bits of string! As I watched – his round pink buttocks (cant have done enough skinny-dipping to get them the rich russet of his legs & torso!) – from gently bobbing up & down like Halloween apples – went into overdrive – & the groans ceased to sound human!

Jesus! – I thought – first Liam up against that tree – now this – maybe Im fated every time I fancy a guy to catch him in flagrante!

Tho I knew the kids were safe I felt a bit pissed that Teds offer of supervision had just been a cover for this – not very logical I know – but I felt personally betrayed – so I tried to announce my presence with a loud cough! But it was drowned in a mighty clap of thunder – & in any case – from the noise Teddy was now making I dont think there was much risk of him noticing anything short of a kick up the backside!

As I made my way back along the ledge – the storm really broke loose – lightning – forked & sheet – played over the sea & the rising wind drove huge drops of rain into my face.

I was mightily relieved to meet the kids hurrying up the path towards me – Minnie & Paul among them – him a bit scared – her really excited. Behind them came Miss Lee & a guy I didnt know.

– that everyone? – I asked Miss L.

– yes – I checked – she said.

By the time we got back to the house – we were soaking. Everyone else had already retreated to shelter – many of them crowded into the huge east facing conservatory – to watch the storm. Others had made themselves comfortable in the deep armchairs in the reception rooms – in one of which Alan Hollis had reassembled the drinks table – & the councillors had settled round it happily!

I reported back to Mary – then took the two kids in search of towels to dry ourselves off. They thought it was a great adventure & Minnie was almost drunk with excitement. In a first floor bathroom I got her as dry as I could – but when I started on her brother she shot off through the door. I dried Paul – gave myself a rub – nothing to do about our damp clothes – but it was still too warm to take much harm from them.

We set off after Minnie. I guessed shed have gone up rather than down – & I found her kneeling on the broad inner sill of a second floor oriel window – staring out – rapt. I couldnt blame her – it was a magnificent & terrifying sight.

Almost as black as night now – lit from time to time by lightning flashes – sheet trembling out over the raging

waters of the North Sea – forked closer at hand –
showing us the woodland surging wildly – as though
dancing in unison with the ocean waves. After the initial
downpour the rain seemed almost to have stopped. We
saw a jag of electricity hit a tall pine – cleaving it in two
from top to bottom – then darkness again – till the next
flash showed us only a mad whirl of leaves & ash where
the tree had been.

What of the pair in the cliff cave? – I wondered.

Did they still shelter there – clinging close as the air
seemed to explode around them? I could almost envy
Clara. To make them take such a risk on such an occasion – their desire must have been elemental – & how
this storm must seem to stamp Gods approval on what
theyd done!

Getting religion? Maybe – weather like this always
makes me feel there has to be something – but what
happened next makes me doubt if I want much to do with
whatever that something is!

Dont know how long we stayed there. Eventually –
thinking Mary would be getting worried again – I made
them go down. Slowly the storm subsided. I began to look
around. Almost at once I spotted Clara – so they must
have made it back. Incredibly she hardly looked damp at
all. Of course – when the storm broke – as well as the
shelter from the shrubs – shed have had her clothes off –
probably underneath her.

Teddy I saw talking to Sid – a long way removed from
Clara. Putting a safe distance between them – in case old
Gorgon-eyes Daphne starts getting suspicious – tho there
was no sign of her at all. Maybe – I thought – she was
entertaining Dr Feldenhammer privately in her boudoir. No
sign of him!

After a while you could feel people looking for someone

to give a lead. Outside the sun was appearing by glimpses – steam was beginning to rise off the sodden grass & shrubbery – the storm was a distant mutter – retreating like a defeated army back to the continent. Should we settle down in the house? Head outside to play the old English game of pretending nothing had happened? Say our thanks & go?

But you need someone to be in charge – someone to make your thanks to – & there was still no sign of Lady D.

It was Teddy – naturally – who took charge.

– Come on people – he cried – sounding a bit manic – theres still drink to be drunk – (there wasnt all that much actually – the councillors hadnt missed their opportunity) – & grub to be eaten – whats a bit of wet to a true blue Englishman? –

He led the way out.

His promise of food didnt hold water – joke – no one had thought to rescue it when the mad rush inside began – & I doubt if soggy canapés would look attractive – even to all those starving children in China the HB is always reminding us about!

Our attention was diverted by a faint cry from the far end of the lawn where it ran into the shrubbery. There was a figure lying on the grass – waving an arm. Some of us moved forward – slowly at first – then – realizing who it was – at greater speed.

It was poor Franny Roote – lying alongside his overturned wheelchair! He looked a real mess – soaked to the skin – & covered with mud. He gasped that his chair had got stuck in the sodden turf – you could see the grooves where it had sunk in – & hed overturned it in his efforts to get it moving – & had been trying for most of the storms duration to get it back upright.

Nurse Sheldon was one of the first to reach him – Im glad to say – as I was thinking I might have to call on my old St J ambulance training again! I helped get the chair upright & the nurse hoisted him into the seat like he was a sack of potatoes. Of course – you nurses have the training for this – explains your well developed muscles!

Once back in the chair Franny resumed normal service – paraplegia dont stop a guy being macho! – & said – thank you – all of you – Im fine now – in fact it was worth a soaking to be bang in the middle of the storm – I may recommend the experience as part of the Third Thought therapy – it was like looking the Almighty in the eye! –

Miss Sheldon – even more used than me to seeing through this kind of male crap – said – you may be seeing him a lot closer up if we dont get you dried off pretty soon –

Fran – determined to stay cool – winked at me – & said – What better to keep me anchored to this world Miss Sheldon than the prospect of being rubbed down by you? –

She grunted – unimpressed – & drove the wheelchair across the lawn towards the house with very little effort.

The rest of us were following when Teddy said – tell you what folks – I could murder a slice of hot pork with lots of crackling – (double entendre or what?) – lets take a look at how Aunt Daphnes pig is doing –

– wont the rain have put the charcoal pit out? – said Tom.

– Ill go & see – shall I? – said Clara.

& off she went – through the copse that concealed the pit from the main lawn.

For a moment – silence. Complete silence. The wind had dropped – the thunder died completely away – no one spoke – no birds sang –

Then – the most terrible sound Id ever heard – a scream – barely human – high – pure – unwavering – a single note just within the range of human hearing – going on – & on – & on –

Teddy was the first to move. He set off running. We all followed – a stampede of humans – running towards what has struck terror into their hearts – because not knowing is worse than knowing. Or so we thought.

What the cause of the screaming was took time to sink in.

I was one of the first to arrive. I saw Clara standing petrified – Teddy beside her – his arms clasping her tight – both of them staring at the metal roasting basket – still slowly turning above the charcoal pit. Despite the downpour – the trees must have given some shelter – the charcoal was still glowing red hot in places. The basket was slowly revolving – & there was a smell of scorching meat.

Someone should have been here to baste the pork – I thought.

& then my mind admitted what my eyes must have registered instantly.

– & now the high scream I heard wasnt Claras – but my own.

Arms went around me. They belonged to Gordon Godley. Didnt realize then – was just glad to have someone to lean up against – even though he was dripping wet.

Tried closing my eyes. Didnt help. Still saw everything even with my eyes closed.

Some yards beyond the pit – under a cloud of vapour – like guttering candle holders – 4 dainty trotters were sticking up out of the lank wet grass.

It was the barbecue pig.

& now – tho I dont think I stopped screaming – the

thought occurred to me that Tom Parker had got the
headline that would really put Sandytown on the map.

Hollis's Ham – the real taste of . . . MURDER!

For the thing being roasted in the slowly revolving
basket was the corpse of Daphne Denham.

Volume the Second

You will never hear me advocating those puerile Emanations which detail nothing but discordant Principles incapable of Amalgamation, or those vapid tissues of ordinary Occurrences from which no useful Deductions can be drawn.

1

'And you're sure this is *our* Franny Roote?' said Pascoe, staring at the name underlined in red on the guest list.

Sergeant Edgar Wield nodded and regarded the Chief Inspector inscrutably. With a face like the dark side of the moon, inscrutability came easy to him. Nevertheless Pascoe scruted reproach.

'Sorry, I'm not doubting you, Wieldy,' he said defensively. 'But *Franny Roote!* I thought he must be dead.'

'Lady Denham's dead,' said Wield. 'Doc says looks like manual strangulation. Dead anything from an hour to three hours when he saw her. Being roasted over a charcoal pit didn't make the timing easy.'

His tone matched his expression. It was Jeevesian in its neutrality. Not a hint of insubordination to the young master. Yet once again Pascoe felt reproached.

And he knew he deserved it.

A Detective Chief Inspector, arriving at a crime scene ninety minutes after his sergeant – courtesy of a flat tyre and an even flatter spare – to discover an Incident Room set up, witness statements being taken, and a CSI unit, clothed in white nylon, mystic, wonderful, busy performing its priest-like tasks, ought to fall to his knees and give thanks.

Of course the fact that the sergeant was Edgar Wield meant that this was only what his bosses at Mid-Yorkshire

CID had come to expect. He was indeed to them what Jeeves was to Bertie Wooster. He performed wonders with quiet efficiency, had a mind which could process information at silicon-chip speeds, and took care never to let his superiority embarrass his superiors.

'Plus,' as Andy Dalziel had observed when the parallel was suggested to him, 'if yon's the first face you see in the morning, you don't need Jeeves's fancy hangover cure.'

Pascoe took a deep breath and pulled himself together. A titled lady roasting over her own barbecue pit was what he should be concentrating on.

'So fill me in, Wieldy,' he said.

It took Wield two minutes. It would probably have taken Andy Dalziel three, Pascoe himself three and a half, most of his junior CID officers five, Uniformed six or seven, an articulate civilian at least ten; and Molly, the HQ tea lady, an hour and a half.

Wield concluded, 'To date, latest reported sighting of the victim is around half three, when she was observed having an animated conversation with one of the guests, a Mr Godley.'

'Animated as in *When I run out of words I'm going to strangle you*?'

Wield shrugged. He liked to advance as far as possible on the firm ground of fact before risking the slough of speculation.

'He's some kind of healer,' he said.

'And isn't death the cure of all diseases?' said Pascoe. 'I look forward to talking to him. I assume, following best Golden Age practice, you've got Mr Godley and the other guests corralled in the library awaiting the arrival of the Great Detective?'

'Didn't realize he was coming,' said Wield. 'No,

sorry. First, there isn't a library. Second, seems a lot of them had already headed off home by the time the local sergeant, Jug Whitby, got here. Most of the rest had drifted away by the time I arrived.'

'This Whitby made no attempt to stop them?' said Pascoe.

'Fair do's,' said Wield, who was very protective of sergeants. 'Not a lot one man could do to keep them here. Can't blame 'em for not wanting to hang around, not with *that* out there.'

They were standing by a window in the Incident Room which was being set up in a disused flat above the stable block. It consisted of a living room, a bedroom, a tiny kitchen and a toilet. By contrast with the well-kept stable below, the flat looked pretty derelict, even though the worst of the dust and debris had been swept away.

Pascoe and the sergeant were in the bedroom. Through the cracked and weather-stained glass they looked out across the lawn to where they could glimpse over the shrubbery the billowing grey of the protective tent erected over the dreadful barbecue.

'So what's Sergeant Whitby doing now?' asked Pascoe, putting off the moment when he'd have to see the horror for himself. 'Gone home for his tea?'

'No, I sent him off to round up one of them that left,' said Wield. 'Chap named Ollie Hollis. He were in charge of the hog-roast. I thought, all things considered, he was one guy we really ought to chat to.'

Pascoe scanned the list.

'Hollis? There's an Alan Hollis here, no Ollie.'

'That's because he weren't a guest,' explained Wield. 'Works for Lady Denham. Gate-man at the Hollis pig unit. That's Hollis's Ham, the Taste of Yorkshire, by the way. Howard Hollis was Lady Denham's first husband and she inherited the business.'

'This is really going to help sales,' said Pascoe. 'Hang on. Wasn't Howard Hollis known as Hog? And wasn't there something odd about his death?'

'He had a heart attack among his pigs. They'd chewed him up a bit afore someone found him. We looked at it, I recollect. Odd but not suspicious.'

'Jesus. I'll be sticking to Danish from now on. This Ollie . . . same family?'

'Aye. And Alan. Landlord at a pub owned by the victim. Seems the Hollises divided into them as cried foul when Hog left everything to his widow, and them as kept their counsel and their jobs. Hog used to stage an annual hog-roast for his workers and the locals. Quite a nifty set-up. As you'll see for yourself eventually, I dare say.'

Pascoe ignored the gentle mockery. His distaste for the nastier sort of crime scene was well known. He'd never got close to the philosophical detachment of Andy Dalziel, who'd remarked on viewing a triple slaying with a chainsaw that he'd seen worse deaths at the Glasgow Empire.

'So Lady Denham kept up the tradition of the annual hog-roast,' he said.

'No. In fact there hadn't been one for years, not since Hog died. This were a one-off. Ollie Hollis used to help in the old days, so he got called in to work the machinery.'

'So where was he when the pig was being removed and the body substituted?'

'Won't know for sure till Whitby brings him in,' said Wield. 'Sheltering somewhere, likely. It was a really violent storm and they got the worst of it here by all accounts. You'd not want to be anywhere near metal with that lightning about and the machine hut's got a tin roof.'

'How'd you know about this Hollis if he's not on the list?'

'There's this relative living with Lady Denham. Clara Brereton, sort of companion cum dogsbody, I reckon. She mentioned Ollie when she gave me the list. I got a preliminary statement from her, and I've set her to preparing a full account of the party, including the run-up to it. With her being in charge of organizing things, could be helpful. Also she were one of the first to see the body.'

'Must be a toughie, discovering something like that but still able to function, produce guest lists, write statements,' said Pascoe. 'Worth a close look?'

'Aye, she is that,' said Wield. 'And you'll find two other relations in the house. Sir Edward Denham and his sister, Esther. Nephew and niece by marriage.'

'They live here too?'

'No,' said Wield patiently. 'Their address is on the list if you look. Denham Park, a few miles along the coast. It was Sir Edward said we could set up our Incident Room here.'

'Didn't want us in the house then,' said Pascoe looking round discontentedly. 'Would have been a damn sight more comfortable than this dump. The horse downstairs looks better situated! So why didn't Lady Denham live at this Denham Park place?'

'Because Edward, being male, inherited the Denham title and estate on the death of his uncle, Sir Henry, the victim's second husband. Sandytown Hall, which is here, Lady Denham inherited from Hog Hollis, her first husband,' explained Wield.

'Hollis family home then?'

'Not really. Hog Hollis bought it when he made his money. Bought himself one of them local titles with it, Lord of the Sandytown Hundred. But Lady Denham's title, which she derived from her second marriage, is real enough.'

'Real? You surprise me, Wieldy. I thought it was well established that one way or another all titles have been bought these days. And this slum that Sir Edward so generously says we can use, I hope no one lives here?'

'Not now,' said Wield. 'Expect it were used by the head groom or some such when they had a lot of horses.'

'Are there any domestics?'

'Nobody living in, unless you count Miss Brereton. She seems to run things.'

'And being a relative probably does it for bed and board,' guessed Pascoe. 'So if Sandytown Hall is part of the victim's Hollis inheritance, and this cousin-companion is so much in charge of things, what makes the nephew feel entitled to order you around?'

And why did you let yourself be ordered around? hung on the air.

But at least it appeared that Pascoe's mind was now fully refocused on the job.

'I did ask Miss Brereton where would be best,' said Wield, 'but Sir Edward cut in afore she could reply. Like he wanted to establish proprietorial rights.'

'Meaning he thinks the house is coming to him,' mused Pascoe. 'Which information a guilty man would be likely to conceal, right?'

'Unless he's a dead clever guy, like you,' said the sergeant.

210

'Thank you kindly,' said Pascoe, though he wasn't sure if it had been kindly meant. 'But alas, I'm not clever enough to see how I can put off the evil moment any longer. I'd better head out to the scene and spoil my appetite. Doctor here?'

'Been and gone. Confirmed death and, like I said, guessed at strangulation, estimated between four and six. Said to ring him if you wanted anything more, but he had people coming to dinner.'

'Hope they're not having pork,' said Pascoe. 'And you've set the ball rolling interviewing the fugitive guests? Great. Who've we got on the team, by the way?'

'I was lucky. Bowler, Novello and Seymour were all available. Told 'em to start with the Parkers. Old Sandytown family, plus there was a close business association with the deceased, I gather. Thought it best to get to them afore they had too much time to sit around chewing over events and coming up with a collective memory.'

Pascoe did the one raised eyebrow trick he'd finally mastered after years of practice.

'A conspiracy, you mean?'

'No. Just human nature,' said Wield. 'Couple of guests from the Avalon Clinic. Head man and head nurse. Thought you might want to tackle them yourself.'

'Because the Super's up there, you mean?' interpreted Pascoe. 'Cap Marvell says he doesn't want visitors yet.'

'Mebbe not, but with a murder on his doorstep, he's likely to come visiting us if he doesn't get put in the picture soon.'

Pascoe shuddered.

'You're right. I'll get over there as soon as I've had a look and talked to the CSI.'

Pascoe, always a touch pedantic, had resisted the Americanization longer than most, but eventually even he had bowed to the power of television.

'One thing more,' said Wield. 'Sammy Ruddlesdin's here. Turned up shortly after I did.'

'Listening in on our wavelength again. Naughty old Sammy,' said Pascoe. 'What did you do with him?'

Ruddlesdin was Mid-Yorkshire's premier crime reporter. He and Pascoe had a good long-standing relationship, which was just as well. Some journalists would have made a lot of being at the scene an hour before the senior detective.

'Saw him off the premises. He's likely wandering around the town now, getting background. Said he'd be back.'

'Could be useful,' said Pascoe.

'Mebbe,' said Wield, sounding unconvinced. 'About Roote, Pete. You want I should take his statement?'

His meaning was clear. With their personal history, Pascoe should stay well clear till Roote had been properly processed.

'I'd be grateful.'

'I'll tell him you'll be round to talk to him some time, shall I?'

'What do you think? What I owe him's beyond payment,' said Pascoe. 'Not that I won't be bollocking him for dropping out of sight like that. Incidentally, that's one thing I'll be asking Fat Andy. Why the hell didn't he let me know Franny was here?'

'Mebbe he didn't know himself,' suggested Wield.

'You're joking! Are not two sparrows sold for a farthing? And if they are, unless the old sod's had a relapse, he'll know which of them's crapped on the washing! No, Andy knew. And he decided I didn't need to. He's got some explaining to do.'

He clattered away down the stairs. Through the window Wield watched as he made his way across the lawn.

To himself he murmured, 'Always thought when we got up before the Almighty, it was us who'd have to do the explaining.'

2

Some thirty minutes before Pascoe arrived in Sandytown, Detective Constable Shirley Novello had parked her Fiat Uno in front of Kyoto House.

Wield had told his trio of DCs to start with the Parkers, but he'd left it to them to sort out their assignments. There were three addresses for the family members and, by right of seniority, Dennis Seymour should have had first pick. But Seymour, old in courtesy as well as service, had said, 'Ladies first, unless you think that's sexist, Shirley.'

'Not from you, Den,' she said, smiling. 'After thirty, you married guys have forgotten all about sex, right?'

As she spoke she was studying the list and assessing the possibilities.

Doing the crappy routine stuff well and without complaint got you marked down as reliable, which was OK, but plucking a precious stone of evidence out of the crap was what got you marked up as bright, which was so very much better. Faced with a choice of witness interviews, the ambitious DC tried to work out where the glittering prize was most likely to lie.

Of the three addresses, only one was permanent and old experience suggested that this was the one to go for. In murder enquiries you started by looking close to home. Relatives were best, but wise old Wield had kept the cousin and niece and nephew to himself.

The other two Parkers were just visitors. Could be their reasons for visiting were worth looking at, but most probably they were just here for the sea air.

She said, 'I'll do Kyoto House.'

As she spoke she covertly watched Hat Bowler's reaction. He was her most direct rival in the contest to climb the CID slippery pole and she had a healthy respect for his ability. She caught a faint smile, instantly suppressed. It worried her for a second. Then she thought, If he'd got first choice I'd have done the faint smile thing too, just to worry him! So, reassured, she set out on the short drive to Kyoto, confident in her own judgment.

As she got out of her car, she glanced eastward. The view was magnificent if you liked mile after mile of water and acre after acre of sky. Novello found it merely boring. She'd never been able to raise much enthusiasm for nature unless it involved muscular young men with a penchant for wrestling. The house, on the other hand, was a bit of all right, its modern lines, big windows and open aspect appealing to her much more than the ivy-draped antiquity of Sandytown Hall.

As she approached the front door, it opened to reveal a girl of eight or nine who demanded, 'Who're you?'

'I'm a police officer,' retorted Novello. 'Who are you?'

If she'd thought to intimidate the child, she was disappointed.

'Have you come to interview us? I'm a witness. I saw everything!'

She stepped forward and would have dragged the door shut behind her, presumably to forestall interruption, but a voice called, 'Minnie, who is it?'

Novello grinned and said, 'Tough luck, kid,' then pushed the door fully open and called back, 'DC Novello, Mid-Yorkshire CID.'

A moment later a man appeared, thirtyish, slim, haggard, with dishevelled gingery hair.

'Mr Tom Parker?' asked Novello.

'Yes. Is it about what happened at the Hall? Of course it is. I'm sorry. This dreadful business has really knocked the wheels off me. Come in, come in.'

As Novello followed him into the house, she glanced back. The child had wandered out to the parked Uno and was eyeing it up with the kind of expression Novello recognized from multi-storey video footage. Had she locked it? Of course she had. Places she parked, both professionally and for pleasure, you did it automatically. So the kid was going to be disappointed, unless she had gone equipped, which in this day and age wouldn't be surprising.

In the house she was led into an airy lounge where a woman rose to meet her.

'Mary, this is Detective Constable . . . I'm sorry . . .?'

'Novello.'

'Yes. Novello. This is my wife.'

Mary Parker was as slim as her husband, with wispy blonde hair and a slightly scrunched-up anxious face, but she looked a lot less haggard.

'Would you like some tea?'

Novello would have preferred coffee but there was a teapot on the table so she said, 'Yes, please,' rather than have a delay. She'd made the quick decision it would be useful to interview this pair together. Some couples you wanted to keep as far removed from each other as possible, but the Parkers, she judged, could be mutually helpful.

This proved to be the case, and soon she'd got what seemed a pretty comprehensive account of their movements during the party. She took particular note of their recollection of times and the location and activities of other guests. With such a large number of witnesses, Wield would be doing a complex reconstruction job on the events at the Hall, ninety-nine per cent of it probably irrelevant to the enquiry, but Novello wanted to be sure that her contribution was detail perfect.

'So the last time you saw Lady Denham . . .?'

Tom Parker was vague.

'There were so many people to talk to, so much to talk about, I'm afraid I lose track . . .'

Novello could believe it. The wife was much more positive.

'Just before four o'clock. Most people were on or around the lawn where the food and drink were. I saw her move away. I assumed she was going to the hog-roast area.'

'Why?'

'There'd been some delay with the roasting and that wouldn't please her. She doesn't – didn't – like things not to go the way she planned.'

Not a big fan of the victim's, guessed Novello.

'Can you be sure that's where she was headed?'

'Only the general direction. You can't see the barbecue from the lawn, it's well removed from the house and there's a deal of shrubbery in the way. Also I wasn't watching her in particular.'

'No? What were you watching in particular, Mrs Parker?'

'The weather,' said Mary Parker promptly. 'I could tell there was a storm brewing.'

'I see. And you were worried it would spoil Lady Denham's party.'

'No. My two older children were down on the beach and I was thinking about them.'

'And that was definitely the last you saw of Lady Denham?'

'Yes. The storm broke about half an hour later. Charlotte said she'd go and make sure the children got back from the beach safely, so I headed into the house with my young ones.'

'Charlotte's the Miss Heywood who lives here? Is she a relative?'

'Oh no. Just a friend who's staying with us for a few days.'

Novello said, 'I'd quite like to speak to her too. Is she around?'

'She's up in her room resting,' said Mary. 'She actually saw poor Daphne's body. It really upset her. Would you like me to ask if she feels up to talking with you?'

'Why don't I do it myself? Then I can explain exactly what I want.'

She got to her feet as she spoke. Her thinking was that it would be very easy for the resting woman to tell Mary Parker, *Sorry, I don't feel up to snuff, tell her to go away!* There would be no appeal against that. *Never give a choice unless it's a test* was something she'd learned early when dealing with witnesses.

She tapped discreetly on the bedroom door, ready to follow up with a proper constabulary bang if necessary, but the door was opened almost instantly to reveal a young woman who stared at her with the

218

same unfriendly expression as the child at the front door, and echoed her words, 'Who're you?'

'Detective Constable Novello,' she said, flashing her ID. 'Sorry to trouble you. I can understand you'd want to lie down after such a shock, but it's important we talk to witnesses as close as possible to the event.'

'Yes, fine. And I haven't been lying down,' said Charlotte brusquely. She hesitated a moment then said, 'You'd better come in.'

Novello guessed she'd decided that if she went downstairs, she'd probably have her anxious hosts hovering. Maybe she had something to tell she didn't want them to hear.

In the room, Novello noted that neither of the twin beds was ruffled, which suggested she was telling the truth. On the dressing table stood an open laptop. The woman closed the lid and nodded Novello to the room's one chair while she sank on to the nearer bed.

'Right, Miss Heywood,' said Novello. 'It's Charlotte, isn't it?'

'Yes. It's Shirley, isn't it?'

'Right,' said Novello, thinking that this was a sharp one, picking her first name from the brief flash of a warrant card. Better stick with Miss Heywood for the time being. 'First things first. You're just staying here, right? Can I have your home address, just in case we need to get in touch after you've gone.'

Charley gave it.

Novello said, 'Not so far then.'

'Seems a long way today,' said Charley.

'That figures.'

The two women looked at each other. Novello saw a rather square-jawed not unattractive young woman with vigorous chestnut hair. She wore enough make-up to soften the jaw line and highlight the intelligent brown eyes. Good shoulder development suggesting weight training or maybe distance swimming; nice figure, would need to watch it when young activity slowed to middle-aged indulgence or she might balloon out.

Charley saw a stockily built woman with short uncombed black hair, wide mouth, watchful grey eyes, not a trace of make-up, wearing a loose off-white top, beige fatigues and black trainers.

Dyke? she wondered. Maybe I should have gone downstairs!

'The Parkers . . . are they friends?' said Novello.

'I suppose so. Why?'

'Just, not your age group. I wondered . . .'

'Yeah? The police are institutionally ageist as well as everything else, are they?'

Novello smiled. It changed her face completely for a moment.

'Student,' she said. 'Either still at it or just finished, right?'

'Why do you think that?'

'If you press the button and get a Twix, it's a chocolate-bar machine,' said Novello, smiling again.

This time Charley smiled back.

'OK, you got me.'

'Studying what?'

'Psychology.'

'Oh my. Need to watch you then.'

'The feeling's mutual.'

The atmosphere was growing more relaxed. Both of them noted it, and noted the other noting it.

'Look, sorry to drag you back to the barbecue, but I do need a statement and I gather you were one of the first on the scene. Don't start there, go back to when you arrived at the Hall, anything you can remember, people, events – doesn't matter how trivial – times.'

Charley rose from the bed and went to the window. The storm had cleared, the evening sky had a fresh-washed look, and though there was still enough wind to give the waves white caps, they were dancing towards the shore rather than roaring in like an invading army.

She said, 'The party started at two, I think. Funny time, neither lunch nor evening meal, but once you get to the back end of August it can start getting chilly after five and no one really likes that kind of English do when you're all standing around the barbecue pit, trying to keep warm . . .'

Her voice tailed off. Novello thought it was because the image of the dead woman's body in the metal roasting basket had returned to her, but when Charley turned to face her, it was irritation not pain that showed in her face.

'This is stupid,' she said. 'I'm really trying, but I can hardly remember a thing. It's crazy, I came back here afterwards – Mary wanted to get the kids away from there as quickly as possible; you can't blame her – and after we'd got them sorted, I headed straight up here, and I sat down at my laptop and emailed my sister, I just had to talk to someone, not talk, you understand, but get it all out to someone close. Cass, that's my sister, and me always told each other every-thing when we were kids, and we still do, even though she's a nurse in Africa. So I spilled it all out to Cass and it's like that's what really happened, I spilled it all out of myself and that's got rid of it and I don't have it in my head any more! Does that sound crazy?'

'You're the psychologist,' said Novello. 'But it doesn't matter anyway. If you've written it all down in an email, all we've got to do is read the email.'

The sharp brown eyes fixed her unblinkingly and the woman said, '*We?*' in a tone cold enough to make an early swallow wonder if this had been such a good idea.

'Sorry,' said Novello, raising her hands in mock surrender. 'Don't want to go prying into your private stuff. All I meant was you could read it over, right? Refresh your memory about what you saw.'

'I suppose so.'

Novello stood up to let Charley sit at the dressing table. She raised the laptop screen and brought up the list of *sent email*. Novello, without making it obvious, clocked that most of the recent ones were addressed to *cassie@natterjack*. Charlotte clicked on the latest of these, regarded it for a moment, then stood up.

'I'm being silly,' she said. 'That poor woman's dead and I'm worried about protecting my privacy. Here, you read it yourself. Best you do anyway, you're more likely to see the gaps you'd like filled.'

'Are you sure?' said Novello, but she was already slipping back on to the chair as she asked the question.

She read quickly, said, 'Wow.'

'What?'

'Those two banging in the cave. They would be . . .?'

'Teddy Denham, that's Sir Edward, Lady D's nephew. And Clara Brereton, her cousin, who lives at the Hall. You don't have to start digging around there, do you?'

She sounded alarmed.

'Not if it's not relevant,' Novello assured her,

thinking, *Two close relations in close relations? Wait till we see the will!*

Something else had caught her attention.

'This guy in the wheelchair. Franny Roote. He a local or what?'

'No, definitely not, though he seems to have been living here a little while. I think he may have had some treatment at the Avalon, that's the clinic just outside the town.'

Franny Roote. Novello remembered a Franny Roote – Pascoe's Franny Roote, as she thought of him. Could this be the same guy? And did the DCI know he was here in Sandytown? Brownie points perhaps for bringing the news! Except, of course, the name would be on the guest list in Wield's possession and certainly would not have escaped those sharp eyes. Anyway, could be Pascoe would regard Roote's presence as bad news, and you didn't win prizes for bringing that.

She asked a lot more questions and made notes. In the process she got the story of how Heywood came to be in Sandytown, and also became aware that the same cast of mind that had made the woman opt for psychology rendered her a sharp and slightly nosey observer of human behaviour. Not only an observer, maybe a recorder too?

She said, 'Charley . . . now we're on email terms, OK if I call you Charley?'

'Do I get to call you Shirl?'

'Only if you can pronounce it with a split lip.'

They shared a laugh, then Novello went on, 'I couldn't help noticing that there were quite a lot of emails to your sister. I'd guess you've been filling her in with your impressions of this place over the past few days, right?'

'That's right.'

'Any chance of getting to see those earlier messages? My impression is not a lot gets past you, and there might be something there that could help. We can ask questions till the cows come home without getting anywhere near an on-the-spot insider's view.'

Charley shook her head vigorously.

'There's private stuff in there. Not just my privacy, it's my sister's too.'

'I understand that,' said Novello. 'Maybe you could print your messages out, do a bit of editing with a black marker if you like. I wouldn't ask, only, from what I've seen, you're good at taking things in and you've got a real gift for expressing it.'

'I'm nebby and gabby, you mean,' said Charley.

'That's it exactly,' said Novello. 'Like me. Only I didn't have the Latin, so that's why I became a cop instead of a psychologist.'

She could see she was nearly there and was wise enough not to push.

Charley said hesitantly, 'And you'd be the only one to read them?'

Novello smiled reassuringly and said, 'You can rely on me. Of course if I spotted anything I thought might be useful, I'd need to pass it on to my boss. I mean, there'd be no point else, would there? Probably won't arise, but in a case as serious as this, we've got to cover every eventuality.'

If the Church ever admits females to the priesthood, I reckon I'll be first in line for the Jesuits, she told herself.

'OK,' said the woman with sudden decision. 'Tom's got a printer in his study . . . I'm sure he won't mind me using it . . .'

'Great! While you're running them off, I'll get my notes organized. I've got this sergeant who likes every-thing squared off with hospital corners, or he sends you to bed without any supper.'

Which was a slander on Edgar Wield, of course, but she'd seen him in the gym pressing weights that made her eyes water just looking at them, so his shoulders were broad enough to bear it.

3

Hat Bowler's smile had not been the subtle attempt at misdirection that Novello suspected.

He'd been the first of the three DCs to arrive at Sandytown Hall. Wield, looking as if he'd been there for hours, was already setting up the Incident Room. He filled the new arrival in with his customary pellucid economy then sent him up to the main house with instructions to pick up a guest list which Miss Brereton, the victim's cousin and companion, was printing out.

'And go easy with her, lad,' said the sergeant. 'She was first on the scene. Mr Pascoe will want to talk to her when he gets here. I've asked her to start working on a full account of the party, the run-up to it and all. See how she's getting on with that and tell her I'm particularly interested in the order the guests arrived, precise times and all.'

'You on to something, Sarge?' asked Bowler eagerly.

'Don't be daft. I've only been here two minutes. I just want to keep the lass busy. Once she stops being busy, likely she'll fall apart and then she'll be no use to any bugger.'

Is it just me, wondered the young DC as he walked away, or have both Wield and the DCI taken on a harder edge since the Super's been away?

To his relief, Miss Brereton still seemed a long way

from falling apart, and what he took for signs of grief – dark shadows beneath her eyes, hair trailing unchecked over her pale face – merely accentuated her good looks. Mindful of Wield's warning and fearful that gentleness might dissolve whatever barriers she'd put up, he passed on the sergeant's message rather brusquely, received the list, glanced down at it, saw that it was headed by a clutch of Parkers, and said, 'Not in alphabetical order then?'

'No. Mr Wield said he'd like it in the order that I put it in when I was working out the list with my . . . with Lady . . .'

Her voice choked and he said quickly, 'So, order of priority then? These Parkers must be important.'

His diversionary tactic worked. Clearly not much got by her, and by the time he returned to Wield he had a pretty good grasp of the relationship between each of the Parkers and the dead woman. Naturally he passed on the gist to Wield, but he saw no reason to add to the sergeant's even gistier digest to Seymour when he instructed the senior DC to organize the witness interviews. Hat could see why Novello went for the local Parkers, but he wasn't at all displeased to be left with the visitors. Nor did he linger long over his choice. Clara Brereton had indicated that Sidney at the hotel was a kind of financial adviser to Lady Denham. She'd only met the sister in Seaview Terrace once, and all she could say about her, without actually saying it, was that she was rather odd.

So no problem for a bright young detective. Oddity could sometimes be sufficient motive for murder, but it was money that made the world go round.

As Hat drove towards the Beresford Manor Hotel, his mind was completely focused on the task ahead.

Then as he turned into the car park, that focus was blurred and diffused by a vision of heart-stopping beauty.

Before him, like a bird of paradise in a rookery, stood a bright red Maserati coupé, worth sixty K of anyone's money, bugger the emissions.

It felt a sacrilege to park his blue Suzuki Swift alongside it.

There was a time, not too long ago, when Bowler had driven a much-loved MG of almost the same colour as the Maz. But he'd wrecked it, and it had never felt the same after the repairs. Or perhaps it was him that never felt the same. Then Wield had suggested someone in his line of work might be well advised to drive a less conspicuous car, which struck him as a bit odd, coming from a guy who roared around town on an old Triumph Thunderbird, but he knew better than to argue. The Swift had been a compromise, great little car to drive, reasonable performance, and it didn't draw too much attention to itself.

But now . . .

He got out and walked slowly round the beautiful red creature, taking in its elegant lines, its promissory power, before coming to a halt directly in front of it.

So rapt was he that he started when a voice said, 'You like the look of her, or are you checking my tax disc?'

Turning, he looked at the speaker. In his thirties, wearing the kind of sweat shirt and slacks that are too expensive to need a visible designer label, he had the easy assurance of a man born to drive a Maserati rather than a wannabe trying to impress.

For a moment the reference to the tax disc made Hat think he'd been clocked, but the smile on the

228

guy's face didn't look like the kind of smile people gave cops.

'She's great,' he said. 'What's she like to drive?'

'A pussycat. Electronic damping control, paddle shift, all the power you could ask for. I've had her up to one fifty with plenty in reserve. Like to look inside?'

It was tempting, but there was work to do. And besides he'd already heard the guy admit one motoring offence and had no desire to lure him into more.

He said, 'Love to, but I don't have the time just now. Thanks.'

He set off towards the hotel. The man fell into step beside him and said, 'You staying here? If you've got time later and I'm around, just give me a wave. Sidney Parker, by the way.'

He held out his hand.

Hat thought, oh shit.

His recrimination was aimed wholly at himself for making assumptions. He'd been looking for a provincial accountant, not the next James Bond.

He didn't take the hand but instead reached into his pocket for his ID.

He said, 'Mr Parker, it's you I've come to see. Detective Constable Bowler, Mid-Yorkshire CID. I'm sorry. I didn't realize it was you back there.'

The smile didn't flicker for a millisec nor did the hand drop, so Hat shook it.

'No need to apologize,' said Parker. 'I didn't spot you for a policeman. That must be useful in your line of work.'

Then his expression turned grave and he went on, 'This is about that dreadful business at the Hall, right?'

'That's right, sir. Just a few questions.'

'Of course. Let's go inside. My room, if that's all right, then we won't be interrupted.'

A couple of minutes later they were sitting in Parker's room, which turned out to be a luxurious suite about twice the size of Hat's flat.

'So what's your line of business, Mr Parker?' said Hat, looking round.

'You mean, what do I have to do to drive a car like that and stay in rooms like this?' said Parker, smiling once more.

'Just for the record, sir,' said Hat, keeping it formal.

'I work for Harpagon's in the City. Here's my business card, and my private card. Just for the record.'

'Harpagon's,' said Hat, looking at the card, which gave no information other than the name and address. 'Doesn't say here what they do.'

'Sorry. It's not anticipated we'll be handing out cards to anyone who doesn't know. We're a finance house. I suppose the easiest way to think of us is as a private bank.'

'Yes. Are you here in Sandytown professionally, or is it a social visit?'

'Bit of both, I suppose. It's home territory for me – the Parkers are old-established Sandytonians – so naturally I like to get back here whenever I can to visit my brother, Tom, and his family at Kyoto House. There is, however, a professional element, insomuch as I act as a financial consultant to Tom. Also to Lady Denham. And to them jointly in their role as co-founders of the Sandytown Development Consortium. But I'm sure a bright young detective like yourself will know all this already.'

This was said with a such pleasant smile that Hat had to work hard to resist returning it.

'Is this consulting stuff a private arrangement, sir, or are you acting as an executive of Harpagon's?' he asked stiffly.

'It's more of a *personal* arrangement than a private one. It's not the kind of area that Harpagon's gets involved in – rather small beer for them – but naturally I keep them informed of all my activities and they have no objection to my using my professional sources and contacts.'

Hat wasn't sure if this was an answer or not.

'So this was why you were invited to the barbecue?'

'Part of the reason, I suppose. Though even without the professional link, the fact that I'm Tom's brother and our family has long connections with this area would probably have merited an invitation – if I were in the area, that is. I admire your thoroughness, Mr Bowler, but can't quite see how this relates to your enquiries into this ghastly affair.'

Hat looked at the elegant figure relaxing in a deep sofa, a long glass filled with some sparkling liquid in his hand. He himself was perched on the edge of an armchair which felt as if it could be very comfortable indeed if he sank back into it. He'd also refused the offer of a drink. In his place, he guessed Dalziel would have downed at least two by now and probably be lying at full stretch on the sofa. Pascoe and Wield he wasn't so sure of.

Didn't matter. He'd learned the hard way that DCs needed to tread carefully if they weren't to sink without a trace. Time enough for eccentricity when he'd got the rank to support it.

He said, 'Just clearing the ground, sir. Now, I'd like you to take me through the events at the barbecue so far as you remember them.'

Twenty minutes later he was done. Sidney Parker's account of the party as he saw it was clear and succinct. Nothing in it, so far as Hat could see, was of any positive use to the investigation. His last sighting of Lady Denham had been as early as two thirty.

'After that our paths just didn't cross,' he said. 'I daresay from time to time I heard her booming away in the background – she has . . . she had a very positive way of speaking – but I couldn't put my hand on my heart and swear to it. I suggest you look to Dr Feldenhammer from the Avalon for a closer account of her movements.'

'Why Dr Feldenhammer in particular?' asked Hat.

Another smile but this one fleeting, private, and perhaps a touch malicious?

'She had, I suspect, formed an attachment for him,' said Parker, watching the young man keenly.

'An attachment? You mean like a . . .' Hat dug for a word and Parker laughed.

'I fear you're being a tad ageist, Constable Bowler. Lady D might have been, in your eyes, an oldie, but she was far from being a mouldie. A lady of strong appetite. But I speak only from hearsay, not experience. You must talk to others better placed and judge for yourself.'

So to family and finance we can add sex! thought Hat. Or maybe Parker had just tossed sex in as a diversion.

He said, 'As her financial consultant, do you have any idea how much she was worth, sir? I mean, just in general terms. Rich? Very rich?'

'That depends on the circles in which you move,' said Parker. 'In the City, I think she'd be rated as very well off. In Sandytown terms, stinking rich.'

'She ever indicate who might get it when she died?' prompted Hat.

'Afraid not, and if she had, I'd have taken it with a pinch of salt. She was not a woman who enjoyed spending money, so she had to concentrate on one of its other pleasures.'

'Which are?'

'Two, principally. The first is giving it away to deserving causes. This, I assure you, was not high among Daphne's priorities. Rumour has it that on Remembrance Sunday, the poppy she sported had been purchased by her father in 1920.'

'And the second?'

'Making people close to you jump through hoops in the hope of inheriting it. Of course, part of this sport is never being too specific about your intentions. I mean, if people know they are definitely not in your will, why should they continue jumping?'

'So you've no idea who'll benefit.'

'Well, it is generally known, because it was part of her first husband Howard aka Hog Hollis's will, that her brother-in-law from that marriage, Harold aka Hen Hollis, will acquire Millstone, the Hollis family farm.'

'Harold Hollis, you say?' said Hat looking at his list. 'Why did he get Hen?'

'He concentrated on raising poultry while his brother favoured pigs. Hence Hen and Hog.'

'I've got an Alan Hollis on my list, but no Harold.'

'Alan runs the Hope and Anchor in the town. Same family, but he had the wit to remain on good terms with Daphne. Unlike Hen. He and Lady D were definitely not on visiting terms.'

'So they didn't get on. And he'll definitely benefit from her death . . .'

He hadn't meant to speak the words out loud, and certainly not so eagerly, but out they came, causing Parker to smile broadly.

'The impetuousness of youth,' he said. 'It would be nice if the solution turned out as simple as that, wouldn't it, Mr Bowler? I hope for your sake it might.'

Hat frowned and tried to retrieve the situation by saying sternly, 'One last question, Mr Parker. Why did you leave the Hall when you did?'

'I had already decided it was time to leave before the . . . *discovery*. I had just asked if anyone knew where I might find Lady Denham to offer thanks when the uproar broke out, and my question was answered. Of course I joined in the general expression of shock and horror, but it soon became apparent that there was nothing practical for me to do. Others were leaving. I saw no reason not to join them. In fact, to tell the truth, I felt that the further I put Sandytown Hall behind me, the better.'

'Not all that far, sir,' observed Hat. 'About a mile and a half.'

'You are being literalist,' said Parker, frowning. 'I just wanted to be away from that atmosphere. Besides, I could hardly go further, not when I knew that eventually someone like yourself would want to interview me.'

'Very responsible of you,' said Hat.

It came out slightly mocking.

Parker said, 'Yes, wasn't it? Tell me, Mr Bowler, did you really not know who I was out in the car park?'

'No. How could I?'

'So your interest in the Maz was genuine?'

'Oh yes. Very much so.'

'Then my offer to look inside, or under the bonnet,

still stands. In fact, if you care to take a ride before you go . . .? I should tell you, by the way, that when I hit the one fifty mark, I was on the circuit at Brand's Hatch. I have a friend who pulled a string.'

I bet you did, thought Hat. Lots of friends, lots of strings.

'No can do, sir,' he said. 'Things to do. Sorry.'

'Of course. It was silly of me. You'll be worked off your feet. But if you do have a respite over the next couple of days, don't hesitate to get in touch.'

'No, sir. We never hesitate to get in touch,' said Hat.

Then, thinking that was a bit sharp, he grinned and said, 'But it would be nice, if I had the time.'

'Good,' said Parker, rising. 'Mr Bowler, it's been nice to meet you.'

He offered his hand again.

This time Hat took it without hesitation.

On his way out he stopped at the reception desk. The young woman there had clearly heard all about the murder and her eyes shone with excitement when he showed her his ID.

Hat leaned over the desk and said, 'You local, are you?'

'Yes. Why?'

"Cos if you were one of these Czechs or Poles you get working in hotels, you'd probably not be able to help me. You sure you're local? I mean, you look a bit exotic to me, those high cheekbones and classy figure . . .'

The girl laughed and said, 'Nice of you to notice, but my family have lived round here for hundreds of years, or so my gran says.'

'Then you're the girl for me. Chap by the name of Hen Hollis, I was wondering where he lived?'

4

Dennis Seymour drove slowly along Seaview Terrace.

Nice, he thought. Narrow Edwardian houses, one big bay window apiece, lovely outlook over the sea, just a short step across the road (a safe cul de sac) and over the shallow wall to the beach – would suit Bernadette and the twins very nicely. Wonder how much they charge in the season? Might not be professional to bring it into a witness interview, but no harm in checking later.

He'd watched the byplay between his younger colleagues with quiet amusement. There'd been a time when he too had strutted and pecked in the cockpit of ambition, but not any more. He was long resigned to the knowledge that what he had was all he was going to get. But how could he be unhappy about that when it included lovely twin daughters and a gorgeous wife whose fiery Irish temperament dovetailed perfectly with his own laid-back easy-over nature? Financially there was no problem either. Bernadette's job as manageress of the restaurant in the city's largest department store meant the family had more than enough coming in to satisfy their needs.

So let Novello and Bowler go scurrying off in search of the subtle clue that was going to unravel the case.

Seymour was more than content to be down here on the seafront to interview the oddball sister.

The door was opened by a small, neatly packaged woman who studied his ID with a keen eye, identified herself as Diana Parker, and said, 'Please, step inside. This is a dreadful business, quite dreadful. It threw everyone into disarray. I could see that chaos was likely to ensue without a controlling hand at the rudder, and I would have stayed at the Hall and offered my services, but my constitution is a delicate machine, easily thrown off balance by any shock or violent turn of events, with deep and long-lasting physical consequences. I needed to be back here in reach of my medicaments. I might not have made it, but happily my friend, Mrs Griffiths, was by my side, giving me support. Here she is now. Sandy, this is Detective Constable Seymour come to question me as a witness to the terrible events at Sandytown Hall.'

This outburst, delivered at a pace which could have got her a job as an announcer on Five Live, had filled the space between the doorstep and a comfortable parlour in which a well-built woman with a strong face and short, curly black hair was standing by an open sash window, smoking a cigarette. She took a last drag, flicked the butt through the opening and turned to greet Seymour with a brusque nod.

Diana Parker went to the window and pulled it down with great force.

'Draughts kill,' she said accusingly.

Resisting the temptation to quip, *But not in the case of Lady Denham*, Seymour said, 'All right if I sit? Thank you. Now what I'm particularly interested in is any conversation with or sightings of the deceased, Lady

Denham, either of you may have had during the course of the party.'

And Diana was off.

Seymour quickly recognized that close questioning wasn't an option. All a man could do was sit with his pencil at the ready and try to bag any potentially significant fact as it flew by.

The one he underlined in his notebook was Diana's assertion that in the middle of the afternoon she had seen Lady Denham having an argument with one of the guests.

'His name is Godley – he is a healer – my brother introduced us earlier – dear Tom suggested that Mr Godley might be able to alleviate some of my chronic symptoms – I said firmly I doubted it – to be honest, experience has taught me that I have to trust to my own knowledge of my own wretched constitution for any relief – but I drift from my story – this Godley and Lady Denham had words – not polite words either, from the look of her after they parted and she passed close to me – she had a high flush – I have always assessed her temperament as choleric and this with her age makes her peculiarly susceptible to the perils of high blood pressure. Concerned, I took it on myself to offer help – not from myself, you understand – I would not be so presumptuous – though with my long experience of illness I think in an emergency I might prove very useful – no, what I did was offer to summon Nurse Sheldon, who was present at the party. I fear Lady Denham did not take my offer in the spirit in which it was given. She said, "I am perfectly well, Miss Parker – and as for summoning that lump, I'd as lief see an undertaker!"'

When the deluge finally abated, Seymour did not

care to risk provoking a renewal with questions but said, 'That's fine, Miss Parker. Now, Mrs Griffiths, I wonder if you have anything you'd like to add?'

The woman regarded him thoughtfully for a moment then said, 'I'm sorry, no. I'm just a visitor here. Miss Parker . . . Diana . . . was kind enough to take me along to the party. I saw Lady Denham when we arrived, but thereafter I can't say I noticed her.'

'You didn't see this encounter she had with Mr Godley then?'

'Sorry.'

'Anything you did see that struck you as unusual?'

'As a stranger, I'm hardly able to say what was usual, am I?'

Seymour was not the most incisive of interrogators, but he knew when he was getting nowhere. He could also see that the other woman was trembling on the brink of another verbal avalanche.

He closed his notebook decisively, stood up, and said, 'In that case, thank you for your co-operation, ladies. If anything further does occur to you, don't hesitate to get in touch.'

Diana followed him to the door.

'One more thing, Constable Seymour,' she said.

He halted and waited. Was this going to be the vital clue that enabled him to solve the case single-handedly and win battlefield promotion to the rank of detective sergeant?

She said, 'It is my experience that red-headed people are particularly susceptible to the evil effects of ultra-violet rays. I cannot help noticing that you are already showing signs of too much exposure to this strong sun. I have found aloe vera gel efficacious in allevi-ating the effects, but with a coarse skin like yours, you might find the simpler and less expensive remedies such as bathing the affected area in cold tea, or applying a vinegar compress – white vinegar, that is – would serve.'

'Well, thank you very much, Miss Parker,' he said. 'I'll make a note of that.'

As he got into his car he noticed that the sash window was open again and Sandy Griffiths was standing there, watching him, another cigarette in her hand.

He smiled and drove away.

5

Pascoe stood and looked down at the mortal remains of Daphne Denham.

The corpse lay on the ground where it had been placed after removal from the roasting cage. In fact, because it was fully clothed and the heat had not been strong enough to fire the clothing, the charring was limited, but with Pascoe a little visual horror went a long way. He'd tried everything from vacuous jocularity to Vedic mantras, but such sights still affected him deeply and later almost invariably replayed themselves on that inward eye which can be the bane of solitude.

It was with relief that, duty done, he authorized removal of the remains and turned his attention to more practical matters.

The Scenes of Crime Officer was an old acquaintance, Frodo Leach, an energetic young man, blissfully happy in his work, whose detractors accused him of being on permanent audition for *CSI Mid-York*.

'You've got yourself a real beauty here, Peter,' he declared almost enviously. 'Nerves of steel, whoever did this.'

'Why so?'

'Think of the time involved. First he kills the victim, no indication where yet, so it could mean he had a long carry. Once here, he has to winch the basket back from the charcoal pit, remove the pig, replace it with the body, and push the whole damn thing back into place.'

'Could one man manage all that?'

'If he were well muscled. Probably not one woman, though.'

'But wouldn't have taken so long with two or more perps, right?'

'No, it wouldn't. Many hands make light work, but many feet make much mud, and there's been so many feet tramping around this damp ground, it's impossible to draw any conclusions about that.'

'Fingerprints?'

'Not much hope. Anyway, he probably wore insulated gloves: we found a couple of pairs in the hut. Standard equipment, I should think. That cage must get pretty damn hot.'

'But if he didn't wear gloves, his hands could be blistered?' said Pascoe hopefully.

'Oh yes, but I shouldn't snap the cuffs on anyone with blisters,' said Leach cheerfully. 'I daresay you'll find quite a few who helped get the old girl out got burned for their pains as well as leaving traces of themselves all over the body. One thing – you probably noticed – extensive red stain down the front of her blouse. I say red – brown now, after exposure to the heat. Thought blood at first, but no such luck. Wine, I think.'

'So she spilled her drink.'

'Maybe. But first thing a woman does when she spills red wine is head for the nearest cloakroom to try and sponge it off.'

'So she spilled it not long before she got attacked. Or maybe the attack caused her to spill it.'

'In that case, where's the wine glass? No sign round here. Could have been attacked somewhere else, of course. In which case, find the glass and you'll find the attack site. But this is just speculation. Watch this space after we get her back to the lab.'

The trouble with Leach's enthusiasm was that it sometimes roused hopes of a banquet when all it actually gave you was a snack.

'So what do you have to show or tell me that's not just speculation?' asked Pascoe.

'Well, there's the shed where the winch is.'

He urged Pascoe towards the shed like an estate agent eager to display the attractions of the property he was trying to sell. Through the open door Pascoe could see a couple of white-clothed figures making a painstaking examination.

'The perp would have had to go in here to work the winch,' said Leach. 'Not much reason for anyone else being in there, except the chap in charge of the pig-roast. Can you dig him out for us so we can take samples for exclusion?'

'Ahead of you there. We've sent someone to bring him in,' said Pascoe, who saw no reason to let the SOCO divas think they had exclusive rights on the high notes.

'Great! Now this is what we've found so far.'

He pointed to a wire tray by the door containing three or four evidence bags.

'Champagne cork. Half a smoked salmon canapé. Bit of chocolate éclair. Some scraps of silver foil, probably from the bubbly bottle. And a couple of cigarette stubs. Prints possibly, DNA certainly.'

Proving that Ollie Hollis hadn't missed out on the refreshments, thought Pascoe. Hardly a breakthrough.

But only a fool or a very grumpy old man would resist Leach's enthusiasm.

They spoke a little longer, then Pascoe headed back to the Incident Room.

As he emerged from the shrubbery, the smell of tobacco smoke caught his nostrils.

He halted and said, 'OK, Sammy. You can stop lurking.'

A long thin figure with a face as unageable as a tortoise slid through the foliage, the cigarette between his lips glowing as he drew in the smoke.

'How do, Pete,' he said.

'You shouldn't be here, you know that, Sammy,' said Pascoe. 'How the hell did you get in?'

It was a redundant question. As Wield had pointed out, the Hall's extensive grounds were bounded along the road with a wall in great need of repair, while its countryside boundary was at best a thick hedge, at worst a dilapidated fence. The gate at the entrance to the drive was hanging off its hinges. The stable apart, Lady Denham clearly hadn't believed in wasting her money on estate upkeep.

Ruddlesdin shrugged and said, 'Got yourself a problem here when the nationals show. Place is easier to get into than Parliament, and any idiot can get in there.'

'So why aren't they here yet?'

'I expect 'cos you ordered a clampdown till you got here yourself and saw what was what.'

This was pretty well the truth, though the clamp-down had been initiated by Chief Constable Dan Trimble, whose wife sat on a couple of committees with Lady Denham. Trimble had rung Pascoe and urged him to get a lid on this one as quickly as he could.

Pascoe had assured him that he would do all in his power to get an early result, not caring to reveal that at the moment of talking he was still some twenty miles from the scene, waiting for a garage truck to arrive with a new tyre.

'And you've been sitting on the news too, Sammy. Kind of you,' he said.

'Got my story all ready to go,' said Ruddlesdin. 'Just wanted to be sure I got your input, Pete. This could be big for you.'

'In what way?'

'Well, you're not peeping out from under the cheeks of yon fat bugger's arse, for one thing. This is your chance to shine.'

While Pascoe and the journalist had struck up a mutually profitable relationship from the start, based on a respect for each other's professionalism that had slowly matured into a cautious friendship, Dalziel believed the only thing the gentlemen of the press understood was fear. Hard to impose this nationally, but at a local level, those who trod on his large toes could be sure that sooner or later they'd feel them applied to their behinds with great force.

'Nice of you to say so, Sammy. You got anything which can give my prospective shine a bit of a polish?'

'Got my headline ready: *Super-sleuth Pascoe solves baffling murder mystery in record time.*'

'Not very punchy, is it? Apart from being even further from the truth than most of your headlines.'

'Now just 'cos you're after the fat bugger's job don't mean you've got to sound like him,' reproved Ruddlesdin. 'Any road, word locally is you've just got to spin a coin between the two most likely suspects. Smart money's on the heir apparent, Sir Edward

Denham, but there's a lot reckon her brother-in-law by her first marriage, Hen Hollis, is worth a look, particularly if what they're saying about the way she died is true. Is it, Pete?'

'Depends what they're saying.'

'Roasted alive on her own barbecue.'

'Thought that might be it. No, it's not true. Yes, that's where she was found, but she was dead before that.'

'How?'

'Strangled, probably, but that's to be confirmed,' said Pascoe. You had to give to get, and in any case the sooner they stopped rumour from making what was bad enough sound grotesque, the better. 'Why should roasting her appeal to this chap Hen Hollis?'

'Hated her guts, evidently. Always ready in his cups to fantasize about her dying. And seems it were him as built the hog-roast equipment for his brother. Also, here's the clincher: by his brother's will, when she died the family farm would revert to Hen.'

'The family farm? You mean Sandytown Hall?' said Pascoe, surprised.

'No! Does this look like a sodding farm? Place called Millstone. Her Ladyship let it go to rack and ruin, by all accounts, but like the song says, there's no place like home.'

They were now approaching the stable block. Wield must have been watching, for now he emerged and came to meet them.

'Sammy, I told you not to hang about,' he said.

'And I heard you. That's why I've been wandering around town picking up some nice tit-bits for your boss,' retorted the reporter.

'For which I'm duly grateful,' said Pascoe. 'Now perhaps it's time to get back to your wanderings . . .'

'Aye, I'll go and polish up that headline. Remember, Pete, with the press behind you, the sky's the limit!'

'Tit-bits?' said Wield as they watched the journalist move off.

Pascoe passed on what Ruddlesdin had said and also what he'd learned from the CSI. In return the sergeant handed him a fairly bulky plastic file.

'Just to keep you up to date with everything we've got so far,' said the sergeant.

'Right, fine,' said Pascoe. 'This Ollie Hollis guy, the CSIs would like to see him ASAP for prints and DNA. I'm quite keen to talk to him too. Any word?'

'Jug Whitby just called in. Hollis lives by himself at Lowbridge, a hamlet a couple of miles along the coast. He's not there, neighbours haven't seen him since this morning. Whitby's tried the local. No sign So now he's casting around the other pubs in the area before heading back to Sandytown. This business must have shook Hollis up a bit, so not surprising if he's gone in search of a drink. And company, maybe.'

'Maybe,' said Pascoe. 'Let's get someone sitting on Hollis's house while Whitby's pub-crawling, OK?'

'It's taken care of. You'll find a note in the file.'

'Anything else?'

'I got one of the lads to feed everyone on the guest list into the computer. It's all in the file.'

'Just give me a digest, Wieldy.'

'The usual stuff came up, mainly road traffic offences. And of course Roote, but we knew about him already. Only other person with a record was the victim.'

'Lady Denham?' said Pascoe. 'Make my day, tell me she's got connections with the Russian Mafia!'

'Not unless the Countryside Alliance is run from

Moscow. Thirty years back, assault on a hunt protester, bound over to keep the peace.'

'And that's it? Great work, Wieldy,' said Pascoe, old acquaintance permitting him to be ungracious to Wield in a way he stopped short of with Leach. 'I think I'll pop across to the Hall to see this companion. You said you got a statement from her?'

'In the file,' said Wield with the relentless certainty of Mephistopheles talking to Faustus.

'What about niece and nephew? Let me guess, in the file too? They still around?'

'I'd bet on it. Scared someone's going to take off with the spoons as soon as their backs are turned,' said Wield. 'You'll be going up the Avalon to see the head quack and his nurse then, will you, Pete?'

'I haven't forgotten. And yes, before you ask, I'll call in and say hello to Andy too. Sammy Ruddlesdin doesn't seem to know he's in the vicinity, thank heaven. Roote neither. I dread to think what he'll make of it when he finds out.'

What can he make of it? And who gives a toss? thought Wield.

He said, 'Talking of Roote, thought I'd head off now and get him out of the way. Oh, and the Chief rang.'

'Checking up on me, is he?' said Pascoe moodily.

'No. Just wanted a progress report. I gather Lady Denham was well connected. I told him you were working too hard to talk just now, but everything was under control and you'd ring back later.'

'To tell him super-sleuth has solved the case in record time. I wish,' said Pascoe. 'See you later, Wieldy.'

The sergeant watched him go with some concern. This case is making him nervous and irritable, he thought. Can't blame him with Roote rising from the grave, the Chief Constable getting anxious, and the Fat Man lurking in the woodshed!

He went to his motorbike and punched the address he had for Roote into his new sat-nav. Specially designed for motorbikes, it was a present from his partner, Edwin. He'd tried it locally and though the upper-class female voice giving the directions was a bit of a pain, it had seemed pretty effective. Getting close to Franny Roote via the notoriously deceptive back roads of Yorkshire would be its first serious test.

For Pascoe too, he suspected.

6

There was a uniformed constable standing guard at the front door of Sandytown Hall. The grounds might be undefendable, but Wield was making sure nobody got into the building without authority.

Pascoe didn't recognize the young PC, but a smart salute confirmed his own recognition. He gave a friendly smile in return and went up the shallow flight of steps to the entrance porch.

The front door was ajar but still he rang the bell. No need to start walking over people till it was necessary.

A tall, slender, palely beautiful young woman in her early twenties appeared. Pascoe said, 'Hello. Miss Denham, is it?'

'No,' said the woman, slightly irritated. 'I'm Clara Brereton. Who're you?'

Pascoe introduced himself, concealing (he hoped) his surprise. Unlike Hat Bowler, who was young enough to have enjoyed the kind of modern English education that didn't clutter the mind with stuff like history and literature, Pascoe had allowed the name Clara and the term companion to create a picture of a desiccated spinster who got her kicks out of needlework. Wield could have put him right, he thought. It was probably in the bloody file!

He followed Clara Brereton through a sub-baronial entrance hall down a wainscoted corridor into a small room furnished with an old sofa, a filing cabinet and a computer station. She sat on the operator's swivel chair and he took the sofa, which meant he was looking up at her.

Her pallor, he judged, was as much her natural skin tone – a kind of pearly glow – as the result of shock. Whatever, it certainly became her. In fact, he concluded, taking in the dishevelled hair and the red-ringed eyes, she was one of those fortunate people whom grief suited.

Or unfortunate, depending how you looked at it.

'I'd like to ask you a few questions, if you feel up to it,' he said.

'Doing things stops me from just remembering,' she said. 'I've just been writing a full account of everything I can recall about Aunt Daphne's . . . party.'

Couldn't bring herself to say *hog-roast*, thought Pascoe, noticing that her eyes had filled with tears at the mention of the dead woman, making them shine even brighter.

'So Lady Denham was your aunt?' he said. Wield had said cousin. A slip?

'No, actually,' said Clara. 'I think my grandfather was her first cousin, so that makes me . . . well, aunt seemed a lot simpler.'

She smiled faintly as she spoke, sunshine through broken cloud, an April sky.

Pascoe found himself wanting to drive away even more cloud.

Whoops! he thought. Remember the words of the master – first bugger on the scene of a crime is chief suspect, till you find someone better.

He said, 'I'll read your account later, of course, but I know how hard it is to do those things. Sometimes talking about events with someone brings back details you might forget in a written account. I expect with an event like this, you were into it more or less from the moment you got up?'

'Oh yes. There's a lot to do. Not that I mean I was doing much of it personally, but it was down to me to make sure that everyone else, like the caterers and so on, were here on time and knew what they were doing.'

'So you supervised, and Lady Denham just left you to it, did she?'

'More or less. Usually she's very hands on, but she seemed a bit distracted this morning. She had a meeting with Sidney Parker, it didn't seem to go too well. Sidney is . . . was . . . usually better than anybody at calming Auntie down if she got in a tizz, but today, it didn't seem to work.'

'This Sidney Parker . . .' Pascoe looked at the notes Wield had given him. 'That's Tom Parker's brother?'

'Yes. He works in the City, and he's a sort of financial consultant to the Consortium, and to Aunt Daphne too – privately, I mean.'

'So this was probably a financial meeting?'

'I expect so.'

'What time was this?'

'About twelve thirty.'

'And the party was due to start at two, right?'

'Yes. The caterers had just arrived. They were setting up their tables. Alan Hollis – he's the landlord at the Hope and Anchor – had just turned up to sort out the drink. Teddy Denham was out there, directing things . . .'

'I thought that was your job?'

She shrugged and said, 'Teddy likes to help. He's family, you know that? Him and his sister, Esther. Teddy inherited the title when his uncle, Sir Henry, died, and took over Denham Park and the estate, not that there was much left of it. Aunt Daphne still kept her title, of course, she was very proud of it . . . sorry, I'm wittering, aren't I?'

'You are doing exactly what I asked you to do,' said Pascoe. 'So carry on wittering. You were saying Sidney Parker's conversation with Lady Denham didn't seem to leave her in a very happy frame of mind. Was that observation, or did she say something to you?'

'No. It was just that Sid came out to the lawn where the tables were being erected and spoke to Teddy. Then from the house through an open window, Aunt Daphne shouted, "Teddy, come in here if you please." And Teddy said, "I'm just making sure that they get these tables in the right position, Aunt," and she said, "I don't know why you should imagine that the organization of my party is any concern of yours. Inside! Now!!"'

'Wow! Did she always speak to him like he was a pet dog?'

He got the April glory again, more sun this time than shower.

'That was how Aunt Daphne spoke to everyone some of the time and some of them all of the time,' she said. 'But she seemed particularly out of sorts with Teddy today. In fact, it started the day before yesterday. I thought at first she was irritated because she hadn't been invited to the Avalon meeting . . .'

'Whoa! I'm an off-comer, remember?'

'Sorry. There was a meeting at the Avalon Clinic.

Something to do with putting the final touches to preparation for the Festival of Health launch next Saturday. That's Tom Parker's pet project; he's very much into alternative therapies. In fact, the whole idea of health and healing is central to his vision of how things should develop here in Sandytown. Aunt Daphne is . . . was a little more commercially minded.'

'But they are partners in this Development thing?'

'The Consortium. Yes.'

'How did that work, then, if they didn't agree on policy? Did they quarrel?'

She shook her head vigorously.

'Oh no. Nothing like that, nothing that would have led to . . . I mean, Tom Parker's the gentlest of men . . . Anyone who's suggested that he would be capable of violence is really out of order!'

Pascoe put on his gently puzzled look and said, 'No one's suggested that, Miss Brereton, and I certainly wasn't implying any such thing. I just want to understand how things stood between Lady Denham and her immediate circle of friends.'

'Well, as far as the Consortium went, it was very much a matter of give and take, I think. As in most relationships. Today's party, for instance. To start with it was going to be a small reception up at the hotel to show appreciation to the main people involved in getting the development plan moving – local investors, the council's planning committee, that sort of thing. But I suspect that, because Aunt Daphne wasn't hugely enthusiastic about the Festival of Health idea, Tom Parker went out of his way to make sure she took the leading role here. So it ended with her having the party at the Hall, reviving her first husband's traditional hog-roast . . .'

She got the phrase out with only a slight shudder. Pascoe nodded encouragingly.

'. . . and generally acting as Lady Bountiful to everyone that mattered, and a few in her eyes who didn't!'

'Very generous of her,' said Pascoe.

'Oh no. That was the beauty of it. She got all the credit, but the Consortium picked up the bill.'

'I see. But despite this, she was annoyed to find she hadn't been asked to this meeting at the Clinic?'

'If it had just been a committee meeting, I don't think she'd have minded. But Dr Feldenhammer had laid on drinks and nibbles afterwards, and various people not directly concerned with the Festival organization were invited to that.'

'So what did she do when she found out?'

'She turned up, of course. And she made Teddy and Esther and me go with her. She liked a retinue.'

'But you feel that she was irritated with her nephew on some other matter?'

'I think so. Summoning him from Denham Park and making him go with her to the Clinic was in part her way of cracking the whip.'

'And did you feel the whip was cracked over you too?' said Pascoe, smiling.

He got a glimmer in return as she said, 'Oh no. A companion's job is to accompany unless commanded not to. But she did seem very out of sorts yesterday. She went off first thing in the morning, I'm not sure where. And when she came back, she seemed very preoccupied. Then she tried to get hold of Sidney, but he wasn't available, and that didn't please her.'

'I see. You say she was still cracking the whip over Teddy today?' he said.

'Yes. When she called him in, I must admit I was glad to see the back of him. He makes a lot of noise, giving directions, but really he's pretty disorganized. Alan Hollis is quite different. He gets things done quietly and efficiently and we were just about finished by the time Teddy reappeared. Not that he showed any interest in resuming control.'

'No? How did he seem then?'

'He looked ready to explode. If I had to guess – sorry, you don't want to hear about my guesses, do you? Just what I saw, that's what Sergeant Wield said.'

'Sergeants aren't allowed to go beyond facts,' Pascoe said gravely. 'Chief Inspectors are permitted to hear a maximum of three guesses a day.'

That earned him another sunbeam.

'He looked to me as if him and Aunt Daphne had just had a big row about something . . .'

Suddenly she stopped and stared at him accusingly.

'Look, this is stupid. I'm not saying . . . I mean, they were always having rows, all of us did. That's the way Aunt Daphne worked. I think she thought of it as keeping people on their toes. You got used to being her favourite for a bit, then you took your turn in the doghouse. It didn't mean anything!'

'No one's saying it did,' said Pascoe. 'So just tell me what you saw. What did Ted do when he reappeared?'

'He just went and stood with Sid Parker and they talked together, or rather Teddy seemed to be doing all the talking . . . Then Aunt Daphne came out to check that everything was in order, which it was.'

'How did she seem?'

'Still a bit uptight, I felt. She gave Teddy and Sid a glower and they moved off out of range. Then she checked everything was ready and she actually said she was pleased the way things were looking. Then she asked Alan Hollis if he had a moment to go over the paperwork relating to the bar with her and they went back to the house together. I finished off outside, then went back to my room to get cleaned up and changed into my party gear. And I got back downstairs a few minutes before the guests started arriving.'

'Tell me about that. Who was first?'

'Miss Sheldon, the Chief Nurse at the Clinic, showed up just a couple of minutes after two, a bit worried in case she was too early. Then very shortly after, Miss Lee, the acupuncturist, then Dr Feldenhammer, he's in charge at the Avalon, and after that they came thick and fast. I've been trying to work out the exact order like Sergeant Wield asked, but it's not easy. In the end we just let new arrivals find their own way round to the garden because we were just too busy making sure everyone got drinks and so on.'

'*We* being you and who else? The Denhams?' suggested Pascoe.

'Well, not really. Teddy and Esther got caught up with talking to people, you see, and of course Aunt Daphne had to say hello to everyone. She was in a much better mood now. Very relaxed, all jolly and good hostessy.'

'So it was just you doing the work then?'

Smile again, a bit rueful this time?

'I suppose so. But very quickly, once people found where the drinks and nibbles were, they looked after themselves so all I had to do was keep a general eye on things.'

'Of course. Did that include the barbecue area?'

The light died in her face, but it had to be mentioned some time.

'No. I don't much care for meat, Mr Pascoe, particularly in a form which displays its source so graphically. Ollie Hollis was in charge there.'

'Tell me about him.'

'He's a gate-man at the Hollis Ham breeding unit out at Denham Park. I think he's a distant relative of Aunt Daphne's first husband who founded the business. Aunt Daphne often gets him . . . got him . . . to do odd jobs around the garden, and I think he used to help with the hog-roast in Mr Hollis's day. It was an annual event then.'

'And your aunt didn't keep up the tradition? Why was that?'

'I suppose because second husbands don't much care to be reminded of their predecessors, and the annual hog-roast was very much Mr Hollis's event.'

Pascoe noted the care with which she put things. She was no one's fool, this girl, he judged, and very far from a sycophantic companion. He doubted if much escaped her. Presently she was too close to the horror of events to be pressed to a full and frank assessment of what made her 'aunt' tick. Later, however, she could be very useful.

'And when did you last see Lady Denham?' he asked.

'Like I told Sergeant Wield, the last time I can be positive about was around three thirty, give or take. She was having a rather intense conversation with Mr Godley . . .'

'An argument, the sergeant said you said.'

'Did I? Well, yes, maybe it was, but I wouldn't like to say . . .'

Frightened once more of seeming to point a finger?

'Mr Godley's a healer, I understand,' said Pascoe. 'I

gather from what you say that Lady Denham wasn't as keen on alternative therapists as Mr Tom Parker?'

'No, she wasn't,' said Clara. 'Frankly, I think Aunt Daphne would rather not have asked any of them to the hog-roast, but as it was being paid for out of Consortium funds, she didn't really have a choice. Anyway she was really very fond of Tom in her own way and wouldn't offend him if she could help it.'

'And you didn't see her again after this?'

'I don't think so. But I was very busy, you see, helping Alan Hollis with the drink. You can leave people to help themselves to food, but unless you keep control of the bar, it gets chaotic. Alan couldn't spare any of his staff from the pub – it's the holiday season – so he needed all the help he could get. Then, when the storm started, we were working like mad to get the bar stuff into the house before it got washed away.'

'That's very helpful. Thank you,' said Pascoe. He studied his copy of the guest list again and went on, 'I notice that the Tom Parkers have a Charlotte Heywood at the same local address. She another relative?'

'No. A visiting friend,' she said. 'Not a poor dependant like me.'

She spoke with a touch of self-mockery.

Pascoe smiled and said, 'That's not really how you see yourself, is it?'

'I suspect it's how I appear in some people's eyes.'

'But not perhaps for long,' he said, watching her carefully.

'I'm sorry?'

'I just meant that, with your aunt's tragic death, your dependency, or its appearance at least, has ceased. As for being poor, I know nothing of your circumstances, nor indeed how Lady Denham's death might affect them.'

'Oh God,' she said incredulously. 'You think I'm at all concerned about that?'

'In the circumstances, it might be natural . . .'

'Natural for you in your line of work, maybe,' she said.

She sounded close to an angry outburst, but took a couple of deep breaths and when she spoke her voice was back under control.

'Aunt Daphne had many faults, and there'll be plenty of people keen to point them out. All I know is she was kind to me, and she invited me to live with her when I needed someone to be kind to me. As to her will, whether she's left me a lot or a little, or nothing, won't make the slightest difference to how I grieve for her and remember her.'

'I'm sorry,' said Pascoe, impressed, though not certain whether it was by the power of her emotion, or the power of her performance. 'I didn't mean to offend you.'

'You haven't,' she assured him. 'Look, I'm as keen as you to see the monster who did this dreadful thing brought to justice. Obviously you'll want to talk to anyone who might benefit from Aunt Daphne's death. I should hate for you to waste time by having me on that list, that's all.'

'Very commendable,' murmured Pascoe. 'Perhaps, having removed your own name from the list, you could suggest some names which ought to figure there?'

She looked at him with an expression which was very much more lady-of-the-house than poor-relative and said, 'Knowing how it feels to be under suspicion, you don't imagine I'm going to point the finger at some other poor devil, do you?'

'No? Then perhaps after all you're not quite so keen as me to see the monster who did this dreadful thing brought to justice,' said Pascoe.

He let her digest that for a moment then went on, 'Thanks for your help, anyway. Now, if Sir Edward and his sister are still around, I'd like a word with them, please.'

She held his gaze steadily for a moment, then rose and led him further down the corridor to a large oak door. She pushed it open and walked away without a word.

Sulking, or just thinking? wondered Pascoe. More to Miss Brereton than meets the eye? And certainly what met the eye was very easy on it.

He pushed the thought to the back of his mind and advanced through the open door.

7

The room he entered was of a different order from the rather poky computer room he'd just left. It was generously proportioned, with a ceiling high enough to take a crystal chandelier, though all that depended from an ornately sculpted boss was the kind of four-bulbed wooden cross-piece fitment you could buy in British Home Stores. The design on the boss and on the matching cornicing was picked out in gold leaf looking badly in need of renewal. Above a huge marble fireplace hung an oil painting of a man in hunting scarlet against a pastoral background across which ran a cry of hounds. The furniture looked old and rather shabby.

There were two people in the room. Stretched out along a chaise longue was a young woman with a tall glass in her left hand. Dressed in baggy patched jeans and what Pascoe thought of as a sloppy Joe sweater, she still contrived to look incredibly elegant as she turned a cold gaze on him and said, 'Who the hell are you?'

'Detective Chief Inspector Pascoe, Mid-Yorkshire CID,' he proclaimed with deliberate sonority.

The second occupant of the room, standing at a tall mahogany bureau with his back to the door, turned round and took a couple of rather aggressive steps forward. He was a fit, muscular young man who moved with athletic ease; very good looking in a slightly outmoded way, this being an age that valued pallid angularity over square-cut five o'clock shadow. His vigorously curly hair was becomingly dishevelled and he wore designer fatigues and the kind of polo shirt that might actually have been worn by a man playing polo, or perhaps it was just a certain arrogance of mien that gave this impression. An expensive-looking watch hung loose on his left wrist as if the bracelet catch had broken, or maybe that was the way the upper set wore their baubles to display their indifference to wealth.

He looked Pascoe up and down and said, 'You the man in charge?'

His tone was on the edge of brusque and very definitely patrician.

Pascoe said, 'Sir Edward Denham, I presume. And Miss Esther? These are sad circumstances in which to meet. I'm sorry for your loss.'

His face solemn with sympathy, he held out his hand.

Like Furtwangler fiddling with his baton in a vain effort to avoid being filmed shaking hands with Hitler, Denham attempted to fasten his watch, but Pascoe kept his hand steady and finally the man gave it a peremptory shake and muttered, 'Thank you.'

Then, presumably as a step to regaining the social high ground, he barked, 'Took your time getting here, didn't you?'

For a second Pascoe looked puzzled, then he smiled faintly, as if spotting an understandable error, and explained, 'Getting here wasn't a priority, sir. My sergeant is more than capable of setting the *mechanics* of the investigation in progress. I logged straight on to the Central Police Computer. Nowadays it's standard practice for chief investigators to acquaint themselves with the known background of significant witnesses before heading for the *locus in quo*.'

He let the implications of this fiction sink in as he took a step past Denham and stared at the bureau. All its drawers were open and the desk was covered with papers, some of which had spilled on to the floor.

'Have you lost something, sir?' he asked politely.

'No!' said Denham. The watch was loose again. He gave up on it and thrust it into his pocket, so not a fashion statement. 'Just checking for Auntie's address book. There are a few people who need to be told the sad news before they hear it on the radio.'

'Very thoughtful of you, sir,' said Pascoe. 'Have you found it?'

'Well no, actually . . .'

'Never mind. Perhaps Miss Brereton will be able to help you. Meanwhile, if I could just get you to answer a few questions . . .?'

Denham took a deep breath then relaxed and said, 'Sure. You've got a job to do, right? Take a seat, Pascoe. Care for a drink?'

The baronet was bright enough to have decided the high hand was going to get him nowhere, thought Pascoe, but the sister still looked as if she'd have preferred to set the dogs on him. The thought took his gaze back to the portrait over the mantelshelf. The man looked slightly familiar. He was staring into the room with a rather quizzical superior gaze and the suggestion of a squint.

'No, I'm OK,' he said. 'Is that the late Mr Hollis perhaps?'

'Good lord, no,' said Denham. 'That's my uncle, Sir Henry. This is Hollis.'

He went to a small ormolu table standing against the same wall as the bureau and picked up a silver photo frame which held the picture of a grizzle-haired man, his weather-beaten and heavily stubbled face glaring out with that narrow-eyed Yorkshire farmer expression that says clearer than words *There's no bugger here getting the better of me!*

Sorry, Hog. Can't win 'em all, thought Pascoe, not without sympathy. If anything of human consciousness survived, what must Hog Hollis feel to find himself gazing across his own drawing room to see pride of place given to his successor!

He turned back to Sir Harry's portrait, then glanced at Edward. No squint but the same superior expression.

'Of course. Now I see the resemblance,' he said. 'Fine portrait. Very . . . big.'

'Should never have left Denham Park,' said the woman. 'It's a daub, you know.'

'Oh surely not so bad as that,' said Pascoe.

The woman gave him a look which would have been contemptuous if she'd thought him worth her contempt. But her brother laughed and said, 'Bradley d'Aube, one of the Huddersfield School, very well thought of, and prices have shot up since he died ten years back. Well, it can go back to its rightful place now.'

'It's here on loan then, rather than part of the late Lady Denham's estate?' said Pascoe innocently.

Esther Denham yawned as if she found the observation too tedious to need a response, but her brother said smoothly, 'Loan covers it, I think. My late aunt naturally wanted to have some memento of Uncle Harry when she returned here after his death and we raised no objection when she chose the portrait. But it was always understood it belonged in the Park. Not a problem. Loan or legacy, either way it will come to me.'

Well, well, thought Pascoe. Cards on the table time, is it? Aimed at making me think no one so open can possibly have anything to hide.

The clever move of a clever mind?

Or maybe subtle sister, reckoning you're not bright enough to deceive me, has advised you to play it this way.

'As to that, I think we should wait and see,' said Pascoe. 'Promises have been broken, wills have been changed. And perhaps, in order not to muddy the waters, and for your own protection, it might be as well to regard all papers and property in the Hall as private until the legal formalities have been observed.'

He let his gaze drift to the open bureau.

Denham looked ready to revert to patrician indignation, but this time it was his sister who chose the conciliatory path.

'Told you not to go poking about, Teddy,' she said. 'That's what we pay the police for. Come on. Let's go home.'

Exit left, leaving the grateful plod spluttering his appreciation, thought Pascoe.

'If I could have a word first,' he said as the woman swung her legs off the chaise.

'Another word? I think I'm worded out, Inspector,' she said. 'You do know we've written our statements and given them to one of your people, I forget his name, the one with the *interesting* face.'

She drawled the adjective in a way that made it sound more abusive than abuse.

'Yes, I know,' said Pascoe. 'And very helpful too. Impressions close to the event are always valuable. But sometimes, as time passes, things surface which the first effort of recall failed to trawl up.'

Esther Denham stood up, shaking her head.

'Sorry, nothing like that,' she said.

The sloppy Joe was so big it hung loose on her with the sleeves dangling a good six inches beneath her hands. But the knit was wide enough for Pascoe to be uncomfortably aware that she was bra-less beneath it.

He was standing between her and the door and when he made no attempt to move, she yawned widely in his face, then said, 'Look, if you're going to keep us hanging around, is it OK if I get another drink, or does that come under muddying the waters too?'

'So long as you don't take the bottle,' said Pascoe, who decided he would be happy to dislike this young woman when he was sure that making him dislike her wasn't simply a distraction tactic.

She smiled faintly and moved across the room to a long sideboard on which stood a vodka bottle and an ice bucket. Her left hand wriggled sexily out of the long sleeve, dropped a couple of cubes into a glass and covered them with vodka.

Her brother watched her uneasily. He didn't have a drink. Keeping his head clear?

'And you, sir?' said Pascoe. 'Anything occur since you gave your statement?'

'Not really,' said Edward. 'Last sightings of poor Aunt Daphne are clearly going to be of the essence and I've been racking my brain to see if I can come up with anything significant in our brief final exchange.'

'Just let your mind go blank, sir,' advised Pascoe, provoking a satirical snort from the sister. 'See if anything pops up.'

Denham closed his eyes for a moment then shook his head.

'No. As I told Sergeant Wield, last time I saw her was quite early on. Some of the children who were there wanted to have a swim from the private beach and I volunteered to help keep an eye on them. I hung around there for a while, then, realizing there were more adults than was really necessary, I thought I'd rejoin the party. Always hate to miss my share of a good bubbly and Auntie had really pushed the boat out for a change.'

'So you didn't notice Lady Denham when you got back.'

'No. Sorry.'

'What about you, Miss Denham?'

'Oh, I glimpsed her from time to time. Noticed her backing poor old Lester Feldenhammer into a corner. Probably inviting him to examine her private parts.'

'Ess, for God's sake!' protested Denham. 'She's only been dead a few hours.'

'I'm sorry,' said Pascoe. 'I'm missing something here. This is Dr Feldenhammer from the Avalon you're referring to, is it?'

'Right. Come on, Teddy, do you imagine the police aren't going to winkle it out? That's your speciality isn't it, Inspector, winkling?'

'*Chief* Inspector, if we are to be precise, Miss Denham. Any assistance you can give me with my winkling would be much appreciated.'

She laughed and for the first time looked at him as if he were possibly something more than a disregardable footman.

'No big secret,' she said. 'Get chatting to anyone down at the Hope and Anchor and they'll tell you that Auntie had set her sights on Feldenhammer.'

'You're saying there was a romantic relationship between Lady Denham and Dr Feldenhammer?'

Esther Denham laughed again.

'Not quite how I'd put it. Daphne liked men. Liked in every sense. But she liked her social standing too, so no Lady Chatterley stuff. Wouldn't have cared to be caught making hay with a well-hung peasant. What she wanted was a consort who could service her both socially and sexually. Hollis, her first husband, brought her wealth and local influence; Uncle Harry, her second, brought her social standing and, because she had a mind like a calculating machine, a lot more profit than he ever managed from the Denham estate. Since his death, she'd been casting around for a successor to scratch all her itches.'

'And why did the election light on Dr Feldenhammer?' wondered Pascoe.

She raised her eyebrows at his choice of words, then said, 'He would make a pretty impressive trophy husband. Not so young he could be called a toy-boy which would have made her ridiculous, but not so old he can't get it up. Not rich, perhaps, but earning enough not to be a drain on her resources, and of sufficient distinction in his profession for there to be plenty of reflected light for her to wallow in. Plus, of course, despite her frequent boast of never having ailed from anything in her life, at her age it must have seemed both prudent and economic to have a doctor perman-ently in the house.'

You really didn't like her, thought Pascoe. But how far would your dislike make you go?

'And Dr Feldenhammer received these attentions . . . how?'

'Like a missionary pursued by a starving cannibal,' responded Esther. 'Seeing that prayer was getting him nowhere, he tried running and even went as far as the Swiss Avalon near Davos on a job exchange for six months, but she was soon in hot pursuit.'

'Don't complain, Sis. We got a skiing holiday out of it,' grinned her brother, apparently happy after his initial protest to endorse her light-hearted openness.

Grief hit people in different ways, thought Pascoe trying to be non-judgmental. At the very least, this pair weren't trying to fake it!

'Why didn't the doctor just say no thanks, I don't want to play?' he wondered.

'Aunt Daph was very good at unlevelling playing fields,' said Ted Denham.

His sister cut in quickly, 'And Lester's no novice at the game. For the past six months or so he has been ducking and weaving pretty skilfully. But box as prettily as you will with Aunt Daph, eventually you end up in a corner. I felt rather sorry for him. It was starting to look as if his only recourse was going to be to elope with Fatty Nightingale.'

'Sorry? You've left me winkling in the dark again.'

'Petula Sheldon, Chief Nurse at the Avalon. Pound for pound she might come close to auntie, and she could give her twenty years in the age stakes, but I think a bookie would have called it a mismatch.'

'This Nurse Sheldon is close to Dr Feldenhammer, is that what you're saying?'

'She'd certainly like to be. Nurses are always on the hunt for doctors, aren't they? What he feels about her, God knows. She probably looks pretty attractive by comparison with Aunt Daph. Could be her attractions will fade now Daph's dead. She is, after all, just hired help. Talking of which, *Chief* Inspector, does your interdict on poking around Aunt Daphne's stuff apply to Clara Brereton too?'

'I'm sorry?' said Pascoe, thrown by the sudden change of subject.

She rolled her eyes as if in appeal to some upper class god for protection from the dullness of the proletariat.

'You seem to fear that my brother might be tempted to poke around the house if he remains here,' she said slowly and very distinctly. 'Miss Brereton actually lives here. What is to stop her from poking around all she likes when she's alone in the house tonight?'

Denham exclaimed, 'Good lord! I'd never thought of that.'

For a moment Pascoe thought he was sharing his sister's uncharitable suspicions. Then he went on, 'Poor Clara won't want to stay here by herself all night, not after what's happened. We must invite her back to the Park.'

He strode out of the room.

Nice to see that one of this pair has got some human feelings, thought Pascoe.

He said stolidly, 'Looks like you've got yourself a house-guest, Miss Denham.'

She drained her glass and smiled at him. It was a mocking smile, no sun through April clouds here, more will-o'-the-wisp through marsh mist. But he couldn't deny that she was a very good-looking woman.

'I don't think so,' she said. 'Five gets you ten she won't come.'

'I'm not allowed to gamble on duty, miss,' said Pascoe.
Which was just as well, as he'd have lost.

'Says she'll be fine here,' said Denham, coming back into the room.

He sounded rather chastened. His sister said sweetly, 'I'm surprised you didn't offer to stay and hold her hand, Teddy.'

He ignored her and said, 'You done with us, Chief Inspector?'

'Just one other thing, sir,' said Pascoe. 'This private beach you mentioned, how do you reach it?'

'There's a path down the cliff.'

'Is there anything at the bottom to stop anyone unauthorized from coming up?'

'What? Ah, I see where you're going. No, apart from a sign saying PRIVATE, and of course local terror at the possibility of encountering Auntie, there's nothing to deter an intruder. You don't think . . .'

'Rest assured, we'll check all possibilities. One thing more, sir. I gather that you and your aunt had a conversation earlier today, before the party started.'

'We were always having conversations,' he blustered. 'We got on very well.'

'I'm sure you did. But the smoothest of relationships can have abrasive moments. I gather this conversation may have been a little heated.'

'Who's been saying that?' he demanded.

His sister, who'd taken the opportunity offered by the extended exchange to refill her glass, let out a snort as if this were the stupidest question she'd ever heard.

Pascoe said, 'So you're saying such a conversation never took place.'

Denham glowered at him for a moment.

He's trying to recall the circumstances, what he can and cannot deny, thought Pascoe.

He said, 'Oh yes. Auntie did give me a bit of a rocket for getting involved in setting out the tables for the refreshments and buffet. I explained that Clara was getting her knickers in a bit of a twist about it and I was just trying to help, but she said that the girl had to learn from her mistakes. End of story.'

An ingenious explanation closely linked to the known facts. Perhaps he was a clever bugger after all.

'Thank you for that, and thank you both for your indulgence,' said Pascoe. 'I may need to talk to you again, so if you could keep me apprised of any plans you may have to be away from Denham Park in the next few days, I'd be grateful.'

'Don't worry. We won't be straying far till things are sorted here,' said Edward.

'We'll be as quick as we can, sir,' said Pascoe, though he did not for a moment think that the man was referring to the investigation.

He stood aside from the door, making it clear he was ushering them out of the room. Esther finished her drink and set her glass down. She'd used only her left hand, Pascoe noticed, both for preparing and disposing of the drink. This he felt was a proper observation for a senior detective to be making, and it helped distract him from the very improper observation of the plump brown breasts pushing like baby seals against the net of wool.

After they left the room he went over to the bureau. He leafed through the papers on view but found nothing that cried for attention. He made a note to tell Wield to get someone to make a detailed list. At least it might tell him what young Sir Edward *wasn't* looking for. The one thing he found which sparked his interest was a small diary, but when he opened it he saw it seemed to contain nothing but appointments. He slipped it into his pocket for further examination.

He left the drawing room and went back to Clara Brereton's room.

'I gather you've turned down Sir Edward's invitation to stay at Denham Park,' he said.

'Yes.'

'Your decision, but it might be better not to stay here by yourself tonight.'

'Better for whom?'

'For yourself.'

'But won't you have policemen patrolling the grounds?'

'Perhaps. Nevertheless . . .'

She regarded him shrewdly for a moment then said, 'Teddy's been poking about, hasn't he? And Esther thinks I might do some poking of my own.'

He still wasn't certain how bright the bart was, nor indeed whether his sister had anything more than that superficial brightness derived from a posh school and an engrained assumption of superiority, but he had no doubts about Clara Brereton.

'Perhaps,' he said. 'If Sir Edward were doing some poking, what might he expect to find? Where for instance might Lady Denham have kept her private papers?'

'I'm not sure. The bureau in the east drawing room, perhaps.'

'That was where I met the Denhams, right? And was the bureau kept locked?'

'Not usually. I doubt if she kept anything there she felt was really confidential. She'd deposit anything like that with Mr Beard, her lawyer.'

'And he's local, is he?'

'Oh no. London. Aunt Daphne didn't believe in employing local firms for confidential matters. That was a piece of advice she gave me. She liked dishing out advice. Local professionals might be very competent but they employ local people. A wise woman takes care that her correspondence with her lawyer cannot be looked at by, say, the daughter of her milliner. That's what she told me.'

'I'm sure you took it to heart,' said Pascoe, smiling. 'Did she go to see Mr Beard or did he come up here?'

'He came here pretty regularly as far as I can gather.'

'She had a lot of legal work then?'

'She enjoyed changing her will, certainly,' she said, pulling a face.

'Really. And the last time Mr Beard was here was . . . when?'

'Week before last.'

'And was that about a will change?'

'You'll need to ask him,' said Clara Brereton dryly. 'I may have been a sort of cousin, but in some respects I was still a sort of milliner's daughter.'

'Do you have Mr Beard's address?'

'Gray's Inn Road, I believe. The number will be in Auntie's address book. Shall I get it for you?'

Pascoe shook his head.

'No. I'd rather you didn't. In fact, Miss Brereton, if you'd care to put a few things of your own together, I really do feel you ought to move out of the Hall for a couple of days.'

'This is beginning to sound more like an instruction than an option. And where am I to go?'

'You could change your mind about Sir Edward's invitation.'

She shook her head and said, 'No, I couldn't.'

'Any particular reason?'

Before she could answer, the phone by the computer rang.

'Am I allowed to answer that?' she said.

'Of course.'

She picked it up and said, 'Hello . . . yes, it's me.'

She listened for a while then said, 'Yes, in fact the police have suggested I move out for the time being . . . that's very kind of you . . . very kind indeed. Thank you.'

She put down the phone and said, 'You haven't been talking to Tom Parker, have you?'

'No, I think one of my officers should have interviewed him by now, but I haven't encountered him personally yet. Why?'

'It was just so timely. That was Tom. He said he and his wife had just realized that I would be all by myself here and they've invited me to stay with them at Kyoto House.'

'That was kind of them. And purely fortuitous, I assure you,' said Pascoe. 'You've no objection?'

'They're kind people,' said Clara. 'No, I've no objection. Right, I'd better go and pack. Are you going to supervise me?'

Pascoe said gently, 'Please, Miss Brereton, don't feel badgered. You've had a terrible shock. I admit there are other considerations but, more importantly, I really feel it's better all round that tonight you should be among friends. Do you have transport?'

'Not my own. I sometimes borrowed my aunt's jeep, but I'd better not risk that or Esther might be demanding you arrest me for theft.'

She said it lightly but Pascoe noted it was the sister she focused on.

'OK. I'll fix a lift for you. Now off you go and pack.'

She nodded, more it seemed to him at some inner decision than in acknowledgement of anything he'd said, then left the room.

Pascoe took out his mobile and rang Wield.

'Car round to the Hall ASAP please to take Miss Brereton to Kyoto House, Tom Parker's residence. And when she's gone, get someone to give the house the once-over.'

'Looking for anything special?'

'Not really, but Sir Ted was looking for something and I don't think he found it. Will maybe. Lady Denham's bedroom might be a good place to start.'

'On the principle that's where women are most likely to keep their secrets?'

'I'm surprised you knowing a thing like that, Wieldy,' he said and switched off.

Clara Brereton came back into the room, carrying a small grip.

'You were quick,' he congratulated her.

'I didn't pack for a long stay,' she said.

He smiled as he recalled Ellie explaining to him that packing for a short stay was much harder than packing for a long stay when you just threw everything in.

How should I pack for this case? he wondered.

'Then let's get you on your way,' he said.

8

As Shirley Novello left Kyoto House, she felt reasonably pleased with herself.

OK, she hadn't lit upon that crucial bit of information that was going to crack the case, but that only ever happened in detective stories. What she'd got were three witness statements, each packed with useful detail, plus the bonus of Charley Heywood's email observations on recent events and activities involving the main protagonists. How useful these might be remained to be seen. Probably just a lot of sisterly gossip.

She opened her car door.

From the passenger seat, Minnie Parker said, 'Hello.'

'How the hell did you get in?' demanded Novello.

'It wasn't locked,' said the girl.

'It bloody well was,' said Novello.

Faced with such vehement certainty the girl didn't argue but said, 'OK. But you left your window open a bit.'

'Yeah? That's forced entry, I could do you for that. What are you doing here anyway?'

'I'm waiting to be interviewed,' said Minnie.

'Sorry?'

'That's what you're doing, isn't it? Interviewing witnesses? Well, I was at the hog-roast too. I'm a witness.'

There was no denying this, thought Novello. The thing was, the children hadn't appeared on Clara Brereton's guest list. And Wield hadn't noticed. No reason he should have, probably. But it gave Novello a frisson of glee to think that even old Super-sarge could have a kryptonite moment.

Also it gave her a problem. Proper procedure was to arrange an interview with a responsible adult present and preferably a specialist officer doing the questioning. Probable result, zilch. But that was Wield's problem. Or Pascoe's when he showed.

No harm in testing the water though . . .

'OK, give me it straight, kid. What did you see?'

Minnie screwed up her eyes in an effort of recall. Or creativity.

Novello said, 'Listen, kid, it doesn't have to be a madman running around with an axe. It's ordinary stuff that helps, so long as it's true. You went swimming, didn't you?'

'That's right.'

'You and who else?'

'Paul, that's my brother, and the Heeley twins – Lynn and Larry, and Tony Jebb.'

Novello made a note.

'How old?'

'The twins are nine, Tony's eleven.'

'Older than you then.'

'Yes, but I'm the best swimmer,' retorted Minnie.

'Great. Any adults?'

'Mr Jebb, Tony's dad. And Miss Lee. Mr Jebb runs the souvenir shop. Miss Lee's an acupuncturist. She's Chinese or something, I think. Oh, and the twins' dad, Mr Heeley, he's a joiner.'

Novello was impressed both by the girl's readiness

to give useful information and the ease with which *acupuncturist* rolled off her lips, but then she was Tom Parker's daughter. She checked her interview list. Jebb was one of Seymour's, Heeley was hers, while Miss Lee was marked down to Bowler.

This meant both her colleagues should at some point discover there'd been children present. How would Wield react to being told he'd missed a bit? Perhaps best to let one of the others find out!

'They swim? The adults, I mean.'

'No. They just sat and talked. Then when the storm started they called for us to come out. That was a real pain. The others got scared but I thought swimming when there was thunder and lightning would be really cool. Do you swim? You look like you could.'

'Oh yeah? Meaning I'm slim and silvery like a trout? Or broad and blubbery like a sea-lion?'

'Well, you look strong,' said the girl cautiously.

'You'd better believe it. OK, so you had to come out of the water. Then?'

'We ran back up the cliff path. Charley was coming down to fetch us and she grabbed hold of me and Paul and we ran into the house and said hello to Mum, then Charley took us upstairs to dry us off and then she let us sit at one of the upstairs windows and watch the storm.'

'Nice of her. You like Charley?'

'She's great. She's going to marry my uncle Sidney, you know.'

'Is that right? No, I didn't know that. She known him a long time?'

Minnie considered then said, 'Not *very* long. And it's a secret, so maybe you shouldn't say anything just yet.'

Novello, recalling that Charley had only been here a week and that by her own account her acquaintance with the Parker family only extended another three days beyond that said, 'This one of those secrets even Charley and your uncle Sid don't know about?'

'Maybe,' said the girl.

'Then I'll definitely keep it to myself. OK, so you watched the storm. And then?'

'Then when it was over we went down to Mum and everyone went outside again and then people started yelling 'cos they'd found Big Bum . . .'

'Sorry?'

'Lady Denham, I mean. Is it true she was roasting alongside the pig?'

'More or less,' said Novello, who thought it was better for kids to get some kind of grisly delight out of horrors rather than nightmares. 'You see her at all?'

'No. I wanted to take a look, but Mum dragged us away straight off,' said the girl regretfully.

Novello gave her a poke and said, 'I mean earlier, dummy.'

'Only when we arrived.'

'How did she seem?'

'She was really nice.'

'Is that unusual?'

'Well, she always makes a big fuss about seeing me and the others when she comes to the house, but it only lasts a few seconds, then she forgets all about us.'

'But this time . . .?'

'She seemed really happy to see us, to see everyone.'

'What sort of happy?'

'You know, like adults get when they've had a couple of drinks, or done sex.'

Trying to shock me? Impress me? Or is she really

281

as laid-back as she sounds? wondered Novello. Anyway, this wasn't a road to go down outside of a properly constituted juvenile interview.

'So who did you see after you came back from the beach?'

'Lots of people. Everyone was rushing around to get sheltered from the storm.'

'Can you be a bit more specific? I mean, can you remember anyone in particular?'

'I know what specific means,' said Minnie resentfully. 'I saw Teddy Denham. He was in his trunks too, but he hadn't been swimming. Not with us anyway.'

No, thought Novello. I know what he'd been doing.

'Anyone else?'

'There were a lot of men, from the council, I think, 'cos the mayor was with them in his chain. And they were grabbing bottles and glasses from the bar to take inside, then Mr Hollis from the pub arrived and said he'd take care of that. No one seemed to be bothering with the food and I wanted to stop and get some 'cos we hadn't had any yet and swimming always makes me hungry, but Charley said no, let's get you all inside.'

'So Charley was in charge of you by then? What happened to the other adults?'

'Mr Jebb was there with Tony, and Mr Heeley was looking after the twins. Didn't see Miss Lee. She sort of vanished when we got to the top of the cliff path. Anyway, when we came out later all the food was spoilt. I think it was Clara's fault, she usually looks after all that sort of thing at the Hall, and I expect Big Bum, I mean Lady Denham, would have given her a right rollicking if she'd seen all that food gone to waste.'

The phrase and the intonation suggested she was quoting something overheard.

Novello glanced at the car clock. It was time to be on her way.

She said, 'Then, after they discovered . . .'

She paused in search of a euphemism and Minnie said impatiently, 'The corpse.'

'That's right. Did your parents take you straight home?'

'Yes. I wanted stay and see what happened next, but you know what adults are like.'

Slightly flattered to be included as a non-adult, Novello said, 'Yeah. I work for a couple of adults and they can be a pain.'

She reached across the girl and opened the passenger door.

'OK,' she said. 'That's fine. Thanks a lot.'

'Are we finished?' said Minnie, sounding disappointed. 'You don't want to hear about the others?'

'What others?'

'The ones I saw out of the window while the storm was on.'

Oh God, thought Novello. I really should have kicked Minnie out of my car straight off, belled Wield, told him about her and the other kids, left him to set up proper interviews.

On the other hand, having got this far, if I dig up something really useful, then any bollocking I get will probably be token.

Probably.

'Tell me,' she said.

The girl screwed up her face in the effort of reconstruction. Or construction. Novello recalled her own childhood confessions when her keenness not to disappoint Father Kerrigan had caused much blurring of the boundaries of fact in search of significant sin. With pubescence the blurring had continued but the motive had completely reversed.

'I was looking out of the window watching the storm and down at the bottom of the lawn I saw Miss Denham . . .'

'Hang on,' said Novello. 'Everyone says it was black as night and the rain was sheeting down and there was a gale filling the air with leaves and stuff. You must have very good eyes.'

'Yes, I have,' said Minnie somewhat complacently. 'And when the lightning flashed, it was as bright as anything.'

'So during a flash of lightning you saw . . . what exactly?'

'I saw Miss Denham. Why won't you believe me?' insisted the child angrily.

Novello replied very quietly, 'What I believe's not the point, Minnie. It's what you really believe. Just remember what we're talking about here. It's something really horrible. It isn't a game. So tell me again what you saw.'

The homily had its effect.

The girl said, more hesitantly now, 'I really did see someone, and I think it was Miss Denham. At least, it could have been, and there was someone with her . . . a man . . .'

'Who?'

'I don't know!' she cried. 'He looked sort of familiar, but I couldn't really say who it was. They were coming out of the shrubbery between the lawn and the hog-roast . . .'

Novello tried to recall the configuration of house, lawn, and hog-roast.

'That would be about three hundred yards. Looking obliquely. That's sideways. Good eyes you've got.'

'Yes,' said the girl complacently.

'And you saw this in one lightning flash?'

'Yes. When the next one came they were gone.'

It was time to finish here, thought Novello. She'd gone a lot further than testing the water. If taken to task, it would have been good to be able to point to some significant discovery, but what she'd got was, in the vernacular, neither owt nor nowt.

She said, 'Anyone else see these two people – your brother or Miss Heywood, say?'

'I don't think so.'

'And did you mention what you saw to either of them?'

'No. I mean, I didn't know it was important then, did I?'

'Kid, you don't know that now,' said Novello. 'Right. Thanks. Off you go.'

'Don't I get to sign something? And shouldn't you have been getting all this on to tape?' demanded the girl.

'Later,' said Novello. 'You may have to go through all this again, with either your mum or dad present. Then you'll probably do the recording and signing thing. Think of this as a sort of rehearsal, OK?'

'OK,' said Minnie, not moving. 'So where are you going now?'

'What's that to you?'

'Maybe I could come with you. I know all the short-cuts round here.'

'Come on! A town this size, everything's so close, who needs shortcuts?' said Novello, who was an urban animal and rated any settlement with a population of less than fifty K a village. 'Anyway, shouldn't you be in bed?'

'I'll be ten next birthday!' declared Minnie indignantly.

'So what do you want? A telegram from the Queen? Go go go, or I may have to arrest you.'

She saw the girl's eyes light up at the possibility and gave her a push which sent her sprawling through the open door on to the edge of the lawn.

'See you later,' Novello called, dragging the door shut, starting the car and sending it racing down the drive in a single gravel-spewing movement.

In the mirror she saw the girl had got to her feet and was running after the car, shouting indignantly.

Receding fast, she was difficult to hear and impossible to lip-read.

But she thought she made out the words, 'You've got a big bum too!'

9

'You have arrived,' said Posh Woman's voice confidently.

'You're a bloody liar,' said Edgar Wield.

He had been impressed as Posh directed him along a skein of unclassified byways mazy enough to confuse a Minotaur hunter, but she'd failed him at the last. The building he had halted beside bore a sign saying Lyke Farm whereas what he wanted was Lyke Farm Barn.

Time for human contact.

He climbed off the Thunderbird and banged on the oak door with a lion-head knocker.

He had his ID open and ready. Normally he expected folk to take him as they found him, but in remote spots the combination of his leather riding gear and forbidding features sometimes required immediate reassurance.

The door opened and the doorway was filled by a huge red-faced man who didn't look as if he'd have been much bothered to find the devil himself on his doorstep.

'Detective Sergeant Wield,' said Wield, just to be on the safe side.

'Oh aye? It'll be about the murder. You'll be wanting young Fran, I daresay.'

Wield wasn't surprised. The speed with which news

travelled across miles of empty space in rural Yorkshire would fill Bill Gates with envy.

'That's right. Mr Roote,' he said. 'I'm looking for Lyke Farm Barn.'

'Well, you've not looked hard enough. Back along the Sandytown road a quarter mile, lane end on your left just afore the dead oak, and there's a bloody great sign for them as can read.'

Wield did not feel reproved. He'd lived in a remote Yorkshire village for a few years now and knew that such apparent aggression was the equivalent of familiar domestic intercourse in metropolitan areas.

'Thank you, Mr . . . er?'

'Sedgwick. Wally Sedgwick. You've not got him yet, then?'

'Got who?'

'Him as did for Daph Brereton, of course.'

'No, we haven't. Do you see a lot of Mr Roote?'

'When he calls to pay the rent. My missus sees a lot more, keeping the place tidy for him like she does.'

'You own the barn then?'

'Oh aye. Got it done up a few years back when this bloody government started making it impossible to make a living by honest farming. Diversify, they said. Tek in lodgers, mek cream teas. Bugger that, I said. I'm not having a bunch of strangers clogging up my bathroom. But we got a grant to convert the barn to a holiday cottage.'

'But Mr Roote lives there permanent?'

'Got a lease for a year, renewable. Didn't think it would work when I saw the state of him, but it's all on one floor and he forked out for a few changes. He said he wanted somewhere quiet so's he could work at his writing. And my missus said it 'ud be a lot easier than having someone new there every week during the summer, then the place sitting empty when the bad weather came. Think she felt a bit sorry for the lad, and he's got a sweet tongue on him when he talks to the ladies, no denying that! So we agreed a price plus a bit more for her doing the cleaning and a bit of cooking sometimes, so everyone's pleased all round.'

'Aye, sounds nice and cosy,' said Wield. 'Bit of cooking, you say? Does a lot of entertaining, does he?'

'Shouldn't think so. What Maisie does is casseroles and such for Mr Roote hisself. Puts them in the freezer. Of course he's well secluded, so I suppose he could be having wild parties every night, but the only folk I've ivver noticed ganging up that lane is Tom Parker and yon Denham lad on his bike.'

'Sir Edward, you mean?'

'Aye. Rides like a maniac. Yon things should be banned, that's what I say.'

He didn't except present company, Wield noted, as he said thanks and climbed back on to the Thunderbird.

A couple of minutes later he slowed down as he spotted the skeletal outline of a huge dead tree against the evening sky. There was the lane end. And Farmer Sedgwick had been right about the sign too, though perhaps not in every particular, thought Wield, as he toed aside some veiling nettles to reveal a lump of granite with *Lyke Farm Barn* painted on it in flaking white gloss.

An ancient gate, attached to an even older flaking sandstone gatepost, barred entrance to the lane. It moved smoothly enough on its rusty hinges but it still must be a bloody nuisance to a guy in a wheelchair.

He rode carefully up the lane. Its surface was rutted

and potholed, fine for a tractor or 4x4 perhaps, but day after day it couldn't do an ordinary car's suspension any good. When it rained, it must be a quagmire. After a hundred yards or so, above the roar of his own engine he heard another engine start up, and as he rounded a bend which brought a building into view, another motorbike came hurtling towards him, moving at twice his speed, with the black-leathered rider crouched low over the handlebars. For a second collision seemed inevitable. Wield came to a halt and prepared to abandon ship. Then the other rider leaned sideways and swept past close enough for him to feel the wind of his passing.

'Wanker!' yelled Wield.

It had all happened too quickly for him to get the number, but at a guess he'd have said the bike was a Buell Lightning, the long-base model.

He set off once more. Soon the track ran into a cobbled yard where a blue Kangoo was parked before the converted barn. Long and low and covered with cream-coloured pebbledash, it showed little of its origins except perhaps for a disproportionately wide front doorway, which must be very useful to a wheelchair user.

The door was open and as Wield dismounted a figure in a wheelchair appeared on the threshold.

'Sergeant Wield! How nice to see you. I wondered who would come. Still riding the Thunderbird, I see. I thought I recognized that throaty growl as you came up the lane.'

The greeting was perfect in its form, but Roote's voice was a little breathless and his face a little flushed.

'I wonder you could hear anything above the noise made by yon Lightning. Was that Edward Denham? I thought he were going to ride right through me.'

'Oh dear,' said Roote. 'I'm sorry about that. Yes. It was Teddy. Well spotted, and you've only been here two minutes! Your reputation for thoroughness is well deserved. I'll read Ted the riot act, or perhaps the Road Safety Act would be more appropriate. Happily you survived and it's so good to see you, Sergeant Wield. How are you? You look so well, hardly changed at all.'

'I'm fine, Mr Roote,' said Wield, wondering what had brought Ted Denham round to Lyke Farm Barn on this particular night.

'Come in, do,' said Roote, spinning the chair around and leading the way into a living room simply furnished with a low table and a wood-framed three-piece suite standing on a granite-flagged floor. The walls were whitewashed and there was no ceiling, just the sharp vee of the cruck-beamed roof, giving the room a slightly churchy feel. The twenty-first century was represented by a small flat-screen TV hung on one of the end walls and a wheelchair-height computer work station.

Observing his visitor take all this in, Roote said, 'There were rugs on the floor to make it all seem a bit more homely, but I asked Maisie if she'd mind taking them away. That way I get a smoother run and she gets more wear out of her rugs.'

'That would be Mrs Sedgwick?'

'Sorry, I should have said. But what need when talking to Sergeant Wield? Anyone dear Peter rates so high is always going to be one step ahead of the game. How is he, by the way? And his lovely wife? And of course, their delightful daughter?'

Wield felt a frisson of pleasure at the praise at the same time as he consigned it to the recycle bin. His personal acquaintance with Roote was much slighter than Pascoe's or Dalziel's, but from listening to them and studying the records, he knew he was dealing with a master of misdirection who made most political spin-doctors look like *Blue Peter* presenters.

'They're grand, all of them,' he said.

'Great! Now, can I offer you some refreshment, Mr Wield?' said Roote. 'No alcohol, of course. You're on duty. But I know how duty can devour time unawares for you chaps, leaving precious little space to devour anything else. So a cup of tea and a slice of cake? Maisie bakes an incredible Madeira loaf.'

'Thanks, no,' said Wield. 'Just a few questions then I'll be out of your hair.'

'No problem there then,' grinned Roote, running a hand over his shaven skull. 'Sorry. Nervous frivolity. This is a truly terrible business with ramifications beyond the immediate ghastly tragedy. But I do not doubt your sensors have already begun to trace those out.'

'Always glad to use local knowledge to point us on the right track,' said Wield invitingly. When witnesses tried to control the direction of an interview, he often found it helpful to give them their head and see where they led.

'Lady Denham is . . . sorry . . . was a very important figure in Sandytown. I don't just mean socially, but economically. The times they are a-changing, Mr Wield, and a-changing faster than ever before. To stand still is to decline. Development is all, and here in Sandytown the main thrust of development has been in the safe hands of our two charismatic figures, Lady D herself and Tom Parker. Have you met Tom yet?'

'No, but he's being interviewed,' said Wield. 'Got on all right, did they?'

Roote frowned and said, 'Impossible not to get on with Tom, though it's true he and Lady D are two very different characters. In the hands of either alone, the good ship Sandytown would probably have quickly foundered – on the reefs of quick profits and personal gain under the captaincy of Lady D, or the shoals of vague idealism and personal obsession under the helmsmanship of Tom Parker. In other words, together they formed a team greater than the sum of its parts. Alas, with dear Daphne gone . . .'

He shook his head and looked tragic. He did it very well, Wield had to admit. Out of the mouth of many people those fancy words would have sounded merely overblown, but Roote gave them real force and life.

He said, 'You're saying mebbe this could be a motive for killing Lady Denham? Wanting to wreck what she were doing in this consortium?'

'On Tom's part? Impossible. But others might see things differently, so it's a possibility. You might want to add it to your list of the usual motives.'

'Them being?'

'Money – who inherits? Sex – who has been scorned or impeded? Mental disturbance – who's off their chump?' replied Roote promptly.

'You've obviously thought a bit about this.'

'I had several years to contemplate the field of murder investigation, Sergeant Wield, with especial attention to the errors that an early false premise can lead even an honest and conscientious investigator into.'

He looked Wield straight in the eyes as he said this.

If he'd been selling me a used car, I'd be reaching for my wallet, thought the sergeant, who found he was almost enjoying himself. Nowt one expert likes more than seeing another at the top of his game.

But enough was enough. He'd seen where Roote wanted to take him, now it was time to rein him in.

'Right,' he said. 'Thanks for that. Now about the party at Sandytown Hall. What time did you arrive, Mr Roote?'

He took out his notebook, opened it, clicked his ballpoint, and held it poised to write. But the young man was not ready so easily to concede control.

'No need for that, Mr Wield,' he said smiling. 'I knew you'd want a statement so the first thing I did when I got back here with everything still fresh in my mind, was . . .'

He picked up a plastic folder from the floor and handed it over.

'. . . write this.'

Wield opened the folder.

Statement of Francis Xavier Roote of Lyke Farm Barn, nr Sandytown, Yorkshire

'Why don't I make us that cup of tea while you cast your eye over it, then you can ask any supplementary questions and I'll sign it in your presence?' said Roote.

'I'm impressed, Mr Roote,' said Wield. 'Bet if I'd come to arrest you, I'd have found you in handcuffs.'

Roote exploded a laugh.

'I can see you and I are going to get along famously, Sergeant,' he said.

He went towards a door which opened at his approach, giving Wield a glimpse into a kitchen. Everything was at wheelchair height: work surfaces, sink, electric oven. Presumably Roote had paid for the alteration and would have to pay for the restoration when he vacated the property. The rumours of the high level of compensation, obtained in part at least through Pascoe's efforts, must be true. A set-up like this, plus automatic doors, wouldn't come cheap. Wield found the low-level oven in particular brought home the change in the young man's life even more than the sight of him in a wheelchair. He concentrated his attention on the statement.

It was clear in language, precise in description, concise in expression. Every sighting of Lady Denham was high-lit. None sounded significant. The only bit that caught Wield's interest came towards the end. When the storm started Roote had taken shelter in the conservatory where he sat in a quiet corner watching the play of lightning in the eastern sky.

As the storm receded, feeling the need for some air, I left the conservatory and went out on to the paved area. I saw someone move in the shrubbery at the end of the lawn. I only got a glimpse and this in poor light at a distance of say twenty-five to thirty metres, but I'm sure he had a beard. The only person I saw at the party with a beard was Gordon Godley, the healer, but I could not say definitely it was him. If anything the man more closely resembled Harold, known as Hen, Hollis, brother of Lady Denham's first husband. Against this, Hen's reaction to his brother's will had led to an estrangement from Lady D and I knew that he was unlikely to have been invited to the hog-roast.

Curious as to why anyone would have stayed out there in the rain, I rolled my chair on to the grass and went to investigate. Unfortunately the lower end of the lawn was so soggy after the downpour that the wheels of my chair sank and I found myself stuck. To make matters worse the rain, which had slackened off to a few negligible drops, suddenly returned for what proved to be a final flurry, provoking me to make such an effort to move that I tipped the whole thing over and ended up sprawled on the lawn. There I remained till others came out of the house and Petula Sheldon, head nurse at the Avalon Clinic, rescued me and wheeled me back to dry land.

Shortly afterwards the body of poor Lady Denham was discovered. For a while all was confusion. In a wheelchair, soaking wet, and extremely distressed by the news, I could see no way that I could assist. So, confident that details of all the guests would be made available to the authorities, I followed the example of many others and went home where, after changing my clothes, I prepared this statement.

Signed in the presence of .... by...............

Roote was still clattering crockery in the kitchen, a little more loudly than necessary?

Mebbe he wants to give me time to poke around, thought Wield. Happy to oblige!

He rose and went to the work station. It was a top-of-the-range set-up. A clued-up operator could probably go almost anywhere he wanted on this. Tempting for a man in a wheelchair . . . no, Wield corrected, tempting for any clued-up operator, as he knew!

'Questions?' said Roote, appearing out of the kitchen with a tea tray bearing mugs, teapot, milk jug, sugar bowl, and a cake set across the arms of his wheelchair.

'Aye. Did you see this bearded man again when you were out on the lawn?'

'No, I didn't,' said Roote. 'I thought I heard some movement in the shrubbery, as though someone were pushing through it, but I actually saw nothing more.'

'Pity,' said Wield returning to his chair. 'And it's a

pity you didn't hang around to give this bit of information to us a lot sooner, Mr Roote. You're not the only person who had time to get home, change his clothes and dry himself off.'

'I've no idea what time you arrived at the Hall, Mr Wield, but I suspect the person I saw would have had ample time to do all that anyway.'

'Mebbe so, but you could have told Sergeant Whitby, who got there a lot sooner.'

'Ah yes. Sergeant Whitby.'

Had he put into words what his tone implied, Wield might have felt impelled by his sergeant union loyalty to offer a defence. As it was he answered silence with silence and accepted the mug of tea that Roote poured for him.

So much for taking control of the interview, he reflected as he sank his teeth into a slice of Madeira cake. At least in his assessment of this Roote had been completely accurate. It was delicious.

'So, may I sign it?' said the young man.

'Aye, it'll do. For now.'

Roote took the statement and signed it with a flourish, then handed it back and watched as Wield countersigned.

Then he said, 'Now tell me about dear Peter Pascoe. Does he know I'm here? When may I hope to see him?'

'Aye, he knows. Sir Edward tell you he was here?'

'Yes, I believe he did. Though I would have guessed. With poor Mr Dalziel *hors de combat* at the Avalon, who else would be entrusted with a case of such moment?'

'You've met Mr Dalziel then?'

'Oh yes. Fate threw us together, though it can't have been too arduous a task for Fate in a place the size of Sandytown. Not altogether himself, I felt, but

297

majestic though in ruin. The second occasion we met, I was glad to see him getting closer to his old self. In fact, the improvement was so marked I felt able to ask his assistance with my appeal.'

'Your appeal?'

'For a review of my conviction, which I hope may result in a pardon.'

Wield drank some tea then said in a voice as flat as Norfolk, 'You asked the superintendent to help you appeal against your conviction?'

'That's right.'

Wield drank some more tea.

'And he said . . .?'

'He undertook to give it serious consideration. I always found him a man open to reason and compassion: His outward semblance doth belie his soul's immensity.'

Wield finished his tea.

There must be something in it, he thought. Magic mushrooms maybe.

He folded the statement, put it in his notebook, stood up and said, 'I'd best be off. Thanks for the tea. And the cake. By the way, what brought you here to Sandytown?'

It was meant to be casual, but Roote grinned broadly and said, 'Of course. You'll need to be debriefed by Peter. The answer is, familiarity and coincidence, Mr Wield. When I finally gave up my quest for a cure and resolved to return to England, where else would I come but Yorkshire, which has played such a significant part in my life?'

'Like getting you jailed, getting you shot and getting you crippled?' said Wield, thinking, If the bugger wants straight talk, let him have it!

298

'Indeed, though I try not to dwell on those things. Fate may have decreed I live my life like a gnome, but I try to record it like a gnomon, telling only the sunlit hours.'

He paused as if anticipating applause, though whether for his mental resolution or verbal convolution wasn't clear. Wield's face remained as unreadable as a footballer's biography. Roote smiled and went on, 'That explains Yorkshire. But why Sandytown? you wonder. During my wanderings around Europe in my vain search for restoration – I even visited Lourdes, God help me! – which He didn't – the best palliative care I encountered was at one of my first ports of call, the Avalon Clinic at Davos. I returned there last year when I finally admitted defeat. Not for treatment – I knew I was beyond that – but because I needed to be somewhere that I would get understanding without pity. To be accepted is the first step to acceptance, wouldn't you agree, Mr Wield?'

Wield said, 'Mebbe,' and glanced surreptitiously at his watch.

'To cut a longish story short,' resumed Roote, 'I was disappointed to find that Herr Professor Doktor Alvin Kling, the Head of the Clinic, with whom I had struck up a good relationship, was away on a six-month exchange with a colleague. But I soon found that the man he'd exchanged with, Lester Feldenhammer, was even more on my wavelength. Talking to him, plus of course my renewed involvement with Third Thought, brought me back fully to the realization that life must be tasted to the full, not wasted in pursuit of a vain dream. And when I discovered that Lester's home clinic was the Avalon here in Yorkshire, it seemed like a sign. So back in

January I relocated here, and it was the best move I ever made.'

Wouldn't be difficult, seeing where your other moves got you, thought Wield.

'How did Dr Feldenhammer take it?' he asked.

'He was delighted. From being a patient, I was converted to being a kind of colleague, unpaid, of course. Lester has such an open and receptive mind. Most mainstream medical practitioners would have found Tom Parker's enthusiasm for alternative therapies at best quirky, at worst positively dangerous. But Lester has thrown his own energy and the resources of the Avalon wholly behind Tom's Festival of Health.'

Wield looked at his watch again, this time openly, and said, 'Very interesting. Now I'd best be off. Thanks again.'

'My pleasure. And you'll give Peter my fond regards, and tell him I should love to see him. But it's his call. If he's uncomfortable with the idea, I shall completely understand. This must be a very important case for him, I'd guess.'

'Oh? Why's that?'

'With Mr Dalziel *hors de combat* . . . need I say more? I very much hope Peter does well.'

'I'll tell him. Bye now.'

As he rode away, Wield tried to score his encounter with Franny Roote. The best he could get it to was a points draw, but in his heart it felt like the man in the wheelchair had shaded it. It was a small comfort to remember a remark of Dalziel's: *If you ever find yourself thinking you've got the better of yon bugger, that's when you're in real trouble.*

His mobile rang as he approached the lane end. He

halted, put the phone to his ear and said, 'Wield . . . what? Hang on . . . reception's lousy.'

He ran the bike out of the crowding trees on to the road.

'That any better? OK, Hat. What were you saying?'

He listened, then said, 'Have you contacted Mr Pascoe? Do it! I'm on my way.'

And thrusting Franny Roote right out of his mind, he set the Thunderbird roaring back towards Sandytown.

10

As Peter Pascoe approached the Avalon Clinic, he had a dilemma.

Who should he contact first – the two witnesses, Dr Feldenhammer and Nurse Sheldon – or Andy Dalziel?

Proper procedure required that as chief investigating officer he made straight for the witnesses.

But Dalziel, though on sick leave, was still his boss, and having been on the spot for a little while he might be able to provide some useful background . . .

No, scrub that!

It was simply an excuse to mask his awareness that one of the horns of his dilemma was bigger and sharper and could penetrate a lot deeper than the other, an awareness heightened by what he now acknowledged was a growing taste for independence.

During his years in Mid-Yorkshire CID, Pascoe had grown used to being answerable only to himself and Dalziel. The Fat Man's absence had left a huge gap which no other senior figure could possibly fill. At first he was always aware of it. But in the last week or so he had felt it less and less, not because anyone was filling it, but because he himself had somehow expanded into the space.

Eventually Daddy Bear would come back home and

bump Goldilocks out of his bed. That was an inevitable part of the scheme of things. But it belonged in the future. In the present Dalziel was a convalescing colleague, taken out of the loop both by medical regime and bureaucratic regulation, and not even the unfortunate coincidence of a big case exploding right on his doorstep entitled him to move back into his old space.

So, dilemma solved. Professional duty first, sick visits second.

The golden gates of Avalon loomed ahead. He peeped his horn. A man emerged from a small gatehouse, opened the gates and waved him forward.

He drew up alongside the gatekeeper and wound down his window.

'Detective Chief Inspector Pascoe to see Dr Feldenhammer.'

Behind him Pascoe heard his rear door open. The car's suspension sighed under a sudden weight. He looked in his mirror knowing what he would see. It was still a shock. Though it shouldn't have been. Why would God leave important decisions to mere mortals when he could so easily take them himself?

'You took your time,' said that all too familiar voice. 'OK, Stan, this is the bugger I were telling thee about.'

'Right, Mr Dalziel. I'll see you later.'

The gatekeeper waved the car forward.

Pascoe obeyed.

'Bear left here,' commanded the Fat Man. 'That's it, towards the old house.'

'Where, no doubt, I shall find Dr Feldenhammer,' said Pascoe, trying to get back on even terms.

'Don't be daft. Old Festerwhanger can wait. Any road he's got Pet up there with him. Probably giving her one. Common reaction to some traumatic episodes, that's what the book says.'

This was the point to stop the car and resume control. Instead Pascoe heard himself ask, 'Whose book? And who is Pet?'

'Pet Sheldon, head nurse. And Fester's own book. *Post-traumatic Stress – a patient's guide*. Catchy title, eh? You'll likely have seen the movie. He gave me a copy. Bet he didn't think I'd read it, but I whipped through it, looking for the mucky bits. Park here.'

Pascoe brought the car to a halt but he kept the engine running. He'd made up his mind. This was as far as he was going.

'Sir . . .' he began, but it was too late. The rear door had opened, and the car almost sighed its relief as the Fat Man got out and set off towards the house, not once looking back to check he was followed.

'Shit,' said Pascoe, and got out.

They crossed a terrace area where a few people sat at small circular wrought-iron tables, drinking coffee or wine. The early evening air was balmy. The storm had merely freshened things up, not signalled the end of summer. The drinkers could have been guests at an Italian villa watching *il Duce* returning from an evening stroll, followed by his faithful bodyguard.

The process ended in a bedroom which looked up to luxury hotel standards. A couple of stars at least above the Cedars, the police convalescent home. Was Cap footing the bill? Couldn't see Dalziel going along with that. Maybe he had insurance. Or maybe a grateful criminal community had taken up a subscription to keep him out of the way.

'Look, sir . . .' he tried again, but the Fat Man cut across, saying, 'First things first. Sit yourself down.'

He opened a drawer and took out a bottle of scotch and two glasses.

Pascoe lowered himself into the single armchair and watched as Dalziel poured an inch of liquor into one glass, three inches into the other.

To Pascoe's surprise, he received the larger measure.

'Slainte!' said the Fat Man, flopping on the bed. 'Welcome to Zombie land. Good to see you, Pete, even though you've not brought any grapes.'

'Like you say, I'm on duty . . .'

'Always mek time to pick the flowers along the way, lad. Or the grapes. Any road, what's the verdict?'

'Early days and I've got an open mind,' said Pascoe.

'Eh? On me, not the case, you daft bugger! You've been running your eye over me like an Aberdeen undertaker wondering whether to charge by the inch or the ounce.'

'I think I'll tell them to put the flowers on hold,' said Pascoe. 'Seriously, you're looking fine. Much more like your old self, and your old self must know that, unless you know something pertinent to my investigation, I should not be here socializing.'

'Pertinent? Socializing? Ee, I've missed you, lad, but not a lot. Right, let's make it official. Questions?'

'Let's start with basics. Were you acquainted with the deceased?'

'Buffalo woman, you mean. Daph Denham. Aye, met her a couple of times. First time were in the Hope and Anchor. That's our local. Nice drop of ale. Landlord knows his beer and knows how to keep his customers happy. Name of Hollis . . .'

'That's a name that keeps cropping up,' said Pascoe, looking at his list. 'That would be Alan . . .?'

'Right. Good lad. They're all relatives of the famous

305

Hog Hollis, tha knows, the Taste of Yorkshire. Any road, that's where me and Daph first met. Didn't make a good impression. In fact she looked at me like I'd just escaped from Dartmoor. Couldn't really blame her as I'd lost one of my slippers. But things were different when I saw her at Fester's party day before yesterday ...'

'Fester's party?' interrupted Pascoe, seeking sense in this surreal flow.

'Lester Feldenhammer's party. It's one mad round of pleasure here. Kill or cure, that's the Avalon motto. Where was I? Buffalo woman. She gave me the glad eye. Naturally I thought mebbe she'd succumbed to me boyish charm – seems she were a bit of a goer, by all accounts – bit long in the tooth, but there's many a good tune played on an old double bass . . .'

'Could we stick to the point?' said Pascoe sharply. 'Presuming there is one!'

'Ooh, hoity toity! What's next? Rubber truncheons? I didn't talk to her at the party. To tell the truth, I weren't feeling too clever. But yesterday morning, she came bursting into my room, like a heifer on heat.'

'Just tell me what she wanted,' said Pascoe wearily.

'Nowt really. Usual daft woman's stuff,' said Dalziel casually. 'She wanted to tap into my constabulary expertise. She'd got some silly notion into her head that someone were trying to kill her.'

I should have known it, thought Pascoe. The old sod enjoys jerking me around, but he'd not get in my way unless he thought it was important.

'You got details, I presume?' he said.

'Oh yes,' said Dalziel. 'I've got details.'

He stuck his right hand under the mattress and came out with what looked like an MP3 player.

306

He's going to play some music in case we're being bugged, guessed Pascoe.

'Meet Mildred, memory on a stick,' said Dalziel almost proudly. 'State-of-the-art recorder, more sensitive than a parson's dick. Present from Fester. Thinks keeping an audio diary could have a beneficiary effect, therapeutically speaking.'

Nice piece of mimicry – if Feldenhammer spoke like W. C. Fields!

What next? wondered Pascoe. Dalziel bragging about state-of-the-art technology was like that first chord from Dylan's electric guitar.

'And has it?' he asked.

To his surprise, Dalziel didn't snort a blasphemous denial, but hesitated a moment before saying, 'Don't know. Mebbe it has. Any road, like I say, it's useful for filling in the gaps till me memory catches up with me bones. More important here, it'll carry on recording even if I've got it stuck in my pocket.'

'You mean you actually recorded what Lady Denham said to you?' said Pascoe, amazed. 'But why . . .?'

'I had it handy when she burst in, and just in case it really were my lily-white body she was after, I switched on. I've got my reputation to think of, tha knows. But for once, I were wrong. Listen.'

He pressed a button and a woman's voice, strong, deep, authoritative, began to speak.

11

I'm sorry to trouble you, Superintendent.

You're not troubling me, not yet anyway. But if you keep catching me in my dressing gown, people may start talking. Have a seat. Oh, you have done. So what can I do for you, luv?

I think someone is trying to kill me.

Doesn't surprise me. Nay, don't take it personal. What I mean is, you'd need to be a saint to get to your age without someone wanting you dead. I can think of a dozen right off who'd dance barefoot on my grave even if I got buried in a midden, which is where the same folk would like me put. But if you're really worried, I'd get in touch with the police.

You are the police.

Nay, lass, tha's right and tha's wrong. I'm an off-duty, convalescing cop. I mean, if I were a convalescing plumber, you'd not ring the Avalon and ask if I could come down to unblock your drain, would you? You want to contact your local station. Who've you got in this neck of the woods? Oh aye, I remember. Sergeant Whitby, old Jug. He's no speed merchant, but he's sound is old Jug. He'll see you right.

He's a nincompoop. I knew his father and he was a nincompoop too. In fact, I don't recollect any of the Whitby family who weren't nincompoops. If I were going to do this officially, Superintendent, I'd ring Dan Trimble, your Chief

Constable, whose wife I know quite well. But the effect would be the same as if I called Sergeant Whitby.

Nay, hang about. I know the Chief's only three foot tall and he comes from Cornwall, but that's no reason to say he's a nincompoop too . . .

That's not what I'm saying. Only that if I make an official complaint, then this becomes . . . official! Policemen about the place, statements, everyone noticing and asking what's going on. That's one thing I know about Sandytown: if they don't know your business before you do it, they'll certainly find out the day after. I don't want whoever's trying to kill me to be alerted. I thought that someone like you, who comes with the most glowing testimonials . . .

Must be them rough towels they give us here. Who's been talking about me, Daph?

I'm not at liberty to say, but I've been assured you are one of the best detectives in the country. I think the exact phrase was, if Sherlock Holmes's elder brother had had an elder brother, it would be Andy Dalziel. There, what do you think of that?

I think you shouldn't take everything Franny Roote says as gospel.

I didn't say it was Mr Roote.

Aye, and the Pope doesn't say he goes to church on Sunday. Listen, here's what I'll do. You tell me what's on your mind and if I think it's worth bothering busy bobbies with, I'll pass it on. Don't worry. I've got this lad I'm training up. He's minding the shop while I'm away and he's so discreet he's got murderers serving life who don't know yet he's arrested them. That's the best I can do. Otherwise it's Jug Whitby.

You don't leave me much choice.

Don't fret. It's over-rated, choice. So what's the tale?

For a start, I'd like you to know you're not dealing with

309

a silly hysterical old woman. Over the years I have grown used to being threatened. Anti-hunt demonstrators and animal rights extremists have been attacking my property and threatening my person almost as long as I can remember. It's water off a duck's back. I take precautions, I am not fool-hardy. But I don't let them spoil my sleep or my appetite. In addition, when Hollis, my first husband, died . . .

Him that got et by his pigs?

That's right. I sometimes think if he'd died trying to save the Queen from drowning, people would have been more likely to forget the circumstances. When he died, I received phone calls and hate mail containing foul accusations and personal threats. Again, when Denham, my second, died . . .

Remind me. Trying to save the Queen, were it?

A hunting accident. Once more there were phone calls and letters, not the same as before . . .

Well, they wouldn't be, luv. Better class of abuse when there's a title involved.

I hope you are taking this seriously, Superintendent.

Of course I am. And stop calling me superintendent. Andy'll do. And you're Daph, right? So can we speed things up a bit? I've not been well lately and it's hard to concentrate.

I'm sorry. I'll try. Eventually the spate that followed Sir Harry's death became a trickle. The trickle is always there. Graffiti, animal parts through the post. The odd phone call. Those I choose to ignore. Then recently these onslaughts began to take another form, much less aggressive on the surface, but somehow I found it more disturbing.

Oh aye. What were that then?

I started getting communications through the post from various animal charities, the mainstream ones, not just the extremists. They said they were delighted to hear I was interested in remembering them in my will and enclosed their bequest packs to show the best way of going about this.

We all get that kind of stuff, luv.

Perhaps. But I must confess it was upsetting. Then last week I got a letter. Its tone was mild yet I felt more threatened by it than anything else I'd ever received. It said the writer hoped I'd taken the chance of modifying my will along the lines suggested in recent mail-shots.

But no specific threat?

Judge for yourself. I have it here. I thought you might need it for examination.

Didn't know I were going to sit one. No, I'm not up to close reading so early in the morning. Just give us the gist.

It says: We all owe a debt to God and the longer we live, the closer the reckoning comes. A woman of your age would be well advised to have her affairs in order. *Then here it says:* It is likely that the door by which you will make your exit from this world already stands unlatched. *Is that threatening or not?*

Poetic, and that can be a bit of a menace. I can see how it might bother someone with a nervous disposition. Can't see it worrying you overmuch, luv.

You're right. I put it aside and went about my business. Then a few days ago, the brakes on my car failed. I was coming down the hill from North Cliff and braking to turn into my drive. I managed to change down and come to a halt by sliding into one of my rhododendron bushes.

That's what the gods invented rhododendrons for, upper-class traffic control. That it?

No, it's not. A couple of times recently I have glimpsed a trespasser in the grounds of the Hall. I realize that these days the law is almost toothless when it comes to dealing with trespass . . .

311

Aye, not like the good old days when a couple of man-traps and a blast with a shotgun would have got things sorted.

Just so. Nevertheless, I would certainly have confronted this person, but he or she took off very quickly when I shouted.

There you are then. No harm done. Likely some poor peasant taking a shortcut.

Perhaps. But yesterday morning I was going down the cliff path from my garden to the beach. It's an easy descent to start with, then you reach a long ledge where the cliff falls away sheer for fifty or sixty feet. A guard-rail starts here and then follows the path for the rest of its descent. I'd just reached the ledge when I heard a noise and looked up to see a large lump of rock bouncing down the path towards me. I leaned back on the rail to get out of the way, it broke free from its support, and I found myself hanging on for grim life looking down at the rocks below. Fortunately the next support held and I was able to pull myself back on to the path without too much difficulty. I am lucky to have a strong constitution. A frailer woman would almost certainly have fallen.

Aye, lot of frail women around, thank God. So what did you do?

I had a look at the rail. The support is a metal stanchion but the rail is made of wood. There was some sign of wood rot, but it looked to me as if someone had carefully eased the rail from its support then put it back so that it looked completely safe.

Don't know why you need a detective, Daph, when you're so good yourself. Can we hurry this up? I'm beginning to remember an urgent appointment. What next?

I rang my nephew, Teddy.

That 'ud be the good-looking lad who fancies himself? So why'd you ring him?

Well, I'm a woman living alone, more or less, so I suppose I naturally turned to a close male relative in time of stress . . .

Bollocks! He's hot favourite in the inheritance stakes, right? So when you got it into your noddle someone had fixed your guard rail and was hoying rocks down at you in the hope of making you fall, you thought, I wonder where young Ted the Heir is?

Mr Dalziel, that's outrageous . . .

No it's not, and you know it's not. And it's Andy. And were he at home?

Yes, he was, though why he was at home when I pay him good money to be at work, I'm not quite sure.

No sense of responsibility, these modern kids. So did you mention your concerns?

No. I got distracted by various things. He told me, I mean he reminded me, about the get-together at the Avalon so I said I'd meet him and Esther there. That's his sister.

Aye, I met her. What about the broken rail? You get anyone to fix it?

Ollie Hollis was at the Hall. I asked him to take a look.

Ollie Hollis? Who's he? A visiting relative?

Not really, though he is a member of my first husband's rather extensive family. He was getting the machinery ready for my hog-roast tomorrow.

So what is he? Carpenter? Mechanic?

No. He's a gate-man at the pig farm.

By God, you know how to pick your experts, luv! So what did he say?

I didn't ask his opinion. I had no desire to set tongues clacking. He bound it up with strong twine and put a warning notice on it. Hardly necessary, as it's a private path and anyone else uses it at their own risk. But with my grounds full of guests for my hog-roast tomorrow, it's better to be safe than sorry.

Good advice, Daph. I think mebbe you should try taking it.

I'm not sure what you mean, Super . . . Mr Dal—, Andy.

What I mean is, likely this is all much ado about nowt. But in the unlikely event someone were trying to top you, I'd say from long experience most likely motive is money. So, though I suspect you've nowt to worry about, just to be on the safe side, simple thing is to take away the motive. Change your will, and make sure you let every bugger interested know! That way it makes more sense for them to keep you alive long enough to change it back again! And that's it, luv. No charge. Now it's time for me to take a shower and get dressed. No need to rush off, I'm too old to be embarrassed.

Good day to you, Mr Dalziel!

12

The Fat Man switched off the recorder.

'There we go,' he said. 'Don't know if I'd have said much different if I'd been really on the ball when she came to see me. But I felt right guilty when I heard the news.'

'You sound as if you rather liked her,' said Pascoe.

'Aye, mebbe I did. She were a big bossy woman, used to rolling over folk who got in her way like an anker of ale, but she must have been a bonny lass once, and she still had a gallon of jimp left in her. It were a lousy way for anyone to go. For someone like Daph Denham, it were a right shame.'

Pascoe said, 'She had a record, you know. Laid into a hunt protester with her riding crop. Fined and bound over.'

'And that means she deserved to end up being grilled on her own hog-roast?'

'I didn't say that, as you well know. I'm just saying there could be more people out there than we think with motives. Did she leave the letter she mentioned?'

'Aye, here it is. Not much good for forensics – I just stuffed it in me dressing gown.'

'Still worth a try,' said Pascoe, taking the crumpled sheet by one corner and slipping it into an evidence bag. He smoothed it out inside the clear plastic. Ink jet printer he guessed, on good quality A5 paper. No date, no preamble, just the message.

You should by now have had time to study the options for leaving legacies to some of the major animal charities, thereby making in death a small atonement for the many cruelties you have inflicted on the animal kingdom in life. Time is short, do not delay. We all owe a debt to God and the longer we live, the closer the reckoning comes. A woman of your age would be well advised to have her affairs in order, for by the time you recieve this letter it is likely that the door by which you will make your exit from this world already stands unlatched.

'Interesting,' said Pascoe.

'That the best you can do?' said Dalziel scornfully. 'So what's next, mastermind? Bring me up to date. This has been one-way traffic so far.'

Pascoe was tempted to point out that this was the usual direction of flow between witness and investigator, but decided not to force the issue. It was hard enough not to sound as if he were seeking approval as he outlined the situation.

The Fat Man said, 'What's this Ollie Hollis got to say for himself? He was in charge of the roast, right? What was he doing when poor old Daph got stuck in the basket?'

'I haven't caught up with him yet,' said Pascoe. 'Like most of the guests, he'd gone walkabout by the time we got there.'

'He weren't a guest. And why didn't Jug Whitby make sure he stayed?'

'I presume he'd already gone by the time Whitby

showed. He's out looking for Hollis now. Why do you call him Jug? Has he got big ears?'

'Whitby, Dracula, jugular, do you know nowt? You need to get a grip on things, Pete. Three hours in and you've still got key witnesses wandering around loose. Pin the buggers down, that's the first rule, and don't let 'em loose till you've squeezed 'em dry!'

'Always good to have your input, sir,' murmured Pascoe, determined not to be provoked. 'And thank you for bringing me up to speed about these threats.'

'Glad to help, lad. Think there's owt there for you?'

'Well, if this letter is anything to go by, the written threats were hardly graphic. As for the alleged attempts, even if they turn out to be genuine, they're of a very different nature from what actually happened.'

'They'd have got Daph dead, that's a lot to have in common.'

'Yes, but the intention was to make it look like an accident. This hog-roast thing is very different. It's theatrical, it's grand guignol, it's sick! And it's unnecessarily risky. Instead of hiding the body and heading off to establish an alibi, the killer removes the pig from the hog-roast basket and substitutes the corpse, all very time consuming. The storm is passing. There's a growing chance of someone strolling along and catching you at it. But it's a risk you are willing to take. Why? It feels to me like there's something deeper and darker than simple greed involved here. This feels like a statement.'

'Ee, you do talk pretty, Pete. Must save you a fortune in tuppeny books,' said the Fat Man.

'That's why I'm so rich. Look, Andy, I need to see Feldenhammer, so unless there's anything else . . .'

'I'll think on. I'm not going anywhere.'

Why did it sound like a threat?

'You've been very helpful,' said Pascoe. 'By the way, it would be useful if I could borrow the recording you made of your chat with Lady Denham.'

Dalziel pursed his lips and said, 'It's not on tape, tha knows. It's a hard disk.'

'Yes, it would be; as you said, state of the art,' said Pascoe, still finding it hard to come to grips with this new technocratic Dalziel. Then it dawned. There was stuff on the disk the Fat Man didn't want him to hear.

He said, 'How about if I get Wieldy along to transcribe it?'

Dalziel considered then said, 'Don't see why not.'

'Great. Now I'll be on my way to see the doctor. Take care.'

In the doorway he paused and said, 'Sir, why didn't you tell me Franny Roote was here? You knew I'd been searching for him.'

The question came despite his resolve to put personal matters on the back burner.

Dalziel didn't answer straightaway but raised his glass to his lips. To Pascoe's surprise, he didn't drink, only sniffed. Then with the clear reluctance of Caesar pushing aside the proffered crown, he set the glass on the bedside table.

'Eyes greedier than my belly these days,' he said sadly. 'Roote says I should think of it as an opportunity, not a problem. But that's the way yon bugger sees most things.'

'Like spending his life in a wheelchair, you mean?' said Pascoe sharply.

'Aye, that too. Get the sympathy vote. Looked to me like he were setting his cap at Clara Brereton. Bit skinny, but I expect her having a rich fat aunt compensated.'

'What are you suggesting, Andy?' demanded Pascoe.

'Me? Nowt! Except maybe he's a cunning bastard, but you know that already.'

Pascoe, refusing to be provoked, said, 'You didn't answer my question. Why didn't you let me know he was here?'

'He told me he'd dropped out of contact 'cos he didn't want you feeling responsible for him any more,' said Dalziel. 'And I believed him. OK?'

Before Pascoe could reply, his mobile rang.

He took it out, glanced at the display, said, 'Lousy signal in here,' waved the phone in farewell and closed the door firmly behind him.

As he strode down the corridor he put the mobile to his ear, and said, 'Hi, Hat.'

By the time he'd finished listening he was alongside his car.

He said, 'I'm on my way.'

For a moment he hesitated, looking back at the building. It felt disloyal to take off without letting the Fat Man know he'd changed his plans, and why.

But as history teaches us, loyalty is always the first casualty of independence.

He started up the engine and headed back towards the main gates.

13

After interviewing Sidney Parker, Hat Bowler had planned to drive down North Cliff Road to call on the next witness on his list, a woman called Lee who lived near the bottom of the hill in a house with the suggestive name of Witch Cottage.

But what Parker had told him, plus some further information extracted during the course of an enjoyably flirty fifteen-minute chat with the hotel receptionist, made him change his mind. The way these country folk gossiped, it wouldn't be long before everyone on the team knew that Hen Hollis who'd designed the hog-roast machinery was a notorious hater of the victim. So no point hanging around if he wanted to be ahead of the pack, by which of course he meant Shirley Novello.

According to the receptionist, Hen lived in a cottage just off the coast road a couple of miles south of the town. Her directions proved less than helpful. She assumed that everyone knew when she said first left, she didn't include a tarmacked lane that quickly turned into a boggy track leading nowhere. And what need to mention what surely everyone was aware of, that the first cottage he'd come to was occupied by a reclusive smallholder with a pack of underfed hellhounds?

Finally, feeling like the pilgrim at the end of his progress, he reached his destination, only to confirm what his ill-divining heart had been telling him for half an hour, that Hen Hollis was not at home.

Now was the moment to put it all down to experience and get back on track by retracing his steps and calling at Witch Cottage, saying a prayer that Wield wouldn't notice the lost time. But seeing that he could re-enter Sandytown by the South Cliff Road, he decided to vary his interview route and call in on Alan Hollis at the Hope and Anchor. Never miss a chance of going into a pub, that's what Andy Dalziel once said in his hearing. Also it might give him a lead on Hen Hollis.

He had no problem finding the pub. On the main street, freshly painted, with a colourful sign showing a scantily clad, curvaceous blonde (presumably Hope) sitting on a rather priapic anchor, it had an inviting look about it, an impression confirmed when he opened the bar-room door. In some Yorkshire pubs, the appearance of a stranger cuts off conversation like a toad in the blancmange, but the atmosphere of the Hope and Anchor wrapped itself around you like a comfortable old coat.

The room was busy with family parties enjoying such delicacies as fish and chips or steak and kidney pie, no Mediterranean salads here despite the warm weather. The cooking smells caressed Hat's taste buds and for a moment he was tempted.

But professionalism won and when a young barwoman, who could have modelled for Hope, asked him what he fancied, he said he was looking for Alan Hollis.

'He's next door in the snug,' she said, sounding faintly disappointed. 'Sure you won't have a drink?'

Hat hadn't bothered much with girls since an earlier relationship had ended in tragedy, but he'd enjoyed his chat with the girl at the hotel, despite its unsatisfactory outcome, and now found himself smiling at this one and saying, 'Later, maybe.'

By contrast with the main room the snug wasn't quite so welcoming. There were only two customers here, one in a corner, his head buried in a copy of the *Mid-York News*, and one leaning on the bar talking to the barman.

On Hat's approach, the standing customer, a man rising seventy, lean and unshaven with a faint odour of the farmyard about him and an ill-tempered face whose sharp angles were accentuated rather than concealed by an ill-kept beard, glared at him as if not best pleased at being disturbed.

By contrast, the man behind the bar gave him a pleasant perhaps even relieved smile and said, 'What can I get you, sir?'

'Mr Hollis, is it?' said Hat.

The two men exchanged glances then the barman said, 'Alan Hollis, yes.'

Hat showed his ID and said, 'Wonder if I might have a quick word, sir.'

The other man raised his glass to his lips, downed the last gill, then made for the door, lighting a cigarette as he exited so that he was illegal for a good couple of seconds.

An act of courtesy? wondered Hat. Or simply nicotine starvation?

'It's about poor Lady Denham, is it?' said Hollis.

'That's right,' said Hat. 'We want to talk to everyone who was at the party.'

'Naturally, though I don't think I'll be able to help you much.'

'It all helps build a picture, sir. So what time did you arrive at the Hall?'

'I had to be there early – about half twelve, I think it was. You see, the drink had all been supplied through the pub, and I needed to set up the bar tables . . .'

'But you were there as a guest, not just as a supplier?' interrupted Hat.

'Right. The hog-roast weren't just social. Idea was to bring all the elements of Sandytown's development plan together: commerce, tourism, the Authority, and so on.'

'And as well as an invite, you were lucky enough to get the drinks concession?'

Hollis smiled.

'Luck hardly came into it,' he said.

'Sorry?'

'You don't know? Lady Denham is . . . was my landlord. She owns . . . owned the Hope and Anchor. I'm just her manager. Owt to do with drink, she made sure the profit came the pub's way.'

'But, as the hostess, she'd be paying for it anyway, right?'

'Wrong. Consortium were paying. Consortium's the private investment side of the development, mainly her and Tom Parker, plus a couple of others.'

'Then she'd still be paying as a leading partner?'

'Aye, but just a share and indirectly, whereas all the pub profits go to her. That's why the bubbly were proper champagne, not the cava she usually feeds her guests. She were a careful lady.'

This wasn't offered in a recriminatory tone. In Yorkshire *being careful* was not regarded as a failing.

'Now take me through the party as you saw it, sir.

Naturally, any contact you had with Lady Denham would be particularly interesting.'

In fact it wasn't. Hollis said he'd only spoken to the woman once and that was fairly early on, to reassure her there was plenty of drink in reserve. As for noticing any behaviour that might be pertinent to the murder, he was a blank.

'I were at it non-stop serving drink for the first couple of hours. Them councillors were putting it away like camels heading out into the Gobi. If it hadn't been for that cousin of Lady Denham's helping me, I doubt if I'd have managed.'

'That would be Miss Brereton,' said Hat.

'Aye. Young Clara. Then when the storm started, the pair of us were scuttling around shifting the drinks table into the house before it got washed away.'

'But not the food?' said Hat, remembering the sight of all that soggy grub resting forlorn on the long trestle tables in front of the house.

'Not my concern,' said Hollis. 'Any road, food spoilt's the same as food eaten, drink undrunk is returnable.'

After the discovery of the body, when he saw people were beginning to leave, he had collected any unopened bottles, loaded them into his van, and driven back to the pub.

'I'd always planned to be back early anyway. This is a busy time of year for us.'

Not so busy you didn't feel able to shut yourself in the snug having a tête-à-tête with your shabby friend, thought Hat.

'Your name, sir,' he said. 'Hollis. Wasn't Lady Denham married to a Mr Hollis?'

'That's right. Her first husband. I'm a cousin, once removed. We're a large family.'

'And close,' said Hat. 'Her taking you on as manager here, I mean.'

'It was Hog, that was her first husband, as gave me the job. But Lady D were happy for me to carry on. She rated family loyalty, so long as it were two way.'

'Like with you, right? But not with her brother-in-law, Mr Hen Hollis, I gather. Wasn't there some tension between them?'

The man looked at him quizzically and said, 'Mebbe there was, mebbe there wasn't. Pity, if he hadn't shot off, you could have asked him yourself.'

Hat digested this then said, 'That was Hen you were talking to when I came in.'

'Oh aye. Didn't you know? No, I suppose you wouldn't have done.'

Shit! thought Hat. I had him in my sights. Wait till Novello hears about this!

'So what were you talking about, sir?' he asked. 'I mean, I'd guess the murder must have been mentioned. What did Mr Hen Hollis have to say about it?'

'Not a lot.'

'Wasn't he pleased?'

Hollis looked shocked.

'Now hold on! All right, they didn't see eye to eye, and I doubt if Hen'll go into deep mourning, but in these parts we know how to behave. We don't go around gloating when folk we don't like get murdered.'

'Sorry,' said Hat. 'All I meant was . . .'

He was saved from having to explain what he meant by the sound of the door opening behind him and Hollis's expression turning from indignant reproach to a broad smile as he said, 'Can't find a copper anywhere then two come along at once. Usual, Jug?'

Hat turned to see a uniformed sergeant coming into

the room. A stockily built man in his late forties, he looked red faced and harassed.

'Aye, and I reckon I've earned it. I've been running around like a blue-arsed flea for two hours now, looking for yon daft cousin on thine. I trailed all the way out to Lowbridge, but he's not been home all day. So I went up to the Lonely Duck to see if he'd fetched up there, and the beck in Bale Bottom had overflowed in the storm, and I got stuck and had to get Jimmy Kilne to haul me out with his tractor. And when I finally made it to the Duck, they'd seen nowt of him, so I came on round by the moor road, not wanting to risk the Bottom again, and thought I might as well try the Black Lamb, but he weren't there either, so here I am back where I started from. You've not seen owt of him have you, Alan?'

Hollis laughed and said, 'Aye, he were in here an hour ago, mebbe a bit longer. You could have saved yourself a trip if you'd only thought on!'

'Excuse me,' said Hat, 'but who're we talking about?'

The sergeant looked at him with distaste and said, 'This is police business, sir. I'd be grateful if you didn't interfere.'

Hat said, 'Yes, I know it's police business, Sergeant,' and produced his ID.

The man studied it carefully then said, 'You'll be one of Ed Wield's lads?'

'That's right. Bowler. Hat Bowler.'

'Oh aye. I'm Whitby. If you work for Ed, I suppose you're all right. What are you doing here then?'

Hat explained and in return learned there was yet another Hollis in the offing, Ollie the hog-roast man. As this exchange took place, the landlord drew two pints of beer. Whitby downed most of his in a single draught. Hat saw no reason not to follow superior example.

The door from the main bar opened and the curvaceous girl came in.

'Running out of Buds, Alan,' she said. 'How do, Sergeant Whitby.'

'How do, Jenny,' said Whitby.

'I'll bring some up,' said Hollis. 'Here, take these to be going on with.'

He plucked half a dozen bottles from the refrigeration unit.

'So, Alan,' said Whitby, 'did Ollie say which direction he were heading in when he left? If I've got to drive all the way out to Lowbridge again, I'll kill him.'

Hollis's brow furrowed as if in the effort of recollection. Jenny paused on her way out, clutching the armful of bottles to her bosom. That will take the chill off them, thought Hat longingly. The chat with the receptionist seemed to have raised his blood temperature a couple of degrees.

She said, 'You're looking for Ollie? Oh, he were in a bad way, weren't he, Alan? Not surprising after what happened up at the Hall. Any excitement and it brings on one of his attacks. He could scarcely breathe, I thought it might be an ambulance job, but he sucked on that device of his and when he got a bit better, he said the only thing that would put him right were a session with Miss Lee.'

Alan Hollis said, 'That's right, Jug. I was just going to say, if you're looking for Ollie, your next stop should be Witch Cottage.'

Witch Cottage. Miss Lee. Whom Hat had pushed down his list. Couldn't make that much difference. Could it?

'Should have thought of that meself,' said Whitby,

finishing his beer. 'Seeing that poor woman dead's stultified me brain. I'll get myself up there and hope he's not left.'

'Hang on, Sarge, I'll come with you,' said Hat.

'If you like,' said Whitby without enthusiasm.

As the door closed behind them, the customer in the corner lowered his paper, finished his drink and took the glass to the bar.

'Same again, sir?' said Hollis.

'Better not. Lovely pint, but I'm driving,' said Sammy Ruddlesdin. 'See you again some time.'

He went through the door.

Ahead of him as he walked to the car park, Hat was saying to Sergeant Whitby, 'This Miss Lee, she does what exactly?'

'Acupuncturist. One of Tom Parker's funny buggers. Don't see how sticking needles into folks works, mesel',' said Whitby. 'But the proof of the pudding's in the eating, and there's no doubt Ollie's a different man after a session at Witch Cottage.'

Any expectations roused by the name were disappointed a few minutes later when Hat got his first clear view of the cottage. OK, it looked pretty ancient, but not very *witchy*. In fact, it looked extremely well kept and rather attractive in an olde worlde kind of way. Of course, appearances could deceive. Perhaps the little garden contained exotic herbs, one sprig of which could put you in a trance or make you fall madly in love or cure you of the quinsy. If so they were well hidden by the hollyhocks and mesembryanthemums.

At the very least there should have been a door knocker in the form of a skull. Instead there was a modern bell push which Whitby ignored, pushing open the door which stood slightly ajar.

They stepped into a tiny hallway, and the sergeant shouted, 'Hello! Miss Lee!'

There was the sound of movement behind a half-open door to the left.

Being the closer to it, Hat pushed it fully open and said, 'Miss Lee?' brightly, because that's what his lips were programmed to say, even though his mind was already calculating the odds against Miss Lee having a grizzled black beard. Still, in this day and age, especially when you were investigating the death of an elderly titled lady roasted in her own hog basket, it would be silly to rule anything out.

Later he realized these irrelevant thoughts were the smoke screen his subconscious was trailing across his conscious mind in an effort to soften the full grotesquerie of what he was seeing.

The bearded man had half turned towards the door, his face a picture of guilt surprised. He was standing next to a table with a padded top. On it, face down, lay a man, stripped to the waist, his head resting on his crossed arms. From his naked back and shoulders protruded perhaps half a dozen of what looked like quills, four or five inches long, stripped of their feathers, leaving just a touch of colour at the tip.

Except for one.

This one, in the middle of the back near the top of the spine, only protruded a couple of inches at most and the bearded man's right hand was still clasped tight about it.

Hat felt himself shouldered aside as Whitby shoved by him.

'Right, you bugger, let's be having you,' he shouted.

The man put up no resistance as Whitby forced his hands behind his back and snapped a pair of handcuffs on his wrists. He then pushed the prisoner towards Hat, saying, 'Watch him!' and turned his attention to the figure on the table.

The bearded man looked straight into Hat's eyes. He seemed to be trying to say something, but no words came.

Whitby had raised the prone figure's head. His fingers ran down the neck, seeking a pulse. Finally he replaced the head gently on the crossed arms.

'He's dead,' he said disbelievingly.

'Is it Hollis?' demanded Hat fearfully.

'Aye, it's Ollie. He's dead!'

It was as if saying it a second time brought home the truth of the situation.

He span round, thrust his face close to the prisoner's and said with quiet savagery, 'You bastard! If there were any justice left in this soft bloody country, you'd hang for this!'

Then to Hat, in a voice full of a frustration which rang in the young constable's ears like accusation, 'Five minutes! If only we'd got here five minutes earlier!'

Volume the Third

*Yes, Yes, my Dear, depend upon it, you will be
thinking of the price of Butcher's meat in time*

1

FROM: charley@whiffle.com
TO: cassie@natterjack.com
SUBJECT: more madness!

Disaster!!

Theyve arrested Mr Godley! I cant believe it – they must be mad – & not just for 1 murder but 2! It was in the *News* this morning – all the details of Lady Ds death – plus another murder last evening. Ollie Hollis – the gateman at the pig farm – who was in charge of the hog-roast – killed on Miss Lees treatment couch – & the article says Mr Godley was caught in the act – sticking one of Miss Lees acupuncture needles into Ollies back!

Its got to be a mistake. OK – hes a nutter – but his nuttiness is believing he has the power to cure people – not to kill them! But the *News* piece is emphatic – goes on about the guy in charge – some plod called Pascoe – & how we can all rest safe in our beds with brains like his on the police payroll. Must be bollocks – stake my professional reputation on it – when I get one!

But – as usual – Im way ahead of myself.

Significant events since my last.

First – this woman cop turned up to take statements from Tom & Mary & me – theyre doing everyone who was at the hog-roast – natch.

She seemed alright – bit understated – no make-up – drab gear – could be one of the sisterhood – butch end – but Im not sure. Name of Novello – rang a bell – some old b&w musical mum once made us watch on the box I think – do you recall?

Anyway – I quite liked her – gave her my statement – using my e to you – hot off the press – to double check memory – & seeing this she asked if she could read it – & next thing Im running off copies of all the stuff Ive sent you with my impressions of Sandytown!

Once she went I soon started wondering if it had been such a good idea. She promised for her eyes only – more or less – but I started thinking of all the crime soaps where the cops idea of a good time is lager & chips while they drool over the latest confiscated porn videos! But she seemed OK – & if us girls cant trust each other – who can we trust?

Pause for mocking laughter!

Anyway – my worries soon pushed to the back of my mind when Mary appeared with a new development. Dear kind Tom had got to worrying about Clara – the poor relation – or maybe not so poor now – who knows?! – down at the Hall all by herself. So hed phoned her & invited her to stay here at Kyoto – & shed accepted. No problem about bedrooms – even with me staying they still have a couple spare – but Mary wondered whether – in the circs – putting Clara into a strange room in a strange house was a great idea & it had occurred to her that maybe sharing with someone her own age – ie me – might not make more sense – no pressure on me to agree. Cant say I really fancied it – but – like we all know – theres no pressure like no pressure – so of course I said yes – fine with me – if Clara herself was OK with it.

I was glad Id agreed when she turned up – she looked

334

wrecked! I reckon all the activity around the Hall when the police arrived had kept her going – but now she was able to relax & take in what had actually happened she was sinking fast through the first stages of shock.

Mary had put her idea to her & shed said yes – but I got the impression that if theyd suggested she slept in the greenhouse shed have agreed. I took her up to my room – Id cleared all my junk off the other bed & she sat down on it. She hadnt spoken a word on our way upstairs – & I didnt know what to say – me – the great psychologist! – so I said Id leave her to sort her stuff out – & I did.

Downstairs Tom & Mary were deep in conversation – with little Miss Minnie in a corner – pretending to read a book but taking everything in. The other children were already in bed – but Min – whos big on rights – like having her own room – insists on staying up half an hour longer. Tonight – in the excitement – shed drawn it out much longer by keeping a low profile – but Mary finally spotted her & said – Minnie you should be in bed.

Looking for a diversion – shes good at diversions – Min burst out – they should have interviewed me & Paul & the others too – we were there – we were witnesses!

Technically she was right – I thought. Tom & Mary exchanged glances – then Tom said – yes – but I dont think you witnessed anything dear –

– yes I did – said Min – loving centre stage. – I saw people wandering around during the storm – at least I think I did –

– did you dear? – said Mary – but I dont suppose thats very important –

– that policewoman thought it was! – riposted Min.

That got their attention.

Tom said – she spoke to you? she asked you questions? –

This was in a quiet scary sort of voice I hadnt heard from him before – & I began to feel sorry for Novello.

– yes – sort of – said Min – she said Id need to do it again properly – on tape – for the record –

She spoke in a different voice too – a bit subdued – like she recognized her dad was really annoyed.

Mary said – all sweet reason – if Minnie wanted to talk to the young woman – thered be no way of stopping her dear –

– perhaps not – but she should have sent for one of us straightaway – said Tom unappeased. Then in his normal tone with a big smile to Min – all right darling – give me a kiss – time you were in bed I think –

This resumption of normal service was clearly a great relief to Min. She hugged him tight – then her mum – then me – saying – will you come & tuck me in Charley? –

I looked at Mary who smiled & nodded.

What Minnie the minx wanted – of course – was a chance to pump me – but when I let her see I wasnt in a pumpable mood she changed tack & said – I wish I could share your room too Charley – Im really scared being by myself tonight – all plaintive enough to melt a glacier!

I said – thats terrible Minnie – tell you what – Ill ask your mum if you can go in with Paul & the others –

That shut her up – & I got out – but not before shed made me promise to take her swimming at the hotel tomorrow! Must think Uncle Sid – being a man – is more pumpable! God – they start young these days!

Before I went down I looked in on Clara to see how she was getting on.

She was lying face down on the bed – long pale legs sprawled wide – & Im shamed to admit at first all I could think of was the barts Halloween apple buttocks bob-bob-bobbing between them.

Then I realized she was crying – no – weepings the word – sobs coming up from deep deep down – like Icelandic geysers.

I sat down beside her & put my arms around her – thinking I might have been a bit simplistic casting her & Lady D as Sara & Miss Minchin in *A Little Princess*. This was real grief. Or if it wasnt – she deserves a barrowload of Oscars!

I said – there there – & other subtly consoling phrases known only to us professionals – but it didnt help that pretty soon I was sobbing away too — interesting form of mimetic reaction – remember how we always used to set each other off? – mum too – like that time she took us to see *The Bridges of Madison County* – & we got asked to leave!

Finally we dried up – & dried off – & with the barriers down – for a moment at least – she told me that she really owed Lady D – whod picked her up at a v low point – just been dumped by her boyfriend – (that brought loathsome Liam into my mind first time in days!) – & not getting on with her mums new partner (dad had done a runner before she was born). Then Lady D showed. Seems Claras grandad had been Lady Ds favourite cousin – & when she said come & live with me it was one of those offers you cant refuse. Not that Clara wanted to.

She told me – if I hadnt come to Sandytown I think by now Id have been – well I dont know what Id have been but it wouldnt have been good. Im really going to miss Aunt Daph – I owe her everything –

& you repaid her by shagging the randy bart – who she was saving up for better things! – I thought – my old mean streak reviving for a moment.

But what the hell – in her shoes – or out of them – Id probably have done the same!

By now we were best buddies – sharing theories about

what had happened – hers being that it was down to some extreme animal rights group – mine that someone shed crossed – with Hen Hollis at the top of the list – had finally flipped. Both theories were based on the grotesque circumstances – Clara seeing the body in the hog-roast basket as an ideological statement – me as demonstrating advanced dementia.

She told me about the policemen whod interviewed her – a sergeant & an inspector – must be that Pascoe – both pretty sharp – she reckoned. I told her about my girl – said Id been impressed too.

Nothing like talking to a trained professional to get you back on an even keel – & eventually she felt well enough to come downstairs & have some nourishing broth – but it didnt surprise me when she excused herself soon after & headed for bed.

When I went up she was sound asleep under the duvet so I wasnt bothered by those long pale legs this time. Thought I wouldnt sleep but went out like a light. Woke early this morning – but not so early as Clara. Met her coming out of the bathroom & we dodged around each other – very much back to our old polite acquaintance. Probably regrets opening up to me last night – common reaction.

But all that was scrubbed from my mind when I got downstairs to find Mary & Tom staring gobsmacked at the *News* article. I could see breakfast was going to be delayed – so I rushed back up to my laptop to give you an update.

Sandytown – Home of the Healthy Holiday! – What a laugh! Bet your daily round of death – disease – & attacks by passing insurgents – feels really dull now!

God knows what today will bring – Im off to breakfast – need to keep my strength up – but watch this space!

Love

Charley xxxx

2

Could hardly keep me eyes open after Pascoe left last night. Had to ring Cap though. Self interest. She doesn't bother much with listening to the news – says most of it's lies and all of it's bad! – but the minute she does hear Sandytown mentioned she'd be on the phone, and I didn't want my beauty sleep disturbed.

I was right. She knew nowt. I filled her in and she went sort of quiet, then said she'd heard of Lady Denham, but no one deserved to die like that. I didn't ask how she'd heard of her 'cos I guessed she were on some ANIMA hit-list! She said she hoped I wasn't going to get mixed up in the investigation. I said no way, I'm only here for the cure. Any road, Pete Pascoe was in charge and he'd made it pretty clear he didn't want me peering over his shoulder. That seemed to reassure her. While her and Ellie have always been a bit suspicious of each other, she seems to think Pete's a good influence!

After we'd finished talking, I fell into bed and slept like a babbie. Woke up bright and early, feeling best I'd done for an age. Thought it must be down to seeing Pete again. Chatting to him about the case had got me back in the groove, just like the old days. Then Pet came along while I were having me breakfast and said there'd been another murder.

I said, Every time I see you these days, you tell me there's been a murder.

Since our session in the shower, Pet and I have been sort of formal friendly, neither of us referring directly to it, but summat like that between you and a lass is always there. At least if you're my age. Mebbe today's youngsters just take it in their stride, like having a tasty takeaway!

Any road, nowt like murder for taking your mind off sex, and when she said it were headlines in the *Mid-York News*, I asked her to fetch me a copy.

Didn't need to look for the by-line. Way it made Pete out to be a cross between Jesus and Hercules Parrot, had to be yon long streak of printer's ink, Ruddlesdin. Him and Pete have always been far too close. For my money, all you get from scratching journalists' backs is dirty fingernails. Hope the sod's got it right this time, else Pete's going to look like a right nana.

Don't know why I was wasting my sympathy on him, but. This must have been that call he got as he were leaving. And the rotten bugger didn't bother to come back in and tell me!

When Pet said Pascoe hadn't been round to interview her or Fester last night, this confirmed it. The cheeky sod were getting ideas above his station. And there was me falling over myself not to get in his way.

Well, all that were changed now. If Ruddlesdin were right and they'd got their man they'd have spent the night grilling him and if he cracked, the celebration could just be beginning!

And if Ruddlesdin were wrong, Pete 'ud need all the help he could get.

I told Pet I needed to get down to the Hall tootie-sweetie, and she said right off she'd give me a lift. I'd like to think it were me manly charm that made her so willing to help, but I soon realized it were interrogation time again, and having me in her car were easier than having me in the shower. She tried hard to find out if I thought the investigation were really over. Mebbe she'd lain awake all night, worrying that, faced with the choice of topping or tupping old Daph, Fester had gone for broke! She must really be hot for the bugger. Has to be true love, being willing to jump into bed with me for his sake! Or mebbe I'm being romantic, and she's got something to hide herself.

As she dropped me off at the Hall, she said to be sure to give her a ring if I needed a lift back, so she were certainly keen to have a second bite at the cherry.

Wouldn't have minded a second bite at hers if I hadn't vowed to be a good boy.

There was a uniform outside the front door, having a quiet fag. Nearly swallowed it when he saw me getting out of the car. Name of Mick Sproggs, I recalled. Nice enough young lad, even if he does come from Mexborough. I asked him where I'd find the DCI. He said he'd called a briefing in the Incident Room. I were surprised to hear that weren't in the Hall itself. Typical Pete that. Me, I'd have been in one of them big drawing rooms with the comfy sofas.

I tapped the young Sproggs's chest afore I moved on and said, 'Listen, lad, if I get there and find I'm expected, I'll come back and by the time I've finished relocating your personal radio you'll be able to get Five Live by farting, right?'

He didn't say owt but I think he got the message.

When I shoved the Incident Room door open, I thought it 'ud be like old John Wayne coming into a bar, everyone freezing then diving for cover. Instead, after a moment of shock, it were big smiles all round and folk telling me it were good to see me and shaking my hand, and I started to feel a right old Scrooge. Mebbe Pete's smile were a bit strained, and it's hard to tell if Wieldy's grinning or passing a hard turd, but I swear young Bowler had tears in his eyes and Ivor Novello even gave me a hug!

I could see at once that this was no breakfast celebration, confirmed when Pete said, 'Good to see you, sir. I presume you've seen this morning's *News*? You probably won't be surprised to learn that the report of my apotheosis has been slightly exaggerated. So sit yourself down, and if you've got anything you'd like to say, I know we'd all be delighted to hear it.'

The lad's good, no denying it. If he'd gone into politics he'd be prime minister by now.

The room set-up were great, just what I'd have expected from them two. I clocked the display boards. Everything neatly laid out, connections made with different colour ribbons, just what the troops need. All right having everything correlated on computers, but a screen's a glass darkly. Seeing it up on a display board is what brings you face to face.

Couldn't fault the way Pete ran the briefing either. Wieldy were a great help, of course, specially when Pete started using words of more than three syllables. He'd got everyone there, even Jug Whitby for local knowledge. Good thinking. A wise cop makes sure his team can see the wood as well as the trees. Let the buggers compartmentalize and they can miss connections. Pete knew that.

Well, he would, wouldn't he? He'd had a wise cop teaching him!

I don't think any on 'em can have slept much, but Wieldy had got a coffee machine organized and there was plenty of it, thick and black and sweet the way cops like it, none of this modern 57 varieties and all piddle.

Naturally Pete started with Ollie Hollis. Everyone there knew there was a suspect in custody, but they could see as well as I could that no one was popping champagne corks and they had to be told why. Or, because it were Pete, made to work out why.

He said, 'The needle driven into his back damaged the spinal cord between vertebrae C3 and C4, causing paralysis of the legs and arms. Also the shock may have triggered a violent asthma attack. Unable to move from his prone position because of the paralysis, he would have experienced grave difficulties in breathing which eventually led to asphyxiation.'

It had taken me a while to realize Pete talking like this were deliberate. Me, I like to give it straight in language the dimmest plod could understand. Pete prefers to make the buggers concentrate real hard, ask questions, draw conclusions. The bright ones like Bowler and Novello knew this was a chance to shine.

Bowler got in first here. Found out later from Wieldy the silly young sod were beating up on himself for not having got to Witch Cottage afore Ollie Hollis got killed. Mebbe that's why he were so pleased to see me – thought I looked like a friendly face!

He said, 'You mean there was a significant gap between him being stabbed by the needle and dying?'

'Possibly as much as thirty minutes,' said Pete. 'Which means . . .'

What it meant to Hat was, the earlier the attack had taken place, the better for his guilt feelings! But he's too bright a lad to say that.

He said, 'Then it's hardly likely that guy Godley would have hung around all that time with his hand on the needle, is it?'

'No, it's not,' said Pascoe. 'Which means his story of discovering Hollis and trying to remove the needle could well be true.'

Even though it was what they'd all been expecting, there was a moan of disappointment.

'We cutting him loose then?' asked Bowler.

'Not yet,' said Pete. 'He may be telling the truth about Hollis, but several witness statements mention him having a violent altercation with Lady Denham and until we get a satisfactory explanation of that, he's going nowhere.'

Understandable but dangerous. When the rest of the press, who'd be feeling a bit disgruntled at being upstaged by a provincial rag, realized Ruddlesdin had got it all wrong, they'd likely put his continued detention down as spite.

Now Pete moved on, or back, to Daph's murder.

Wieldy had the PM details and laid them out with his usual precision.

Cause of death strangulation. Contusion on brow looked more likely to have been sustained by, say, falling against a hard object rather than being hit by a weapon. Whatever, someone had almost immediately decided to finish the job off with his bare hands. Or, seeing as Daph weren't in a state to fight back, with *her* bare hands. Good news were that she was dead afore she started grilling. Heat made establishing an exact time of death hard, but they reckoned between thirty minutes and an hour before she'd been discovered.

And there were seminal traces in her vaginal passage.

'You mean she'd been raped?' interrupted Novello, not clever as Wieldy prides himself on saying what he means.

Pete cut in, 'There were no signs of violence around the genital area, and the estimate was that the coitus had occurred some hours before death, so it seems likely it was consensual.'

Wield resumed.

Clothing was charred but a large red stain on the front of her dress had been identified as red wine. Spatter pattern suggested it might have been thrown rather than simply spilled. No glass found at scene, though a champagne cork, some silver foil, cigarette stubs and food remains were recovered from the hut. Possible DNA samples from food. Partial fingerprint on the foil.

'So we'll need prints from everybody who was at the party,' said Pete.

'In hand,' said Wield.

'Where else would they be?' said Pete.

They did a nice double act, those two, and it got an appreciative laugh.

'Questions, comments,' Pete invited.

Bowler got in quick.

'Sounds like someone had been having a bit of a

345

party in the hut, then did a tidy-up, got rid of any glasses or bottles. Wonder why.'

'And what's the result of your wondering, Hat?' asked Pete.

'Could be there was someone else there as well as Ollie Hollis, but they didn't want to draw attention to it,' he offered.

'Good point,' said Pete. He'd got there already, of course, but like I say he loves to make the buggers think.

Novello now got in on the act. Nothing like feeling upstaged by your rival for putting the brain cells into overdrive.

She said, 'If Ollie Hollis suffered from asthma, it's not likely that he smoked, is it?'

I was pretty sure Pete would have worked this out for himself too, but he gave Ivor a big smile and said, 'Excellent point. We'll check it out. Not so many smokers around these days. Something to ask everyone you interview. Now let's think about motives in both cases, which may or may not be connected. I don't want anyone making assumptions till we have firm evidence of a connection. So, motive.'

According to Pete, there were two main lines, the most obvious the usual one: money. Who profited? Daph's lawyer, Beard, wouldn't discuss the will over the phone but was on his way north already. Meaning there has to be serious dosh involved. Them London briefs charge an extra one per cent for every mile they go north of Hampstead.

Till he got here, the only person definitely benefiting from Daph's exit was Hen Hollis. (When he were mentioned, Novello shot young Bowler a grin and I saw him wince. Besides not getting to Witch Cottage early enough, seems he'd also run into Hen last night without knowing it. Crap never hits you in single dottles, it comes in volleys!) Jug Whitby, who it seemed to me were a lot guiltier than Bowler for not getting to Ollie earlier, were told off to fetch Hen in. Don't hold your breath, I thought.

The other line was animal rights activists. Hollis's Ham had been targeted, Daph herself had been personally threatened and various alleged attempts on her life were being examined. (Caught my eye as he said this, like he were signalling, Keep quiet about your part in this – so I did.) Placing her body in the hog-roast cage suggested a possible link here.

Now Pete paused again for questions and comments. Straight off the young 'uns were at it again, scoring Brownie points. Bowler tried to make up some of his lost ground by bringing up Tom Parker's bro, Sidney. Way he dresses, the car he runs, obviously lives high on the hog. Pete winced – doesn't like jokes in bad taste – but I reckon it were an accident. Happens to me all the time. Bowler pressed on: as the victim's financial adviser, maybe it was worth looking at the way he was handling her money? Novello chipped in with the notion that maybe Sid Parker and Ted Denham had some deal cooking behind Lady Denham's back. She just happened to know that they'd had a secret meeting at Denham Park, and she speculated that it could have been about the possibility of turning the Denham's stately home into a gambling casino or a care facility. Instead of asking her where the fuck all this were coming from, Pete nodded approvingly, so he must have some idea.

'Let's look hard at these Parkers,' he said. 'Lots of connections with the victim, with some suggestion of tensions in the Sandytown Consortium between its two leading members, Tom Parker and Daphne Denham.'

Seems Seymour had interviewed dotty Diana and her chum. Dennis had been sitting there, playing with his laptop, not getting involved as the younger DCs bickered about who were king of the castle. Pete asked rather sarcastic if he had owt to add to the 'somewhat pithy' statements he'd taken. It didn't faze the lad. He just gave his big friendly grin and said, 'Not really. Struck me Miss Parker were a flush short of a toilet, but harmless with it.'

'Well, thank you for your always helpful analysis, Dennis,' says Pete, and I saw Novello and Bowler glance at each other, this time in harmony, agreeing that old Dennis weren't a threat in their private little Olympics.

Then Seymour said, 'One thing, though, sir, this animal rights stuff . . .'

'Yes?' said Pete.

'I were looking through the case file earlier and I noticed that stuff about Lady Denham having a record . . .'

I could see this were news to most of them there.

Wield said, 'Hit a hunt protester with her riding crop, got bound over to keep the peace. This were thirty years ago, don't see how it can be relevant now, unless you can tell us different, Dennis?'

With Pete, that would've sounded sarcastic, but with Wieldy you never can tell.

'Just thought I'd check it out,' said Seymour. 'The protester were a sixteen-year-old lass, Alexandra

348

Lambe. She were squirting some spray stuff up the hounds' noses to put them off the scent when Lady Denham hit her. Back then she'd likely have got off, case dismissed, except the girl turned up in court with a severely blackened left eye.'

'Dennis, I'm losing the will to live,' said Pascoe. 'Get to whatever point there is to your tale, will you?'

Seymour said, 'Thing is, sir, this Mrs Griffiths I talked to at Seaview Terrace, her first name's Sandy.'

He paused and gave us his smile like he were expecting a kiss on both cheeks and a medal.

'The point,' said Pete wearily.

'I got a niece called Alexandra, she always gets called Sandy,' said Seymour.

'And your niece is relevant how? Convictions for murder? An urban terrorist, perhaps?' said Pete.

I saw Novello and Bowler grinning like a pair of chimps.

'No, sir. She's only eight,' said Seymour. 'It were just that this Mrs Griffiths had a funny eye. Not funny ha ha, but it didn't move in synch with t'other.'

I thought, Christ, that explains her weird stare. Here's my big ego putting it down to meeting me, while uncomplicated Dennis spots straight off it's her eye! Not only that, he jumps to a connection, 'cos now he was saying, 'When I checked out this Lambe girl, it turned out a few years later, she lost the use of the same eye that got blacked. On the record 'cos she wanted to claim compensation and her brief asked for court records of the case and police evidence. Never came to anything. Too much time had passed, and they couldn't find a doc to swear that was the cause anyway.'

Now the DCs had stopped grinning and Pete's

voice had lost that sarky edge as he said, 'So what you're saying is, maybe this Sandy Griffiths and this Alexandra Lambe are one and the same person?'

'No, sir. Not maybe. Just got confirmation on my laptop. Definitely,' said Seymour. 'Got married in 1987, widowed eight years later. Bit more too, sir. She's got a record. Animal rights activities, so she didn't grow out of it. Bound over a couple of times, three fines, four weeks' community service, and six months suspended for harassment. She's a member of some group called ANIMA. So unless it's just a coincidence she's holidaying in Sandytown . . .'

Got to admire Pete. Not the slightest eye flicker in my direction even though he knew as well as I did that ANIMA were the protest group founded by my Cap!

'Good work, Dennis! The rest of you take notice. You can't make this kind of useful connection unless you've taken on board all the facts. Let's have her in, see what she has to say for herself. Dennis, it's your shout, you do the honours.'

'Should I go too, sir?' said Ivor Novello. 'A woman's touch might come in handy.'

Doesn't want to miss out, I thought.

'No,' said Pete. 'I've got another job for you. OK, people. That's it. Check with Sergeant Wield here if you've any doubts at all about what you're doing. And, like I said, let Dennis be your shining example. I want results! Shirley, a word.'

He gathered his bits of paper together, jerked his head at me, and wandered off through a door behind him. Novello followed. So did I. Must have been the flat's bedroom. No bed now, just a table, couple of chairs and a recorder. Made our interview rooms back at the Factory look like suites at the Ritz.

Pete registered my presence but said nowt.

To Ivor he said, 'I want you to head on up to Kyoto House and invite Miss Heywood down for a chat.'

Ivor said, 'Yes, sir. Sir, about the emails . . .'

'No need to mention them, Shirley,' he said. 'Off you go.'

The lass left.

'What emails?' I said.

'A Miss Heywood, whom I believe you have met, is presently a guest of the Parkers and she has been sending a fairly detailed email account of her time here to her sister. She is, it seems, a psychology student, and Novello, thinking that her outsider's view of the set-up here in Sandytown might be of interest, persuaded her to let her glance at the emails. And very interesting they are too, for all kinds of reasons.'

He patted a stack of print-outs on the table.

'Let me guess,' I said. 'Ivor did the all-girls-together thing and got a hold of those on the understanding they were for her eyes only. No wonder she ain't looking forward to seeing young Heywood again.'

'Shirley's a Catholic, they know how to deal with guilt,' said Pete indifferently. 'She is also, I'm glad to say, a very sharp, very ambitious young detective. Anyway, Andy, it's really good to see you here. You're looking a lot more like your old self this morning. You slept well?'

'Yes, I did. And yes, I've been, and yes, I take sugar,' I said. 'Nice of you not to worry me poor invalid mind with more bad news afore you took off last night.'

He shrugged and said, 'Andy, I'll be glad of any input you can offer, and you're very welcome to sit in on briefings, as you've just done, but I can't be making diversions to bring you up to speed on every new development.'

Me, I didn't rate two steps back into my room as diversion, but I guessed the poor sod were under enough stress without me piling it on. No need to let him off scot-free, but.

I said, 'Desperate Dan been in touch, has he?'

He winced and said, 'Yes, the Chief Constable and I spoke briefly early this morning.'

'And how about Sammy Ruddlesdin? He been round for his daily briefing yet?'

I thought I'd pushed him too far, but he's a hard man to topple over the edge.

He said, 'No doubt Sammy and I will talk later. Meanwhile, as I say, Andy, I'd be really pleased to have any input you may care to offer.'

He sounded so sincere, I'd have bought a timeshare off him.

I said, 'You didn't mention Roote out there.'

'I couldn't see how he might be relevant.'

'No? There were a time when we couldn't talk about an outbreak of shoplifting in Woollies without you bringing Roote into it,' I said. 'Now we've got him on the scene at a murder and you don't want to talk about him!'

'Wieldy's spoken to him already, as you know,' he said. 'And I'll be talking to him myself later. Don't worry, Andy, If I feel that he's involved in any way, I shall know how to do my duty.'

I clapped my hands a couple of times. There's not another bugger I know in the Force could have delivered that line like Pete Pascoe!

'Right, that's that sorted,' I said. 'So are you going to let me take a look at Charley Heywood's emails then?'

He looked doubtful and said, 'Not sure if I should do that, Andy, in view of the personal connection.'

'Eh?' I said.

'You know her father, I believe. And also you are mentioned in the text.'

'Jesus is mentioned in the gospels, that mean he can't take a look and see what they've been writing about him?'

'A persuasive parallel,' he said. 'But we really shouldn't forget the assurance of confidentiality that Novello gave Miss Heywood. Shirley has passed them on to me under the same condition. In other words, they won't be passed around every Tom, Dick and Harry. Miss Heywood sounds an interesting girl.'

Decided to ignore the Tom, Dick and Harry crack, but it's not often I get the chance to trip Pete up with this daft PC stuff so I said, 'Shouldn't call her a girl, if I were you. She's a bright young woman.'

'Thanks, Andy, I'll try to remember that. Though, like so many these days, despite all that time in our expensive education system, she still can't spell.'

'Pete,' I said, 'you're a real tonic to a sick old man. You make me feel young!'

He said, 'Always glad to help. But it's not just a grumpy old man moan. You recall that letter that Lady Denham got, the one you handed over to me? In it, the word *receive* was spelt with the *e* and the *i* the wrong way round. And its that particular error we find in these emails.'

'Oh aye?' I said, unimpressed. 'But according to you, most of the young buggers nowadays can't spell. Think you'll need a bit more than that to send her down for a lifer.'

'There are other interesting things here as well,' he said, a bit coldly. 'I don't see much point in discussing them till I've talked with the girl. I mean young woman.'

Wield came in.

He said, 'Shirley's just told me you've sent her to bring Miss Heywood in.'

Hello, I thought. Pete making decisions without consulting Broken Face. The times they are a-changing.

'That's right. Is there a problem?'

'Just wondered who you wanted to deal with first, Miss Heywood or Mrs Griffiths.'

'Heywood,' said Pete. 'Let Griffiths stew. Andy, anything else? As you can see, we're up to our eyes.'

I said, 'Nowt, except I'd go easy with the Heywood lass. Like I say, she's bright.'

'Be nice to bright people. I'll note that,' said Pascoe. 'Anything else, sir?'

Trying to make me piss off by provoking me! There's folk tried that with cattle prods and failed!

I said, 'Aye, and Godley the healer's fallen for her in a big way, only she's too bright to have noticed. So if you really think he's holding something back, mebbe you could use her somehow to get him to open up.'

He said thoughtfully, 'Thanks, Andy. I'll make a note of that,' this time sounding like he meant it.

So while I was in credit, I took me chance and said, 'Pete, I can see you're up to your neck here. I were thinking: Fester and Pet up at the Home are likely feeling a bit out of it 'cos you haven't got round to interviewing them yet. I'm on the spot, and I know what makes 'em tick, so why don't I have a chat, get a preliminary statement, like you get from Novello or Bowler, then you can decide whether you need to follow it up yourself.'

I chucked in the last bit about Hat and Ivor 'cos I thought the notion of using me like a DC might appeal, but, give him his due, he didn't hesitate for a second.

He said, 'That would be very helpful, Andy. Thank you. But by the book, eh?'

'You mean I can't use the rubber truncheon? Oh shit,' I said. 'What about my little friend?'

I pulled out Mildred.

'Oh yes,' he said. 'Might be useful. At your discretion.'

Wield gave a sort of snarly grunt that meant, What the fuck's this about?

Pete said, 'Forgot to mention in last night's excitements, Wieldy. Andy's gone hi-tech. He's got Lady D recorded in conversation with him. Be good if you two can get together some time and transcribe it. But not now. You've both got better things to do.'

Wieldy and me can both take a hint. He left and I said, 'Right. I'll be off. And thank you, too.'

'What for?'

'Not mentioning Cap and ANIMA,' I said.

'No need to,' he said. 'Like me and Franny Roote, I know you won't let a personal relationship stand in the way of your duty.'

By the cringe! I thought, the bugger's really determined to put me in my place.

Then he grinned like a schoolboy and produced this green plastic file.

'Here you are,' he said. 'I'll be interested to hear what you make of them.'

'What?'

'Miss Heywood's emails. You didn't really think I'd not let you see them? I made a copy for you.'

'But you didn't know I were coming down here,' I protested.

'Of course I didn't, Andy,' he said, still grinning. 'Like I don't know the swallows are coming in the spring.'

Oh, you clever bugger! I thought as I left. What'll you be like when time's set a grizzle on your case?

Sooner I get back on the job the better, else I might be finding the place filled!

FROM: charley@whiffle.com
TO: cassie@natterjack.com
SUBJECT: things get worse!

Hi!

Im really frustrated. Lots happening – some fascinating stuff – its like being in a Miss Marple movie – but the screen goes fuzzy when youre not actually in shot!

Breakfast was a bit of a scratch affair.

Tom gobbled his then shot off to see what he could find out – & more importantly to reassure his troops that the violent events of the previous day were just a glitch in the triumphal progress of Sandytown! Mary made polite conversation – trying not to sully the ears of the children. Neednt have bothered. The younger kids had decided whatever was going on was adult stuff – disregardable so long as it didnt get in the way of their own plans – & they shot off outside as soon as theyd stuffed their faces.

Minnie of course was having none of that – & it took a couple of – for Mary – sharp rebukes to keep her from cross examining Clara.

Then we heard the sound of a car coming up the drive & Min looked out of the window & screamed – its Novello – come to take me for my interview! –

Mary ordered her to sit still & went to the door – & we all waited – with bated breath – to see how she would handle things. If Tom had been home – Im sure thered have been a confrontation – but Mary kept her voice low & a few moments later she reappeared with Novello – looking a bit chastened – by her side.

Min jumped up – face bright with expectation – but it was me the DC was looking at.

Good morning Miss Heywood – she said – very formal – that should have warned me – Mr Pascoe our DCI would like to talk with you –

– here? – I said stupidly – like he might be travelling in the boot of her tiny car.

– no – down at the Hall – as soon as you can – if thats OK –

I shrugged & said – why not?

Min – who was standing there like an actress whos got to her feet in anticipation of winning an Oscar only to hear someone elses name – burst out – but you promised wed go swimming! –

– later – I said – I dont expect Ill be long – will I? –

I looked at Novello who shrugged.

We went out to her car. Behind us – from the doorstep – Mary said – you will remember what I said Constable Novello? – If at any time in the future you should wish to talk to any of my children – I would appreciate it if you contacted myself or their father first –

No special voice here – just her normal gentle conversational tone – but I saw Novello wince like shed been whipped. She turned & began to speak – but Mary was already closing the door.

On the way down the hill – I said – whats this all about Shirley? Is it true youve arrested Mr Godley? –

– sorry – I cant discuss the case – she said – still

formal. I put it down to being told off by Mary – & we did the rest of the short trip in silence.

I expected to find the police had taken over the Hall. Instead I was taken to a flat above the stables block. Looked in on Ginger. Seemed like someone had remembered to feed & water him – so not all townie morons!

The flat was a decent size but run down. First room I entered looked like it had been a living room – now it had computers & telephones & display boards on all the walls. There I met 2 men. One was thickset with the kind of face people will eventually be paying me good money not to dream of! By contrast anyone would have looked good – but the other really was quite dishy – slim – mid 30s – a shock of pale brown hair either attractively dishevelled – or carefully arranged – narrow intelligent face – bright blue eyes that ran me up & down without undressing me – which I found rather disturbing – or disappointing? – & a nice smile as he said – Miss Heywood? Im DCI Pascoe – & this is Detective Sergeant Wield – so good of you to come –

So this was the super-sleuth – I thought. Easy to believe now Id seen him – except of course I was still certain hed got it dead wrong with regard to poor Mr Godley.

He took me into another room – bedroom I suppose – peeling wallpaper – smell of damp – just enough room for a small kitchen table – several hard chairs – a clutter of recording equipment on a recessed shelf.

The ugly sergeant was with us – but not Novello.

We sat down – me opposite Pascoe – the sergeant to one side.

For a few moments no one spoke – old psychologists trick – trying to let silence push me into speech – so – childishly – I resolved not to say anything before he did.

Finally he opened a folder hed brought with him & spilled on to the table several sheets of closely printed paper. Even upside down I recognized them. The print-outs of my emails that Id given to Novello. Suddenly I had a bad feeling & forgot my resolve.

I said – where did you get those? –

He said – from DC Novello of course – where else? –

I thought – that dykey cow! (sorry – but even psychologists relapse into non-PC thinking at moments of stress!) No wonder she was a bit off with me this morning. Guilt!

I said – well hold on there. I want to make it clear – I let DC Novello look at them on the strict understanding that shed only extract from them anything she thought might be useful & not pass it on without keeping me informed –

– indeed – he said – so we may assume she found it all useful – & as for keeping you informed – thats whats happening now – isnt it? –

This with the smile again – but I was on to him now. He wasnt trying to charm me into accepting Novellos shattering of my foolish trust. No – hed probably listened to her account of me & decided – rightly – I wasnt going to fall for the all mates together line again. So – get in my face – provoke a reaction – get it out of the way – then down to business.

Not bad psychology – I thought. OK – I wasnt going to forgive bitch Novello in a hurry – but he knew that – & why should he care? In fact her getting all the crap left a clear field for him to be nice cop & get all the benefit of my interesting insights!

I gave him a faint smile – & could see he was pleased.

But every *quid* has a *quo* – as the HB used to say – & always make sure you see the *quo* before you let any sod get his hand on your *quid* –

Not big on *double entendre* our dad – & Im sure hed have been shocked to have heard you & me giggling every time you came home from a first date & Id ask how big was his *quo* – & did he get his hand on your *quid*!

I said – before we start – is it true youve arrested Mr Godley? –

– hes been helping us with our enquiries – yes – he said.

– then you must be mad – I said. If he wanted blunt – he was going to get it!

– why? –

– cos theres as much chance of him committing murder as the Pope! – I said.

– which pope would that be? – he said – John Paul the 2nd? Or Alexander the 6th? –

I didnt get the reference but did get the message – I was dealing with a real clever bugger here – a category that ranks just above daft buggers in the HBs hit list!

He hadnt finished either. He went on – in any case Miss Heywood – why would you think it impossible that a man you find distinctly odd – *mad as a hatter* was your description I seem to recall – should commit murder? –

I said – youre right Mr Pascoe – I did find him odd – still do – but if – as I presume – youre trying to impress me with your total recall of what youve read in my private emails – you will also have noticed I modified my first impression considerably as I came to see his oddness was mainly the oddness of goodness & innocence in a corrupt & guilty world –

There! Let him see he wasnt the only clever bugger around!

Of course all I was saying – when you dumped the fancy packaging – was – dont know how I know it but I just *know* Mr Godley couldnt kill anyone!

He gave me a *get-her!* kind of look – then said – goodness & innocence can be motives too – but lets not get bogged down in psychology & metaphysics – lets look at the facts. Godley was found by 2 police officers beside Hollis's body – with his hand on the instrument that killed him. My officer searched the house immediately after the discovery. There was nobody else there –

– which indicates – if you know your Agatha Christie – I interrupted – that he certainly did not do it! –

A stupid thing to say – but he nodded as if really pleased – & said – you read Christie do you? I collect her first editions – Ive got one or two rarities –

– no – I dont read the books – but Ive seen a lot of the movies – I said.

– yes – like Jane Austen – she films surprisingly well – he said – But you will recall that occasionally – as in *The Hollow* – the character you dismiss from the frame because theyve been caught apparently in flagrante can turn out to be the perpetrator after all –

– youre suggesting Mr Godley let himself be caught – to divert suspicion! – I mocked.

– in a way – yes – he said. His story is – he called at Witch Cottage – Miss Lee was out – he let himself in – sat in the living room to await her return – thought he heard a noise – got up – went across the hall into the consulting room – discovered Ollie Hollis on the treatment table – realized there was something wrong & was just on the point of trying to remove the fatal needle when interrupted by two of my officers –

– its a good story – I said – but I expect youve got a better one –

– an alternative certainly – he said – Mr Godley enters the cottage – discovers Hollis on the table – kills him with a needle – then hears my officers car pull up outside. The house has no rear exit. He could of course have let himself be discovered in the living room & claim he knew

362

nothing of the body in the consulting room – but he knows
what forensic science can do & he has not had time to
reassure himself he has left no traces of his presence on
or near the corpse. So he grasps the nettle – & the
needle – & lets himself be discovered allegedly trying to
pull it out of Hollis's back –

– this is Mr Godley youre talking about – not Professor
Moriarty – I said – why on earth do you imagine he would
want to kill Ollie? –

– perhaps because of something Mr Hollis saw at the
hog-roast? – he suggested.

I was gobsmacked.

– you mean you think Gordon had something to do with
Lady Denhams murder? – I cried – now youre being
really crazy! – what the hell could put a stupid idea like
that into your head? –

– well – for a start – *you* – he said – shuffling the
email print-outs – first you mention seeing Godley & the
victim having an argument – an incident confirmed by
several other witnesses. Then – after the discovery of the
body – you describe how you found yourself being
comforted by Godley – & he was dripping wet –

– it had been raining! – I yelled – rain makes you wet
– or havent you noticed? –

– indeed – & the normal reaction is to head for shelter
– he said – unless you have some good reason to stay
out in the downpour –

– anyone can get caught in the rain – I protested –
what does he say? –

– he says that he was preoccupied with his thoughts & did
not notice it was raining – till he was soaked to the skin –

– & whats wrong with that? – I demanded – are you so
completely unimaginative that youve never got so deeply
involved in something you didnt notice the weather? –

– oh yes – he said – last time it happened I was lying in wait for a murderer –

I suddenly realized – for a long time now hed been totally in control – while Id been on the defensive – with lots of yelling – & heavy sarcasm.

I took a deep breath & said – so that was his motive for killing Ollie – but what would be his motive for killing Lady D? – Hed only ever seen her twice! –

– twice when youd been present – you mean? – he said.

– well yes – I said – but I know he had never been to Sandytown till Tom Parker persuaded him –

– you know – how? –

– because he hadnt – I said feebly.

– I see – but didnt you think it odd that he hadnt when clearly – as you yourself so astutely observed – his relationship with Miss Lee was so . . .

He was shuffling through the print-outs again.

– *lovey-dovey* – he read – *bit of mutual alternative therapy going on there perhaps?* – so – 2 people in a close personal relationship – living within half an hours journey of each other – yet ignorant of the significant details of each others life? Doesnt seem likely – does it? –

He was right – it didnt.

I said – OK – but it seems to me that its Miss Lee you should be looking at – if youve been reading my private correspondence as closely as you claim youll have noticed she wasnt exactly Lady Ds greatest fan! –

He smiled – turned to the ugly guy & said – Novello was right sergeant – Miss Heywood would make a very good detective –

I noted the subtle attempt to repair feet-of-clay Novello – maybe he hopes I can be set up again for her all-girls-together act. Well forget it fellow! Remember

Suzie Bogg who threw my favourite Barbie in the duckpond when I was 7? I still hear the splash every time I see her in the village.

I said – so whats her story then? –

– she says that Mr Hollis came to her in the throes of a bad asthma attack – she alleviated the worst symptoms by her usual treatment then had to go out for a regular appointment with some old lady who suffers badly from arthritis – .

– youve checked this? – I said.

That got another approving smile & nod – & he went on – she left Mr Hollis on the table in the treatment room – she had no concern about doing this as in Mr Hollis case retention of the needles for up to ninety minutes had proved to be efficacious – & she expected to be back within the hour. Mr Godley meanwhile had been having problems with his motorbike. Realizing he couldnt fix it himself he abandoned it at a local garage – which was closed – with a note asking them to check it out in the morning. Then – needing a bed for the night – he walked to Witch Cottage. When he realized Miss Lee wasnt home – he let himself in …

He paused. I took the cue.

– he had his own key? – I said.

– no – but he knew that a spare key was left on the stone ledge above the front door – which implies a considerable familiarity does it not? Then he sat in the kitchen drinking Miss Lees whisky – till he thought he heard a noise. He went into the passage – saw nothing – returned to his whisky. Then a little later – twenty minutes perhaps – he wanted to go to the toilet. In the passage he noticed that the door of the treatment room – closed before – was now ajar. He looked inside – saw Mr Hollis on the table – realized there was something seriously

365

wrong – that one of the needles was plunged in far too
deeply – & he was attempting to pull it out when my officers
interrupted him –

– how did they get in? – I asked.

– another good question! – they found the front door
open – he said.

– does Mr Godley say he left it like that? – I asked.

– no – he is adamant he closed it behind him – he said.

I said – when your men brought Mr Godley in – did he
need to go to the toilet? –

He looked surprised – then checked his notes & said
– in fact yes he did – urgently – I see what youre getting
at – this supports his story – on the other hand – with
us men – stress often brings on the need to urinate or
defecate – & killing somebody would be most stressful I
imagine – especially for a healer. But that was a good
point Miss Heywood – do go on –

He was inviting me – almost provoking me – to speculate
– which was rather flattering. But I wanted to get away & mull
over these things by myself.

I stood up & said – where is Mr Godley now? – would
it be possible to see him? –

To my surprise he said – no problem – in fact one of
our cars is giving him a lift to his home in Willingdene –
so they can drop you at Kyoto House en route –

Gobsmacked – I said – you mean youre letting him
go? –

– we dont hold people unless weve got good reason
Miss Heywood – he said.

Which – of course – wasnt really an answer.

Pascoe now shook my hand & said – thank you for
helping us. I may need to talk to you again – if thats all
right – & dont worry about your emails. Need-to-know is
my watchword! Shirley! –

Hed opened the door into the bigger room. Bitch Novello was there – still not meeting my gaze.

Pascoe said – drop Miss Heywood off as you pass Kyoto – will you? –

Neither of us spoke as Novello led me down the stairs & across the lawn to where a police car was waiting. I could see Mr Godley sitting in the back. Novello opened the rear door for me & I got in.

Every time I see Mr Godley I seem to adjust his age downwards. Id got him down to nearer thirty than forty – but today when he turned those gentle grey eyes on me – if it hadnt been for the grizzled beard – he could have been a frightened teenager. In fact – up close – I could see that the beard wasnt so much grizzled as gilded – the lighter coloured hairs amidst the dark brown being bright gold rather than grey. Some genetic quirk – I thought – or maybe hes got highlights! He was wearing jeans & a t-shirt – the former a bit too big – the latter a bit too small. Meaning theyd got his own clothes for examination – so he was still some way from being out of the woods.

He did his usual shrinking away thing – & when I said – how are you? – he said – fine – in a choked sort of voice – & turned his head to look out of the window.

Novello had got in the front passenger seat. She looked round & said to Mr Godley – wheres our driver then? –

– he said something about getting a cup of coffee – said Mr Godley.

– Jesus! – said Novello – whats he think hes on? – a coach tour of the dales? –

Then she got out & strode off back towards the garage.

I said – nows our chance – we could make a run for it –

He looked round at me & said – why should I want to run? –

I said – I didnt mean anything – look Mr Godley while Ive got the chance – I just want to say I think its absolutely ludicrous suspecting you of being involved in Lady Denhams murder –

He looked at me blankly for a moment – then he smiled – & bang went another 5 years!

– thank you – he said – thank you –

To my horror I realized that – above the smile – there were tears in his eyes.

– sorry – he said – brushing them away – its just that – a kind word – from you –

I wasnt really listening – I was too busy staring at his hands. It wasnt till he raised them to his face that I realized he was wearing handcuffs!

I burst out – I thought they were letting you go – Pascoe said they were taking you home –

– oh yes – he said – so that they can search it with me there –

– what a bastard that man is! – I cried.

– hes doing his job – he said resignedly.

– Im going to put in a complaint! – I fulminated.

Hed been looking at me sort of assessingly – rather disconcerting – seeing hed never managed to meet my gaze for more than a split second on our previous meetings.

He said – Miss Heywood – could you do something for me? – if you see Doris – could you tell her Im alright? – & no matter what they say – I havent said anything? –

I said – Doris? –

He said – Im sorry – Miss Lee –

I said – but I thought she was called Yan –

He said – thats her professional name – she was christened Doris –

– christened? – I said. For some reason I found myself

368

thinking — Miss Lees converted so that they can get married in whatever happy-clappy chapel Godly Gordon worships at — but whos daft idea was it to lumber her with a name like Doris?!

Then I pulled myself up & said — sorry Mr Godley — your private relationships are your own business — yes — of course Ill pass on your message —

He was looking all anguished — us trick cyclists are good at spotting that kind of thing — the facial spasms & writhing lips are the subtle clinical signs we look out for — then he burst out — shes my sister! —

Well I was fair gobsmacked! — stunnered! — dunder-cowpt! — all those other things dad is whenever something happens to remind him its the 21st century!

— but youre not Chinese — are you? — I said stupidly.

At least that made him smile again.

— youve noticed — he said. 1st time Id heard him make anything like a joke.

Then it all came out.

Miss Lee is really Doris Godley — Gordons half-sister! His dad married the daughter of a Taiwanese couple who ran a takeaway in Leeds. They produced Doris. When she was 9 — her mother died. Cancer. Gordons dad married again a year later. Shortly afterwards Gordon appeared. When he was 5 his mum ran off with a salesman — & Gordon was more or less brought up by his half sister — Doris. Age 16 she started working in her grandparents takeaway — till they sold up & went back to Taiwan. After that she was a check-out girl at Tescos — but shed got interested in acupuncture through some practitioner her grandparents used — name of Yan Lee — & acted as a sort of part-time assistant cum apprentice. When Yan Lee died a few years later — Doris thought of taking over but found the old ethnic clientele didnt much fancy being stuck

369

with – & by – Doris Godley from Tescos. By this time Gordon – now 19 – had discovered his – alleged! – healing powers – though this was a talent not much valued in the Council wages office where he worked.

Then – a few years on – their dad died leaving them a surprisingly large insurance pay-out & the family home – a terrace house in a bit of Leeds which was in the process of being gentrified. So – with a bit of money to play with – they each decided to follow their true calling. Doris headed upmarket – first moving to Harrogate & taking over her old mentors name – Yan Lee – even recycling some of her professional certificates for added authenticity.

Eventually she fetched up in Sandytown – because a patient whose arthritis she did wonders for turned out to be Lady Denhams land agent! He was the one Lady D told off to do the deal with Avalon while she was putting Sir Harry through his paces in the Caribbean! Hearing Doris was looking for new premises he said – why not relocate completely? – Sandytowns on the up – exaggerating a bit probably cos he wanted his own treatment source handy! As a sweetener he offered a generous 10 year lease on Witch Cottage.

She thought it all looked a bit too Sleepy Hollowish to start with – but clever agent made sure she met Tom Parker – already a crazy fan of alternative medicine. So she stayed – & when the Great Consortium sprang into being – with Toms plans for promoting alternative therapies – she thought shed really got it made.

But there was a downside. Lady D now began to look at all her many land & property holdings in the light of the new marketing opportunities on offer. Eventually it occurred to her that Witch Cottage – picturesque & historical – was a potential mini-goldmine. Guided tours – local fare – a gift shoppe! The only trouble was Miss

Lees lease – watertight – & with renewal options. Doris was unbudgeable. She knew a good thing when she saw it. But dear old Daph was no slouch when it came to finding angles! Somehow she found out the truth about Doris & she put it to her – if she insisted on the terms of her lease – Lady D would go public – taking the high moral ground – insisting that the good name of Sandytown would be soiled forever – if they permitted a known con-artist to continue practising her unqualified medicine there!

Nothing Doris could do but agree to move out. When she told Gordon he was furious – hence the row with his hostess at the hog-roast.

But none of this did he want the police to know – because of what it would do to his sisters reputation if it got out.

I told him he was crazy – he was under suspicion of murder for Godsake! – he had to come clean. But he was adamant. He owed Doris more than he could ever repay. In any case – he said – in this country innocent people dont get condemned for crimes they havent committed.

I started to say – if you beleive that youll beleive anything.

Then suddenly Novello & Wield appeared.

The sergeant said – change of plan – we need to talk to you a bit more Mr Godley –

& he started to help Gordon out of the car.

At the same time Novello opened the front passenger door. I saw her pick something up from the seat – & start slipping it into her pocket.

I leaned forward & got hold of her wrist.

It was a mobile phone – & it was switched on.

Novello didnt pull away or anything – just turned bright red – confirming what my mind was telling me.

Id been put in the car with Gordon Godley to get him to talk – & uglymug Wield & cunningbastard Pascoe had been listening in on everything he said!

What was worse – Gordon had paused half out of the car & was taking in this little scene – only – from the way he turned those big eyes on me like a dear old Labrador whose owner has inexplicably given him a hard kick – he had jumped to the conclusion that I was in on it!

I yelled – no! I didnt know! – really! –

But already Wield was marching him away from me.

Novello started to slide across into the drivers seat – saying – right – Ill drive you home now –

I opened the door & got out.

– fuck you – I said – fuck you & all the rest of you – Ill walk –

OK – not the most elegant of put-downs – I thought of several much better on my way back up the hill – but none of them good enough to damp down my anger. When I got back to Kyoto Minnie was waiting for me – gagging for a blow-by-blow account – but I brushed past the poor kid & came straight up to my room to e you. O God Cassie – I wish you were here so we could talk – face to face. Something like this happens & suddenly everyone looks different – everything has at least a double meaning – theres nobody to trust. Id pack my bag & head for home – except I know that Id just take all this other baggage with me. You used to say one day it would get me into real trouble – always putting the most sensational interpretation on the most ordinary of incidents. But this time Im not fantasizing.

Shit has happened – is still happening – here in Sandytown – & Im not leaving till Ive helped clean it up!

Lots of love

Charley xxxxxx

4

I need to watch myself!

Felt a bit knackered when I got back and had my last chat with Mildred, and thought I'd take forty winks. When I woke, it had been at least an hour and I'd have been happy to make it longer! It felt real good lying there on my bed – like a day off at home when there's no reason to get up afore opening time.

But I knew it weren't really good. In fact, it were downright bad. When a Home starts feeling like home, that means you're getting institutionalized! All them proud words to Pascoe about being a cop first, a patient second, seemed just hot air. Didn't have a good CID thought in me. Needed to snap meself out of that, so rolled off the bed, doused my head in cold water, and settled down to read the Heywood lass's emails.

That helped a lot, made me ashamed of myself. I mean, here's me, the great detective, can hardly drag himself out of bed, and here's this young lass, bright as a button, sharp eyes taking everything in, nebby as a norrie, always making connections, not scared of two and two making five, in fact sometimes she could jump to conclusions for England!

I laughed out loud at the bits she wrote about me.

Could Pete be right about her writing that note to Daph? Not likely, I'd say. Any lass brought up on Stompy Heywood's farm's going to have a right down-to-earth attitude to the animal kingdom. No cruelty, but no sentimentality either. Mind you, owt's possible when you've been a student. Whatever, it's real good intelligence, this stuff. Bet she hates Ivor's guts for spreading it around! Hope Pete's got the sense to be straight with her. Could be useful if he keeps her onside.

But I can't sit around here all day when there's work to be done. I told Pete I'd take statements from Fester and Pet. Who should I start with? Pet's handiest, but I reckon the longer I keep her waiting, the gabbier she'll be. So I'll take a stroll up to the Clinic and see if I can wipe that smile off them teeth! I'd best take these emails with me. Don't want Pet doing a search for illegal substances and coming across these. Any road, man carrying a file always looks more official.

And just in case Fester breaks down and makes a full confession, I'll stick my friend Mildred in the file and leave her running!

5

Andy! I didn't hear you knock.

Knock? Oh aye. Short-term memory still on the blink. Sorry.

Never mind. It's good to see you. How're you doing? You look well. Come on in, take a seat, let's review your progress.

Nay, Lester, that's not why I'm here. Not doctor and patient this time. This is official. I'm back on the job. Mind if I put another cushion on this chair, raise me up a bit? That's better. Always like to look a suspect straight in the eyes.

Suspect?

Did I say suspect? Witness, that's what I meant. No way you could be a suspect, is there? Not the way you felt about poor old Daph.

And what way was that, Andy?

Best make that Superintendent, just for the record. You loved her, didn't you?

Loved her? Good God, no! Not in any romantic sense. We were friends, I hope. And I admired her energy, her drive. But as for love . . .!

You mean you weren't secretly having a passionate affair then?

No, we weren't! I can't imagine who's been saying these things!

Well, let's think. That would be . . . everybody!

Then everybody was wrong. It does happen, you know.

375

Oh aye? Like in elections your side of the pond, you mean? Whoops, let's not get political, eh? But you can see how folk got the wrong end of the stick. I mean, I only saw the two of you together a couple of times, and both times she were giving your tonsils the old tongue massage. And then again, when you went to Switzerland on exchange last year, didn't she straight off book a holiday so she could be on your doorstep? From where I'm sitting, looks like a straight case of love to me.

Not on my side. I can't answer for what Lady Denham may have felt, but there was no reciprocation, I assure you.

Recipro— what you said. That a trick cyclist term for shagging?

Don't pretend to misunderstand my vocabulary, Superintendent. *I have read your case notes, remember? I know just how bright you are.*

Does that mean I can use you for a reference? All right, no bullshit. Just to get things quite clear, she fancied you, but you didn't fancy her, right?

Yes, I think that captures the essence.

So all this face-sucking, you put up with it for the sake of politeness? Or what?

I certainly didn't wish to offend her.

Why not? The woman's stalking you. Why didn't you wish to offend her?

I think stalking's putting it a tad high.

Following you halfway across Europe ain't stalking?

She was on holiday! Our Swiss clinic is located in a very popular winter sports area.

Nay, don't get your stethoscope in a twist. All right, have it your way. She weren't stalking you and you weren't running away from her.

Running away? Who said that?

No one said that. I said you weren't *running away. Man*

in your job mebbe ought to listen a bit harder. Patient tells you he likes fluffy towels and you hear he likes fucking owls, that could get you into real bother with the GMC. Listen, Lest, let's play this straight. Poor old Daph's dead. I want to find out who killed her. You too, right? So cut the crap, let's talk turkey, no witnesses, no recording, just thee and me, man to man.

You're quite right. Murder's more important than personal vanity. I'm sorry. Yes, Daphne fancied me; yes, I was happy to encourage her because she was generous in her support of the Avalon; and yes, I probably allowed what to me was merely a flirtatious relationship to go too far. I prided myself that my daily experience dealing with the clinically deluded and deranged meant I could quite easily take care of a fond old lady. I use fond in all its senses. Originally it meant . . .

No need to explain, Lest. I got a lad working for me who can conjugate and. *But you were wrong, right?*

Oh yes. I was wrong. I was horrified to discover that her sex drive, far from being in abeyance, was . . . rampant. And yes, I did run away. Not openly, of course. There were good clinical reasons, my exchange with Dr Kling of the Davos Avalon was always on the schedule. But deep inside I knew I was running away.

And she followed you.

She brought her niece and nephew out to Davos for a skiing holiday, yes.

How did you feel about that?

Shocked when she turned up at the clinic – a courtesy call, she termed it – but also somewhat reassured that she was still sufficiently in control of herself and sensitive enough to the opinions of others to have cloaked her visit under the guise of a holiday. She was not yet quite Venus toute entière à sa proie attachée.

She weren't going to jump you in public, you mean?

That's it. She was very conscious of herself as Lady Denham of Sandytown Hall, the apex of the social pyramid in this neighbourhood. She had needs which age had not diluted, I can confirm that. I suspect she must have satisfied them somehow, but it would be done with the greatest discretion. No, my attraction was social as much as sexual. She didn't just want to ravish me, she wanted to marry me.

Oh aye. I've been there. The ravishing's not so bad, but bugger the marrying!

That's not quite how I saw it.

No. I understand. Tell me, Lest, just between mates, you said she had to be getting it somewhere, so what about you? Did you ever, tha knows, give her one?

Please! I really don't care for the way you phrase that question . . .

That means tha did! Good for thee, lad! No need to look embarrassed. To them as asks, it ought to be given, at least once. So what happened?

I am not going into details. There was drink involved. I don't think my performance matched her expectations. But it didn't seem to put her off. She still acted as though we had an understanding if not quite a formal engagement.

Expect she felt that once she got you under her wing and med sure you started the day with a proper Yorkshire breakfast, she'd soon bring you up to scratch. In fact, she probably wanted a progress report. How'd you measure up yesterday?

I don't follow you.

Yesterday, when you banged Daph for the second time. How was it for her?

Now see here, I don't know what you're . . . Wait, I get it. The autopsy indicates sexual activity, right? Dear God, you're not saying the poor woman was raped?

378

No, it looks like she did it with someone she wanted to do it with, and that made me think of you.

Well, you can think again. No, categorically. Not me.

No? Oh well, nowt that a DNA test won't prove. Right, let's get on to the hog-roast, Dr Feldenhammer.

What happened to Lester?

Nay, that were me being chummy with a witness to get the best out of him. After everything you've just told me, the case is altered. Congratulations, sunshine, you've got yourself promoted from witness to suspect! Always start off polite and formal with suspects, that's my way, just in case there's any complaints later.

Is that so? Then shouldn't you read me my rights?

What's them when they're at home? Listen, lad, we both know if tha starts getting seriously worried, you'll be waving the star-spangled banner and demanding to see the sodding US ambassador. So just tell me all you can remember about the hog-roast.

I'm ahead of you there, Superintendent. Knowing the police would want a statement eventually, and wanting to capture my memories before they began to fade, I wrote this out not long after my return yesterday.

Oh aye. Neatly typed, and not a lot of long words either, by the look of it. Just the job for a country cop. Matter of interest, did you write it before or after Pet called in to see you?

Sorry?

Ms Sheldon, your Chief Nurse. She came over from the Home after she got back from the Hall. I just wondered if you wrote this before or after you had a chat.

Now listen in, Mr Dalziel, I don't know what you're implying . . .

Implying? You've both been to a party where your hostess got lightly grilled over a barbecue – Jesus, even folk in your line of work can't be so used to cadavers you wouldn't talk about that!

Yes, of course we talked about it. I think I'd started writing my statement when she turned up, and I finished it later, quite unaltered by anything we may have discussed.

That's fine then. You didn't give her a lift to the hog-roast? Or her you?

You know I didn't. Why do you ask?

Seems odd, that's all. Both invited, coming from the same place, I'd have thought you'd likely have tossed for who was going to drive, who was going to get rat-arsed.

Perhaps neither of us looks on such occasions as an opportunity to get rat-arsed, as you so elegantly put it.

No? May be wrong, but Pet strikes me as a lass as can sup her yard of ale, and from what you just told me about you and poor old Daph, you're not averse to tying one on. Mebbe you just didn't want to be seen arriving with her in case that rattled Daph's cage. Got to be careful with a possessive personality like Daph's. But you'd know all about that, you've got the certificates.

Interesting speculation, but I'm sorry to say it was just a matter of convenience. In our line of work, we are both always on call and either of us could have been summoned away early.

Fair enough. See much of her at the party?

In fact, yes. We have a lot in common – work and such, you understand. I circulated, the way you do at a party, but once the storm appeared on the horizon and everybody headed into the house, I was happy to find myself with Nurse Sheldon, sheltering in the conservatory. In fact, we were together until we went outside again when the storm passed, and they discovered the body.

Great. That's that sorted then. Wish it were always as easy as this. What about dear old Daph, see much of her as you circulated?

A little. We talked, but only in passing. She was very much the gracious hostess, seeing to the needs of all her guests.

Didn't see to her own needs, or yours mebbe, a bit more privately, Lest? You know, invite you up to her room? Or mebbe you were a bit bolder, nowt like a good shag out of doors, long as the mercury's high and the midges aren't biting.

For God's sake, I've told you already. We did not have sex at the hog-roast, indoors or outdoors. What do you think I am?

I'm not sure. A man, certainly. What kind of man, that's the question. Mebbe I should ask someone who knows you a lot better than me. Nurse Sheldon, for instance.

What the hell does that mean?

It was you who said you'd a lot in common. Makes sense, I'd be surprised if your head nurse didn't know you inside out. Like I expect, as her employer, you'll know her inside out. Aye, I daresay the pair of you know each other's ins and outs very well.

Now listen here, Dalziel, I'm getting just a tad tired of all this innuendo . . .

Innuendo? That a board game? No, now I recall, it means going round the houses to suggest summat. Nay, I'm sorry if you don't think I've been direct with you. Easily remedied, but. So tell me, Lest, are you and Pet at it?

At it?

Screwing, shagging, jig-a-jigging, making love, having intercourse, exchanging bodily juices – you choose the phrase, then answer the question. Are you at it?

I've had enough of this! You may be a policeman, Dalziel, and you may be a patient, but I don't have to take this kind of prurient crap from you under either hat . . .

Now ho'd on there! Fair do's. I ask if you've banged old Daph and you answer me sort of embarrassed but polite. Now I ask the same about Pet and you're all in a lather.

Why's that? Me, I could understand anyone getting annoyed to be asked if they'd banged some woman old enough to be their mother, but not a grand lass like Pet! It's not this doctor–nurse thing, is it, Lester? Didn't think you Yanks did snobbery. Shame on you!

Enough! Just two last things I want to say to you, Andy, before I get on with my work. The first is I don't need anyone to tell me what a fine woman Pet Sheldon is, especially not in the vulgar provocative tone you have chosen to adopt. Secondly, from my clinical observation during this so-called interview I'd say that physically your convalescence is progressing very well, but mentally there are many issues still to deal with. Don't worry. We don't give up on people at the Avalon. We'll get there in the end.

Is that right? I'm glad to hear it. Got a lot in common, me and you, Lester. Reckon that will do for now, then. Won't keep you from your work any longer. Thanks for your time. Oh, just one other thing, you'll let me know if you're planning to leave the country in the near future, won't you? Catch you later, lad. Cheers!

Come on! Come on! Answer . . . ah, there you are, Pet. It's Lester. Listen, not a lot of time. Dalziel has just been interviewing me . . . yes, interviewing, or perhaps interrogating would be a better word. I think he's on his way to see you now, I thought I should warn you. Don't be taken in if he tries the patient-flirting-with-nurse approach. He's very much back in policeman mode. He talks like he knows about you and me, but he's only guessing. Admit nothing. And remember, after the storm started, we were together till they found the body. Whatever else you do, don't give an inch on that . . . yes, I know . . . yes, yes, it's going to be OK . . . we'll talk after he's seen you . . . No, best leave it till our usual pre-rounds consultation . . . we have to be careful. He may come across as a fat clown, but believe me, this guy is really dangerous . . . yeah, me too. Take care. Bye.

Lester! Sorry to bother you again, but I think I left me file in here. Be forgetting me head if it weren't screwed on. Age, eh? Pity you buggers couldn't find a cure for that, other than the obvious one, I mean. Ah, there it is. I'll leave you in peace now. Cheers, again!

6

Well now, Mildred, that made interesting listening, didn't it? So what are they up to? One thing's clear, they weren't together all the time after the storm started. But who's alibiing who? Or could they both be in it together?

Going to be a hard habit to get out of, this thinking aloud business. Place like this, no one takes much notice of old fogeys sitting in the sun, talking to themselves, but if I try it when I get back on the job, I'll be on gardening leave afore you can say mesembryanthemums.

Clever bugger, old Fester. Had him going for a bit, but he came back strong. Liked the way he stuck up for Pet – mebbe he's not just in there for his jollies. And that crack about me having mental issues, that were a clever bit of counter-punching. Like a sharp intake of breath from a car mechanic, not what you want to hear from a shrink!

And mebbe he's right. Mebbe I have gone a bit doolally. I mean, what the fuck am I playing at, sticking my neb into this case? Nowt I can do that Pete isn't capable of doing himself. He wanted to keep me out of it, but no, here I come, swinging through the trees, beating my chest and yodelling!

But I've made my bed – Jesus Christ, how I'd

love to be lying on it! – by myself. Lead us not into temptation. At least what happened with Pet's reassured me my bit of bother with Cap ain't permanent. It's a worry, but. Suddenly I could see all them viagra jokes coming back to haunt me! It'll never happen to me, you think, when you're still getting a hard-on just walking through the lingerie department in Marks and Sparks. But, like the tax man, it'll get you in the end. Right in the end! Women are lucky. Don't matter how old they are, if they've still got the itch, all they've got to do is find a hard pecker to scratch it with. Like old Daph. Though it don't sound like it were Fester that were doing the scratching.

And now she's dead. That's all that matters, Dalziel. Get your mind back on the job. She might have been a right old bruiser, but she didn't deserve what happened to her. So let's take a real close look at Fester and Pet, and ask what motive could either one of them have strong enough to make them decide Daph had to go?

Pet's way ahead here. Combination of jealousy and doing your loved one a good turn has often done the trick, specially in a strong-willed passionate woman. No problem physically – she'd know all the right places to squeeze, and she'll have had lots of practice lugging bodies around.

Fester's different. Unless it turns out Daph's remembered him in her will, I can't see any reason why his fancy should have lightly turned to thoughts of murder. In the end he could just have walked away from Daph, shipping out back to the US if necessary. Maybe he'd even hinted this to Pet. Maybe she'd begun to worry that getting his jollies from her didn't include any long-term plans for their relationship. Wouldn't surprise me if she were right. Being keen to hear a luscious handful like Pet say *yes please!* is a long way off wanting to hear her say *I do*! In fact, if my reading of Fester's right, I'd say he were the type who were more likely to use his position and standing to get himself one of them trophy wives, some nice young juicy bit of tottie as 'ud hang on his arm in public and flash her tits and make all the other men drool with jealousy!

Easy to imagine Pet thinking, Walk away from Lady D if you want, but you're not going to walk away from me! And a wise woman might find herself looking for something that ties a tighter knot than slippery love.

Like shared guilt.

So Pet does the deed, then makes sure Fester gets involved in the cover-up. Easy enough in the heat of the moment, and she knows once Fester has taken a step down that road, there's no going back. Pet gets a bit mucked up dragging poor Daph around, so when she sees Roote's fallen out of his chair later, she moves right in and picks the muddy bugger up, and now she's got a reason for being all wet and clarty herself.

What about Ollie Hollis, but?

Could be he saw summat, enough to worry him, but not enough to make him head for the police. Rings up Pet or Fester, tells them he wants to talk, says he's going round to Madame Lee's. One of them takes off down there, the other stays up here, sets up the mutual alibi again.

If I hadn't hijacked Pete when he came to take their statements, we'd have known which one was doing which!

Shit. Don't expect he'll be backward about pointing that out to me.

But I'm getting ahead of meself.

Looks like Godly Gordon's out of the frame. Never did fancy him myself. I know there's no art to read and all that, but I just can't see a guy who looks like that being a killer! Bet the bugger has a hard time stomping on a beetle!

So who does clever old Pete see as the front runner now?

Not Fester and Pet, I'd guess, else he'd not have agreed to turn me loose on them.

Seems to have serious doubts about the Heywood lass, but I reckon he's up the creek there. Spent too many of his formative years with prancing ponces in education who reckoned bad spelling was a capital crime! No, I'd put money on Stompy's lass being OK. My only worry about her after reading her emails is that round Sandytown just now it might not be too healthy to be so nebby and bright!

Make a note, Dalziel. Have a friendly word.

Back to Pete's hit list. At the moment I'd guess Hen Hollis and Ted Denham are neck and neck. Then there's all them Parkers. Or mebbe it's the obvious for once and it were down to that animal rights woman Seymour spotted. Not likely, in my book, but mebbe I'm prejudiced 'cos of Cap.

One name that won't figure high on Pete's list.

Franny Roote.

Hard to believe he's here for the good of his health.

Except of course if that's exactly why the poor sod's here!

Need to watch developments there carefully. I've

invested too much good drinking time bringing Pascoe on to see him brought down 'cos he feels he owes a slippery bastard like Roote.

Any road, time to stop talking to myself.

Interrogation ain't much different from fornication. Keep 'em waiting till they want it as much as you!

Nurse Sheldon should be on the boil by now, so here I come, ready or not!

7

Pet! There you are, lass. All right if I come in?

Looks like you're in already to me.

*So I am. Must be your animal magnetism that does it.
You've got us poor sods skittering around like iron filings.*

*All right, Andy, or should I call you Superintendent? You
can cut the crap. Lester's warned me you were on your way,
and why.*

*Warned? Nay, that's not a very friendly word, and me and
him the best of mates. Must have got it wrong, luv. Likely he
mentioned in passing I might be dropping in – and would you
co-operate? – that 'ud be a quite natural thing for a boss to tell
one of his staff, letting her know it would be fine to take a few
minutes off her professional duties to co-operate with the police.*

*Nice try, Andy, but I'll make up my own lies, thank you.
Talking of which, as I'd take odds you already know, Lester
rang to ask me to back up the lies he told you and, if necessary, add any of my own to support them. That's not a look
of real surprise on your face, is it, Andy?*

*Not just on my face, luv. A lot further down than that.
You've not just taken the wind out of my sails, you've bent
my rudder! So you've decided to turn poor old Fester in, have
you? Good thinking, Pet, on every count. You're doing your
duty as a good citizen, and you're keeping yourself out of the
clag. So what's the lying bastard been up to?*

Nothing, except trying to watch out for me. Which is really nice of him, and I must admit it gives me a warm glow to know he's willing to go out on a limb for me . . .

No more than you've done for him, Pet, and very nice limbs they are. Sorry, that weren't very gentlemanly, were it? I don't mean to upset you . . .

Andy, I've been nursing a long time now and I've had to deal with patients who've used everything from filthy slander to assault with loaded bedpans to try and upset me. Got me going a couple of times too, but I soon learned that all you need to do is remember them lying face down with a thermometer up their backsides, and you soon see things in perspective. So stop trying to be provocative and just listen for a change.

I'm listening, I'm listening.

Right. I love Lester.

Oh aye? That why you jumped me in the shower?

Look, I'm sorry about that. I don't know what came over me. I was feeling a bit down, things didn't seem to be going too well with Lester. We should have seen each other the night before, but he called it off – I think Lady Denham crashing his party had upset him – and then when I saw her coming into the Home next morning, I thought, has she been here all night? So when I looked in on you and realized you were in the shower . . . I'm sorry . . .

Nay, lass, don't fret. So long as it's not spoilt it for you with other men. You were saying, you love old Fester . . .

Yes, I do. Don't know where it's going exactly, but even if it goes nowhere, I think far too much of him to let him put his reputation at risk defending me. I'm not trying to make myself out to be some pillar of virtue here either. Last night after we came back from the Hall, I was more than willing to accept Lester's offer to cover up for me. Like I said, it really made me feel good knowing he'd do that for me. But this morning, specially after I heard about poor Ollie Hollis, I got to thinking, this is more than just a simple case of someone knocking off a nasty old woman who'd been asking for it anyway. Telling you lot the truth is important, if only because not telling you the truth could slow down your investigation, and if someone else gets killed, I don't want to feel in any way responsible. What's up? You might look a bit pleased instead of sitting there groaning like I'd just told you we were going to have to operate on your piles.

Nay, lass, of course I'm pleased you're going to come clean, only I were half expecting the way you've been rattling on that you were building up to a full confession!

Then you're going to be disappointed. But two things you ought to know. One is that not long before the storm broke, Lady Denham and me had a bit of a storm of our own. No prizes for guessing what about. I'd been having a wander round the grounds and I came back by the stables. No hunters there any more since she called it a day after Sir Harry broke his neck, but she still kept her old hack, Ginger. Liked to feel something between her legs, and I bet if she'd ended up in a wheelchair she'd have had it built twice as high as normal so's she could still look down on the peasants.

Didn't like her much, did you, luv?

You really are a great detective, aren't you, Andy! Anyway, I thought I'd say hello to the horse. I like horses, specially when they don't have idiots perched on their backs. But as I got near I saw the door was ajar and I could hear a voice inside. It was Daph Denham, though I didn't recognize it straight away, it sounded so soft and sad – human, you know, not her usual way of talking, like you were a public meeting she'd rather not be attending.

Oh aye. And who were she talking to?

Ginger, of course! Everyone says . . . said that the horses were really the only things she loved. She could treat humans like dirt, but her horses got the best of everything. Perhaps this was where she headed when she was unhappy . . .

Nay, lass! Don't go sentimental on me.

Why not? There's good in all of us, Andy, though it takes a clever surgeon to find it in some.

I'll remember that. So what was this sad human stuff she were saying?

Didn't hear much of it, it was the intonation that struck. But I did catch something about trusting people, and a pig squealing, I think.

Mebbe she were thinking the animal rights people were right and she should give up the pigs and go veggie?

Didn't get the timing right then, did she? Like I say, I surprised myself by feeling a bit sorry for her, her own party, lady-of-the-manoring it over the hoi polloi, and still she ends up talking to a horse! I'd have moved away quietly, only there was an old feed pail by the door and, as I turned, I gave it a kick. The horse neighed — must have thought it was feeding time — and Lady D called, 'Who's there?' I'd still have made my getaway if there'd been time, but she was at the door in a flash. Looked me up and down, then said, 'Oh, it's only you, Nurse Sheldon.' She always called me Nurse Sheldon, like it was a put-down.

And were you? Put down, I mean?

No. I was still feeling sorry for her. I took a sip of my wine — I had a glass of red — champagne goes to my head — and I said, 'Hello, Lady Denham. Just admiring your grounds. Looking really lovely, aren't they?' That seemed to provoke her.

Why? Sounds pretty bland to me.

I think that may have been the trouble. I usually look her in the eye, give as good as I get, without being openly rude. This time, I don't know, maybe I sounded too polite, a bit friendly even, as if I was feeling sorry for her. I think she caught that, and that's what got her rag.

So what did she do?

She lost it. Thinking about it later, I reckon that whatever

*it was sent her to the stables, it was something that had made
her very angry and very sorry for herself at the same time. It
was the unhappy bit that came out as she was talking to
Ginger, but now all the anger came bubbling up – no, not
bubbling, exploding! I couldn't believe what I was hearing!
She told me I had no right to go wandering round her property at will, I was only there on sufferance as a paid employee
of the Avalon, to represent the nursing staff, and if I had any
true sense of my place I'd be back on the lawn, making sure
the important guests like Dr Feldenhammer got properly looked
after, instead of wandering round, half inebriated, sticking
my nose in where I had no right to be.*

By God, lass! And you stood there taking this?

*Well, no. After a bit I got angry too. Do you blame me?
I said things I shouldn't have said.*

Like what?

*That she thought she was so special but in fact she was
a laughing stock. A geriatric nymphomaniac running after
a man twenty years younger than herself, a man who found
her at best ridiculous, at worst revolting.*

You don't take prisoners, do you, Pet!

*I'm not proud of some of the things I said, Andy. I ended
by telling her it was time the world knew exactly what kind
of monster she was and then even her sodding title wouldn't
protect her. By this time she'd stopped yelling back at me.
She just stood there, looking at me like I was a piece of dog
dirt. And she said something like, 'What I am, I am, Nurse
Sheldon. I do what I need to do and I accept the consequences.
Now go away. You are pathetic.' Suddenly I ran out of things
to say. That's when I threw my wine over her.*

*Why? I mean that was nowt compared to what you'd
been saying to her. A geriatric nymphomaniac! She must
have said summat more than, 'you're pathetic'. Summat
really offensive. Or threatening. Come to think of it, this thing*

393

about letting the world know what kind of monster she was – what's that mean? Just fancying old Fester doesn't make her a monster, not in my book, anyway.

You know what it's like in a row, Andy. Words just come out.

Mebbe. OK. Then what? You and her ran at each other and started pulling each other's hair?

No. She stood there like the wine was nothing, I was nothing. I walked away. All right, maybe I walked away because I was afraid of what I might say or do next, but I didn't do or say it. I went and found Lester and told him what had happened.

Looking for a comforting hug, were you?

To warn him that the big moment had likely come. He was going to be faced with a choice, her or me.

Rarely a wise move, luv, facing a man with a choice. What did he say?

He said he'd have a word with her, get things sorted. I was still pretty wound up. I said he better had, and quick, I wasn't going to put up with that old biddy treating me like dirt any longer. Then the storm started and everyone rushed back to the house. I made for the conservatory. It was dark in there and I found a corner hidden away behind a shrub.

By yourself?

Yes. I didn't want to talk to anyone. Other people came into the conservatory, but I don't think any of them saw me. I just sat there and fumed till the storm passed. Then I went outside.

So Lester was telling a porkie when he gave you an alibi?

Yes. I didn't want him to, but when we got back here last night, he said that if Daph Denham had mentioned our bust-up to anyone, it might look bad. It was simpler if he said we'd been together in the conservatory during the storm and it would save the police wasting time going down a dead end.

Very civic-minded of him. And after the storm? Were you there when they found Lady D?

In fact, no. Someone spotted your friend, Franny Roote . . .

Nay, lass, not my friend.

Sorry. He speaks very highly of you. Anyway, his wheelchair had got stuck at the bottom of the lawn, which was really boggy after the downpour, and the poor lad had managed to tip it over trying to get it to move. I don't know how long he'd been lying there, trying to get the chair upright and drag himself back in. He was a right mess, soaking wet and covered with mud. Someone had to look after him, and I was the obvious choice. I got him back in the chair and a couple of us manhandled it on to firmer ground. Then I pushed him back to the Hall. I heard this uproar behind us — that must have been when they found Lady Denham's body — but I was concentrating on getting poor Franny back inside where I could check him out properly.

Ay, quite right, the patient comes first, eh? So how was poor Mr Roote?

Fortunately he didn't seem to have done himself any real damage, so it was just a case of cleaning him up and drying him down as best I could. And while I was doing this, people started coming back inside, all talking about the murder, naturally.

That must have been a shock.

Of course it was a bloody shock! She was an old monster, but that didn't mean she deserved to be killed and roasted like a pig! I couldn't take it in. I just concentrated on getting Franny sorted. He was really upset, didn't want to leave, but I told him if he didn't get himself home and into some dry clothes, I wouldn't answer for the consequences. A man in his circumstances is very susceptible to pneumonia. I wheeled him out to his car and helped him in. I offered to go with him, but he said no, he was fine now. Then he drove off. I was going to go back into the house, but suddenly I couldn't face it. Also I'd got myself all mucky cleaning up Mr Roote. So I got into my own car and drove back here. I got myself cleaned up, then I had a word with you, remember?

A pleasure as always, Pet, but why did you do that?

I don't know. I thought, being a policeman, you ought to know what was going off. After we'd talked, I went up to the Clinic, saw Lester's car there so knew he was back. And I went in and we talked things over.

And cooked up your little story, to save us poor overworked bobbies from wasting time down a dead end. Kind of you, except of course you haven't done it. Does Lester know you've changed your mind and are telling me what really happened?

Yes. After he rang me to warn me you were coming to see me, I looked out of the window and I saw you sitting out there on the lawn, and after a while, just watching you, I found myself thinking, that doesn't look like a man I want to lie to. So I rang Lester back and told him I'd decided to come clean.

Did he give you an argument?

Not really. He said it was up to me, he was still ready to stand by our story, even if it meant lying in court. I said I was really grateful but I didn't want it to come to that, and he said in that case it was probably for the best, and to tell you he was sorry, and if you wanted to see him again, this time he'd be completely frank with you.

Big on him! So then it was love and kisses down the line and promises you'd meet up later for something a bit more substantial. Nay, don't look offended, lass. With old Daph out of the way, you don't want to hang about. Strike while the iron's hot. And when you've both got your breath back, you can tell Lester I'll look forward to talking to him again, but meanwhile I've got other fish to fry. Right? Now I'll be off. Take care, Pet. And try not to kill any patients, eh? Not with the boys in blue all over the town! Cheers!

396

8

So what do you make of that, Mildred? I could do with a bit of female input.

Nowt worries me more from a woman than a sudden rush of honesty. Usually means they're hiding something, in my experience!

Old Fester, too. Mebbe after I went back in to pick up my file and Mildred, he got to thinking I could have been eavesdropping on his call to Pet. Mebbe it weren't Pet's idea to come clean, but Fester's. Mebbe there's something he's more worried about me finding out than that the two of them were both wandering round loose during the period when Daph got topped. I'd put money it's got summat to do with that song about the Indian Maid, the one that got Fester so upset when Ted the bart whistled it in the pub. I were singing it in the shower when Pet jumped me. Got to give it to her, the way she explained doing that were pretty convincing! Don't know why they give Oscars to them Hollywood stars for spouting some other bugger's lines when half the women I know could act 'em off the screen without breaking sweat! No, it was Daph visiting me, then me singing 'The Indian Maid' as did it.

My guess is Daph must have got something on Fester, something that meant he couldn't just tell her to sod off and bother some other bugger. She wants him, but she can't buy him, 'cos, first off, he seems pretty comfortable already, and second, it's clear the one intimate part of herself she kept out of everyone's reach was her purse! Nay, it had to be summat really personal to keep him dangling at the end of Lady D's string.

Likely Pete'll think I'm delusional if I tell him any of this. Any road, last thing I want is him getting a sniff of my knee-trembler with Pet. Don't think he's got any secrets from Ellie. OK, she wouldn't go running to Cap, but by God, the reproachful glowers I'd have to put up with! So I'll sit on that till I know what it is I'm sitting on, as the actress said to the bishop.

What Pete will like is knowing how the wine got on Daph's dress. I can see his eyes lighting up as he thinks, What if it went further than wine throwing and ended up with Pet on top of her, throttling the poor old biddy? Doesn't mean to kill her, but when she realizes how far things have gone, she rushes off to fetch Fester. So they decide the best thing is to stick her in the hog-roast!

Doesn't sound all that likely to me. And it 'ud mean all that stuff about fixing then unfixing their stories was even more complicated than it looks! No, like all the best lies, I reckon most of Pet's story is true, up until the storm starts anyway.

So what was all that stuff about squealing pigs she overheard? Mebbe the animal rights nutters had got close enough to really put the frighteners on Daph. But you don't soften people up, then top them, do you?

So where now? Report back to Pete?

Nay, he'll have plenty of other things to worry about. And I don't want to look like I'm hanging around, all pathetic, like them poor old sods who sit on park benches watching the lasses playing tennis.

Not that I'd mind the company of a bit of young stuff for a change. That lass of Stompy Heywood's now, she's got an interesting way of looking at things. And a nice turn of phrase. If I'd caught her a bit younger, she might have trained up into a good cop. Said I needed a bit of female input, didn't I, Mildred? And talking to her 'ud give me the chance to take a closer look at the Parker set-up. Sounds like if anyone will benefit from poor old Daph's departure, it's Tom Parker. Now he'll have free scope to put all his daft ideas into action!

So Kyoto House it is. But how am I to get there, that's the rub? No problem, Pet 'ull fix me up a lift. Her and Fester will be only too glad to see me off the premises.

And if I time it right, I might get a bite of lunch too!

FROM: charley@whiffle.com
TO: cassie@natterjack.com
SUBJECT: whos a big twit then?!

Hi!

Ive done it again! Why should I be surprised? This started – more or less – with me dropping the old lemonade jug & seeing it hit the one stone remaining in Mill Meadow like Id aimed it. That should have been a warning. Charley girl – you dont want to get mixed up in this – but mixed ups what I am!

Sorry – waffling – dont worry – Ive not been arrested or anything like that – tho maybe I should be.

Back to the beginning – after I shot my last off to you I felt a lot better – also felt in need of coffee – so went downstairs to find Mary preparing a tray with a cafetiere & some choc cake – which she was going to bring up – in case I wasnt well! Typical – time to think of others – even in the middle of a crisis – which it is for them. Got to remember that. For them its a crisis – for me its just grand opera. I can leave the theatre any time I like – head for home – get my life back – turn all this into an anthology of entertaining anecdotes for my mates.

But Tom & Mary will be back here on the stage – having to deal with whatever comes up.

The kids were playing somewhere in the garden — making a lot of noise. Id seen Minnie briefly as I came downstairs. Shes seriously pissed with me — returned a glower for my friendly smile — & vanished. At Marys suggestion I took my tray outside on to the terrace — & she joined me — & I got stuck into the coffee & cake — yummy! For a few minutes it was easy to forget everything that had happened. The sun was shining — the sea was sparkling blue like a Riviera tourist poster — not a hint of yesterdays storm — & the visibility was so good you could probably see all the way across to Holland — if (I recalled Sids remark) you really wanted to.

Then Tom came up the drive.

Nice to see him — of course — but it did mean end of quiet interlude time. Even as he walked across the terrace towards us — he was launching into a blow by blow account of his morning so far.

Spent most of his time — I gathered — making sure everyone affected by the development plans understood Lady Ds death didnt change anything. Comfort & light pedlar — thats Tom. His message to them was — Lady D would have wanted them to go ahead with the Festival of Healing as planned — put the tragedy behind them — full steam ahead to the Promised Land — with Sandytown on the map as its unrivalled capital — a fit memorial to dear dead Daphne!

Sunny optimisms no substitute for the real stuff — & it was maybe irritation at having my sunlit moment so quickly interrupted that made me object — but surely everything depends on the will? What if Lady Ds heir — or heirs — dont care to continue supporting her investment?

He said — theyd be mad not to — the future was gilt edged — & there were safeguards built into the

401

Consortium agreement – to protect a survivor if one partner died.

Instantly – you can see how my minds working! – I thought that sharp-eyed Pascoe would see this as a motive – specially once he ferreted out how Tom & Daph used to fight about various details of the scheme.

Didnt say anything of course – but could see Mary was worried about what was going to happen next. As Ive said before – suspect she feels – for all her reservations about Daph – that at least the old girl acted as a counter-balance to Toms flightier notions! But it soon became clear he wasnt so naively optimistic that he hadnt been thinking about the will also. He said hed been in touch with his solicitor whod made contact with Lady Ds London lawyers – whod told him that their Mr Beard was already on his way up to Yorkshire. No details of the will were forthcoming.

– but I do not doubt that Edward will inherit the bulk – they have been so close since Sir Harry died – said Tom.

– & what about poor Clara? – said Mary – doesnt she deserve some compensation for what she has had to put up with? –

Which prompted me to wonder where poor Clara was.

I was told she had gone out shortly before I got back.

– I think she just wanted to get some fresh air & walk around by herself – Mary told us – she said she thought she might pick up some of her things at the Hall later – the poor child looked as pale as a snowdrop – tho of course some people do have that natural subtle skin tone –

There can be few people less capable of malice than Mary Parker – but I still felt my ruddy sun-smacked cheeks were being glanced at!

Tom went on to say that hed met Sergeant Whitby –

whod told him he was searching for Hen Hollis – to help with enquiries – but he wasnt at home & no one seemed to have seen him since he left the Hope & Anchor last night.

I think we all thought – last time Jug Whitby went looking for a Hollis – he found him dead!

Tom had also checked out Diana. Shed sent apologies for not calling at Kyoto House this morning to offer moral & medicinal support – but her friend Mrs Griffiths had started packing to go home & Di was trying to dissuade her – presumably not wanting the word to spread that S-town was the new murder capital of the UK – & then the police had turned up to take Sandy in for more questioning! This had naturally thrown Di into a decline – from which she was still recovering – poor thing!

Mary rolled her eyes heavenward as she listened to this – whether in exasperation at the hypochondria – or gratitude at being spared the visit – I couldnt tell!

I noticed Minnie had done her stealth bomber thing at this point & materialized within eavesdropping distance – not wanting to miss hearing any fresh news her dad brought. Looking at her I felt a sharp pang of guilt – adults shouldnt offload their crap on to kids – I can recall mum sermonizing the HB on that very subject!

Time to build bridges.

I said – hey there Min – what time are we going then? –

She glowered at me & said – going where? –

– thought wed arranged to go for a swim in the pool – I said – I know I said this afternoon but I could manage now if you like – of course if youre too busy . . .

I could see her shilly-shallying between the chance to put me down & the prospect of going to the hotel & maybe seeing Uncle Sidney. No competition really. With a

weary curl of the lip she could have sold to Ice Queen
Esther – she said – oh all right – Ill get my things –

– let Charley finish her coffee – commanded Mary – &
say thank you –

Minnie glanced at me sullenly & muttered – thanks –
almost inaudibly.

– didnt quite catch that – said Mary sternly.

Tom & Mary both had their attention fixed on their sulky
daughter – so I took the chance to put my fingers in my
mouth – pull my lips wide – & roll my eyes – in my
famous Mad Mavis act that always used to get you
corpsing when I did it behind the HBs back!

I judged my girl right. Her eyes opened wide – then
she dissolved into peals of laughter – ran up to me –
gave me a hug – & said – thanks a million! – before
taking off into the house.

– there – said Mary – its marvellous what a few well
judged words will do – isnt it dear? –

– how true – said Tom – You know – I think Ill stroll
along with the girls to the hotel – I want to have a word
with Sidney & get his take on what effect this business
might have on the investment programme –

I could tell Min wasnt too delighted to have her dad
tagging along – she was probably hoping to squeeze
every last detail of my interview with the police out of me
– but she did pretty well by making sure whenever the
path got too narrow for 3 abreast – Tom was always the
odd one out.

To start with I went for an edited version – but eventually
– maybe cos shes so sharp at spotting omissions – & also
cos I dont think anyones too young to learn what cunning
bastards the police can be! – I found myself telling her just
about everything.

Her shriek of indignation when I told her about Novello

404

passing my emails to all & sundry had to be explained to Tom. He was less openly indignant – saying – if youd told me why you wanted to use the printer Charley I think I would have advised against it –

When we came in sight of the hotel – & Minnie ran ahead as if she hoped Sidney might be waiting for her in reception – Tom went back to the subject saying – re those emails Charley – it might be well to think carefully in future about what you say to your sister –

Behind all his sometimes daft optimism – Tom Parker is pretty sharp!

– you mean theyd hack into my computer? – I said – horrified!

He didnt answer direct but said – tell me about your security set-up –

So I did. When I told him that Id kept on getting blue screen which the accompanying message blamed on my firewall – so Id disabled it – he groaned.

– Im going to get it sorted – I assured him.

I didnt tell him that I was so non-tec that in fact it had been loathsome Liam who disabled it when I mentioned my problem. Hed been going to download another firewall for me – but that went out of the window when I caught him poking my ex-pal up against that tree!

– meanwhile youre an easy target – he said – for anyone! –

Would the bastards really do that? – I wondered.

Of course they would! I almost hope they do read this. BASTARDS! BASTARDS! BASTARDS! There – now I feel better!

In reception we found Minnie chatting to the girl at the desk – who was telling her that she knew Sid wasnt in his room cos hed told her if anyone wanted him hed be in the Recreation Centre.

As we approached the pool area we could see a towel spread out on one of the luxurious sunbeds the hotel supplies for its well heeled clients but no sign of Sid.

Then Min screamed – there he is! Not in delight – but horror!

Lying on the water – face down – quite still – arms & legs spread wide – was a pale naked body.

Before we could stop her – Min had run forward & jumped straight in. I think Tom might have followed – but as the shockwaves from the splash reached the body – it turned slowly over – & Sid Parker – shaking the water from his head – said – well hello young Minnie! – havent you forgotten something? – like taking your clothes off? –

Cradling Min in his arms – he waded to the side. The girl was choking with relief – or maybe shed just swallowed a lot of water. I realized now Sid wasnt in fact nude – but wearing a pair of trunks – creamy coloured like his skin – & tight enough to leave little to the imagination.

Not that the sight engaged mine anyway. Suddenly Sid was no longer an object of my lustful fantasy. Indeed – memory of its enough to make me cringe with embarrassment! What an idiot I am Cass! – seeing everything – understanding nothing – but always 100 per cent certain Im right.

What Im 150 per cent certain Im right about now is that those long white limbs Id glimpsed in the cliff cave – spread-eagled beneath the barts bouncing buttocks – hadnt belonged to Clara Brereton – but to Sidney Parker!

Now I recalled him walking away from me at Denham Park – his arm draped round Ted Denhams shoulders. Oh God! Me thinking the only reason for them to be closeted together was to hatch some cunning financial plot – then trying to decide which one of them I found the more gorgeous! Twit twit twit!

& Esther, welcoming me into the house & flinging open doors. Bet she hoped she might let me catch them at it! Maybe it was her way of being kind. Cow!

Well, I did catch them at it, didnt I? Only as usual my mind wouldnt let me compute what it didnt want my eyes to see.

Didnt stay long at the pool. Tom was insistent on talking to Sid – & the pair of them went off to his room. Minnie not pleased – started a sulk – but Sid knows how to smooth her feathers – promised her he wouldnt be leaving Sandytown for at least another two or three days – & hed take her for a drive in the Maz. Gave me a sort of rueful glance – like hes caught on Ive caught on! At a guess Id say Sids dedicated High Church gay while Teds a lot more ecumenical. Not that that makes any difference to the way I feel about him now. Dont mind a boy freind who thinks my lovely sisters a knock-out – but I couldnt put up with one who started making eyes at George!

Somehow neither me nor Min were in a mood for swimming – so after a few lengths we were both ready to head back home. More chance of getting updates here than at the hotel anyway – & if something interesting happens you dont want to be caught lying around in a wet swimming cozzie!

Gap there. Minnie came bursting in at speed of sound – meaning I didnt hear her knock! She gasped the police were here – asking for me again. I said – who? – Novello? – & she said – no – a big fat man – could be Shreks brother if you painted him vomit green.

Has to be Mr Deal – however you spell it. Whats he want? Minnie didnt know – so I chucked her out – said Id be down in a moment. But with him sniffing around – not to mention the rest of his gang – Im not risking leaving

this around for anyone to see. Send & delete! You do the
same, OK? Thatll show the bastards!
    Love
    Charley xxx

Volume the Fourth

*My feelings tell me too plainly that in my present state,
the Sea air would probably be the death of me.*

1

'Peter! *Salvere iubeo! Willkommen! Bienvenu!* In any language, I am glad to see you!'

Franny Roote was sitting in his wheelchair on the threshold of his cottage, so for a moment as Pascoe swivelled his legs to get out of the car, they were face to face and eye to eye.

From many a mouth, such a greeting would have seemed over-effusive, even synthetic. But the glow of pleasure on the young man's face was beyond fabrication.

Wasn't it?

Pascoe said, 'Good to see you, Fran.'

He meant it, but with reservations.

He'd been genuinely concerned to lose touch with Roote, and his relief at discovering he was alive and relatively well was equally genuine. But to see that slight figure sitting there in a wheelchair sent a pang through his heart at the memory of how he had got there. And then there were the circumstances of their meeting.

He'd listened to Wield's account of his interview with the man and read his witness statement, and with some relief had found nothing to suggest that Roote was anything more than a peripheral witness in the case.

But now that he laid eyes on him again, for some reason there popped into his mind the famous response of the great Bill Shankly when asked if in his opinion a player who was not interfering with play could be judged offside.

If a player's not interfering with play, he ought to be!

Around a crime – and Pascoe's encounters with Franny always seemed to take place around a crime – somehow it was hard to believe he wasn't interfering with play.

He got out of the car and they shook hands, each bringing the free hand to intensify the greeting, both apparently reluctant to break the contact.

Finally Roote said, 'I thought we'd sit outside and enjoy the air, if that's all right?'

There was a rustic table with a bench set against the cottage wall. On the table stood a coffee pot, two mugs and a cake on a plate.

He was expecting me, thought Pascoe. Interesting.

'Maisie's Madeira, I presume,' he said.

'I'm impressed. Sergeant Wield, of course? If I read him right, no detail of my simple life here will have gone unrecorded or unreported.'

'That's Wieldy,' agreed Pascoe. 'Anything he misses won't be missed.'

'I see you still love a paradox,' said Roote.

'In the abstract. But in reality, they can be a problem. For example, the paradox of why you, having made so much more progress than seemed likely, and knowing how concerned I was to keep track of this progress, should apparently have vanished off the face of the earth. And on top of that, why you finally should have settled down within a short car ride of where I live and never made contact.'

Roote poured the coffee and cut the cake.

Then he said, 'Maybe I wanted to walk into your office one day under my own steam and say, "Hi! Here I am! Good as new!" And lift the guilt from your shoulders.'

'Guilt? You think I feel guilty?'

'Sorry. Wrong word. Responsibility? Something like that. Whatever it is you feel whenever you see me. I wanted to take that away. And having got that scenario in my mind, I couldn't settle for less. Sorry. It was silly. Egotistical, even.'

'Seems pretty unegotistical to me,' said Pascoe. 'Even Mr Dalziel was impressed.'

'Dear Andy! What a joy it was to see him again. I couldn't believe my eyes when I rolled into the pub that day. Do you know, I was so pleased to see his face, at first I didn't notice he was wearing a dressing gown and slippers – sorry – one slipper!'

Pascoe murmured, 'He'll be flattered to know he had that effect on you.'

'He's one of the great originals, isn't he? But part of my pleasure, a large part, was knowing that chance had done what I myself should have done months earlier. To see him was at one remove to see you, and whatever I said, I knew it could not be long before that remove was removed.'

Pascoe took a large bite out of his slice of the cake because he had no idea how to respond to this intensity. Was there a homosexual element in it? There were so many ambiguous areas in Roote's personality that it wouldn't be surprising . . .

'Peter, just for the record, I don't fancy you,' said Roote. 'Not touchy-feely fancy, so no need to worry lest I might leap from firm handshakes to slobbery kisses.'

413

Pascoe swallowed a large bolus of Madeira and washed it down with coffee. He should have remembered that talking with Roote could be like having your mind scanned.

'I never imagined . . . well, maybe I did wonder . . . look, I'm sorry, but to be honest when you first started writing those letters to me, I thought you were taking the piss!'

Roote grinned.

'Maybe I was, a little. But that's what friends do to each other, isn't it? Listen, I think it's your job that gets in the way. Imagine we'd just met, on a campus, say, at a gallery, in a theatre, anywhere. You might have found me a touch eccentric, but amusingly so. And I might have found you a touch buttoned up, but intriguingly so. And if we met again a couple of times, I reckon we'd have drifted into being friends, which is how friendship happens, isn't it?'

'But . . .?'

'But we met in circumstances which demanded you saw me as a suspect. And when the vagaries of English law saw me sent down, that initial relationship was frozen, apparently beyond all hope of dissolution. Myself, I soon realized that I needed to move on from any feelings of resentment and blame. But when I met you again, I saw that it was going to be much harder for you to move on from suspicion and distrust.'

'So you thought, hey, I can change this guy!' said Pascoe, trying to lighten things up. 'Was that because of some evangelical imperative, or simply as an entertaining intellectual exercise?'

'Bit of both,' said Roote. 'Then I began to realize this was really important to me. Without getting anywhere near slobbery kiss territory, I found I really did like you, and it's a shit feeling when you know someone you really like regards you as the pits.'

'You're saying what you did for Rosie you did to make me like you?' said Pascoe.

'No,' said Roote. 'I did it because that's what friends do. And hey! Let's not make too big a thing of this. I didn't know that part of the deal was a madman with a shotgun who hated my guts!'

'But when you found out, you still put Rosie first,' said Pascoe. 'She talks about you, you know.'

'Does she? I'd rather she forgot me. That's another reason I didn't want to roll in on you. Bad enough having you look at me with those big guilty eyes. No reason to load that stuff on a kid.'

They sat and drank their cooling coffee in silence for a few minutes.

Pascoe thought, Please God, don't let me find that Franny Roote has anything to do with this case. Don't face me with that choice!

Which he knew wouldn't be a choice.

He set down his mug and said, 'Tell me about your wanderings and how you came to settle in Sandytown. I got an outline from Wieldy, but I always prefer original sources.'

'You and I both,' said Roote.

He started talking. The style was anecdotal, the tone light and amusing. It was, thought Pascoe, like listening to a young gent of an earlier age just back from doing the Grand Tour. Where the reason for his journey was touched upon, it came over as hardly weightier than a visit to various spas to take the waters.

Pascoe finally interrupted.

'So in the end, there was nothing that gave any hope?'

He hadn't meant to be quite so blunt, but that was how it came out.

Roote's eyes widened in a parody of shock.

'Do you think you might be spending too much time with dear Andy, Peter? I should watch that. In answer to your question, hope never dies, though sometimes it changes. I have the consolation of philosophy, of course.'

'This Third Thought stuff? Andy told me you tried it on him.'

'Did he indeed? Perhaps the seed has found a crack in even that stony ground. Yes, that was something else I approached not altogether seriously but which has since proved stronger than I imagined. Like my friendship with you. Whoops, sorry, I don't want to embarrass you again. Getting back to hope, Peter, there was something which I'm reluctant to share with anyone, yet you of all people deserve to share it. Not hope exactly, but hope of hope. I hardly dare think about it, let alone talk about it.'

He paused as if marshalling his words, then resumed.

'In terms of care and consideration, the Avalon Clinic at Davos was by far the most comfortable institution I visited. I don't mean just physically, but psychologically. I felt at home there, but of course I didn't want to feel at home in a clinic, so eventually I moved on, always searching. One man's name kept cropping up – a Dr Hermann Meitler. I found him in a small research establishment near Dresden. His official area of expertise was sports injuries, would you believe? If you recall, the old Democratic Republic had a rather dubious reputation for their attitude to performance-enhancing treatments. In terms of medals, they were always looking for the philosopher's stone which would turn everything to gold. And they didn't let consideration of things like casualties along the way hinder their research.'

'Sure this guy was called Meitler, not Mengele?' said Pascoe with distaste.

'Behind his back, possibly,' laughed Roote. 'He was certainly a man who regarded humans as problems to be solved rather than individuals to be cared for. The demolition of the Berlin Wall and the invasion of Western standards of accountability had deprived him of his endless supply of experimental material. Once he got the idea that in me he'd found someone ready to go the extra mile, and willing to pay for the privilege, we got on famously.'

'But he didn't do the miracle,' said Pascoe.

'No,' said Roote. 'And yes. He treated me in ways that would certainly have got him struck off in the UK. I didn't mind. And I was right not to mind. For eventually he made me feel again, Peter. I'd always kept up the electrical toning routines even though I couldn't feel a damn thing. I was determined that if the miracle ever did happen, I wasn't going to fall over because my muscles had completely atrophied. Then one day, I felt a tingle. A comic word, tingle, isn't it? Certainly made me laugh with joy. I felt a tingle where I had felt nothing since I got shot.'

'But that's marvellous!' exclaimed Pascoe. 'So what happened?'

'Nothing happened. I spoke with Meitler. He made it clear there was a choice involved. Not be killed or cured. That I'd have gone for, no hesitation. No. It was between the possibility of cure and the equal possibility of being left as a thinking vegetable. That gave me pause. Was I ready to take that risk?'

'And you weren't?'

'I needed time to think before I took it. I went away, and spent the next six months making up my mind and changing it. Eventually I returned to the Davos Avalon where my previous stay had suggested I might find a solution to my problems. When I got back there, I discovered my old mentor, Dr Alvin Kling, had done a six-month exchange with Lester Feldenhammer of the Sandytown Avalon. Happily, Lester and I soon found we were on the same wavelength and I struck up an even closer relationship with him than I'd had with Alvin.'

'So you asked for his advice?'

'No,' said Roote. 'Shortly after I met him, I read in the papers that Dr Meitler was dead. He'd been under investigation by the German medical authorities for some time. It seems that finally the police were getting involved. One night Meitler's laboratory went up in flames. His body was found in the ashes. Accident, suicide, it was impossible to tell. All his research records were destroyed, among them, I assume, mine.'

Fleetingly the thought that death seemed to follow Franny Roote around drifted across Pascoe's mind, but there was no room for it to lodge there alongside this hint of a possibility of further recovery.

'That must have been a terrible shock, Franny!' he exclaimed.

'I think I'm beyond shock now, Peter,' said Roote.

'But this tingle, is it still there?' demanded Pascoe.

'Ah, the tingle! Is it the real tingle of renewal or just the delusory tingle of hope? Peter, perhaps I shouldn't have spoken to you. Third Thought has taught me to deal with hope, but now I fear I've set all its chimeras loose to trouble you.'

'I just don't see how you can feel this tingle and not do anything about it!'

'Let myself be poked and prodded and X-rayed and analysed again? I would need to think long and hard about that. What if they told me nothing has changed? Goodbye hope. Or what if they confirmed there has been a change? Wouldn't I once again be faced with some form of the choice Meitler spelt out to me?'

'At least you could talk to this Dr Feldenhammer. Or isn't this his field?'

'In fact Lester specialized in neurology before turning to psychiatry. He would be the perfect man to consult. Indeed, as I hesitate to decide my future, Lester is one of the best of my reasons for remaining here in Sandytown.'

'Just one of the reasons?'

Roote smiled and said, 'Oh yes, there were many others. Lester told me about Tom Parker and his plans for the town. He was confident that my Third Thought ideas would be greeted enthusiastically by Tom, and he was certainly happy to let me have the chance to air them in the Clinic to those who wanted to hear. In addition I found after my long sojourn abroad, I was homesick for England, and especially for Yorkshire, where so much significant in my life has happened. So when he returned to Sandytown at the end of his six months, I came with him.'

It all sounded perfectly logical, but when did any information vouchsafed by this young man not appear so?

The thought felt like a disloyalty, but until the brutal killings of Lady Denham and Ollie Hollis had been resolved, Pascoe knew he had to follow every line of enquiry.

He said, 'Franny, this is more than just a social call, you understand that?'

'Of course. I'd be worried if it weren't. This is a dreadful business. Anything I can do to get it out of the way, you've only to ask.'

'OK. Now you first met Lady Denham when you came to Sandytown at the start of this year, right?'

As trick questions go, it was hardly the trickiest. Indeed, there was no reason Roote should have met the woman during the trip to Switzerland mentioned in Heywood's emails, nor, if he had, why he should want to conceal it, but the faint smile that touched the young man's lips suggested he appreciated the prevarication.

'No, I met her first at the Davos Avalon towards the end of last year,' he said. 'She was on a skiing holiday with her nephew and niece and she made a courtesy call on Lester Feldenhammer.'

'Courtesy?'

Roote laughed out loud.

'Peter, you are so good! Here less than twenty-four hours and you've already winkled out that dear old Daphne had serious designs upon Lester. Yes, I'd guess her choice of locale for her holiday – probably the main reason for taking it at all – was her desire to keep tabs on her chosen one. Conversely, I would speculate that one of Lester's reasons for organizing the exchange was to put him out of Daph's reach for a while.'

'You know this for a fact?'

'No. Lester has never confided anything about his private life,' said Roote. 'I used the word *speculate* advisedly, just as I used the word *courtesy* to describe Lady D's call. Her ultimate purpose may have been predatory, but on the couple of occasions I saw her, she was accompanied by her niece, Esther, so unless what she had in mind was a *troika*, I would be wrong to imply on that occasion a deeper motive.'

'Franny,' sighed Pascoe, 'you're not at some academic conference. Just tell it as you'd tell it to . . . Mr Dalziel, say.'

Roote laughed again and said, 'OK. Daph was a woman of strong appetites, none of which was diluted by age. She loved wealth, status and sex, not necessarily in that order. Hollis gave her wealth, and a bit of status. He'd bought Sandytown Hall and the Lordship of the Hundreds. Denham gave her a title and she manoeuvred the poor devil so that she squeezed what profit she could out of him. And Feldenhammer is wealthy enough both from his earnings and money he's inherited from his family connections – he's one of the Milwaukee dairy product Feldenhammers – blessed are the cheesemakers for they shall be stinking rich – you'll have heard of them?'

Pascoe shook his head.

'Never mind. Point is, Daph liked it round here 'cos she was the local great lady. She enjoys status, and another thing about Lester is he has an international reputation, so she could envisage a future travelling to conferences in exotic places, and if her English title didn't get the natives kow-towing, her celebrity husband would.'

'She sounds a bit . . . calculating,' said Pascoe.

'None more so. But let's not forget the sex. She was, I'd say, an enthusiast. She had to have the hots for any guy she went after, meaning that money and status weren't enough, they had to be able to do the job.'

'Does this mean she was promiscuous?'

'I thought we were talking *à la Dalziel*! You mean, was she putting it about? Who knows? But she'd have made sure she did it so discreetly, no one noticed. As I say, she was hugely jealous of her status.'

This fitted in with what Esther Denham had told him. She and Roote might not share much else, but they shared a sharp eye.

Thinking of Esther brought her brother into his mind and he said, 'So, no toy-boys? I hear her nephew liked to flash the family jewels on her private beach . . .'

'My, Peter, how do you discover such details? Yes, it's true, and I'm sure Daphne was not averse to admiring the display. But as for touching, as well as the risk of looking ridiculous if it got out, that would have meant giving up the power she had over him. That was the unifying element of her three passions – wealth, status, sex – they all gave her power. In the end, slaves revolt, worms turn, lap-dogs foul the silken laps they rest on. Look for someone who'd had enough and you'll find your killer!'

That was as far as Roote was willing to go, despite Pascoe's invitation to him to suggest possibilities. But he was happy to give thumbnail sketches of all the locals. What struck Pascoe was the general absence of malice, indeed the many hints of affection, in his comments. He sounded at ease with himself and his life, almost happy. Perhaps he was in love, thought Pascoe, who had learned never to ignore the conventional. Remembering Dalziel's suggestion that Franny might have his eyes on Clara Brereton, he listened carefully for any underlying note of special interest when he talked of her, but detected none. In fact his most open admiration was reserved for Charley Heywood, whom he could only have met a couple of times.

'A bright girl, sharp eyes and a sharp mind; give her a few more years and I wouldn't mind lying on her couch myself,' he concluded.

Pascoe laughed and said, 'She rates you pretty highly too. Up there with Ted Denham and Sidney Parker in the list of Sandytown's top attractions.'

'Well well,' said Roote thoughtfully. 'Poor lady, she were better love a dream.'

This fell more sadly on Pascoe's ears than anything he'd heard the young man say.

He glanced at his watch and said brightly, 'Time to go, I'm afraid.'

'You'll come again?' asked Roote.

'Of course. Now I've found you, I'll keep real close tabs on you. One thing, Franny. Is it true you're thinking of mounting an appeal against your conviction? Or were you just winding the Super up?'

'Would it surprise you if I were serious, Peter?' he asked.

Pascoe shook his head.

'I'm long past being surprised by you, Franny.'

'I'll take that as a compliment, shall I? Let's say it depends on how I feel when I wake up in the morning. Sometimes it seems a great idea, sometimes it seems pointless. Bit like waking up, I suppose. Don't worry. Whatever I do, I'll try to keep you out of it. And whatever I tell you will be the truth, the whole truth, and nothing but the truth.'

Then he gave his birds-out-of-the-trees charming smile and added, 'But not necessarily in that order. Goodbye, Peter.'

They shook hands.

As Pascoe got back in his car, Roote called, 'One thing I wondered about. Of course you and clever

Sergeant Wield have probably got it sorted already, but why was the hog-roast timetable delayed? Might be worth a look. Take care, Peter.'

Pascoe drove away down the rutted lane.

On the road, he got out of the car to close the rickety gate. As he did so, his eyes quartered the surrounds. No problem once you started looking. In one of the cracks in the old sandstone gatepost, a sensor glinted, and high in the holly bush, painted the same shiny dark green as the leaves, a tiny CCTV camera looked down on him.

He smiled at it and waved.

Franny liked to know who was coming up his drive. Why not? A man in a wheelchair must feel very vulnerable. Particularly a man with enemies.

And one thing was certain.

Being in a wheelchair wasn't going to stop Franny Roote from making enemies!

He got back in the car and glanced at the clock. It was an hour and a half since he'd told Wield, 'It's no use. I've got to see Franny, get it out of the way.'

What *it* was, he wasn't quite sure. Relief, responsibility, guilt, gratitude, doubt, suspicion, they were all there. Now added to them was hope.

His mobile rang as he was pulling away. Being a law-abiding citizen he steered into the side and switched off the engine before he picked up the phone.

It was Wield.

'Pete,' he said, 'you need to get back here. There's been another incident.'

Law-abiding citizenship forgotten, he switched on, started up and sent the car screaming along the narrow road as he said into the mobile, 'Fill me in, Wieldy.'

2

Sergeant Wield had had a trying morning.

Peter Pascoe wasn't running this investigation the way he'd expected. Normally they made an excellent team, their peculiar talents and skills dovetailing nicely, while the knowledge that they were working under the shadow cast by the Olympian bulk of Andy Dalziel acted as a bonding agent that drew them even closer together.

Pascoe's reaction to Dalziel's close encounter with death had taken him down roads where Wield had been reluctant to follow, but once the Fat Man had started to recover, it seemed that normal service was being resumed. The obsessional behaviour which had marked Pascoe's pursuit of the truth about the explosion had pretty well vanished, and a period of relatively conventional work for Mid-Yorkshire CID had allowed everyone to settle back into their well-oiled grooves. Even the gap left by the Fat Man had begun to gape less widely.

Then had come the summons to Sandytown.

Pascoe's late arrival had allowed Wield to get things set up in a way that would normally have won him nothing but praise and gratitude. Fair do's, there had been expressions of both. But there'd also been a sense of something held back, of *I know I can't complain because*

I got here late, but if I had got here earlier I'd have done this differently.

The scattering of the witnesses had occurred before Wield's arrival, but he felt that to some extent Pascoe held him responsible. At the same time the DCI managed to suggest that his attitude to those who had remained – especially Edward Denham – would have been much firmer. For one thing, he clearly hadn't much liked the locating of the Incident Room in the flat above the stables.

His attitude to Andy Dalziel's presence was also an area that gave Wield concern. Dealing with the Fat Man was never going to be easy, but in Wield's view, the only way to do it was by the book.

At the present time, Dalziel was in a non-operational state. You paid him all the formal respect due to his rank, you might even have an off-the-record chat with him from time to time about how things were going, but you shouldn't let him get within sniffing distance of an official function. Precisely how he'd managed to hijack Pascoe on his visit to the Avalon the previous night Wield did not know. OK, some useful information had come out of it, but with that extracted, Pascoe should have drawn a line and said, *From now on in, don't cross it.* When Dalziel turned up at the briefing, he should have been asked to wait somewhere else. And when he volunteered to interview Feldenhammer and Nurse Sheldon, Pascoe should have told him thanks, but definitely no thanks. At the very least he should have received a firm warning about using that fancy little recorder during the interviews. How the hell did the Last of the Luddites get his hands on something like that? Wield asked himself. And he shuddered to think of the legal standing of such recordings, made without the knowledge or permission of the recordees. Perhaps his brief period working with the Combined Anti-Terrorist Unit had blurred too many edges for Pascoe. When Wield had hesitated support for Pascoe's ruse of getting Novello to leave an open phone in the car with Godley and Heywood, the DCI had smiled rather condescendingly and said, 'If it works, Wieldy, great. If it doesn't, who gives a toss?'

In the event it had worked. But only at the expense of really alienating Charley Heywood, already seriously pissed at what she regarded as misuse of her email correspondence with her sister, and even provoking the hitherto mild and subdued Gordon Godley into demands for his solicitor. Pascoe had used a carrot and a stick to restore his former docility, the stick being the threat of a charge of obstruction for concealing his relationship to Miss Lee, the carrot the promise that future co-operation should mean his half-sister's background did not have to become public knowledge.

Wield later expressed doubts about the wisdom of such a promise if the CPS decided Miss Lee had laid herself open to charges of obtaining money by false pretences. Pascoe had laughed and said, 'Come on, Wieldy! Either curing people by sticking needles into them is always false pretences, or it's not. Sticking needles into someone and killing them is murder and that's all we need to be thinking about.'

The way Pascoe was dealing with the woman from Seaview Terrace was another cause of concern to Wield. By the time they finished with Godley, Mrs Griffiths had been sitting around for the best part of an hour. Seymour had found her all packed up and ready to leave. Cleverly he'd insisted on bringing the luggage along, for security, he assured her. What it meant was it now had the same status as a handbag and was thus much easier to search than if it had remained in the house, in which case they'd have needed a fully sworn warrant.

Of course a personal search would require a significant change of status. At the moment she was there as a voluntary potential witness. Keeping her hanging around this long was a dangerous strategy. If she took it into her head to insist on leaving, only arrest could keep her there. But Pascoe still didn't seem in any hurry. He'd opened a file which Wield recognized. There'd been no opportunity in the immediate aftermath of Ollie Hollis's murder for the sergeant to write up his account of his interview with Franny Roote. He'd done it before he got his head down for the few hours' sleep he'd managed last night. And he'd presented it along with Roote's own statement to Pascoe first thing this morning.

Now, seeing the DCI so rapt in his reading, Wield saw his chance to restore an equilibrium he felt was in danger of being lost.

He said, 'Tell you what, Peter, you'll be wanting to see Roote yourself some time. Why not shoot across there now and get it out of the way? I'll deal with Griffiths, put her in the frame or out of it. If in, she'll still be here when you get back. If out, then you've missed nowt.'

Pascoe raised his bright blue eyes and looked at his sergeant. For a moment Wield felt as if that unblinking gaze was tracking every last convolution of his thought. In the past, only Dalziel had ever managed to make him feel like this.

Then Pascoe grinned and said, 'Think I'll faint if she takes her glass eye out, is that it, Wieldy? You may be right. And I must admit I am starting to find it irritating the way my thoughts always drift back to Franny.'

'I honestly don't see how he can be involved in any of this,' said Wield.

'Me neither, but I do need to check it out myself. And I want to see him anyway. OK. She's all yours.'

It had been that easy. Perhaps the distraction of Roote's reappearance had been at the bottom of Pascoe's slightly eccentric conduct of things so far. Time would tell.

He waited till he'd seen Pascoe drive away, then he said, 'Right, Dennis, let's go chat to Mrs Griffiths.'

Wield's strength as an interviewer was his face. It was as unreadable as a brick wall. Except, as Dalziel put it, a brick wall was a lot prettier. Abuse, accusation, dramatic revelation, subtle legal argument, full confession, passionate denial, all bounced off that unchanging visage. Silence was no weapon because he could return silence till it became a howling chorus. He never used verbal menace. His favourite strategy was to invite interviewees to talk about themselves, then concentrate on what they missed out.

The moment he took his seat in front of Sandy Griffiths, he knew this wasn't going to work.

She was reading a magazine called *Animal Rights*. She was wearing a T-shirt bearing the legend *hey hey BMA how many rats have you tortured today?* And on the table in front of her was a bunch of keys which he didn't doubt included the key to her suitcase.

Seymour started the recording machine and spoke the introductory ritual.

Wield said, 'Rats?'

'Better with sweet cuddly kittens, you think? Our arguments are ethical not sentimental, Sergeant. Rats have rights too.'

'Rights in defence of which you've broken the law on – how many is it? – five occasions, I think.'

'Lot more than that, but five where it came to prosecution. Six, if you include my very first demo here in Sandytown, back when I was a young girl. Except of course it wasn't me who got prosecuted that time, but Lady Denham.'

He'd been right. She wasn't going to leave him any aces in the hole.

He said, 'Tell me about that.'

'I was spraying this anti-scent stuff on to the hounds' noses. She took a swipe at me with her riding crop, laid my face open along the cheekbone and over the right eye. She said I was aiming the spray at her horse and she was just trying to knock it out of my hand, but the horse reared in fear as she swung, so the crop caught my face by mistake.'

'But that wasn't true?'

'Why would I want to spray a horse? They don't scent the fox out! No, she knew exactly what she was doing.'

'And she was found guilty?'

'Sight of me in the witness box with twenty-seven stitches and my face like an explosion in a paint factory did the trick. That sentimentality I was talking about.'

'Did you feel the sentence was severe enough?'

'For assault on me?' She shrugged. 'Couple of weeks in a dirty cell would have been nearer the mark, but at least it was a conviction. For the more serious crime of inflicting pain on innocent animals she should have gone down for life.'

'But she wasn't accused of that.'

'Not by you lot, she wasn't.'

'Meaning there's some other tribunal in which she may have been accused, tried, and condemned?'

'Depends if you're a religious man, Sergeant.'

'I were talking this life, not the next. So, as far as the actual assault on you went, you felt justice had been done, more or less?'

'I suppose.'

'Despite the fact that you later lost the use of your eye?'

'No connection, the doctors said.'

'These same doctors whose knowledge is based on cruelty to rats?' he said, glancing at her T-shirt.

'They're the ones.'

'But you didn't agree, I presume, else you wouldn't have wanted to sue Lady Denham in the first place?'

She smiled and said, 'No, not my idea at all. A lawyer in our group – we get all kinds, Sergeant; I've even known some policemen who were sympathetic – this lawyer saw a chance for some publicity, good for us, bad for the huntin' and shootin' fraternity. But when they couldn't find a medical expert willing to connect the assault and the loss of sight, they had to give it up.'

'How did you feel about that?'

'Relieved. I didn't fancy going to court.'

'No? Doesn't seem to have bothered you much those other five times.'

'I was there as a protester standing up for my beliefs, not a victim playing on a jury's feelings.'

'So what are you doing in Sandytown, Mrs Griffiths?'

'Holiday,' she said. 'With my young nieces.'

'How young are they?'

'Late teens. Eighteen, nineteen.'

'Not so young then.'

'By comparison with you and me, Sergeant, mere children.'

'Brother's kids? Or sister's?'

For the first time he scored a hit.

'Sister's,' she said after a hesitation.

'That would be sister in what kind of sense? Religious? Feminist?'

'I don't follow.'

'Your file says you were an only child, Mrs Griffiths.'

She smiled and nodded.

'So I was. Am. I should have said, sister-in-law's. Sorry.'

That might check out. Probably not. Didn't matter.

Wield said, 'I gather one of your nieces hurt her leg and had to go home. Dog bite, was it?'

'A fall.'

'Dog bite, fall, I'm sure she could have been treated in Sandytown.'

'You know what young people are like. She felt she'd rather be at home in Leeds.'

'Less chance of attracting attention there than here, I suppose. Get treated for a dog bite here in Sandytown and I expect Sergeant Whitby would learn about it in a couple of hours.'

She didn't reply, just smiled at him as if to say, Where's this all leading?

He said, 'Why did you choose Sandytown? Lots of unhappy memories.'

'It's the coming place, Sergeant, haven't you heard? The healthiest place on earth, according to the publicity handouts. If I stayed here long enough, who knows, I might even get the sight of my eye back!'

432

A bitter note. But bitter enough to lead to murder?

He said, 'Had you ever been in the grounds of the Hall before you went to the hog-roast?'

'It's possible,' she said. 'I'm fond of walking. I may have strayed into the grounds during one of my strolls.'

'Surely you'd have known?'

'Why? Like yourself, Sergeant, I'm a stranger here.'

Like an expert dancing partner, she was moving exactly in time with him.

He said, 'How did you feel about Lady Denham?'

'Some distant personal resentment, naturally.'

'Enough to make you target her in your capacity as an animal rights activist?'

'Certainly not,' she said. 'Her ownership of the Hollis pig business is enough to earn her that privilege without anything personal coming into it. Conditions on that site are a disgrace. I have some photographs in my case if you would like to see for yourself.'

There it was, an invitation to look in her case. Could be a double bluff, of course, in the hope of putting him off.

He said, 'Thank you. Yes, we'd like to search your luggage, if you don't mind.'

She pushed the key-ring towards him.

'Be my guest.'

He didn't touch the key but said, 'Is there anything you'd like to add to the account you gave DC Seymour here of your attendance at the hog-roast yesterday?'

She said, 'Only that after a good night's sleep, I woke this morning feeling I'd walked into someone else's drama and the best thing for me to do was head off home.'

There was a tap at the door and Bowler stuck his head in and mouthed, 'Got a mo, Sarge?'

433

'Interview suspended,' said Wield. 'Dennis, why don't you take a look through Mrs Griffiths' case while I'm gone?'

He stood up and went out of the room without even glancing at the woman.

He would have liked to think he was getting on top here, but the best an honest assessment could give him was a score draw so far. His gut feeling was that Lady Denham's death had nothing to do with animal rights, but gut feelings weren't for sergeants. His job was to advance cautiously through the darkness, step after blind step.

The old proverb popped into his mind – *In the country of the blind, the one-eyed man is king.*

Make that *woman* and *queen*.

3

Hat Bowler greeted him with a smile too bright to be genuine.

Wield said, 'Right, Hat. What's so important?'

'Nothing important, really, Sarge,' said Bowler. 'It's that Miss Brereton. She's at the Hall. Says she wants to collect some of her clothes and personal belongings.'

Wield in both his personal and his professional life had developed a sensitive ear for an evasion. He said, 'You mean Miss Brereton's being detained outside the Hall by PC Scroggs who is under strict instructions to admit no one without contacting me?'

'Not exactly,' said Bowler.

'Then let's start again, this time exactly,' said Wield.

It turned out that Bowler had glimpsed a figure passing behind an upstairs window and when he asked Mick Scroggs who he'd let in, he received the answer, 'No bugger.' Investigation revealed Clara Brereton. She said she'd entered by a rear door to which she had a key. In Bowler's eyes this cleared Scroggs of any blame, but the fearful constable, in unsolicited testimony to Wield's reputation as Pascoe's enforcer, had said, 'Doesn't matter, yon ugly bastard will kill me!'

Bowler had a kind heart and Scroggs was a like-able youngster and the DC might have been tempted simply to approve the young woman's request to pick up her clothes, then escort her off the premises, but for one thing.

'Thing is, Sarge, it wasn't her room she was in, it was Lady Denham's.'

'How do you know?' asked Wield.

'Didn't look like the kind of room I'd have expected someone like Miss Brereton to have,' said Bowler. 'Too fussy. And the wrong stuff lying around.'

'Mebbe she's an old-fashioned girl.'

'No. I got Scroggsy to take her downstairs and I had a poke around. It was definitely the old lass's.'

'You ask Brereton what she was doing there?'

'No. Thought if she was looking for something, it was best not to alert her we knew, not without talking to you first.'

'The room's been searched, you know that? DCI was very particular about that. Nothing found that seemed relevant, so what could Brereton have been after?'

'Maybe these,' said Bowler.

He produced a manilla A5 envelope from which he spilled four photographs on to a table. The colour wasn't great and they'd been printed on ordinary cartridge paper, but the images were clear enough. Taken from above they showed a middle-aged man lying on top of a young woman. They were both naked. The shadows suggested the sun was high in the sky. The ground beneath them looked sandy, possibly a beach.

Wield examined them. Bowler's awkwardness was explained now. He'd done well to unearth these, but claiming the credit meant dropping Scroggs in it.

'It's not Brereton,' said the sergeant.

'No. She looks Asian to me. You know the man, Sarge?'

'No. Where were these?'

'In this antique writing desk.'

'So why weren't they found during the search?' asked Wield in some irritation. 'Some bugger's been careless.'

'Don't think so, Sarge,' said Bowler. 'There's a drawer hidden beneath a drawer. My granddad was a cabinet maker and I used to enjoy helping him when I was a kid and he taught me all about this kind of secret drawer. Everyone thought I'd probably go into the business, but it wasn't the woodwork that fascinated me, it was the business of hiding things and finding them out. Sorry . . .'

He tailed off, thinking this was more than the sergeant probably wanted to hear, but Wield nodded as if he understood, and said, 'Good work. So what would Lady Denham be doing with mucky pictures?'

'And why would Miss Brereton want them?' said Bowler.

'If that's what she were after,' said Wield. 'Did she have a bag?'

'No.'

'What's she wearing?'

'Sun top, loose cotton jacket, lightweight fatigues, the kind with the big pockets down the front.'

'You had a good look at her then?'

Hat flushed, then grinned.

'Close observation, that's what you taught us, Sarge.'

'That's right. So you go back and closely observe Miss Brereton till I finish up here. I shouldn't be long.'

He went back into the interview room. On the table were spread the contents of Sandy Griffiths' case, clothes, toiletries, a notebook, a couple of paperbacks, and a laptop which was switched on.

He looked questioningly at the woman, who said, 'I told Mr Seymour it was all right to look.'

She kept a tidy machine. Her address book was minimal, the recycle bin was empty, and her documents contained only a single folder entitled *Hollis*.

He opened it. There were photographs of pigs, close crowded in metal pens. His mind registered distaste though his face showed nothing. He didn't know if any welfare regulations were being broken here, but this was not a sight anyone who enjoyed a pork chop wanted to see. Some of the pictures showed dead piglets, lying in filth.

'Did you take these?'

She shrugged.

'Is this why you came to Sandytown, so you could do a raid on the pig farm?'

'Has there been a raid?'

'Someone defaced the sign at the main gate, I understand. The night of your arrival, I think it was.'

'There you go. We're not alone,' she said, smiling.

'So you're denying it was you and your *nieces*.'

'Of course. We want to use the law against these people. Why should we alienate it by committing criminal damage?'

He said, 'Mebbe because the law is slow and messy and you get your kicks out of direct action.'

'Is that how you feel about your job, Sergeant?'

'No,' said Wield. 'I like slow and messy. Dennis? Anything you want to ask Mrs Griffiths?'

Seymour, knowing the tape was off and the interview had not been formally resumed, took this as an invitation to sign off. He closed the notebook he'd been studying and set it on the table.

'No, Sarge,' he said.

'Good. Thank you for being so helpful, Mrs Griffiths.'

'I'm free to go?'

'Of course. Like a hand repacking your case?'

'No. Men can manage unpacking all right, but putting stuff together again is best left to a woman.'

'I think you're right. Each to his own, eh?'

'Indeed. Which is why it strikes me as odd – during our little chat, you didn't once refer directly to the fact that Lady Denham was murdered yesterday.'

For the first time a flicker of what his close friends and associates might recognize as a smile ran over Wield's face.

'No,' he said. 'What's really odd is neither did you. Let DC Seymour know when you've finished repacking and he'll drive you back to Seaview Terrace.'

With the door closed behind them he said to Seymour, 'So what do you think, Dennis?'

The DC's answer was typically prompt and direct.

'Almost certainly responsible for the spray job on the pig-farm notice. She probably drove the car, let the youngsters do the climbing. And I'm pretty sure she wrote the letters Lady Denham got. Noticed you didn't mention them, Sarge.'

'No, I didn't. She was ready for everything I was likely to ask, so she'd have been ready for that too. Best thing with her was to frustrate expectation. Anything more than gut feeling she wrote the letters?'

'That funny spelling. That notebook I was looking at, nothing significant, just jottings, reminders, that sort of stuff, but I did notice she spelt *diet* and *receipt* both with an *ei*.'

'That is how you spell *receipt*, Dennis,' said Wield gently.

'Is that right?' said Seymour, unfazed. 'I'll try and

remember that, Sarge. But *diet's d-i-e-t*. Isn't it? Not *d-e-i-t.*'

'Right. So she wrote the threatening letters and we've got her at the scene. Why don't you see her in the frame for the hog-roast murder?'

'Don't reckon her as a killer, that's all,' said Seymour.

He was, judged Wield, the only one of the DCs who would have ventured such an unsupported judgment. Sometimes, by contrast with Novello and Bowler, he might come across as a bit naïve, but what you got from him was always simple reaction without hidden agenda.

'There's been a lot of cases across the world where animal rights extremists haven't fought shy of killing and maiming,' said Wield. 'And I got the feeling she wasn't as laid-back about losing her eye as she let on.'

'OK, she might have lobbed a rock down at the old lady. Might even have broken the cliff fence to give her a fright. But strangling her . . . not a woman's m.o., is it?'

Wield tried to work out if this was sexist or not. Either way, he tended to agree. Could even be that the fence and the falling rock were pure accident. Interfering with the car brakes would have been a serious attempt at causing harm, but the local garage had poured scorn on the notion that anything other than Her Ladyship's reluctance to pay for maintenance was needed to make them fail.

'Right, Dennis. Once you've got Lady Nelson back to the Terrace, start getting this lot down on paper for the DCI to look at. I'll be over at the Hall talking to the poor relation.'

But when he got across to the Hall, there was no sign of Clara Brereton.

'Gone for a swim,' said Bowler, trying for bright and breezy but not getting close.

'She's what!'

'I told her she had to wait for you and she sat around for a bit, then a couple of minutes ago she suddenly got up, said she was getting hot and would it be OK if she popped down to the beach for a swim and waited for you there? I said I didn't think that was a good idea, but she was already moving off. I didn't see how I could stop her without arresting her.'

'So why didn't you go with her?'

'Thought I'd better let you know what was happening.'

'You've got a phone.'

'Yeah, I know. Thing was, Sarge, she's not got anything with her, so unless she's wearing a cozzie under her clothes, I thought maybe she wanted to skinny-dip . . .'

Jesus, thought Wield. What was it with these sensitive young straights? Tongues hanging out at the sight of a scantily clad lass, but overcome with embarrassment at the prospect of seeing one naked!

'That's her problem,' said Wield. 'Come on.'

With a promissory glance at Scroggs, who was discreetly keeping his distance, he set off towards the cliff path.

As they walked Bowler continued his defence.

'Anyway, I couldn't see it made much difference, Sarge. I mean, we've got the photos . . .'

'How do you know it was the photos she was after?' interrupted Wield. 'She might have left them because they weren't what she wanted.'

They reached the top of the path and paused. Before them lay the sea, gleaming silky blue under the noon-high sun, stretching away to a heat-smudged horizon. For a moment they were lifted far above the sordid concerns that had brought them here.

Mebbe, thought Wield, letting the peace and beauty of the scene wash over him as he drew in a deep breath of the famous sea air that Tom Parker claimed cured everything, mebbe what we're meant to do is go down this path and if we find yon lass skinny-dipping, we should strip our clothes off too and join her!

He shook the daft fancy out of his head and started the descent.

Gradual at first, it soon began to steepen, not enough to be a problem unless you had vertigo, for time had worn good footholds in the rock. Nevertheless a wise man concentrated on his footing and forgot the view. Bowler was ahead, moving with the easy confidence of youth, but suddenly he stopped and called, 'Sarge!'

Below them the cliff was now steepening to a degree sufficient to cause concern even to the young and active. There was a ledge beyond which it seemed to fall away sheer and here the path turned sharply right to follow the ledge and then descend the cliff face by zigs and zags. Along the ledge and all the way down the remainder of the path, a wooden fence had been built to give protection from the drop.

This was the fence that Lady Denham suspected had been sabotaged. No doubt now, though sabotage was perhaps too subtle a word. The top bar of the fence had been shattered and hung drunkenly from its stanchions.

Bowler leapt down the last few feet, steadied himself against one of the uprights, peered over and said, 'Oh shit!' Then he was off along the oblique path at a breakneck speed.

Wield reached the broken fence and looked down and saw what had provoked the young DC's reaction.

Below him, sprawled face down across a huge sea-smoothed boulder, was the body of Clara Brereton.

4

When Charley entered the lounge, Dalziel, occupying one of Tom Parker's low-slung Scandinavian chairs like the USA occupying Iraq, tried to lever himself upright but had difficulty formulating a satisfactory exit strategy.

'Please,' she said. 'Don't bother to get up.'

'Nay, I'll not be beaten,' he said. 'There! Done it! Good to see you again, Miss Heywood. How are you bearing up?'

'I'm fine, Mr Deal.'

He took the deliberate mispronunciation in his stride and said, 'Nay, lass, let's not be formal. I'm an old friend of your dad's. Call me Andy. Uncle Andy, if you like. And I'll call you Charley, right?'

Uncle Andy! Jesus Christ!

She replied pertly, 'Of course, Andy. Any friend of dad's is a friend of . . . my father.'

He roared with laughter. Mary Parker, pleased to see them at ease with each other, said, 'If you'll excuse me, I've things to do. Then I'll throw together some lunch. Just something light. Would you care to join us, Mr Dalziel?'

'That's real kind of you, missus. Nowt I like better than a light lunch. Except mebbe a heavy one.'

Mary smiled politely at what she hoped was a joke

444

and said, 'Good. I'll bring it outside, shall I? Such a lovely day.'

Charley led the way out on to the terrace. Minnie followed, but not on their heels. She was expert in assessing distances. Too close drew attention and got you dismissed, too distant and you couldn't hear a damn thing. She was helped in her efforts at un-obtrusiveness by the distant ululation of a siren.

'That you lot disturbing the peace?' said Charley.

Dalziel cupped his sagacious ear and said, 'Not one of ours. Ambulance, I'd say. Sounds like it's down in the town. Probably some daft sod's got sunstroke on the beach.'

Under cover of this exchange, Minnie squatted down on the edge of the terrace, about ten feet away, making herself as small as possible and keeping very still.

'So what did you want to talk to me about, Andy?' asked Charley, determined to seize control of the conversation.

'Murder,' he said.

'Oh. As a witness? A suspect? Or because of my psychological training? I'm afraid I have no background in criminal profiling.'

'Nay, but you've got sharp eyes, a sharp brain and you're nebby.'

'That's your assessment after what? Two brief encounters? No wonder the police have a track record of getting things wrong!'

'It happens. Like them trick cyclists who set homicidal maniacs loose to kill some other poor bugger.'

'Hardly the same.'

'No. Your lot don't do it after two brief encounters, you've usually had years to study the case-notes and still get it wrong. Any road, I'm not making snap judgments about you, Charley. I've been inside your mind; I've read your emails.'

'Jesus!' said Charley angrily. 'Is there anyone left in Sandytown who hasn't?'

'Oh aye. There's always a few folk who wait for the movie,' said Dalziel, grinning. 'Never fret, lass. I'm not going to sue you for defamation. Listen, serious now afore our light lunch comes. I think it could be useful if we pooled our resources.'

'Oh yes? Like I let that Novello bitch see my emails, you mean?'

'No, not like that. Don't be hard on poor Ivor. She's a nice lass and a good cop, but she's still at the bottom of the heap. She's got to do what other people tell her.'

'And you're at the top, I take it?'

'Oh yes. King of the castle, that's me,' said the Fat Man complacently.

'Then it was your idea to eavesdrop on me and Mr Godley talking in the police car, was it?'

'Eh?'

There was a massive conviction about that *eh?* which persuaded Charley more than oath or argument that Dalziel was truly ignorant of the mobile phone ruse.

Briefly she explained what had happened. She saw no reason not to tell him what Godley had said. All it did was explain the oddities of the healer's behaviour, and that sly sod Pascoe probably had it on tape anyway.

Far from disapproving the ruse, Dalziel seemed inclined to take some credit for it.

'Nose like a retriever, Pete,' he said complacently. 'Give him a sniff of a hint and he's up and after it instantly.'

'It was a monstrous thing to do. And probably illegal,' she retorted.

'Steady on, lass. It's a cop's job to get at the truth any way he can.'

'Even if it means hurting people!'

'Can't see why Godley should feel hurt. It were him holding back that made it necessary in the first place.'

'I'm talking about me! It looked like I was part of the deception. That's what Mr Godley went away thinking, anyway!'

'Oh dear,' said Dalziel. 'Now I can see how that would really hurt him. Never mind. Yon shit-lit's full of misunderstandings, isn't it? Makes it all the sweeter when he finds out the truth and realizes you weren't in on it.'

Charley, assuming he meant chick lit and also assuming he knew what he meant, tried to work out the implications of this.

'Hang about,' she said. 'You said it was you gave Pascoe the hint. What hint was that?'

'I think I said summat about Godley fancying you rotten, and that probably set Pete thinking he might open up to you. Clever, eh?'

Charley shook her head violently. She felt control of the conversation slipping irretrievably from her grasp. She tried a laugh – truly what he'd just said was daft enough to laugh at – but somehow she couldn't manage it.

'You're mad,' she said. 'He thinks I'm a waste of space, takes him all his time to stay in the same room as me.'

'Takes some lads like that,' said the Fat Man. 'Crazy for you but doesn't think he's got a cat in hell's chance, you being so attractive and superior and way out of his league.'

'*Me*?'

'Aye. Love's a bit short-sighted, isn't that what they say? Come on, young Charley. Driving a young man to distraction's not all that bad, is it?'

'Not a *young* man, maybe,' said Charley, still trying to get her head round what he'd said. How did he manage to assert what was so manifestly crazy with such authority?

'Picky, are we?' said Dalziel. 'Thirty's young by my standards.'

'Thirty?'

'Just turned, I saw his details on the Incident Room board. OK, that face fungus makes him look older, but that's likely why he wears it. Gives him a bit of gravitas.'

Charley tried to envisage a shaven Mr Godley, but it wouldn't come. In any case, it didn't matter. Thirty, forty, fifty, even in the remote contingency Dalziel was right, the poor sod was doomed to suffer till he got over it.

'Look,' she said. 'None of this matters, does it? The important thing is, what he told me puts him out of the frame, as you lot say, right?'

'You reckon?' said Dalziel dubiously. 'Should have thought it gives him and Miss Lee a good motive for being seriously pissed off with Lady D. He were seen quarrelling with her, tha knows. In fact, I think you were one of them as fingered him.'

'No I didn't,' she protested angrily. 'All I said was . . . and I didn't know it was going to be grand jury testimony . . . anyway, it was hardly a killing matter, was it?'

'I've known folk kill for less,' he said. 'And it could have been an accident.'

'An accidental strangling? Come on!' she mocked. 'And what about Ollie Hollis? That was no accident. Why would Mr Godley want to kill him?'

'Mebbe Ollie saw something that could tie Godley in to the murder?'

'That's stupid! If his motive for quarrelling with Lady Denham was to protect his sister, he's hardly going to commit murder in her treatment room, is he?'

Dalziel nodded his great grey head approvingly.

'There,' he said. 'Knew I were right about you, Charley. Good bit of logic to back up what both of us think without benefit of logic – that Mr Godley ain't no killer. So who's next?'

'You're the detective,' she said. 'Also I'm getting a bit fed up with this one-way traffic. You've got my emails plus a tape of a private conversation. Time to share a bit of what you know, I'd say. Or is this *ee by gum lass, I think thee and me could make a grand partnership* stuff just another ploy like Novello's and Pascoe's?'

'Fair enough,' he said without hesitation. 'Turn and turn about it is. And I promise you, nowt you tell me will get passed on without your say-so. Right?'

'Right,' she said. 'So now it's your turn, Andy.'

'OK. Let's go through the suspects. Best get you out of the way first, I suppose.'

'Me?'

'Aye. Pete Pascoe reckons your lousy spelling puts you in the frame.'

He explained about the anonymous letters with their spelling error.

'I've always had bother with e's and i's,' she said. 'But no one bothers in an email, right?'

'Don't say that to Pete Pascoe,' said Dalziel. 'If he left a suicide note, I'd know it were forged if there were just one semi-colon out of place. Not to worry, but. My reading of you is that if you did decide to write an anonymous letter, any clues it gave wouldn't be mistakes but deliberate red herrings.'

He seemed to intend it as a compliment.

'You're saying I'd make a good criminal?' said Charley.

'That's what it takes to make a good detective,' he said. 'Look at me. One gene more or less and I could have been the Napoleon of Crime!'

He put his hand under his shirt and looked out to sea with such a lugubrious expression, she laughed out loud.

'If that's meant to be Napoleon, remind me not to ask for your Jimmy Cagney!'

'Jimmy Cagney? Bit old for you. No, hang on, it's all them movies your mam loves to watch, right? Sorry, didn't mean to tread into the personal stuff, but it's all tangled up in your emails, isn't it? Listen, I'll give you another one for free, just to prove good faith. Fester and Pet!'

'Who?'

'Dr Lester Feldenhammer and Nurse Petula Sheldon. You met them at that do in the Clinic. And you saw them at the hog-roast.'

'That's right. What about them?'

'Come on, luv. In your emails you mention Mary Parker filling you in on Daph having the hots for Fester. And his affections being engaged elsewhere.'

'Elsewhere being Nurse Sheldon? So what are you saying? A crime of passion? Aren't they a bit old for that?'

'Christ, you really are ageist, aren't you? Pet and Fester are younger than me, and I can still tear a passion if I put my mind to it. They had a bloody great row at the party that ended with Pet hurling her wine over Daph.'

'Hardly lethal, is it?'

'No, but it's a step in the wrong direction.'

She shook her head.

'No. A woman chucks wine 'cos she's pissed off with someone. Killing them takes passionate jealousy, and I can't see Sheldon being jealous of someone thirty years older than she is. Anyway, sticking her in the hog-roast cage suggests intent rather than impulse, doesn't it?'

He nodded complacently. He was right. She was quick. Pete would probably kill him for giving away confidential info about the case, but he had the feeling that young Heywood would sniff out prevarication like the Holy Inquisition.

He said, 'Maybe there was intent. Maybe Pet and Fester were more than just irritated by Daph.'

She said slowly, 'Yes, I've been wondering about that. If Feldenhammer wanted to stop Daph bothering him, why not simply tell her it was no go? OK, she was persistent. Most women would have taken the hint when he ran away to Switzerland for six months. And when she followed him out there, why not just say, Enough's enough, act your age, woman! Unless . . .'

Dalziel leaned forward and nodded his head encouragingly.

'Unless what?' he said.

'Unless,' said Charley, 'unless she had some sort of a hold over him. From the way she set about getting Miss Lee out of Witch Cottage, she clearly wasn't above a bit of blackmail!'

The Fat Man sat back in his chair and beamed at her.

'If I weren't promised, Charley, I might ask Stompy for leave to marry thee.'

'If you did, I'd run a lot further than Switzerland,' she retorted. 'OK, so that's the conclusion you've reached too, so it has to be right! Have you any idea what?'

'Not yet, but I'll find out. Then we'll see if what she was using to pull his string were important enough to make him want to cut hers.'

The wail of the ambulance siren came floating up from the town again.

Dalziel let it fade away then leaned forward in his chair and said, 'So what do you think about all this, Minnie?'

Charley turned her head and for the first time observed the small figure hunched up at the end of the terrace. Slowly the girl straightened up, stretched her arms and yawned, as if just awaking from a deep sleep.

'Sorry?' she said.

The Fat Man clapped his hands together thunderously.

'By God, she's good, ain't she, Charley? Maggie Smith watch out! Come on, luv, you've won your Oscar, now you can join the party. Owt you can tell us about poor old Lady Denham, or about any bugger, that might help?'

Minnie, like Charley, didn't waste time weighing decisions.

Looking fully alert, she scrambled to her feet and came to join them.

'What sort of thing?' she said.

'Anything at all, long as it's stuff no one else is likely to know.'

Minnie's face screwed up in concentration for a moment then she said, 'Well, what you were saying about Big Bum . . . sorry, Lady Denham . . . and Dr Feldenhammer, I think she really liked him a lot, 'cos when Miss Watson our head teacher caught Mr Standfast, our deputy head, doing sex with the dinner lady, she sacked them both, even though she was doing it with Mr Standfast too.'.

Charley looked at her in shocked bewilderment, but Dalziel nodded his huge head as if this made perfect sense and said, 'Lady Denham didn't mind, though?'

'Well, I don't know if she didn't mind exactly, but she still kept on liking Dr Feldenhammer even after she saw him doing it with the Indian lady.'

This was getting seriously weird, thought Charley, and she sent her mind scuttling through her textbooks in search of a subtle psychological technique for getting the girl to open up further.

The Fat Man said, 'The Indian lady . . .' as if this rang some kind of bell, then he bared his big yellow teeth in the kind of anticipatory rictus that might twitch the jaws of a somnolent crocodile identifying the rhythmic splashing noise that has been disturbing him as the sound of an approaching swimmer.

He said, 'Oh aye. Now I remember. Old Fester and the Indian lady. Right! Don't think Charley knows about her, but. Why don't you tell her the story?'

Did he really know what Minnie was talking about, or was this just his own personal technique, worked out without benefit of textbooks, for getting the girl to reveal all? The latter, she guessed. The old sod was a lot cleverer than he looked. Not too difficult, of course, when you looked like Cro-Magnon man!

Minnie, revelling in the spotlight, said, 'It was my last birthday, Uncle Sid bought me a new bike, a proper one, not a kid's. Mum said it was too expensive and Uncle Sid said nonsense, he always bought the people he loved best a bike, he thought it should be a family tradition. Anyway, Mum and Dad bought me a digital camera and that was quite expensive.'

'Aye, well, the best deserve nowt but the best, eh?' said Dalziel.

Minnie looked pleased and continued, 'I went for a ride along the coast, and after a bit I stopped for a rest and I saw Big Bum . . . sorry, Lady . . .'

'Big Bum'll do, luv,' said Dalziel. 'Don't think she'll mind now. When is your birthday, by the way?'

'September ninth, next month. I'll be ten,' she said hopefully.

'I'll not forget,' said Dalziel. 'St Wulfhilda's feast day. She were a real smart lass too. Go on with your story.'

'I saw Big Bum's horse, Ginger. I'd seen her over the hedge earlier. Only now Ginger was just cropping grass. I thought I'd take a picture of him and while I was doing it, Big Bum came up, and I said thank you for your birthday card, but she didn't look like she knew what I was talking about. Then she asked if she could borrow my camera for a moment. I didn't really want to let her have it, but she just sort of took it and went off again.'

'Where did she go?'

'Towards the cliff. It's not very high there, not like North Cliff, more like a big sand dune. And after a few moments she came back and she said she'd need to keep the memory card. I said that meant I wouldn't be able to take any more photos and she said all right, she'd rent it off me, ten pounds for the day.'

'Ten pounds? And did you get the ten pounds?'

'No, I got fifteen,' said the girl. 'Uncle Sid says that when anyone makes an offer always ask for twice as much and never let them knock you down to less than half the extra.'

Dalziel glared a warning at Charley who was stifling a laugh.

'So what happened next?' he asked.

'I rode on a bit, but when I looked back and saw that she'd gone, I went over to take a look at what she'd been photographing.'

'And what was it?'

'It was Dr Feldenhammer with the Indian lady on the beach. They were doing sex.'

'You're sure it was Dr Feldenhammer?' said Dalziel, forgetting he was supposed to know all of this anyway.

'Oh yes. Dr Feldenhammer had been round to our house for dinner a couple of nights earlier. He gave me a twenty-pound note when he heard it was my birthday soon and he said I had to spend it on something I really wanted, but Mum made me put it in my savings account.'

'That's the trouble with mums,' said Dalziel. 'Always thinking of your future. Go on.'

'Well, I knew I'd get into trouble if they saw me, so I just crawled away and got back on my bike and rode off home.'

Charley said, 'Minnie, when you say they were doing sex, what exactly . . . do you mean, they were kissing, or . . .'

'They had all their clothes off – that's how I knew it was the Indian lady; she was really brown all over

455

– and they were bouncing up and down together. It's all right, Charley. We learned all about it at school.'

She spoke so condescendingly that Dalziel laughed out loud.

Charley said quite sharply, 'This Indian lady, does she have a name?'

'I expect so,' said Minnie. 'Everyone has a name. I expect hers is Indian.'

'But who was she?'

'She was from the clinic. I'd seen her in the town once, dressed in one of those lovely silk things they wear, but I haven't seen her for a long time, so perhaps she got another job. Does that help, Mr Andy?'

'I think it might, Minnie. What do you think, Charley?'

'Could do,' said Charley. 'Did you ever talk to anyone about what you saw, Minnie?'

'I told Sue Locksley, my best friend at school, but she said that her babysitter does it with her boyfriend every Saturday night in the living room and it's really boring. So I didn't bother telling anyone else. Except Uncle Sid.'

'You told your Uncle Sidney?' said Charley. 'Why did you do that?'

'He was there when I got home and he asked me how I liked the bike and I told him it was the best present ever and he asked how far I'd ridden on it, so I told him. Uncle Sid and me tell each other everything. I wish I was old enough to marry him.'

No you don't, love, thought Charley.

Dalziel said, 'And what did Uncle Sid say, lass?'

'He told me that doing sex was really only the business of the ones doing it and I shouldn't tell anyone else. But you don't count, do you, Mr Andy, because you're a policeman?'

'Right, luv. I don't count,' said the Fat Man. 'Did he say anything else?'

'No. I said thank you again for the bike and he said I was a special girl and I said does that mean when I'm eighteen you'll buy me a motorbike too? And he laughed and said maybe he would.'

Charley asked, 'What made you think of a motorbike, Min?' then wished she hadn't.

The girl said, 'Because he bought Teddy one for his birthday, only when I heard Teddy thanking him, they said it was a secret, so maybe I shouldn't have told you.'

'Think of me as a policeman too,' said Charley.

She didn't look at the Fat Man, but felt his eyes on her.

He said, 'What about your mum and dad? They must have wondered when Big Bum gave you fifteen pound for using your memory card.'

'I didn't tell them,' said Minnie promptly. 'They'd just have made me put it in the savings bank like Dr Feldenhammer's twenty pound, and I had things to spend it on.'

Like what? wondered Charley. And do I really want to know?

Dalziel said, 'That were real interesting, Minnie, very helpful. Now, would you do me a favour? All this talk's made me thirsty. Why don't you run along to your mam and ask if there's any chance of a light beer with my light lunch?'

Minnie offered no objection but sped away into the house.

When she was out of earshot, Charley said sharply, 'If you knew she was listening, why didn't you send her away before?'

'And miss that little nugget?' said Dalziel. 'Soon as I clapped eyes on young Min, I saw that here were the ears and eyes of Sandytown! Only understands half of what she knows, but it all gets stored away, understood or not. Bet you were just the same at her age. Well now, I reckon that might solve our little problem of the hold Daph had on Fester.'

'Catching him screwing one of his staff isn't much of a hold,' said Charley.

'What if she weren't one of his staff?'

'I thought . . . oh, I see what you mean . . . she might have been a patient? But surely . . .'

'Surely a nice upstanding pro like Dr Feldenhammer wouldn't screw one of his own patients, is that what you mean? Listen, luv, if you're going to make it in your line of business, you'll need to be ready to hear far worse things than that. Stuff that is a thousand miles away from the way you yourself act and think.'

'Oh. You mean like you knowing about that saint, you mean?' retorted Charley.

'Wulfhilda?' Dalziel laughed. 'Nay, we've a lot in common. Bright lass, very moral. She escaped through the drains when the king wanted to shag her. And she could multiply her stock of booze when guests turned up unexpected. That's a trick I'd love to learn.'

There was definitely more to this guy than met the eye, thought Charley.

She said, 'Very interesting. But I still think it was irresponsible to let Minnie carry on eavesdropping when you knew she was there.'

'Don't think she heard owt that's not on the curriculum these days!' said Dalziel. 'Mebbe Mr Standfast and the dinner lady were a visual aid. Any road, that's why I've sent the lass off now. It's clear she thinks the sun shines out of her Uncle Sid's bum and I didn't want her earwigging while we talked about him. What was all that about him giving Ted the bart a motorbike?'

'No idea. First I knew about it,' said Charley, affecting indifference. 'I really hardly know Sid.'

'Apart from him having a red Maserati and being absolutely gorgeous, you mean? Come on, lass. You do not knowing about as well as Minnie does not listening!'

Oh shit, thought Charley. In principle she agreed with Sid, sex was nobody's business except the couple doing it. And their psychologists, of course. And maybe the police, if there was some connection with a serious crime . . .?

The bottom line was the cops had read her emails. OK, she was still pissed off about that, but it was a fact. And she'd accidentally misled them in two ways, first in the closeness of the relationship between Ted and Clara, and secondly in the location of Clara and Sid when the storm started. Probably unimportant, but with two people dead already . . .

'Spit it out afore it chokes you,' urged Dalziel.

'Sid's gay,' she said. 'Ted too. Don't know if they're exclusively so – I'd guess not in Ted's case.'

She hadn't expected him to look surprised and he didn't.

'Oh aye? Lot of it about. Not catching, thank God, else we'd probably all be wearing tutus down the nick. I can see it'd be a bit of a shock to you when you found out, fancying 'em both like you did. How did you find out, by the way?'

'This morning. I saw Sid in the hotel swimming pool, and I realized what I'd said in my email about the hog-roast was wrong. It wasn't Clara Teddy was banging in the cave on the cliff, it was Sid!'

Dalziel whistled and said, 'Quite a mistake that, lass. Bit short-sighted, are you?'

She told him the story and felt indignant when he still regarded her doubtfully.

'It was dark in the cave,' she declared. 'I only got a glimpse, he was on his face, I just saw those long white legs, and when I saw them again in the pool, I knew beyond all doubt that's what I'd seen in the cave. I think he must shave them!'

'Bloody hell!' said the Fat Man. 'Wonder how far up he goes?'

They were saved from further pursuit of this interesting speculation by the roar of an engine. It didn't sound like the Sexy Beast, more like an asthmatic eunuch. Charley knew who it was long before the familiar bike and side-car combination hove into view around the side of the house and slewed to a halt in a spray of gravel. Gordon Godley vaulted off with a display of athleticism that suggested the Fat Man was right about his age, and came striding on to the terrace. His gaze was focused on Charley, but he didn't seem convinced he was seeing her till he got within a couple of feet. He reached out his hand as if he was going to touch her, then he collapsed on to a chair and said, 'Thank God! It's not you!'

Charley, scrolling through her course notes again for some tip on how best to deal with such a situation, could come up with nothing better than, 'Well, it is, actually.'

'No, sorry,' said Godley breathlessly, never taking his eyes off her. 'It's just that when they finally turned me loose I went to the garage to pick up my bike and the

460

police were holding up the traffic to let an ambulance come off the beach, and when I asked a policeman what was happening he said that a girl had fallen off the cliff and I said which girl and he said he didn't know anything except he thought she'd been staying up at Kyoto House so I jumped on my bike and headed straight up here because I thought . . .'

He stopped, either for want of breath or because he didn't want to give what he'd thought the weight of utterance.

As Charley and the Fat Man looked at each other with wild surmise, Mary came hurrying out on to the terrace, closely followed by Minnie.

The child was bright-eyed with excitement, the mother pale with shock.

'Mary, what is it?' demanded Charley.

'It's Clara,' cried the woman. 'I've just had Tom on the phone. There's been a dreadful accident at Sandytown Hall. It's poor Clara. She's fallen over the cliff, and they think she's going to die.'

5

After Peter Pascoe set off down the drive, Franny Roote had poured another cup of coffee and rolled his chair into the barn. He pointed a remote control at the LCD panel on the wall and watched as a sharp picture of the entrance gate came into view.

Pascoe's car appeared.

He nodded approval as he saw Peter looking for the sensor and when he waved at the camera, Roote smiled and waved back.

When the car pulled away, he sipped at his coffee and gave himself over to self-examination. He was not by nature introspective but the instinct of self-preservation had long since persuaded him that knowing himself was the key to successful action. Without being a sociopath, he recognized what might be termed sociopathic elements in his make-up. Society to him was an ocean which could either buoy you up or drive you down. He knew how to work with its currents and tides so that they took you where you wanted to be rather than fight against them and risk ending up beached and exhausted. But this did not mean he felt himself detached from society's conventions and relationships. His immorality had limits and his amorality stopped a long way short of total indifference to ethical judgments. For him the human race was a source of constant entertainment rather than a pernicious race of odious vermin. There were a few of them who inspired in him feelings of loyalty and of love, and even those he regarded as side-show monsters he could view with an almost affectionate amusement that occasionally came close to sympathy.

Lady Denham had stood high in his list of monsters but he admired her energy, her uncompromising forth-rightness, and, though he was thankful not to have run the risk of becoming its object, her undiminished sexual drive. She was like a great bulbous view-blocking beech tree whose removal opened up all kinds of distant vistas, but whose absence you could still deplore. That she'd had some hold over Lester Feldenhammer he was sure. What it was he hadn't been able to discover, but he'd back Andy Dalziel to suss it out, if he hadn't done so already. That was the mark of the man, to know things after less than a fort-night in Sandytown which the famous Roote nose had not sniffed out with six months' start! You had to admire the fat bastard. OK, like Lady D he belonged to the genus *monstrum* – and he was ten times more dangerous than she was – but though Roote might fear him, he could not get close to hating him.

But it was neither of these monsters who had trig-gered this bout of self-examination.

It was Pete Pascoe. No monster this, but a man he'd started by respecting and ended by loving.

Not in any physical sense. He hadn't been lying when he assured the detective that there was nothing of homo-eroticism in his feelings. He knew all about sexual love, the lullings and the relishes of it. This wasn't it. No, the measure of his feelings for Peter was the pain he felt in having had to lie to him.

Normally in the world according to Franny Roote, success in deceit was a source of delight, a whimsy in the blood, leaving him so limber he felt that, snake-like, he could skip out of his skin. But not this time. He had tried to salve his unease with prevarication – *but not necessarily in that order* – clever stuff, but he no longer wanted to be clever with Pascoe, he wanted to be open. He had tasted the clean savour of openness and it was addictive. There were monsters enough in the world to play mind games with, but the heart was too soft a ground not to be damaged by such sharp twists and turns.

He longed for an end to deceit and happily the time was now ripe to end it. But not by confession. In his observation and experience of the world, the truth rarely set you free. Indeed it was more likely to get you banged up!

No, by one of those paradoxes he loved, his route to openness lay through that super subtle labyrinthine hinterland of his mind ruled by Loki, the Nordic spirit of trickery and mischief. He did not doubt that his old familiar would show the right moment, the right place.

Meanwhile, as in all areas of human endeavour, the key to success was information, and not being too scrupulous about how you got it. Every good police-man knew this, and Peter Pascoe was a very good policeman. He hadn't actually said it, but somehow it was clear that he had access to Charley Heywood's emails, and that he found them useful. Presumably she was using her laptop linked to her mobile. He went to his work station and from a drawer retrieved the piece of paper bearing her email address and mobile number. He didn't anticipate meeting any of the problems that accessing Wield's system at the Hall had given him, and in fact, as he worked, it almost seemed as if Charley, with the arrogance of youth, revelled in her insecurity!

Twenty minutes later he made himself another cup of coffee and settled down to read.

6

Once again Pascoe arrived at Sandytown Hall to find Wield in full control.

'She didn't look good,' said the sergeant. 'Head injuries, God knows what bones are broken, very faint pulse. Didn't dare touch her because of worrying about her spine. Ambulance service said it would be half an hour minimum, mebbe more. Big pile-up north of York. All the roads snarled up. Didn't know if she'd last half an hour. Thought of trying to whistle up a chopper, then Bowler said, "What about the Avalon?" I rang them, seems they've got the lot up there, small ambulance, paramedics, plus fully kitted Intensive Care Unit. Fortunately the tide was way out so the ambulance could get round the rocks. Never thought I'd say thank God for private medicine!'

'So what do they think?'

'No feedback yet. I've sent Novello up there to keep an eye on things. I've secured the whole of the cliff path and the private beach. And I've recalled the CSIs.'

They were standing on the ledge looking at the broken rail. The wood had certainly rotted where the screws fastening it to the metal stanchion had penetrated. The cord that had been used to make it good was still in place round the stanchion, but the rail had snapped off a few inches further along where the wood was reasonably sound.

'Would need quite a bit of pressure to break this, I should have thought,' mused Pascoe. 'And wasn't there a warning notice?'

'Over there,' said Wield, pointing to a square of hardboard lying face down a couple of feet along the ledge. 'Could have got blown down during the storm.'

'And the pressure?'

'Stopped to take a breather and admire the view. Leant her full weight against the rail. Crack, and she's gone.'

'She didn't look all that heavy to me. Could there be someone else involved?'

'Me and Bowler can't have been more than a couple of minutes behind her. No way anyone could have evaded us by coming up. If they went down, they must have moved like lightning. The beach was completely empty when we reached the ledge.'

'But you still called the CSIs?'

'I'd have called them even if I'd seen her fall,' said Wield. 'When you're investigating murder, every death's suspicious.'

'Quite right,' said Pascoe, starting to climb back up to the garden. 'It doesn't sound like Brereton will be answering questions for a while, if ever. You say she was found in Lady Denham's room. What we need to work out is what she was after there.'

'Mebbe she were looking for these,' said Wield, producing the photos. 'Bowler found them. He spotted a drawer in the desk we'd missed. Seems his parents wanted him to go into the family cabinet-making business.'

'Maybe he should have taken their advice,' grunted

Pascoe ungratefully. He examined the photos. 'They look like they're having fun. Any identification yet?'

'Haven't had much time since I got them,' said Wield. 'Been a bit busy.'

'Sorry. Leave them with me then. And I'll get Frodo Leach to check out the drawer. Now let's talk to Bowler, see if there's anything more he can remember.'

Wield said, 'Young Hat's a bit shook up, Pete. I think he reckons he should have got to Witch Cottage earlier and possibly have saved Ollie Hollis. Now he's blaming himself for not stopping the lass when she said she was going for a swim.'

'That sounds like a step in the right direction,' said Pascoe indifferently.

They found Bowler at the top of the path. He looked close to the point of collapse. Wield's heart went out to him, but Pascoe said, 'You look like shit, Hat. Either snap out of it, or go home. You're no use to anyone like this.'

There had been a time, thought Wield, when he'd have held the lad's hand and tried to talk him out of his depression.

On the other hand, this new approach seemed rather more effective. Bowler straightened up and said, 'I'm fine, sir. Really.'

'That's the ticket,' said Pascoe heartily. 'So let's go through it all again, from the moment you noticed someone in the Hall.'

He took the young DC through events step by step. When they'd finished, Pascoe said, 'Thanks. Now go and write your statement while it's still fresh.'

'Yes, sir. Thank you, sir,' said Bowler.

He still did not look happy, but at least he no longer looked defeated.

'Mebbe when he's done, he should go home,' suggested Wield.

'What on earth for?' said Pascoe. 'We need all the bodies we can muster.'

'Way things are going, seems we're getting a steady supply of them,' retorted Wield, for once letting himself be provoked.

Pascoe looked at him unblinkingly for a second then his face relaxed into a rueful smile.

He said, 'Sorry, Wieldy. Maybe it's me should be sent home! Three bodies and counting. Oh shit. And here's three more I could do without.'

They looked across the lawn. Around the side of the house, a motorcycle combo came labouring. The reason for the strain on its engine was not far to seek. Behind Godley on the pillion sat Charley Heywood, her arms wrapped round the healer's waist, while in the side-car, like the effigy of some oriental god paraded to bless the rice crop, rode a serious-looking Andy Dalziel. By contrast, Gordon Godley wore a blissful smile.

The combo came to a halt. PC Scroggs, eager to atone for his earlier dereliction, came hurrying forward, his face stern with the resolution of Horatio about to confront the ranks of Tuscany. Then he spotted Dalziel, skidded to a halt, and went into reverse.

Pascoe did not move but let the Fat Man come across the lawn to him.

'Pete, lad,' he said. 'Just heard the news. How's the poor lass?'

'We're waiting to hear. Andy, what are you doing here? And why have you brought those two?'

'Fair do's, I think they brought me. And not to worry, I think I've talked them out of making a

469

complaint against you. In fact, if you've got any sense, you'll kiss and make up with yon Charley and get her on board. She's bright as old Fester's teeth. Oh aye. That's one of the reasons I'm here. You asked me to talk to Pet and Fester, remember? But first things first, this Clara, did she jump or were she pushed?'

Pascoe noted the old familiar imperious tone and recalled his feelings of loss and despair when he'd first seen the Fat Man stretched out in Intensive Care, as lifeless and forlorn as some deserted hulk found floating on a silent sea. To see him now, masts restored, wind filling his sails, should have been an undiluted joy; but was that just a small breath of nostalgia he felt ruffling his soul?

He ignored it and said, 'Looks like an accident. She was going down the cliff path, reached the ledge with the dodgy rail, leaned against it and it gave way. But we're keeping an open mind.'

'For God's sake!' exclaimed Charley Heywood, who'd followed the Fat Man across the lawn. 'Can't you two stop being cops for a minute? Who gives a fuck how it happened? How's Clara? That's the main thing.'

Pascoe stared at her for a moment then said quietly, 'Of course it is, Miss Heywood. But as none of us can know how she is until we hear from the Avalon where she's been taken, forgive me if I carry on being a cop for the time being.'

Dalziel made a face at Charley which she read as an admonition to keep her mouth shut, then he said, 'So what happened then?'

In response to a nod from Pascoe, Wield told his story.

Dalziel said, 'So if there had been anyone else

involved, they'd have had to get down the cliff almost as fast as the poor lass to be out of sight by the time you got there?'

'That's right, sir,' said Wield. 'And there definitely weren't anyone down there.'

'He could have hidden in the cave.'

All eyes turned on Charley.

She said, 'If someone pushed Clara over, he could have heard you coming down the path and hidden in the cave till you went rushing down to the beach after Clara, then climbed up here and headed off through the woods.'

Dalziel regarded her with a parental pride.

'Told you she were bright,' he said.

Pascoe said, 'Oh yes. The cave. I remember. In your email. The cave where you claim to have seen Sir Edward and Miss Brereton *in flagrante*.'

Charley noted the *claim* and recalled the Fat Man telling her that Pascoe was inclined to take everything she said with a pinch of salt.

Before she could give battle, Wield said, 'Where exactly is this cave, miss?'

'It's off to the left from the ledge,' she said. 'Up a bit, among the shrubs. If you look, you can see a faint track.'

Pascoe and Wield exchanged glances.

Wieldy said, 'Shall I . . .?'

'No,' said Pascoe. 'Just in case, let's not risk contamination. Leave it to the CSI. Thank you, Miss Heywood. Anything else you'd care to contribute?'

His tone was even and polite, but to Charley it felt as if it were dripping with sarcasm. She looked at the Fat Man. He returned her look blank-faced but she read there an assurance, *I promised I'd say nowt without your say-so. Up to you, lass.*

She said, 'There is something else, Mr Pascoe. About the cave. I made a mistake. It wasn't Clara I saw there with Teddy Denham. It was Sidney Parker.'

Pascoe passed his hand over his face, hiding any reaction.

'Not Clara Brereton but Sidney Parker. I see,' he said musingly. 'Well, that was certainly quite a mistake, Miss Heywood. What relevance it might have I don't know, but before we draw any conclusions from it, we need to be absolutely sure . . .'

Dalziel, seeing the young woman was once more ready to be provoked, got in quickly, 'We've been through all this, Pete. Miss Heywood's sure. Me too.'

'In that case, sir, the matter is, of course, beyond all doubt,' said Pascoe, draining all irony from his voice. 'To be quite clear, Miss Heywood, your error was only in the personnel involved, not in the activity? The two men were also *in flagrante?*'

Charley said, 'Yes. Ted was definitely buggering him.'

The Fat Man grinned. He was beginning to really like this lass.

Pascoe showed no emotion. 'So in the light of this, are you now saying that all that stuff in your emails about Ted Denham coming on to Miss Brereton, not to mention yourself, was probably a misinterpretation also?'

Charley looked as if she might be considering physical violence for a moment, then said, 'No way. All right, to some extent it might have been a smokescreen to put Lady Denham off the scent, but at a guess I'd say Ted's bisexual.'

Pascoe echoed, 'A smokescreen? To hide what? And why?'

'From what little I got to know about Lady Denham,

I'd say there wasn't much chance of her leaving anything to a gay,' said Charley.

'Except mebbe a couple of her evening gowns,' said Dalziel cheerfully.

Again Pascoe looked from the woman to the Fat Man.

He said, 'If I could have a word in private, sir?'

He set off walking towards the Hall. Dalziel winked at Charley and followed.

'So you weren't here when the lass got attacked?' he said as he caught up.

'No,' said Pascoe shortly. 'I was visiting Franny Roote.'

'You mean interviewing him?'

'That too. It's all right, Andy. As I told you last evening, I can keep my personal feelings and professional responsibilities separate.'

'As the bishop said to the actress,' said Dalziel. 'So, this private word you want – not in trouble, am I?'

'Only like Brer Rabbit in the bramble bush,' said Pascoe, halting and turning to face the Fat Man. 'I'd like to get back to your agreed professional involvement in the investigation, if you don't mind. Perhaps you'd care to tell me how you got on with the interviews you volunteered to do at the Avalon?'

Dalziel grimaced and said, 'Getting a bit above myself, am I? Old habits, eh? Like me, they die hard. From now on in, I'll play it by the book. You're the boss.'

'I know I am,' said Pascoe. 'The interviews. Sir.'

Dalziel gave him a digest of his conversations with Sheldon and Feldenhammer.

'And your conclusions?'

'Ho'd on. I'm not done yet.'

Now he gave an account of his visit to Kyoto House. As he related Minnie Parker's contribution, Pascoe groaned.

'Jesus, Andy,' he said. 'We've already had Tom Parker banging on about Novello interviewing the girl without a responsible adult present. If he finds out you've been questioning her about people screwing on the beach, you could be in big trouble.'

'It weren't like that,' protested Dalziel. 'She just came out with it. Could be completely the product of her imagination for all I know.'

'I don't think so,' said Pascoe, producing the envelope with the photos. 'Anyone you recognize here?'

Dalziel examined them for a moment then said, 'Hope old Fester rubbed some sun block on to his buttocks.'

'Fester? This is Dr Feldenhammer, is it?'

'Oh aye. No doubt. And the lass must be this Indian lady Minnie told us about.'

'Indeed. I'm afraid this means we'll have to talk to the girl again. I'll try to play down how we got the info, but maybe you'd better start working on a good explanation of how you came to be talking to her unofficially without a responsible adult present.'

'Don't preach to me, lad, not till you've started shaving,' retorted Dalziel, forgetting his recent resolution to play the underling. 'Any road, Charley Heywood's a responsible adult, and a bright one too. I'm not the only one straying off the straight and narrow here. She lays a complaint about you bugging her private conversations, you'll know what trouble is. If I were you, I'd start building bridges with that lass.'

'No conversation with a suspect in custody can be

called private,' declared Pascoe, trying for the forensic high ground.

'In custody?' snorted Dalziel. 'Crap! You knew Godley were in the clear as evidenced by the fact he's now running around loose.'

'Which he wouldn't be if I hadn't used Miss Heywood to get to the truth of his relationship with Miss Lee,' riposted Pascoe. 'You never used to be so pussy-footed, Andy.'

'And you never used to make your own sodding rules, lad!'

The two men glared at each other for a moment, then both began to grin.

Pascoe said, 'Anyway, he certainly doesn't look like he wants to complain now.'

They both glanced towards Charley and Godley, who were having an animated conversation in the middle of the lawn.

'That's 'cos the poor sod thinks the sun shines out of her ears,' said the Fat Man. 'If you'd dropped him in a bog and young Charley were in it too, he'd have been grateful. But she's still a long way from being your greatest fan.'

'And you think she's the complaining type?'

'Mebbe not, but if her dad, Stompy Heywood, hears you've been messing his daughter around, I'd make sure your BUPA payments are up to date. Think on, and while you're thinking, here's the way I see things. Festerwhanger's right in the frame. Daph were coming on at him hard and he didn't dare fend her off too strong 'cos she knew about his little bit of naughty with the Indian patient.'

'Whoah!' said Pascoe. 'We don't know she's a patient. Could be a nurse.'

'She were a patient, I can feel it in my water,' said the Fat Man.

'Offer the same argument for God and I'm sure the whole world will turn religious,' said Pascoe.

'Ha ha. Listen, she has to be a patient. Doctors don't get struck off for shagging nurses, else the NHS would be in an even worse state than it is!'

'And you believe Lady Denham was capable of telling Feldenhammer that if he didn't marry her, she'd publish those pictures of him on the beach? I mean, they would put most women right off!'

'Not Daph,' said Dalziel almost admiringly. 'Probably took them as a testimonial he were fit for purpose! Seems the one time she did manage to get him into bed weren't all that satisfactory, so it must have been nice to see him on top form, so to speak.'

Pascoe shook his head and said, 'But he's a doctor.'

'He's a man!'

'No. I meant, doctors don't strangle people. They give them poison, or bring on heart attacks with a large bill.'

Dalziel laughed and said, 'Aye, but they can be provoked like anyone else.'

'I suppose so. Who else knows about this putative patient? You say Minnie told Sid Parker?'

'That's right. And my guess is he told Ted Denham. The poor sod's obviously crazy about Ted! Bought him a mo-bike called Sexy Beast, didn't he? Wants to make him happy, that's what love's about, right? Nice presents, help with problems like what to do with a rotting old house, sweet nothings whispered in his ear, pillow talk, aye that'll be how Ted got to hear about the Indian maid.'

'Stop there, Andy. Why has she suddenly become

a maid? I thought the whole point was she was a patient.'

'Sorry. Word association, that's all.'

He whistled the opening bars of the rugby song. Pascoe, an unreconstructed soccer fan, looked blank. So Dalziel sang the words. Pascoe, who was slightly prudish, looked blanker.

Dalziel said, 'First time I set eyes on Denham and Fester together, Ted whistled that song and old Fester nearly blew a gasket. I reckon when Ted first let Fester know he knew, he rounded it off by singing the song, and thereafter whenever he wanted to wind him up, he'd whistle the tune.'

'That sounds as if it might be a motive for getting rid of Denham too, but as far as I know, he's alive and well.'

'Pete, what's happened to that sharp mind of thine? It's talking to Roote that's done it. Always acted on you like salt on a slug.'

'I don't quite care for the slug image, but do put me straight, Andy.'

'Last thing Teddy would want is for Daph to get Fester down the aisle. What might that do to his hopes of inheriting? So Ted would use the Indian Maid to warn Fester he'd better keep his hands off Daph or else. Randy Daphne were likely doing the opposite, using the Indian maid to pressure Fester into laying his hands on her! Poor sod. Two blackmailers, neither of 'em he can satisfy without pissing off the other! Must have felt like they both had their hands on his bollocks and were pulling different ways!'

'So you're saying that, with Lady Denham gone, Feldenhammer would have no more need to worry about Ted?'

'Well done, lad! Long time coming, but you get there in the end . . .'

'. . . as the actress said to the very old bishop.'

'By the cringe, stealing my lines now!'

'You once told me, Andy, if it's useful, use it, doesn't matter how polluted the source. Miss Heywood!'

Charley looked in their direction, then finished off what she was saying to Gordon Godley before walking slowly towards them. Pascoe, who knew how to manage these things, didn't let her come all the way but took a few steps to meet her.

'Miss Heywood,' he said. 'I'd like to say that I'm sorry if I have appeared rather cavalier in the way I've dealt with you.'

'Not cavalier. I've got you down more as a roundhead,' said Charley. 'If you think it's right, do it, and to hell with other people's rights and feelings!'

Pascoe ran his hand through his hair as if to check it hadn't all been shaved off.

'Perhaps, but more protestant than puritan, I hope. I certainly think it's right now that I should apologize for listening in on your conversation with Mr Godley without your consent.'

'That's nice. He's here too, you know. You going to apologize to him as well?'

'No,' said Pascoe. 'If he'd been open with us from the start, the situation would not have arisen.'

Then he grinned his famous boyish grin which Dalziel claimed could charm warts off witches and added, 'I think in any case he may be inclined now to regard it as *felix culpa*, seeing that it seems to have brought him rather closer to yourself.'

Charley felt herself blushing.

'What is it with you people?' she demanded. 'I thought

this was a murder investigation you were running, not a dating agency!'

'Sorry again. Yes, that was a rather archly *cavalier* sort of thing to say, wasn't it?'

He put on his rueful self-mocking look and Dalziel saw the girl stifle a smile.

Then the entertainment was interrupted by the sound of a car. Not that it made much sound. It was a dove grey Daimler with tinted glass that made it hard to see the inmates. The driver when he got out was perfectly cast. Tall, slim, wearing a dark suit that came close to being a uniform, an impression confirmed when he put on a peaked cap before going to the rear door and opening it.

'You didn't say the Queen were coming, Pete,' said Dalziel.

The passenger's legs appeared. Unless Her Majesty had taken to grey pinstripes, this was not going to be a royal visit.

And now the man himself appeared and stood upright. But not very far upright. He was broad and squat and had a bushy black beard, trimmed square. And he came up to the chauffeur's third rib.

'It's Gimli from *The Lord of the Rings*,' said Charley.

At the same time, almost unnoticed, a slightly built young woman, wearing a heron grey business suit and carrying a black leather briefcase, slid out of the other passenger door.

PC Scroggs once more advanced officiously and addressed the man. Words were exchanged, Scroggs looked chastened. He pointed towards the group in the garden, and the man marched towards them with a step that, though not actually ground-shaking, gave the impression that if it wanted it could be.

As he got near, he gravelled out a single word. 'Beard!'

Pascoe's susceptibility to sudden strange fancies was sometimes a plus in his profession, but just as often it could be a potentially fatal distraction. Now instead of concentrating on seeking a stratagem to identify the newcomer who looked important enough to be a new Home Secretary (or even an old one – who the hell was Home Secretary anyway?), he found himself thinking that maybe this was one of those magical encounters when failure to utter the correct counter-word could bring disaster. He was still vacillating between *bareface!* and *sporran!* when the Fat Man stepped forward and said fulsomely, 'Good to see you, Mr Beard. We've been expecting you. I'm Dalziel, and this is Detective Chief Inspector Pascoe who is in charge of the enquiry.'

Pascoe came back to earth. This was Lady Denham's lawyer, Mr Beard of Gray's Inn Road, and Dalziel was keeping his promise of keeping his place, even though it meant being polite to a solicitor, quite something from a man who regarded Dick the Butcher's proposal to kill all the lawyers after the revolution as an act of clemency.

'I'm glad to meet you, sir,' said Pascoe, shaking hands. 'And your colleague.'

He glanced towards the woman. Beard didn't.

'Secretary. Sorry I didn't get here earlier. Roadworks.'

His voice was so deep and vibrant that it almost massaged you, thought Charley. Talk to this guy on the phone and you'd date him any time, even though he did use the same dismissive tone for both *secretary* and *roadworks*.

'Let's step inside,' said Pascoe.

As they set off he glanced round at Charley, made a rueful face and murmured, 'Sorry. The will. Hang about and we'll talk later. If you can, that is. Thanks.'

What had Dalziel called him? *Old silver tongue*. Well, she'd never been a pushover for a smooth talker. On the other hand, if his smooth talking was going to include some gobbets of info about the will, she certainly wasn't going to miss the chance to hear that.

She turned round to find Godley standing so close to her she took an involuntary step backwards. At the same time he did a backward hop of twice the distance.

She said, 'Mr Godley, if you're going to make a habit of sneaking up on me, you're really going to have to do something with that beard.'

'Yes. Sorry.'

He looked so hangdog, she felt as guilty as if she'd given him a kick.

Thinking only to make amends she said, 'I was wondering – you must have heard all about Tom Parker's plans for Sandytown from your sister . . . half-sister . . . Doris. Right?'

'Yes. Doris was very enthusiastic about the festival and everything.'

'But you weren't?'

'Not really. Not my kind of thing. Don't like a lot of people around. Don't like a fuss. And with Doris being . . . well . . . being Miss Lee . . .'

She saw what he was saying. He loved his half-sister very much, but he didn't do deception. Being around her professionally must have been a real trial.

'So what made you change your mind?'

Silly question. She knew the answer even as she asked it, but it was too late.

He wouldn't look at her but stared at the ground and gabbled something inaudibly.

Inaudible was fine by her so she didn't say, 'Pardon?' or 'What?' but he took her silence as, 'Sorry, I didn't get that,' and straightened up and looked her in the eyes.

'Because when you and Mr and Mrs Parker called at the Mill and Mr Parker said you were going to stay with them for a few days, I thought if I accepted his invitation I might get to see you again. That's why I came.'

'But that's just . . . daft!' said Charley.

'Yes, I agree,' he said instantly. 'And I thought, the simplest way for me to see how daft it was would be to see you again and wonder why I'd bothered.'

It was silly for a sensible adult woman who really didn't fancy being fancied by a weirdo to feel disappointed, but Charley definitely felt a pang of something a lot like disappointment.

'Good thinking,' she said heartily.

'Not really. It doesn't seem at all daft to me now,' he said. 'In fact, it seems perfectly logical. And I'm sorry I thought even for a second you might have been in on that trick the police played to get me to talk. When I thought about it later, I knew I had to be wrong, and when I heard you stand up to the pair of them just now, I was certain. So there you go. What I feel about you might be hopeless, but it certainly isn't daft. Now I've got to go.'

'Where? Why?' she demanded.

'To the Avalon. You were right, that girl Clara should be our main concern now.'

He turned and walked swiftly away.

She felt an impulse to shout after his retreating

figure, to say they needed to talk more, but she was fearful that anything she said might be taken as encouragement. If he knew it was hopeless already, why risk changing that?

As he climbed on to the bike, a familiar dusty old Defender drew up alongside the lawyer's Daimler and the driver jumped out. He was a tall young man with broad shoulders and a smile to match as he strode across the lawn towards her.

'Hi, Charley,' he said as soon as he got within distance. 'Don't be mad, but when we got your news, the only way to stop Dad coming straight over here to make sure you're all right was for me to come, and I reckoned that was the lesser of two evils!'

He was right. She should have felt mad, or at least hugely exasperated to know that the Headbanger still thought of her as a helpless child in need of protection.

Instead, as her brother reached her and put his arms around her, she surprised herself even more than him by saying, 'Oh, George!' and bursting into tears.

7

In the large drawing room, the late Sir Henry Denham looked down upon the newly entered quartet of men with a patrician indifference.

Was the slight squint evidence of Bradley d'Aube's determination to paint a true portrait, warts and all? wondered Pascoe. Or had he just got fed up with being patronized?

The drawing room had been Mr Beard's choice. He had led them there without consultation. Presumably this was where he usually encountered Daphne Denham. Also he was clearly a man used to being in charge, even or perhaps especially in the company of policemen.

He sat down on a huge sofa. His secretary placed the briefcase beside him as an unambiguous signal that he intended single occupancy, then she sat down at a small ormolu table by the wall near the big bureau, pad and pencil at the ready.

Pascoe and Dalziel and Wield rearranged three armchairs so they centred on the lawyer and took their seats with a synchronicity worthy of Busby Berkeley.

Beard said, 'I take it, Mr Pascoe, that you do not yet have the perpetrator of this monstrous crime in custody?'

'Afraid not,' said Pascoe.

Beard nodded as if this came as no surprise.

'And you have not seen a copy of Lady Denham's will?'

'No.' Else we wouldn't be wasting time sitting here with you, thought Pascoe, giving Dalziel a quick glower to stop him saying it out loud.

'I see,' said Beard, not sounding surprised, but sounding as if he might be if he let himself. 'In that case, assuming that you regard all of those who might reasonably expect to profit from my client's will as possible suspects, I think I am justified in revealing its contents to you in advance of the beneficiaries.'

Dalziel scratched the folds of double chin with the baffled air of one who couldn't see how the fuck the lawyer should imagine he'd got any choice in the matter even if he did look like a self-portrait of Toulouse-Lautrec.

'That would be most helpful,' murmured Pascoe.

Mr Beard unlocked his briefcase and extracted a folder that looked as if it were made of vellum. Out of this he took a document.

He proclaimed, 'I have in my hand what is, presumably, the last will and testament of Lady Daphne Denham.'

'Presumably?' said Pascoe. 'Any reason to think there might be a later one?'

Beard sighed like a French horn and said, 'No specific reason, else I would have mentioned it. But in her latter years Lady Denham had got into the habit of writing wills. It is not uncommon. Some ageing people solve crosswords, some do cross-stitch, a few take to the composition of haikus. But a large number devote themselves to the writing and revising of wills. Basically, size does not matter. As long as there is portable property of any nature and any quantity, the habitual will-writer gains hours of pleasure from distributing and redistributing it. But where the estate is, as in this case, substantial, there is the additional element of exercising real power.'

'So how often did Lady Denham revise her will?' asked Pascoe.

'Four times this year that I know of,' said Beard. 'By which I mean, four times when her purposed modifications were major enough to require my professional assistance. I suspect, nay I am sure, that there have been frequent minor changes, or even major ones that did not stand the test of time and bring her to the stage where she consulted me. Such documents of course would have no status unless properly signed and witnessed. So, as I say, this to the best of my knowledge is the last will and testament of Lady Denham. It is a document of considerable detail, and commensurate length. Do you wish to hear it all?'

Dalziel let out a sighing groan, or a groaning sigh, the kind of sound that might well up from the soul of a tone-deaf man who has just realized the second act of *Götterdämmerung* is not the last.

Pascoe said, 'I think you might spare us the fine detail, Mr Beard. The principal bequests are naturally what I am most interested in.'

'As you wish. At what level would your definition of *principal* begin?'

Another sound from Dalziel, this one more ursine than human.

Hastily Pascoe said, 'Start at the top and work your way down.'

'That would in fact mean starting at the end,' said Mr Beard with distaste. 'But if you insist. "To my

486

nephew by marriage, Sir Edward Denham of Denham Park in the county of Yorkshire, all the residue of my estate real and personal . . ." You see the problem, Chief Inspector? Without the details of the other bequests, the term is meaningless . . .'

'I'm sure you've made an estimate,' said Pascoe. 'We won't hold you to it.'

'It isn't easy, property and the market being constantly in flux. I would say at least ten million. In fact it could be as much as . . .'

'Ten million will suffice,' said Pascoe. 'Go on.'

He went on. Esther Denham got a million and all her aunt's jewellery except for the single item Clara Brereton was invited to choose to accompany her five thousand.

'Five thousand,' interrupted Pascoe. 'Not five hundred thousand?'

'No, five thousand,' said Beard.

'Not a lot, considering. By comparison, I mean.'

'It is not a lawyer's duty to consider, Chief Inspector. Nor to compare. I will say that this was typical of the changes Lady Denham made in her will from time to time. The principal beneficiaries tended to remain the same, but the pecking order varied considerably. There have been times in the last twelve months when Miss Brereton was in line to inherit the Hall and a couple of million beside. Presumably when my client prepared this will, she felt she had reason to feel ill disposed to her cousin. Had she survived another week or so, no doubt it would have changed.'

Pascoe said, 'Would these beneficiaries know of the changes Lady Denham made from time to time?'

'I don't think she made a public announcement, but I do not doubt she made her dispositions known to those most nearly concerned.'

This would explain Ted Denham's confidence that the Hall and the bulk of the estate were coming his way, thought Pascoe. But why was he rifling through the bureau in the drawing room? Looking for the copy of the will, perhaps? But what need, if he knew its contents? And in any case Beard would be in possession of the original.

Mysteries – but they were what kept him in gainful employment!

'May I proceed?' said Beard, bringing him back to the present.

'Please do.'

'The other substantial beneficiary is Mr Alan Hollis, who gets the freehold of the Hope and Anchor.'

'The pub, eh? Worth killing for,' said Dalziel. 'Looks a tidy little business to me.'

'Indeed it is, as I can testify. I always stay there on my visits to Sandytown.'

'Oh aye? Had you down as more the Brereton Manor type,' said Dalziel.

'I have been coming here for many years now, and the hotel, of course, has only just opened,' said Beard. 'In any case, I prefer the simple life.'

'So what do you do when the pub's booked up?' said the Fat Man.

This sounded like irrelevant chitchat, but years of watching the Fat Man's apparently aimless wanderings bring him to some longed-for shore kept Pascoe quiet.

'The two letting rooms at the Hope and Anchor are used solely by myself and Miss Gay or any other visitors stipulated by my late client. I am sure Lady Denham made sure Mr Alan Hollis did not lose by the arrangement, and in any case his great expectations must have made him more than willing to oblige his patroness.'

There was a noise from the ormolu table. The secretary had let her notepad slip to the floor. She stooped to pick it up, her cheeks flushing as she mouthed an apology.

'Great expectations equal bloody big motive to me,' said Dalziel heavily.

'As a general principle, I would have to agree with you. In this case however Mr Hollis is very comfortably situated and his expectations have never been in doubt. He seems to have possessed the happy knack of never falling out with his employer and this bequest has been the one constant in all Lady Denham's wills, which strikes me as a clever move on my client's behalf, giving Mr Hollis a powerful incentive to run a business that would one day be his as efficiently and as honestly as possible.'

'Trusting him didn't stop her checking the accounts at least once a week,' observed Pascoe dryly, recalling the dead woman's diary.

'Aye well, she were a Yorkshire lass. Belts and braces, tha knows,' said Dalziel, a phrase which drew an appreciative smile from the secretary.

Pascoe said, 'Anything else you'd like to draw our attention to, Mr Beard?'

'As I indicated earlier, the length of the will derives from the small detail,' said the lawyer. 'None of the lesser bequests are such as to provoke a crime of greed, but one or two of them you may find peculiarly indicative of Lady Denham's state of mind as she made her dispositions.'

'For example?'

'To Harold Hollis, the shaving mug, badger hair

shaving brush and cut-throat razor belonging to his late lamented half-brother, my first husband, that he might have the wherewithal to make himself presentable should he care to attend my funeral. Also the sum of five pounds which should suffice to buy enough soap to last the rest of his life.'

'Wow,' said Pascoe.

'Wow indeed. They were not on good terms, but as you may already know, by the late Mr Howard Hollis's will, on his widow's decease the Hollis family farmhouse reverts to his half-brother.'

'Yes, we knew that. Anything else you'd like to draw our attention to?'

'Let me see. To Miss Petula Sheldon of the Avalon Clinic she leaves a bed.'

'A bed?'

'Yes. A single bed, specified as *the narrow hard single bed which will be found in what used to be the housemaid's room.* I do not completely grasp the significance of this, but doubt if it is kindly meant. The Parthian shot from beyond the grave is a not uncommon testamentary feature, attractive in that it is unanswerable.'

'Except by dancing on the grave and living another fifty years,' said Dalziel.

'Not perhaps an option for all of us. But I do not wish to give the impression that my late client's small bequests were always motivated by malice. There is for instance the sum of one thousand pounds left to each of the children of Mary and Tom Parker of Kyoto House, the money to be invested on the children's behalf till they are eighteen, with the rider that a small portion of the interest may be used to buy them ice cream on their birthdays. Another legatee is Mr Francis Roote of Lyke Farm Barn, who gets a thousand pounds towards the purchase of a motorized wheelchair. And a sum of ten thousand pounds is left to the Yorkshire Equine Trust on condition that they take care of her horse, Ginger, for the rest of his life.'

This made Pascoe smile. Franny had been right. A monster with a heart.

'Mebbe the horse did it,' muttered the Fat Man.

Pascoe frowned his distaste. His mobile rang. He looked at the display, mouthed *Novello* at Dalziel and Wield, and excused himself.

Outside he said, 'Hi, Shirley. What's the news?'

'Good and bad. Bad is she's broken her right leg, her right arm and collarbone, plus several ribs and she's cracked her skull right open. Good news is that they don't think there's any serious damage to her spine and she's stable.'

'Conscious?'

'No. And until she is, they won't be able to assess the full extent of the damage to her head. Worst case is, she could be brain damaged.'

'Are they planning to move her to a specialized unit?'

'Not till they're certain they won't do more damage by moving her. Anyway, I'm no expert, but this place makes the last NHS hospital I visited look like a doss-house. Dr Feldenhammer's whistling up relevant consultants from the Central and other places. Seems they do this all the time for their rich clientele. He'll wait till he gets their advice before deciding. Unless Clara's got good medical insurance, the sooner she gets out of here the better, else the sight of the bill will probably kill her!'

'I hope no one's relying too heavily on her expectations under Lady Denham's will,' said Pascoe.

'Why's that, sir?'

'She gets a bit but not a lot.'

'This will, when's it dated?'

'Couple of weeks ago? Why?'

'Something else I was ringing to tell you. I had a look at her clothes. In the patch pocket on her trousers I found a handwritten will, signed by Lady Denham, and dated the day before yesterday.'

'What does it say?'

'Not a lot,' said Novello, clearly enjoying her spotlight moment. 'It leaves everything to something called the Yorkshire Equine Trust. And here's the really interesting thing, sir. The witnesses are Mr Oliver Hollis and Miss Clara Brereton. So she knew about it, and my guess is, if the earlier will leaves her anything at all, something's better than nothing, and she wasn't about to let this one see the light of day!'

Pascoe didn't say anything for a long moment while he tried to take in the implications of this.

'Sir? You still there?'

'Yes, Shirley. You haven't let anyone else see this will, have you?'

'No, sir,' said Novello, sounding hurt.

'Good. Find anything else that might be useful?'

'Just her mobile.'

'Right. Where are you now, Shirley?'

'I'm in the corridor outside the Intensive Care Unit.'

'Excellent. Stay there. Make a note of everyone who has anything to do with her, and let them see what you're doing. I'll send someone to relieve you, then get yourself back here ASAP. Something you can do to pass the time is check who Brereton's been ringing today, who's been ringing her, with times. Can you manage that?'

'Think so, sir,' said Novello with the long-suffering tone of one to whom taking moving pictures on her

492

mobile while playing su-doku, listening to Nickelback, and checking her emails was second nature.

'Fine, but above all don't let Brereton out of your sight for a second. If you want a piss, ask for a bottle!'

He used the vulgarism deliberately to reinforce his command. From Dalziel it would have passed unnoticed.

He didn't go straight back into the drawing room but headed outside. PC Scroggs snapped to attention. He saw that Charley Heywood was now sitting in the middle of the lawn talking earnestly, but not to Godley. Her companion was a tall, broad-shouldered, clean-shaven young man. There was no sign of the healer.

'Who's that?' he said to Scroggs.

'Miss Heywood's brother, sir. Thought it would be all right as she came along with the Super.'

Some things didn't change. If the Prince of Darkness came along with the Super, that would be passport suffi-cient for all subsequent horned and hooved arrivals.

He realized Scroggs was regarding him fearfully.

'Yes, that's fine,' he said. 'You hurt your back or something? You're standing awfully stiff. I'd get it seen to, son. No shortage of therapists round here.'

Leaving the bewildered constable, he made his way to the Incident Room, where he found Seymour and Bowler.

To the latter he handed the envelope containing the photographs. He said, 'The man is Dr Feldenhammer. Blow up the best view of the woman's face, get rid of the doctor, then take it to the Avalon. Could be she was a patient there last autumn, perhaps an Indian. We need an ID. But be discreet. Check for rumours, but try not to start any.'

'Right,' said Bowler, clearly taking this as a sign that he was forgiven.

Pascoe turned to Seymour and said, 'Dennis, I want you up at the clinic too. Relieve Novello. You'll be watching Clara Brereton. And I mean watching. No one goes near her without a good medical reason. But watch the staff too, OK?'

'Yes, sir. Presume there's a good police reason why I'm doing this?'

Pascoe smiled and said, 'Sorry. I think she may have been attacked and I don't want it happening again. Now go!'

'Hello again,' said a voice behind him. 'We can't keep on meeting like this, Pete.'

He turned to see the cheerful face of Frodo Leach, the CSI.

Pascoe walked outside with him, explaining what had happened.

'So did she fall or was she pushed? Won't be easy, Pete, but who likes easy?'

'It would make a pleasant change,' said Pascoe. 'One more thing, if she was pushed, there's a cave in the cliff face where the perp may have hidden before making his escape. Have a good look there. That young woman can tell you where it is.'

He pointed towards Charley Heywood.

'Will do. Rest quiet, my chief, the experts have the task in hand!'

'I'm pleased to hear it. When you're done there, I'd like you to take a look at Lady Denham's bedroom in the Hall.'

'Thought your lot had searched it already?'

'They managed to miss a secret drawer in the old desk. Fortunately another of my lot spotted it later.'

'I love a secret drawer!' said Leach. 'What did your clever DC find in it?'

'Some photos,' said Pascoe. 'But I think something may have been taken out of it. That's your task, Frodo. I want to know who's been in there besides Lady Denham, OK?'

'If there's been a mouse in there, we'll have its DNA and prints,' declared Leach confidently. 'Talking of which, those bits and pieces we got from the shed – a few partials. Two matches with the samples your guys supplied, both named Hollis. One was the poor devil who got killed last evening, the hog-roast man, so it's not surprising. The other was a Mr Alan Hollis. That was on a piece of silver foil from a champagne bottle.'

'He runs the local pub, they supplied the booze, so that's not surprising either,' said Pascoe. 'I hope you are going to surprise me.'

'Sorry! One other thing, on the victim's blouse, on the front where the red wine stain was, we found a small tear, as if something had caught there.'

'Something like . . .?'

'God knows!' said Frodo cheerfully. 'Probably not a thorn, or a fingernail – they would have left traces. Metal, perhaps.'

'Great,' said Pascoe wearily. 'Don't think we're going to hang anybody on that.'

'Hanging's your job. Me, I just tell you what I know,' said Leach. 'See you later!'

As Pascoe returned to the main house, the front door opened and Mr Beard stepped out followed by his secretary.

He said, 'There you are, Chief Inspector. I think I have waited long enough. I cannot see how I can do more to assist you and I need to make arrangements to let the beneficiaries hear the terms of the will, and then, as an executor, I shall begin the complex task of tying up Lady Denham's estate.'

Behind the lawyer, Pascoe could see Wield and Dalziel, their faces in their very different ways conceding defeat. Beard must be a very powerful personality indeed to walk away from these two, thought Pascoe.

There was an ever so well brought up click from the Daimler as the chauffeur opened the rear door.

Pascoe said, 'In that case, thank you for your help, sir.'

'Yes. Goodbye.'

Dalziel now wore an expression that said that if he'd been unable to keep the lawyer from leaving, it was little surprise that Pascoe should fail too.

'One thing though,' said Pascoe to the lawyer's back. 'Perhaps you shouldn't be in too much of a hurry to summon the presumed beneficiaries. You said yourself, the will you have is the last one *that you know of*. Always a mistake to raise false hopes, isn't it?'

He didn't wait for an answer but walked into the house past his two colleagues and returned to the drawing room.

First Wield followed, then the Fat Man. The three of them resumed their previous seats.

After about thirty seconds, Miss Gay entered, gaze fixed on the ground, like a shy bride, and took her seat at the side table.

A pause, and then the lawyer appeared.

Pascoe waited till he was once more seated on the sofa.

Then he said, 'Right, let me tell you what I know.'

8

Charley and George sat on the lawn and talked. Occasionally a police officer passing to or from the Incident Room looked at them doubtfully, but a quick consultation with PC Scroggs confirmed their surprising legitimacy. At least it was surprising to Charley. From being treated as a reluctant witness cum suspect, she was now being given free rein to bask in the sunlight within striking distance of two crime scenes. In her own mind she was quite convinced that Clara's fall had not been an accident. This was something she would like to discuss with Fat Andy. She knew Pascoe was the man in charge, but far from reassuring her, his change of attitude had made her even more cautious. She was beginning to realize there was a lot more to Dalziel than appeared at first glance, but she felt that each new revelation simply revealed more of the truth of the man. Pascoe's changes were more protean. She was a long way from getting a grip on the central core.

For the moment she concentrated her attention on convincing her brother that her outburst of weeping was a natural female phenomenon, of no deep psychological significance. The trouble was he had hardly ever seen her cry as they grew up. Her stoicism was famous, and when pain or frustration had brought

George close to tears, he'd become used to the admonition, 'Look at Charley – do you think this would
make her cry?' His alarm now was both touching and
irritating.

The last thing Charley wanted was a negative report
to get back to Willingden. An independent adult woman
she might be, but if the Headbanger thought his little
girl needed protection, nothing would stop him from
descending on Sandytown like the Stompy of old, bent
on teaching a pint-sized scrum-half a bit of respect.

She had a great advantage in that, as the closest to
George in age, she had been his most frequent
guardian, mentor, entertainer and fellow conspirator.
The habit of subservience was deep ingrained, and
soon he was reassured that her tears had merely been
one of those woman things that cloud a man's hori-
zons briefly but quickly pass if you pay them no heed.

George was a simple soul in the very best sense of
the phrase. He was bright enough, in the top half of
class at school, and from an early age demonstrating
a firm grasp of both the practicalities and the economy
of farming. But his attitude to life was one of sunny
optimism. He saw everything in black and white; he
liked everyone he met until they proved themselves
unlikeable, upon which he shrugged and moved on,
his conviction that the world and its inhabitants were
on the whole bloody marvellous undinted. Girls loved
him and he loved them back, but so far he'd never
gone steady with anyone, declaring that he'd need to
find someone like his sister Charley, and there was
only one of her.

Away from home at college, Charley's explorations
of what made human beings tick had for a time woken
awful doubts about incestuous love, but soon as she

came home for the vacation and saw his open honest face and broad grin, all such fears had fled away. Seeing him enjoying himself like a kid in a sweetie shop during their skiing holiday at Davos, and hearing her lucky friends' rapturous reports of their encounters disposed of any residual worries.

Memories of the ski trip were triggered now as she gave him a blow-by-blow account of the events of the past two days. Death didn't mean a lot to George, unless it was the death of someone he knew personally, and his reaction to her account of Lady D's passing had more of X-movie shock/horror than of genuine human empathy in it.

Then he said, with the cheerfulness of one whose personal compass always turns towards the brightest quarter, 'At least it means Ess and Em won't need to go skulking around any more.'

'Sorry?'

'You said when I told you about seeing Emil, he were likely embarrassed at running into someone he knew 'cos him and Ess would want to keep things quiet for fear of Auntie's reaction. Now she's dead, they needn't bother, need they?'

'No. You're right. They needn't . . .'

Her mind was racing. How come she hadn't thought of this before? Until she had the details of the will, she had no idea to what extent Esther would benefit from the murder. In any case, despite her instinctive dislike of the woman, she felt unable to believe her capable of a cold-blooded killing just for a bit of money. On the other hand what must have really pissed her off was having to skulk around, as George had put it, just because this bossy vulgar parvenu woman wouldn't approve her chosen mate.

Also she'd have an ally, a young fit man who, for all that Charley knew, was as cold blooded as they came. Though it must have been Esther's special knowledge of her aunt's struggles with the animal rights people that had suggested putting her in the roasting frame instead of the pig . . .

She tried all this out on George, who listened as raptly as he used to when she invented bedtime stories peopled with local characters to send him to sleep, only to find that her penchant for gothic excitements had quite the opposite effect.

'Yeah, that's great,' he said. 'You certainly haven't lost your touch, sis.'

'My touch? No, George, this isn't one of my stories, this is a hypothesis. This could actually have happened!'

His expression changed.

'I just thought you were making it up, like the vicar and the vampires, or that one about Miss Hardy at the school and the poisoned milk. That was my favourite . . .'

'They were different. They were just daft stories. What's happened here is real.'

'But what you're saying about Emil . . . he seems such a nice guy, I really liked him. No, I think you've got it all wrong, sis. Not Emil. He's not like that.'

She looked at him with exasperated fondness and said, 'How can you know that? You only met Emil a couple of times at Davos, right? And you've seen him once since . . .'

'Twice,' he said.

'Twice?'

'Yeah. Remember I gave him my number when I bumped into him at the filling station, asked him to ring if he was anywhere near? Well, he rang Friday afternoon, said he was on his way home, catching a ferry later that night, and did I fancy a quick drink early on? So we met up at the Nag's Head.'

What did this signify? Charley tried to compartmentalize her thoughts, rational inference on the one side, imaginative speculation on the other. It wasn't easy. One of her tutors had rather dryly remarked, 'The beginning of all analysis is self-analysis. In your case, Miss Heywood, perhaps it should be the end as well.'

'So what did you talk about?' she asked.

'Talked a lot about you, actually,' grinned George.

'Me? But I only knew him by sight. I mean, there was no way for any other girl to get near him with poison ivy Ess twined round him the way she did!'

'Well, you certainly made a big impression, he wanted to know all about you.'

Charley found this incomprehensible. She was sure Emil hadn't even noticed her!

Then it struck her. Friday was the day she'd gone to Denham Park and out of sheer bloody malice reminded Esther that she'd seen her and Em last December in the Bengel-bar. Suddenly her creative imagination was racing. In Ess's shoes, she'd have taken the first opportunity to pass this on to Emil. He, recalling his recent encounter with George, had scented danger. Digging out George's telephone number, he'd made the phone call and fixed a meet. Charley knew her brother. By the time Emil finished chatting to him, the Swiss would know every detail of what George had told her and how she'd responded. Em was probably reassured that she wasn't going to go running to Lady D with the news that he was in the county, but just to make assurance doubly sure, he'd suggested to Esther that it might be time to mend a few fences, which would explain her sudden attack of amiability at the hog-roast!

None of this fitted in with a picture of the frustrated lovers having hatched a cunning plan to top Lady Denham later that afternoon. But that didn't matter. To Charley the whole business felt extempore. Maybe for some reason Emil had come to see Esther at Sandytown Hall . . . maybe Daph had surprised them . . . maybe . . .

'Oh, I nearly forgot, a letter came for you. Mum said it looked like Liam's handwriting,' said George with a grin.

Her mother of course had been right, thought Charley as she took the envelope. I bet she was tempted to steam it open!

She tried not to check for signs of tampering as she tore it open, but found she couldn't help it! There were none.

She read the single sheet quickly. It was a full, frank and fulsome apology. All his fault, he was a heel, didn't know what had come over him.

Dirty Dot, that's what, thought Charley savagely.

But as grovels went, it was a pretty good grovel, ending with assurances that he'd realized he couldn't live without her and a plea to be given one more chance.

'Who's this then?' said George.

She looked up to see Andy Dalziel coming towards them and quickly thrust the letter into her pocket.

'Superintendent Dalziel, dad's old rugby mate,' she said.

George rose to his feet and held out his hand. Dalziel was no dwarf, but Charley was secretly pleased to see he had to look up at her brother.

'Hi there, Mr Dalziel,' said George, beaming his irresistible smile. 'I'm George Heywood. Dad's told me a lot about you.'

'Oh aye? Never told me he were breeding giants. Glad to meet you, lad. What position do you play?'

'Second row at school, but I don't play any more since I left.'

'No? What's Stompy thinking of? Can think of half a dozen top teams as 'ud give their eye teeth for a youngster built like you.'

Charley could have told him that her father had reluctantly come to terms with the fact that his giant son had everything except the killer instinct. Opponents might bounce off him as he moved forward, but instead of trampling them underfoot, George was more likely to help them up and ask if they were all right.

But there was no time for that.

She said, 'What's happening? Have you seen the will?'

'Seen *a* will. Sir Ted gets the lion's share. Sis gets a hefty chunk, Clara a lot less. But it seems there's another will and, if that holds, nobody gets owt except for a bunch of broken-down horses. Mebbe we should be questioning yon nag in the stables!'

Charley smiled and asked, 'You say *if* it holds. Is there a doubt?'

'Don't know till yon hairy lawyer takes a look. Yon lass Clara had it. Your mate Novello's bringing it back from the clinic. Thought I'd get a breath of air and bring you up to speed.'

He's sticking to our bargain, thought Charley. Telling me everything. At least it sounds like he is. My turn now.

'George,' she said, 'tell Andy about meeting Emil Kunzli-Geiger again.'

When her brother had finished she added her own gloss.

The Fat Man rubbed his face, the flesh moving beneath his fingers as if it were a rubber mask he might pull off to reveal . . . she stopped the fancy there. Imagination could take you too far.

Dalziel looked as if he felt fancy had already taken her far beyond the facts.

'But . . .' he began.

His but did not get butted. A car pulled up outside the Hall and Shirley Novello got out. She glanced their way, showed no reaction, and went inside.

'Best get back in,' said Dalziel. 'You'll wait?'

'You bet.'

'See you later then. You too, lad. Hope you'll have time for a pint. Few tales I can tell you about your dad that I bet you've not heard from him!'

He found Pascoe and Novello in the passage outside the closed drawing-room door. Pascoe was studying a document.

'That the will?'

'Yes,' said Pascoe. 'Take a look.'

Dalziel studied the document. Handwritten on a stationer's will form, it was signed and witnessed. It was dated Friday, the day she'd visited him in the Home and he'd choked her off with the advice that she should change her will and cut out anyone she felt threatened by. Remove the motive, and you remove the danger, he'd said.

His mind ran round in circles seeking ways he could have handled it differently.

He said, 'Looks fine to me.'

Pascoe said, 'Let's see what Beard says. Shirley, you manage to check Brereton's phone calls?'

'Yes, sir.' Novello produced her notebook. 'This morning at nine fifteen, she received a call from a mobile registered to Sir Edward Denham of Denham Park. Duration, ten minutes. Nine thirty, she made a call to a mobile; I've got the number but it's an unregistered pay-as-you-go job. Duration five minutes. Five past ten she called Edward Denham's number. Duration three minutes. Twelve seventeen she rang him again. Duration fifty seconds.'

'Good work, Shirley,' said Pascoe. 'Another job for you. Go to Denham Park. Pick up Ted Denham. His sister too, if she's there. Invite them here for a chat.'

'Invite?' said Novello, wanting to be certain of her brief. 'Like, ask them nicely?'

'I hope you always do that, Shirley,' said Pascoe, smiling. 'Yes, ask them nicely. Once. If they prevaricate, arrest them. Cuff them if necessary. Or even if not.'

He looked at the Fat Man challengingly.

Dalziel said, 'Your call, lad. But they come here in handcuffs, you're going to have the media all over you.'

'So what's new? Looking at the timings, Brereton made that last call while she was in Lady Denham's bedroom. Way I read it is, Lady D, even if she wasn't completely convinced it was Ted who was threatening her, was so pissed off when she got the notion he and Sid Parker were plotting some financial deal behind her back, that she decided to follow the advice of her local resident expert – take a bow, Andy . . .'

'Put a sock in it!' growled the Fat Man, who didn't find the subject amusing.

'So she made a new disinheriting will and showed it to him before the hog-roast, to give him a salutary kick up the behind. Naturally, Ted's first thought after her death . . .'

'You saying he killed her?'

'He's high on my list. His first thought was to find and destroy the new will. But it was nowhere to be found. No great cause for panic. If *he* couldn't find it, who could? When he inherited the Hall, he'd be able to search at his leisure. The only fly in the ointment was the witnesses. If they spoke up, then a serious search might be instigated. Happily, one of them quickly followed Lady Denham across the great divide . . .'

'You saying Teddy killed Ollie Hollis as well?'

'He certainly had a motive,' said Pascoe. 'Which left Clara, the other witness. Not only did she know about the second will, it occurred to him, or maybe his sister, that she was the person most likely to know where Lady D had hidden it. On the other hand, she also would lose out if the will surfaced. The sensible thing to do would be nothing, relying on self-interest to keep Brereton quiet. I suspect this is what the sister advised.'

Dalziel nodded. This fitted with his reading of Esther too.

He said, 'But Ted thinks he can charm the knickers off any woman he meets . . .'

'Right. And he's not really going to rest easy till he's burnt the will. So he rings Brereton, and chats her up. She says yes, reckons she knows where the will could be hidden, and suggests they meet after she's had a chance to check it out.'

'What for? Why not just say she'll destroy it, if that's

the route she's going down? Or she'll hand it over to Mr Beard, if her conscience is too ticklish.'

'Because,' said Pascoe, 'her conscience isn't all that ticklish. She reckons she's earned her inheritance, putting up with Aunt Daph's little ways all these months. But it really gripes her that her reward is going to be just a few thousand while the randy bart and his sister get millions! So she goes to the Hall, checks the secret drawer, finds the will, rings Ted and says she's found it and she's on her way to meet him on the beach. However, he's waiting for her on the ledge.'

'And he pushes her over? Why'd he do that before he'd got his hands on the will?'

'Maybe it really was an accident,' said Pascoe. 'Or maybe she didn't say she had it in her pocket but that she'd left it in its hiding place where she could lay her hands on it whenever she wanted. He thought, if it's so well hidden, I don't need to worry. And I certainly don't need cousin Clara twisting my balls for a share of my inheritance. So over she goes, then he ducks into the cave when he hears Wieldy coming. That's the way I read it anyway. What do you think, Andy?'

'More loose ends than you'd find at a tinker's wedding,' said Dalziel. 'But I suppose it's worth pulling the bugger. Not sure about Esther, but.'

'No? Well, I think she's implicated up to her swan-like neck,' said Pascoe. 'When I interviewed her in the Hall, she'd changed her clothes. I know that because of what Charley Heywood says in one of those emails Shirley so cleverly got her hands on.'

Dalziel saw Novello wince at the reminder. Or mebbe she was just looking modest at the compliment!

'So she got wet, it were raining.'

'According to her statement she went straight into the Hall as soon as the storm began. Also I think she'd hurt her right arm. I think she may have burnt it.'

'Like on the hog-roast cage? OK, she got a burn when they found the body and that's when she got mussed up, helping to get it off the barbecue pit.'

Pascoe said, 'You're very defensive of the lady, Andy. Not becoming chivalrous in your old age, are you?'

God, he's getting right cocky! thought the Fat Man. In front of the servants too!

'I think that what with Daphne coming the duchess and her useless brother buggering around in every sense of the phrase, she's had a lot to put up with,' he said.

'My points exactly. Provoked by her aunt, protective of her brother, I reckon she'd be up for anything. Incidentally, no one reports seeing her around when the body was discovered, and she herself says she stayed in the house when the others went outside again after the storm stopped. Any other comments, Andy? Always glad of your input.'

'Only that with two such desperate criminals to bring in, mebbe I'd better go along with Ivor.'

Watching their faces as he spoke, he savoured their reactions to his generous offer of help. Pascoe looked doubtful, Novello looked disgruntled. Her, he could understand. From being the arresting officer, she'd be demoted to junior assist. As for Pascoe, he was probably thinking, is there no way I can stop this fat bastard from getting in on the act? No, a bit more than that. From pissing on my parade!

He said, 'Pete, it's your call. You're the man. And it'll be Ivor's collar. I'll just be along as the heavy.'

'Fine,' said Pascoe with sudden decision. 'Do it. One

thing more. Bring Ted's watch, big chunky Rolex. If he's not wearing it, look for it.'

'Without a warrant?' said Dalziel.

'Use your imagination,' said Pascoe coldly.

'Why do we want the watch, sir?' said Novello, as always eager to learn.

'Something had snagged the victim's blouse, and when I interviewed Sir Edward, he was having trouble with his watch clasp.'

'You don't break a Rolex catch by snagging it on a bit of silk,' objected Dalziel.

'No. But as clever Miss Heywood pointed out for us, this is a fake, remember?' said Pascoe triumphantly. 'Probably you could bend the catch by breathing on it. Now, I'd better get back in there before Wield and Beard come to blows over who's prettiest.'

He returned to the drawing room where, far from fighting, he discovered the lawyer and the sergeant having an animated conversation about Gilbert and Sullivan.

'Sorry to interrupt,' said Pascoe, 'but I'd be grateful if you'd cast your eye over this, Mr Beard.'

The lawyer took the will form and read through it carefully. He snapped his fingers and Miss Gay passed him a magnifying glass through which he scrutinized parts of the will even more closely.

Finally satisfied, he put down the glass and sat back on the sofa.

'What we have here,' he said, 'is a will, simple in purpose and unambiguous in language, revoking all previous wills and appointing myself as sole executor, in which the entirety of the late Lady Denham's estate is left to the Yorkshire Equine Trust. It is handwritten and I can confirm beyond any reasonable doubt that the writing is Lady Denham's, as is the signature. It is dated two days ago, and therefore post-dates the will in my possession whose dispositions we discussed earlier.'

He paused.

'So, for the avoidance of doubt,' said Pascoe, 'you can confirm that the will you read to us is no longer valid and that, unless yet another will surfaces, what we have here is legally the last will and testament of the late Lady Denham?'

'I don't believe I said that, Chief Inspector,' said Mr Beard.

'I'm sorry? I thought you said you were convinced the signature was genuine?'

'Indeed I did, and indeed I am. Lady Denham's signature this certainly is. But then we come to the two witnesses who are given as Mr Oliver Hollis and Miss Clara Brereton. I have had occasion to see Miss Brereton's signature only once before, so I cannot be absolutely certain, but it does not accord with memory. As for Mr Oliver Hollis, he was, coincidentally, or perhaps significantly, along with Miss Gay here' – the secretary bobbed her head in unsmiling acknowledgement – 'a witness to the will I have in my briefcase. You may, if you wish, compare his signature there with what I see before me here. Myself, I have no such need. I can affirm beyond all doubt that it was not written by his hand.'

Beard and Wieldy were right to be talking about Gilbert and Sullivan, thought Pascoe. We're in Titipu!

He said, 'So what are you saying, Mr Beard?'

For the first time the lawyer smiled, white teeth gleaming through black beard, as though he'd been waiting all his life for this.

'I am saying that Lady Denham appears to have forged her own will!'

9

Dennis Seymour wasn't good with hospitals. When his twin daughters were born, he'd managed to witness the arrival of the first, but by the time the second emerged, he was lying on the floor, receiving treatment himself. So it was with no great enthusiasm that he'd made his way to the Avalon and asked to be directed to Intensive Care.

Shirley Novello had shown no reluctance to be relieved. The only hope she could offer of anything to dilute the boredom was a warning that Gordon Godley had appeared and asked if he could have a few minutes with the patient.

'Sounded harmless, but the nuts often do,' said Novello. 'I sent him packing, but keep an eye open. Never trust a man with a beard; he's usually got something to hide.'

'Means I'm there with a chance then,' grinned Seymour, stroking his chin.

'Oh no. Clean shaven's worse. Means you've got nothing to hide. Cheers, Dennis.'

Since then he had sat on a hard chair in the corridor with nothing to occupy him but the beep from the life-support system to which the still figure on the bed was hooked up. The arrival of a nurse to check that all was as it should be came as a welcome relief. She was rather pretty and he tried to flirt with her, but she was young enough to regard a man in his thirties as a lost cause and merely looked embarrassed. When she appeared again some fifteen minutes later, he tried the poor old man approach and asked if there was any way of getting a cup of coffee.

She pointed down the corridor and said, 'Visitors' lounge, third on the right, help yourself.'

She went into the room. Based on her previous visit, she'd be in there for several minutes, so Seymour wandered off along the corridor. The visitors' lounge was unlike any hospital waiting room Seymour had ever been in. His feet sank into a thick piled carpet, a scatter of richly upholstered armchairs invited him into their depths, along one wall ran a rack of up-to-date newspapers and magazines, and on an antique sideboard against the opposite wall rested a plateful of what smelt like freshly baked scones and a state-of-the-art percolator.

Used to pressing a button and watching a plastic cup fill with brown sludge, Seymour was still puzzling over the mechanics of the device when the door opened and the pretty nurse looked in.

'Bet you're good with cars though,' she said as she made him a cup of delicious coffee.

'Yeah, keep getting head-hunted by Ferrari, but I don't care for their team colours.'

He reckoned it was quite a good line but he only got a polite, slightly puzzled smile. He helped himself to a scone and made for the door. It opened and Hat Bowler came in.

'Hi, Dennis. Might have guessed I'd find you stuffing your face. My uncle not bothering you, is he, miss?'

The nurse laughed out loud and said, 'Is there a police convention here they didn't tell me about?'

'No, I've just been sent to make sure this guy's doing his job. Also I'm looking for someone. Bet those bright blue eyes don't miss much. Ever see her around?'

He put the edited photo into the nurse's hand then made himself a cup of coffee with an ease that even more than the nurse's reaction told Seymour he was getting old.

The nurse said, 'I think it could be Miss Bannerjee. She was a patient when I started a year ago, but I didn't really know her as she moved on not long after I came.'

'Moved on? You don't mean she, you know, *died*?' said Hat, mouthing the last word lugubriously.

'No, of course not. I mean she left,' said the nurse, laughing.

'Thank God for that!' said Hat, laughing with her. 'Had me worried for a moment. So she was discharged, everything in working order? That's great. I expect they'll have a forwarding address in the office.'

'I expect so,' said the nurse. 'Though there might be a problem. If I remember right, she wasn't discharged as such, more sort of like I said . . . left.'

'Left? You mean like . . . disappeared? Here one moment, gone the next? Indian rope trick?'

'No, don't be daft! I think her family decided she should go, there was a bit of bother . . . Look, I shouldn't be talking to you about a patient really . . .'

'You're not, 'cos she's not a patient, is she?' said Hat triumphantly. 'Anyway, if you're talking about the rumours about her and Dr Feldenhammer, no one pays any attention to that sort of thing. Happens all the time with doctors, and with policemen too. I mean, here's you and me talking away, all innocent, but if someone decided to start spreading a rumour that I really fancied you, there's nothing we could do about it, is there? Specially 'cos a rumour like that would be really easy to believe. I've just heard it myself and I'm starting to believe it!'

It was ludicrously corny, but that didn't stop it from working, thought Seymour half enviously. Another couple of minutes of this should be enough for Bowler to have extracted everything she knew about the rumoured relationship between Feldenhammer and Miss Bannerjee.

Time to give him a free run.

'Best be getting back,' he said.

He stuck the scone in his mouth to free a hand to pick up a newspaper. That might win him a few precious minutes in the fight against boredom.

As he reached the Intensive Care Unit door, he glanced through the glass panel and suddenly boredom seemed a condition devoutly to be wished.

There was someone in there, stooping over the recumbent figure on the bed, his hands hovering over her head.

It was Gordon Godley.

Dropping his cup and newspaper, and letting out a bellow of, 'Hat!' that Dalziel would have been proud of, Seymour pushed open the door and rushed in.

'What the hell are you doing?' he demanded, grabbing hold of the man and dragging him away.

Godley offered no resistance.

'It's OK,' he said. 'Really. It's OK.'

'It better had be, you bastard,' grated Seymour, pushing the man up against the wall and holding him there with one hand on his chest, the other ready with clenched fist to deliver a disabling punch if he tried anything.

Hat Bowler burst through the door, followed by the pretty nurse.

'You need any help there?' demanded Bowler.

'No. I've got him,' said Seymour, irritated to realize he was much more out of breath than Godley. 'Just check that she's OK, will you?'

He glowered at his unresisting captive till the nurse said, 'Everything looks fine. No harm done.'

'Good,' said Bowler. 'Well done, Dennis. You got him before he had time to do anything.'

'Thank Christ for that,' said Seymour, shuddering to think of Pascoe's reaction if he'd been too late.

But Mr Godley was shaking his head.

'No, I don't think so,' he said. 'It felt like I had plenty of time.'

'For what, you bastard?' demanded Seymour, alarmed once more. 'What were you trying to do to her?'

Then the nurse cried, 'Look!'

He turned, fearful of what he might see.

Clara Brereton had opened her eyes. They were moving rapidly, taking in the room, the people there. She brought her fingers up to the tube down her throat as if she wanted to speak.

The nurse said, 'I'll get a doctor,' and pressed a button on the wall by the bed.

Seymour looked back at Godley.

The man was smiling and nodding his head.

'There,' he said. 'I knew I'd had time.'

10

Seymour was by nature and by nurture an honest, straightforward man, so much so that it never even occurred to him, as many of his colleagues theorized, that if he'd had just a little capacity for deviousness, he might have risen a lot higher in his career.

When Pascoe turned up at the Avalon, the DC made no attempt to conceal the dereliction of duty that had allowed Godley access to Clara Brereton, only perhaps slightly overstressing in mitigation the miraculous nature of the woman's recovery.

But Pascoe was in no mood either to administer bollockings or to debate miracles.

'Is she talking yet?' he demanded.

'Don't know. Dr Feldenhammer made us leave the room.'

Another thing Pascoe wasn't in the mood for was being obstructed by doctors whose professional expertise was no match for the mumbo jumbo of a hairy healer.

He strode into the Intensive Care Unit. Clara Brereton was lying there, still looking very pale, but unencumbered by breathing or feeding tubes. He saw her intelligent eyes register his arrival.

There were several nurses and doctors around the bed. One of them said indignantly in an American accent, 'Now see here, whoever you are . . .'

'Pascoe. DCI Pascoe. It's Dr Feldenhammer, isn't it? I've seen your photo.'

'That's right. So you're Pascoe. I've heard about you.'

'And I about you,' said Pascoe significantly. 'I'd like to speak to Miss Brereton.'

'Not possible till my people are done here.'

'If she can talk, it's possible,' said Pascoe.

The men glared at each other, but the struggle was ended by a whisper from the bed.

'Mr Pascoe . . .'

'Yes. I'm here, Miss Brereton.'

'I'm sorry,' she said, her eyes full of tears, 'but I can't remember anything . . . What happened to me? . . . I can't remember . . .'

Pascoe allowed himself to be escorted out of the room by Feldenhammer.

'So what's the prognosis?' he asked, his tone now conciliatory.

'Surprisingly good. As you saw, she can breathe unaided and though her fractures and possible internal injuries will probably keep her bedridden for some time, her mind seems unimpaired. Memory loss is common in such cases. Often it returns eventually, at least in part, but you'll just have to be patient.'

'One of my officers will be with her, or close to her, at all times. I'd like your assurance that anything she says to any of your staff will be passed on immediately.'

'We have a duty of confidentiality, Mr Pascoe . . .'

'I'm glad to hear you take your responsibilities to your patients so seriously, Doctor,' said Pascoe heavily. 'Regardless of race or creed. It's a concept I may need to discuss with you some time in the future. Meanwhile, if I can have your assurance . . .'

Feldenhammer looked at him uneasily, perhaps recalling the remark about seeing his photo. Finally he said, 'Yes, of course, we'll be happy to co-operate. Now excuse me.'

He went back into the room.

Pascoe said, 'Dennis, no cock-ups this time, right? Next time you may not be so lucky.'

'Yes, sir.'

'Now where's Hat?'

Bowler was sitting in the visitors' room, drinking coffee.

'Like a cup, sir?' he asked. 'It's really good.'

'No thanks. I take it from your demeanour, Hat, that you've got some news for me.'

'Yes, sir. The lady in the picture is Miss Indira Bannerjee, a former patient here. Her problems were psychological, my source didn't have any detail and in any case she didn't want to say . . .'

'Yeah yeah, patient confidentiality, I know all about it,' said Pascoe.

'But she didn't mind a bit of gossip. Evidently, Miss Bannerjee was what you might call hot stuff . . .'

Pascoe noted the young man's effort to find an idiom he might understand.

He said, 'You mean, she put it about a bit?'

'Yeah,' grinned Bowler. 'Started young, I gather. She was only seventeen when she was here. Evidently the nurses called her the Bannerjee Jump.'

'Very witty. And her and Feldenhammer?'

'Oh yes. There were rumours. Nothing positive, but it was generally agreed that what Indira wanted, Indira got.'

'What about the family? If they suspected . . .'

'They might have been suspicious, but they wouldn't

have been surprised,' said Bowler. 'What they weren't going to do was demand an investigation and encourage the tabloids to dig up all the others. So they simply took her away.'

'Great. Well done, Hat. Another job for you. You seemed to get on all right with Sidney Parker? Well, get yourself up to the hotel and talk to him again.'

'Yes, sir. Sir, is it right what they're saying, that he's gay?'

'Doesn't bother you, does it?'

'No, sir,' said Hat indignantly.

'Oh, I get it. You thought he liked you for your cultural depth and witty conversation! Don't brood on it, Hat – use it! Undo another button on your shirt if it helps. I want to know precisely when he and Ted Denham stopped screwing in their little love nest on the cliff. Maybe Sid likes to keep check of how long it takes. He is, after all, an accountant. OK?'

'Yes, sir,' said Hat unhappily.

'If he doesn't want to be co-operative, you might like to wonder why, when his niece Minnie told him she'd stumbled upon Dr Feldenhammer performing an act of indecency with an under-age girl who also happened to be his patient, he didn't inform the authorities.'

'But Miss Bannerjee was seventeen, sir,' objected Hat.

'You know that and I know that, but there's no reason for Sidney Parker to know that, is there?' said Pascoe. 'Call me if you get anything.'

He rose and went out to his car. When he got back to the Hall he found as expected that Dalziel and Novello had returned with the Denhams. He'd left instructions with Wield to keep them separate, Ted in the Incident Room, Esther in the Hall.

Dalziel was sitting on the lawn talking to Charley Heywood and her brother. There was another figure with them. Sammy Ruddlesdin.

'What the hell's he doing there?' Pascoe demanded of PC Scroggs.

'Said he was waiting for you, sir. Said you were expecting him.'

In a sense it was true. But he was in no mood to exchange pleasantries with the journalist just now.

Dalziel had spotted him and rose not without effort from the grass. Ruddlesdin started to get up too, but the Fat Man put his hand on his shoulder and pushed him back down.

'So what's she say?' he asked as he joined Pascoe on the steps.

'A convenient CRAFT moment,' said Pascoe.

'Nay, don't be cynical,' said Dalziel. 'Experience like that, nasty knock to the head, does funny things to the mind, as I know. Even now most of what happened afore I got blown up is like an old movie I saw years back and didn't much care for. Any road, why should she lie?'

'Because she's not yet sure which way the wind is going to blow,' said Pascoe.

'Which wind's that?'

'The wind that Ted Denham blows out of his mouth when he talks. How did he look when you picked him up? Any problem?'

'Came like a lamb. When I mentioned his watch, he went and got it for me. Gave it to yon Frodo to check out, but you were right, the broken catch were dead flimsy.'

'Excellent. And Esther?'

'No problem either. At a guess I'd say being brought

in didn't come like a bolt from the blue to either of them.'

'Meaning they've probably been doing a bit of rehearsal,' said Pascoe. 'With the woman as director and scriptwriter. Be interesting to see if Ted can remember his lines. I think I'll start with Esther. That way I'll know what the lines are.'

Dalziel said, 'Pete, about Ted and Clara, you're forgetting one thing, aren't you? When me and Ivor went off to Denham Park, you didn't know then the will wasn't valid.'

'So?'

'So that fancy tale you wove doesn't make sense if, soon as the bart mentions the will to Clara, she says, "What the fuck are you talking about?" I mean, once he catches on that her signature must be a forgery, he's home and clear, isn't he? Let them find the will! It changes nowt!'

Pascoe was unconcerned.

'Makes no difference. Clara's a very bright girl. I can imagine Denham rattling on at great length, putting on the charm, imagining he was overcoming her scruples with his subtle arguments, while all the time he was only giving her space to get her head round what he was saying. She tells him she'll need time to think. He thinks she means whether to be a good honest citizen or to tear up the will. Whereas what she's really thinking is: I need to see this will. And by the time she finds it, she's worked out it doesn't matter if it's valid or not, as long as Sir Ted thinks it is! Like I say, a bright girl.'

'Not all that bright,' said the Fat Man. 'Else she'd have also worked out Ted were the person benefiting most from Daph and Ollie's deaths, so maybe it weren't so clever meeting up with a possible killer on an empty beach. And another thing, if Ted thought he'd been disinherited, why the fuck would he want to kill his aunt anyway?'

'I don't know, Andy,' said Pascoe, irritated. 'Perhaps it was a spur of the moment thing. I'll ask him about it when I interrogate him, shall I? By the way, was Ruddlesdin here when you brought the Denhams in?'

''Fraid so.'

'Shit. Tell him I'll kill him if he prints anything before he gets my say-so.'

'Pete, it's no use gagging the *Mid-York News*. By now the national vultures will be dropping down on Sandytown. If I were you, I'd think about a Press Conference.'

'Never thought I'd see the day when you suggested that, Andy.'

'Never thought I'd see the day when you didn't, Pete.'

The two men looked at each other in silence for a while then Pascoe forced a smile and said, 'Well, I'd better not keep Esther waiting any longer.'

'You don't want me to sit in then?'

Pascoe said, 'I think not. But thanks for the offer.'

'Any time,' said the Fat Man. He turned and walked away to rejoin the trio on the lawn. As he reached them, he said, 'Twang!'

'What?' said Charley.

'Nowt. Just the sound of an umbilical cord snapping.'

'So what's happening, Mr Dalziel?' said Ruddlesdin. 'How soon can we expect to hear that Sir Edward's been charged?'

'Don't think you'll be able to hear owt for the sound of my stomach rumbling,' said Dalziel, 'I'm fair clemmed.

Charley, George, you can't lie around here all day, cluttering up a crime scene. On your feet. We're all off to the Hope and Anchor. Mr Ruddlesdin's treat.'

Sammy Ruddlesdin looked ready to object. Then he looked up at Dalziel's bulky figure, looming over him like the Old Man of Hoy.

'My pleasure, Mr Dalziel,' he said. 'My pleasure.'

11

Pascoe had his strategy all carefully worked out as he made his way to the big drawing room. Esther would be sitting on the sofa that Beard had occupied, her expression a mix of weary indifference and intellectual superiority. Novello would be sitting watchfully opposite her. On his entrance, the DC would rise and vacate her seat. He would sit down, smile, apologize for keeping Esther waiting. And then he would take her through her initial statement, getting her to reconfirm every last detail. Eventually he would start gently nudging her into making alterations. Why, if she'd avoided the storm, had she felt the need to change her clothing? How, if she hadn't been among those who removed the body from the hog-roast basket, had she come to burn her arm? What was that? You haven't burnt your arm? Perhaps you'd care to roll up your right sleeve . . .?

Eventually she would have to abandon her script and move on to his and then the drama was ready to unfold.

But when he pushed open the door, he realized that he'd been rehearsing the wrong play.

Esther Denham wasn't sitting on the sofa but was at the open bureau, writing. She wasn't wearing an arm-concealing blouse, but a sleeveless top, revealing a neat dressing on her right forearm. Novello, standing behind her, looked round at Pascoe's entry and shrugged helplessly.

'Miss Denham,' said Pascoe.

'Almost finished,' said the woman without looking up. 'When they said you were delayed, I thought it would speed things up if I wrote out my revised statement. There, that's finished.'

She signed her name with a flourish, gathered together the sheets of notepaper and handed them to Novello.

'Shouldn't you sign as a witness?' she enquired. 'I think we've probably had enough problems with forgeries for one day.'

Novello glanced at Pascoe again. He nodded, and she took the pen and signed, then handed the papers to Pascoe.

How co-operative everyone was being in this case, he thought. Roote had had a statement prepared for Wield; Feldenhammer had handed his to Dalziel: now here was Esther Denham getting in on the act.

He sat down on an armchair. The woman came from the bureau and reclined elegantly on to the sofa.

So now the scene was physically as he'd envisaged it, but even before he studied the sheets in his hand, he guessed that his prepared script was out of the window.

Written on Sandytown Hall headed notepaper in an elegant cursive hand, the new statement was both confession and rebuttal. To Pascoe the style bore the mark of the lamp.

Making my way back to the Hall after a stroll round the grounds, I stumbled upon the body of Lady Denham concealed in some long grass in the vicinity of the hog-roast machinery. Having ascertained that she was dead, my first thought was to call for help. Then I became aware of a man's wrist watch snagged on her blouse. On closer examination, I realized that it belonged to my brother, Sir Edward Denham. Knowing that earlier he had been involved in an angry altercation with Lady Denham over changes she had made to her will, I began to fear that he might have something to do with her death. Marks around the body's neck made me suspect there had been foul play. With time for leisurely thought, I am sure I would have reached the conclusion that my brother was incapable of such an act, but I did not have this time. My only thought was for Edward. I removed the watch. Then I tried to think of other ways in which I could misdirect any investigation. Knowing of her long-standing feud with animal rights extremists, I looked for a means to suggest their involvement here. The hog-roast machinery was close by. It occurred to me that substituting Lady Denham's body for that of the pig in the basket could be seen as a clear statement of the motives behind the murder. There was no sign of Ollie Hollis who was in charge of the actual roast, and the developing storm made it unlikely that anyone else would come this way to disturb me, so I winched the basket off the pit, and, using the heavy insulated gloves I found in the hut, I managed to remove the pig and substitute the cadaver, burning my forearm slightly in the process.

I then made my way back to the Hall, entering unobserved by a rear door, and went to the room I knew my brother used for changing in when he went swimming. I found him there, towelling himself down. It soon became clear to me as I told him what I had *done that he had no idea what I was talking about. He in fact had spent the last hour or so in the company of Sidney Parker, his homosexual lover. He was completely bowled over when I told him about Lady Denham. I was convinced of his innocence, and I realized the presence of his watch on the scene meant that someone was trying to point the finger of suspicion his way. Not knowing what other false clues might have been deposited, it seemed best to say nothing but try to outthink the perpetrator. To this end, we agreed that Edward must be among the first on the spot when the body was discovered so that any other physical evidence of his involvement that might have been planted could be explained by contact made in removing it from the basket. Edward, though not the clearest of thinkers, has always had a great deal of self-possession in trying circumstances, so, though naturally deeply distressed, he was able to carry this off with relative ease.*

I had hoped that the police investigation might have led rapidly to discovery of the real culprit and that my role in this affair would never need to surface, but clearly this has not happened. In fact, I am glad of this opportunity to get this burden of concealment off my chest. I regret that any action of mine should have muddied the waters, and hope that by volunteering this statement, I might leave the way clear for the police to get on the trail of the real perpetrator.

Pascoe sighed deeply as he finished reading and said, 'Miss Denham, you realize that, however we take this statement, in it you are admitting to a very serious offence?'

'Yes.'

'And if in fact your assertion that you were

527

mistakenly trying to cover up for your brother turns out itself to be an attempt to cover up for your brother, you are committing an even more serious offence?'

'I had worked that out. But my statement is true.'

'Really? Work out a lot, do you, Miss Denham?'

'I'm sorry?'

'Visit the gym two or three times a week? Weight training, that sort of thing?'

'Certainly not.'

'I didn't think so. I don't observe any of that definition of the biceps, triceps or deltoid muscles that usually accompanies such exercise.'

'How about my pecs, Chief Inspector? Are they defined enough for you?'

'Excellently defined, if God did all,' said Pascoe. 'But my point is, young, healthy and fit though you appear to be, I find it hard to believe that you could have done all you claim to have done without assistance. Your aunt was no spring chicken. The winch and the pulley systems, even though well oiled, still require a fair amount of strength to work them.'

'Your point being?'

'My point being that it seems to me far more likely that this was the work of you and your brother working in concert.'

'You think we conspired to murder Lady Denham?' She smiled. 'I assure you if my mind had ever turned that way, I would have come up with something a lot less muddled than this!'

'I believe you,' said Pascoe, smiling in his turn. 'This smacks of masculine anger and impulsiveness. I think you probably chanced upon the event as it reached its climax. Too late to prevent the murder, you immediately set about setting up the diversions. That much of what you write is true, except of course that Edward was with you, following your instructions.'

'No,' she insisted serenely. 'I was alone. Teddy was never there. I'm sure that Sid Parker will be able to provide him with an alibi.'

'So am I,' said Pascoe. 'If the love of a sister can do as much, then surely the love of a lover will not fall short. Mr Parker's story will, I fear, carry as much or as little weight as yours.'

'You don't seem to regard love very highly, Mr Pascoe.'

'Oh, but I do. It comes second only to truth in my Pantheon,' said Pascoe. 'I'm going to talk with your brother now. Knowing him as you do, how do you think he's going to stand up to interrogation?'

'Very well. All he's got to do is tell you what little he knows. As such a devout worshipper of truth, eventually you'll have to acknowledge the presence of your deity.'

He felt he was beginning to see what Andy Dalziel had clearly seen from the beginning, the real woman beneath the polished shell. From the Fat Man she won sympathy. From himself she won merely admiration.

Her one point of weakness was Ted. He did not doubt for a moment that she was trying to cover up for him.

But he didn't doubt either that her serene confidence in her brother's ability to be able to withstand close interrogation was misplaced. That was the trouble with love. It made you do silly things. But worse, it made you blind to weakness.

He said, 'I'll let you know how I get on then, shall I?'

Then he stood up and left the room.

12

As they approached the gate of Sandytown Hall, Sammy Ruddlesdin's battered old Fiesta leading the way, George's Land Rover behind, Dalziel saw that he'd been right about the growing media interest. Their way was barred by a pack of journalists and photographers.

Sammy began to brake, but the Fat Man's hand fastened like a clamp about his thigh.

'Accelerator, Sammy, not brake,' said Dalziel. 'If the buggers don't get out of the way, run 'em down. Then turn left up the hill.'

At the top of North Cliff, he directed the Fiesta along a skein of country lanes till thirty minutes later he was satisfied they'd shaken off any journalist attempting pursuit. Then he navigated the car back to the coast road and re-entered the town by way of South Cliff with the Land Rover close behind.

They parked behind the Hope and Anchor and went into the pub by the rear door. A clever journalist who knew him might have been waiting in the snug, but only Ruddlesdin fitted that bill, and when they entered the room, they found it empty.

'That was fun,' said George Heywood with a grin. 'I expect you've worked up a thirst, Mr Dalziel. What are you having?'

Dalziel nodded approvingly. This was as it should be, young man eager to buy drinks for his elders. But not in this case.

He said, 'You can buy me one later, lad. This round's Mr Ruddlesdin's.'

Sammy said, 'Name your poison,' with the complacency of one who knew that any expense docket marked *drinks for DS Dalziel* would be passed on the nod.

He took the order to the bar and rang a bell for attention. After a pause, Jenny the barmaid appeared.

'Sorry about that,' she said. 'Bit shorthanded. Alan's popped up to the Avalon.'

'Oh aye?' said Dalziel. 'Not badly, is he?'

'No, have you not heard? That cousin of Lady Denham's, Clara, she's up there. She had a fall. We got word she recovered consciousness and we had a whip-round for some flowers and Alan said he'd run them up there.'

'Friend of his then?'

'We all liked her and we felt a bit sorry for her too, specially Alan, knowing what Lady Denham could be like. He used to say she went over his accounts like a spy satellite, she could spot an error from fifty miles up. I hope the old cow – sorry, shouldn't speak ill of the dead – I hope the old lady's left Clara comfortable in her will. Worth millions, they say?'

She ended on a question mark, looking hopefully at Dalziel.

Bet everyone in Sandytown knows exactly who he is by now, thought Charley. And they assume that, if anyone knows anything, it will be him.

Curiously she found herself assuming much the same.

But all he said was, 'Aye, wills are funny things. But isn't Mr Beard staying here? You'd best ask him.'

'More chance of getting my granda to speak, and he said nowt but *bugger Blair!* for ten years,' said Jenny. 'Now he says nowt but *bugger Brown!*'

She took the order and began pouring drinks. The door opened and Franny Roote rolled through it. His jaw dropped in a show of stagy surprise that felt to Charley as if it concealed the real thing.

'All my favourite people under one roof,' he said. 'Mr Dalziel. Charley. And George. This has to be George, I assume? I see a family resemblance, and Charley's told me so much about you, I feel as if I know you already.'

He reached out and the two young men shook hands. Ruddlesdin came back from the bar, bearing drinks. Roote grinned up at him.

'And it's Mr Ruddlesdin, star reporter of the *News*, if I'm not mistaken. Long time no see, Mr Ruddlesdin.'

Sammy said, 'Eh?' looked more closely, then glanced from the man in the wheelchair to Dalziel and back again.

'It's Roote, isn't it?' he said cautiously. 'Franny Roote?'

'Yes. You interviewed me once, or was it twice? Good piece, lousy photo.'

'I recall. What are you doing here then?' He tried to sound casual, but his eyes were bright with speculation.

'Oh, a bit of this, bit of that,' said Roote, smiling. 'So how're things going up at the Hall, Andy? I hear they've taken the bart and his sister in for questioning. Serious stuff, is it? I mean, can we expect a statement soon?'

Again all attention was on the Fat Man.

He took a long draught of his beer, then said, 'I dare say.'

'Make a note of that, Mr Ruddlesdin. Quote of the week. Detective Superintendent Dalziel says, "I dare say".'

It struck Charley that Roote was in a slightly manic mood. There was a sense of barely repressed energy about him in contrast with his usual aura of cool control.

Dalziel didn't react. His attention was concentrated on the door which Roote had left open. Suddenly he put his glass down, said, 'I need a leak. And I've spat in that beer,' stood up and went out. Charley saw him step into the path of a young woman who'd just come down the stairs into the passage between the snug and the main bar. He paused as if to apologize, then the door swung shut behind him.

'So, George,' said Roote, 'have you come to rescue your sister? Must be worrying for your family when suddenly the Home of the Healthy Holiday turns into the *Costa de Muerte*!'

'Rescue Charley? You must be joking,' laughed George. 'As far as I'm concerned, she's always been the one who did the rescuing.'

'I can believe it,' said Roote. 'Ever since she came here, we've all felt ourselves very much the object of her attention. We shall miss her when she finally goes.'

Charley felt herself disproportionately complimented by what was after all a mere polite token of regret.

She said, 'So what was this interview about, Mr Ruddlesdin? I didn't realize Franny was famous.'

Roote looked quizzically at the journalist who,

perhaps for the first time in his adult life, felt embarrassed.

But he was saved from replying by the door opening again, this time to admit Alan Hollis.

'Sorry, Jenny,' he said. 'Been rushed off your feet?'

'No, it's been fine. How's Clara?'

'Broke an arm and a leg and some ribs, still pretty shocked, but they say they're pleased with her,' replied Hollis. 'They just let me in long enough to pass on everyone's good wishes, and the flowers, of course. She said to tell everyone thank you, and that was about as much as the poor love could manage.'

'Anyone got any idea what happened yet?' asked Ruddlesdin.

'Not yet. Seems she can't recall a thing.'

'Folk are saying that the Hall was never a lucky place for them as lived there,' said Jenny. 'That's why it stood empty so long afore Hog Hollis bought it. And look what happened to him. Then Lady Denham. Now poor Clara.'

'You saying she's inherited the Hall?' said Ruddlesdin sharply.

'I've no idea,' said Jenny. 'If anyone deserves it, she does.'

'Don't worry, lass. Everyone will get what they deserve,' said Dalziel, who had somehow re-entered the room without attracting attention. Nimble on his pins for a big man, thought Charley.

The barmaid looked unimpressed by the Fat Man's assertion and Hollis said, 'Right, Jenny, I'll take over here. You get back to the bar.'

'How do, Mr Hollis,' said Dalziel. 'Everything all right up at the Avalon?'

The landlord repeated what he'd told the others,

adding, 'All the nurses were talking about that healer fellow, Godley, him as is one of Tom Parker's circus. Seems they were all dead worried she'd never wake up, or not be right when she did, then after he'd been with her a couple of minutes, she opened her eyes and was fine. Makes you think, doesn't it?'

'Godley? This the same guy they thought they'd caught in the act at the acupuncturist's last night?' asked Ruddlesdin, his nose twitching at the scent of a good human interest story.

'The guy *you* thought they'd caught in the act,' said Dalziel heavily. 'If he decides to sue the *News* for that piece you wrote about him, likely you'll need his healing touch once your editor's done with you.'

He sat down, drained the rest of his beer, looked at George, and said, 'Now you can buy me that pint, lad.'

As George went to the bar, the Fat Man said to Charley with a ponderous archness, 'Does make you think, but. Handy chap to have around, yon Godley, if he's really got the gift.'

Charley yawned to indicate her indifference to this geriatric match-making.

Roote said, 'Might come in handy for your thesis, Charley. Or have the last couple of days redirected your interest away from alternative medicine to offender profiling?'

She said coldly, 'I'll be glad to get back to my own work.'

'Ready to come home then, Charley?' said George, placing a foaming pint in front of the Fat Man.

She became aware that Roote and the Fat Man were both looking at her, waiting for her answer.

She said, 'Yes, but I'll stay as long as I think I can

be useful at Kyoto House. This business has put a lot of strain on poor Mary.'

It sounded nice and altruistic, she thought, so long as no one cared to enquire if sitting in a pub supping ale was the best way of helping a friend take care of her family.

The door opened again. In stepped Sergeant Whitby. He clearly had the tunnel vision of one who has spent too much time fantasizing about a drink so cold you could trace your name in the condensation on the glass.

With never a side glance at the seated drinkers, he made straight for the bar, sank on a stool and said, 'Pint of the usual, Alan. I've bloody well earned it.'

'Bad day, Jug?' said the landlord who'd started drawing the pint as soon as the door opened.

'Bad!' echoed the sergeant. 'I've been running around half the county looking for that daft cousin of thine, all because yon fancy Dan from CID says *its imperative we talk with Mr Hen Hollis.*'

As parodies of Pascoe went, it wasn't bad, thought Dalziel. He wondered if he should interrupt before the sergeant got more personal, but decided it might be fun to wait.

'The bugger's nowhere to be found, so finally I gives up and goes along to the Hall to report in. And what do I find? Only that they've arrested yon Ted Denham and his sister and they're taking them off to Headquarters for questioning. Did anyone think to give me a call and let me know? Did they buggery! No, all that long streak of gull shit and his bunch of fairies can think of is –'

'JUG!'

The word fell on Whitby's ears like the clap of doom.

He spun round on his stool. The expression on his face made Munch's *Scream* look like a smiley.

'Mr Dalziel,' he stammered.

'Outside,' said the Fat Man.

He slammed the door behind them so hard those inside felt the increase in air pressure.

'How long to retirement, Jug?' he asked.

'Nine months, sir.'

'Full sergeant's pension?'

'Yes, sir.'

'No, sir! I ever get as much as a sniff of a whiff of a rumour that you're standing around a pub bar, badmouthing your superiors and letting all and sundry in on confidential police information, you'll find yourself booted out so hard, you'll need a cushion when you're sitting in the benefits office trying to persuade them to give you the dole. Understand me, lad?'

'Yes, sir.'

'Right. Get back in there then and finish your drink. Say nowt to no bugger. If the pub bursts into flames, don't even yell Fire! You got that?'

'Got it, sir.'

He waited till the chastened sergeant had re-entered the snug, then he walked outside into the street and thumbed a number into his mobile.

'Pascoe.'

'What the fuck's going on?'

'Good day to you too, Andy. Glad you rang. I was just going to call you and bring you up to speed. I've decided that we need to move things on a bit. The Denhams have both been arrested and are presently en route to HQ for formal interviews. We don't have the facilities here and of course we don't have secure accommodation.'

'You're going to bang them up?' asked Dalziel incredulously.

'I don't anticipate releasing them in the next few hours,' replied Pascoe carefully.

'So what brought this on?'

Pascoe related Esther's version of the discovery of Lady Denham's body.

'She's stuck to it. Her brother sticks to his story, i.e. that he was banging Sidney Parker till the storm broke. Parker confirms the timings. And both Ted and Esther assure me they were together all day till you picked them up, thus alibiing him for Clara Brereton.'

'The phone calls?'

'Oh yes. He had pat answers there too. He rang her in the morning to see how she was. She was interrupted in her reply and promised to ring him back later, which she did, to say she was fine.'

'Bit risky if it's a lie, when he don't know what she's going to say when she wakes up.'

'Perhaps he did know. We got hold of his mobile. Last call he made just before you and Novello turned up at the Park was to the Avalon. I reckon he got hold of Feldenhammer, whistled a couple of bars of that vulgar song you told me about . . .'

'"The Indian Maid".'

'Indeed. Then he invited the doctor to give him a full and frank account of the patient's progress. *Miraculously conscious* must have been bad news. But *total memory loss* must have fallen on his ears like the Pilgrims' Chorus.'

'That another vulgar song then? Isn't this all a bit clever-clever for someone who keeps his brains in his boxers?'

'Not when you've got your sibylline sister murmuring in your ear.'

'Thought her name were Esther.'

538

'Oh, Andy, Andy. I have to go now. Naturally I'm heading back to HQ to take charge of the interrogations.'

'Naturally. You talked to Desperate Dan yet?'

'Of course. I promised the Chief he'd be the first to know about any significant development. He was pleased to hear there's been progress.'

'I bet he was. Progress is grand, but don't get ahead of yourself. Take care.'

'You too, Andy. See you soon, I hope. Next time I'll remember the grapes.'

Dalziel switched off and stood in thought for a couple of minutes. What he was trying to think about was the case, but what kept getting in the way was the fact that suddenly he felt bloody knackered. Could this uneasiness he felt about the investigation just be a symptom of his own debility rather than a sign that Peter Pascoe had got things wrong?

'Andy, are you all right?'

He turned to see Charley Heywood regarding him with concern. He must have been standing here a bit longer than he thought.

'Nay, lass, I'm fine.'

'You sure? We got worried, you were so long.'

We, he saw, as he accompanied her back into the snug, consisted of the Heywoods and Franny Roote.

'Where's Ruddlesdin?'

'He took off a couple of minutes back.'

Shit. He must have gone out of the back door into the car park and was probably heading back to town now, wanting to be on hand if and when any news came out of HQ. Even if nothing new broke in the next few hours, the Denhams' arrest would give his fertile imagination more than enough material for a sensational headline.

Not your problem, he told himself.

Charley said, 'Would you like George to give you a lift back up to the Avalon?'

He said, 'Not afore I've finished the pint your brother were kind enough to buy me.'

Hollis and Whitby had been head to head over the bar, but any conversation between them stopped as soon as the Fat Man re-entered.

After a moment or two, the landlord said, 'Point of law, Mr Dalziel. I were just asking Jug: what would happen to all the money Lady D left Ted if it turned out he did have something to do with her death?'

'I'm not a bloody lawyer,' growled Dalziel. 'And if I was, likely you couldn't afford me.'

A sup of his beer as well as smoothing his ruffles reminded him what a good cellar Hollis kept. Also this was a landlord who'd taken him in without comment or objection when he was dressed in jim-jams, dressing gown and one slipper. Such a man did not deserve rudeness.

He said, 'But if Sir Ted *were* convicted of murder, he can never touch the money, that's for sure. I reckon that the other legacies would stand, so you'll be able to sort out yon dungeon you call a cellar, if that's what's bothering you.'

Alan Hollis regarded him coldly.

'No, it wasn't bothering me, Mr Dalziel, and I won't let it bother me till Lady Denham's decently buried and the bastard who murdered her's behind bars.'

'I'm sorry, lad,' said Dalziel fulsomely. 'I were out of order. I reckon Ted's share would be treated like Daph had died intestate. So the family could claim. Blood family, that is.'

'You mean the Breretons?' said Hollis.

'Aye. Doubt if the Hollises would have a claim,' said Dalziel. 'Sorry, there I go again. Us cops have big feet.'

'I'd guess you usually know where you're planting yours,' said Hollis with a faint smile. 'But I really am happy with what I've got. I was wondering about young Clara.'

'Depends,' said Dalziel. 'How close related is she? And how many more of the Breretons are still alive and kicking?'

Whitby gave a cough and looked at the Fat Man like a schoolboy putting his hand up in class.

Dalziel gave him a permissory nod.

'Daph Brereton were an only child,' he began, 'but there were two uncles and an aunt, all dead now I should think. Derek, that's the eldest, he had two daughters and a son, while his brother Michael had at least one boy, mebbe more, and Edith had three boys. I think Clara is grandchild to Derek's eldest son, which makes her a cousin twice removed, is it, or three times . . .'

'Too far already,' interrupted Dalziel. 'If there's full cousins still alive, plus their children, then Clara's so far out of the running, she wouldn't even figure in the betting.'

'For God's sake!' snapped Franny Roote. 'We're talking about a murdered woman here! We're talking about people we know who are under arrest, rightly or wrongly – not that that matters, once the law in this country gets its claws into you. The system needs its victims and sometimes it's not too choosey who they are!'

He ended abruptly, looking rather flushed.

Dalziel looked at him goggle-eyed.

'Bloody hell, lad,' he exclaimed. 'I thought it were

yon Third Thought crap you'd got mixed up with, not Amnesty International!'

'You know me,' said Roote, recovering his normal control. 'Always sensitive to an injustice. Not that I anticipate one here. Not with Peter Pascoe in charge, and you getting back to your normal rude health, Andy.'

'Less of the rude,' said the Fat Man. 'Sergeant Whitby, now that you've displayed your local knowledge, how about putting it to some practical use? When you came in you were moaning on about wasting your time looking for this guy Hen Hollis. Has anyone told you to stop looking for him?'

'No, not as such, but I thought . . .'

'Don't start thinking at your age, Jug, it'll get you confused. Just do what you're told. Carry on looking.'

'But I've looked everywhere,' protested the sergeant.

'Have you looked at Millstone?' asked Alan Hollis.

'No. He's not been out there since Daph chucked him out after Hog died,' objected Whitby. 'It's been let go to wrack and ruin. Why'd he want to go out there?'

'Because,' said Hollis, 'it's his again now, isn't it? At least it will be, once the will's settled.'

'What's Millstone?' asked Dalziel.

'Millstone Farm, where Hog and Hen grew up,' explained Hollis. 'Hog left it to his wife, but just for her lifetime. Now it reverts to Hen.'

'And you reckon he wouldn't worry about waiting for the legal stuff to get settled afore moving back in?'

'Not too big on legal stuff, Hen,' said the landlord, smiling.

'There you are, Jug. Get yourself out there, take a look. And if you find the bugger, bring him in and let me know.'

'Yes, sir. Where will you be?'

Where will I be? wondered Dalziel. Not at the Hall for sure. The circus and its new ringmaster had left town. No point in hanging around there like a left-over clown. He could sit around here another hour or so, supping pints. That was tempting. But not as tempting as the prospect of that nice comfy bed up at the Home.

He said, 'Likely I'll be up at the Avalon, taking a well-earned rest. Young George, what fettle? I think I'm ready for that lift now.'

'My pleasure,' said George Heywood.

13

Sergeant Jug Whitby was not a revolutionary. No way was he going to break out the flag of freedom and lead a charge against the monstrous regiment of Andy Dalziel. By rank, by personality, by sheer bulk, the Fat Man held him in thrall.

And yet he was carved from the same hard stone as the superintendent, he belonged in the same long tradition of independent bloody-mindedness, he looked at the world through the same dark-shaded spectacles. In short, he too was a Yorkshireman. Come to think of it, as a Whitby, he was probably a truer bluer Yorkshireman than the fat old sod. What sort of name was Dalziel anyway? Touch of the tartan there, hint of the whacky macs from over the Border.

So though he was never going to face up to the Fat Man and say *bugger off!*, with every yard he put between himself and the actual terrifying presence, his sense of what was due to him as keeper of the law here in Sandytown and district these twenty-five years reasserted itself.

Yes, he'd carry out the order, pointless and stupid though he reckoned it were. But he'd do it in his own time, at his own speed. First he'd assert his statutory right to refreshment by heading home to the Sunday joint cold cut plus bubble and squeak his wife prepared for him every Monday, regardless of season or weather. Then he'd exercise his statutory right to rest by taking his usual thirty-minute nap in his favourite armchair, followed by his statutory right to recreation by watching his favourite American cop show on the box.

And only then, refreshed and restored, would he go and take a look at Millstone Farm to confirm what he was certain of, that it was unoccupied by anything but rodents, bats and spiders.

'You're nivver gan out now?' his wife demanded as he began to pull his boots on about nine thirty.

'I told you. Got to take a look out at Millstone.'

'It'll be pitch black by the time you get out there. Not a spot I'd want to be in the pitch black,' she said. 'Won't it keep till morning?'

After the long and outwardly visible internal debate necessary before any self-respecting Yorkshireman accepted female advice, he nodded and said, 'Happen tha's right. But if the phone rings, you answer it, and if it's yon fat bastard, tell him I'm out!'

Upright, in the light and warmth of his sitting room, this boldness felt good. Prone in the dark of his bedroom, it soon began to feel foolhardy, and every time he woke during a restless night, it felt foolhardier.

Not long after dawn he rose, resolved to get the useless task out of the way before he was required to explain his dilatoriness.

It occurred to him as he drove slowly up the long, deep-rutted, weed-overgrown lane to Millstone Farm that the last time he'd made this journey, he'd been bringing the sad news of Hog Hollis's death.

Hen, sole occupant of the house since his brother's success had taken him to Sandytown Hall and the Lordship of the Hundred, hadn't invited him in, notwithstanding it was a bitter day and a gusting wind was shooting volleys of sharp sleet against his unprotected back. So he'd wasted no words as he broke the news on the doorstep.

'Hog's dead.'

'Dead,' said Hen.

There was no question mark but Jug had treated it as a request for confirmation.

'Aye,' he said. 'Stroke. Pigs had started on him when they found him.'

'Right then.'

And the door had closed.

Maybe Hen Hollis had retreated to his kitchen and sat there recalling younger happier days with his brother. Maybe he had wept.

More likely, according to local speculation, he had wandered round the house thinking, It's all mine now!

If so, there were bigger shocks than his brother's death to come.

The revelation that everything had been left to Hog's relict had devastated Hen, but the local speculators weren't short of explanation.

'Hog reckoned nowt to most of his family. He used to say young Alan were the only one as he'd trust to boil water. He knew what he wanted, in business or bed, and he went straight for it, and the thing about Daph Brereton were that she was usually on her way to meet him! Wife like that were a godsend to Hog, and he always paid his debts.'

But family was family, for all that, and the locals agreed that justice had been done by the clause which gave the widow only a life's interest in Millstone with the house reverting to Hen if he survived her.

So all he had to do was bide his time, continue to

live in the family home, and mutter the odd prayer that fate or a high fence would bring his sister-in-law low sooner rather than later.

But though he lacked his half-brother's business acumen, he shared his impatience with delay. He took Daphne on in the courts and he lost. Then he took her on out of the courts, laying accusations of murder against her with the constabulary, the press and anyone else who would listen. And here he lost also.

Everything, including his job and his home.

He'd tried to claim he was a sitting tenant, but as he'd never paid a penny's rent this got him nowhere. He tried to claim residence at Millstone was part of his contract of employment with Hollis's Ham, but as he'd walked out of his job of his own accord, that didn't wash either.

So he'd been evicted and the house had stood unoccupied these many years. Here in the countryside nature is always waiting to reclaim what man has taken from her. A human presence with its need for warmth and shelter and some degree of cleanliness can establish a long truce, but drop your guard, withdraw even for a few months, and nature starts to retake possession. Whether out of meanness or malice, Hog's widow hadn't undertaken even the minimum maintenance necessary to keep weather and wildlife at bay. Slates blew off, window frames rotted, glass cracked, cladding was pierced, pipes froze, rats gnawed, rabbits burrowed, beetles tunnelled, and not a thing was done to remedy or resist any of these depredations.

Not yet quite a ruin, it needed only another decade of neglect to render it so.

A man would have to be dafter even than Hen Hollis to spend a night here afore the builders had worked on the place for a long fortnight, thought Sergeant Whitby as he saw the cluster of house and shippens loom gothically out of the morning mist.

There was no knocker on the front door, just a darker oval to show where one had been fixed for a hundred years or so till the screws had worked loose in the rotting woodwork.

Whitby clenched his fist and brought it crashing down on the oak panel with a force that shook the door in its frame.

The noise of the blow seemed to reverberate a long time, as if winding its way around the interior room by room, seeking life to absorb it.

Finally, finding none, it died away of its own accord.

Satisfied he didn't need to knock again, Whitby considered his next move. It might be fun to get fat Dalziel out of bed to tell him there was nowt to tell! But while he was debating if he had courage enough for that, he felt a powerful need to empty his bladder.

He unbuttoned, then, some old social inhibition making him reluctant to piss even on Hen Hollis's ruinous doorstep, he stepped round the side of the house.

And there it was, hidden by the angle of the wall on his approach to the front door.

Hen's ancient bike.

He postponed thinking about this till he'd hosed the ground.

A last shake, then it was time for action. One step at a time, no need to jump ahead to possible conclusions, that was for poncey CID kids like Pascoe.

First another thunderous blow on the front door accompanied by a cry of, 'Hen! You in there? It's Jug Whitby! Don't muck about!'

Again only the echo of emptiness.

He walked round the house, peering in the small-framed, small-paned windows, but even where the sun shone full upon them, they were too dusty and weather grimed to let him see beyond.

The back door was a simple piece of kit. No lock, just a latch. And of course a couple of hefty bolts inside, so's an untrusting Yorkshire farmer could sleep secure in his bed.

He lifted the latch. There was no resistance. The door creaked open.

Now even a hard-headed, ageing Yorkshire sergeant couldn't stop his mind taking a couple of steps to a most unwelcome conclusion.

He entered the big farmhouse kitchen.

This would have been the centre of life in the days when the Hollis family lived at Millstone. There was the old range where old Ma Hollis would have cooked the family meals, there was the long scarred table where the men would have sat to eat them, there was the great arched fireplace before which they would have crowded to dry themselves after a day in the thin cold rain or sat to stare at their futures in the glowing embers during the cold winter evenings.

At a corner of the table stood an overflowing ash-tray. Alongside it a glass tumbler, turned upside down. And dead in the centre, an empty whisky bottle weighing down a sheet of paper.

Jug ignored it. Time enough to read when he was certain that reading was all that was left to do.

He knew from long experience that when a farmer came to the end of his tether, if there were family around, he'd take himself to the barn or byre where only the beasts would see him set the shotgun barrel under his chin.

But if he were alone, then it was here on his own familiar hearth that he'd take his farewells.

So it was a cause for relief to find the kitchen empty.

You're just letting this gloomy old place get to you, he admonished himself. I mean, why the hell would Hen choose the moment Daph Brereton's death had so improved his life to decide to end it?

Mebbe after marking his recovery of the family home by a typically solitary celebration, he'd staggered upstairs and was lying senseless on his old dusty bed.

He shouted, 'Hen! You there?'

Loud as he shouted, he couldn't drown out the thought that Hen couldn't have chosen to shoot himself because he didn't have a shotgun.

This he knew because he himself had confiscated it the year after the eviction. In recent years, local police kept a very close check on gun ownership. When Hen hadn't renewed his licence, Whitby had visited him and, after listening to his catalogue of grievances, had come away with the weapon.

So in the unlikely event he'd decided to kill himself, it wouldn't have been by shooting.

And once again long experience of the traumas of rustic life projected images in the sergeant's mind.

If not the gun, then the rope. A high-beamed barn was the favoured site here. Most of these old low-ceilinged farmhouses didn't have any vertical space deep enough for a grown man to drop into, but in some instances the situation of the stairs meant that a short rope carefully affixed to a beam across the landing would allow a determined man room to dangle into his own entrance hall.

But there was no reason for Hen to kill himself,

not now, not here! his thoughts reiterated. No reason at all.

One way to be sure.

Slowly Jug Whitby lifted the latch on the inner door that opened into the hall. Slowly he pushed it open.

'Oh shit,' he said. 'Oh shit shit shit shit shit!'

14

Andy Dalziel sat in the morning sunshine on the doorstep of Millstone Farm and read the note through the transparent plastic of an evidence bag.

It was written in pencil in a round, unjoined-up hand.

> it were all an accident I only went there to help after Ollie had bother with the hog roast machnry and rang me to say could I give a hand.
>
> Then Daph saw me there and we got into a row and she told me shed make sure I nivver set foot in Millstone again even if it meant she had to burn it down with her own hands and I ran at her and she fell over and banged her head and as she lay there looking up at me she laughed and said so what are you going to do now Hen Hollis? Strangle me? Everything went black in my head then and when it got light again I found Id done just that. Id strangled her. Ollie were in a right stew wanting to run for help. I said dont be daft they'll do for us both. No one knows Ive been here. Let someone else find her theres plenty with good cause to want Daph Brereton dead like yon Ted Denham for one. Saying that made me wonder

552

if there were any way I could point a finger at him. He always tret me like dirt. Ollie said he thought hed gone off swimming with some kids and he knew where he left his clothes in the house. I sent him off there to fetch summat of Denhams we could leave around to fool the cops and while he were gone I dragged the body away from the hut. When Ollie came back with that fancy watch Denham wears I told him to bugger off and say he went to shelter somewhere away from the machnry because of the lightning. Then I snagged the watch on Lady Mucks clothes and headed off myself leaving her lying in the grass. How she got in the hog roast cage I don't know unless Ollie sneaked back and put her there for some reason. But he said it werent him when I found him at Witch Cottage. I wanted to be sure hed stick to his story but the soft bugger had got himself in such a state he said he were going to see Whitby and tell him everything soon as Miss Lee got back and took the needles out. He said hed mek sure the police understood it had been an accident. I said you stupid sod how the fuck can you strangle some bugger by accident? And I felt the blackness coming over me again and I picked up one of them needles and stuck it right into his back. Didn't mean to kill him like I didn't really mean no harm to Daph Brereton not to start with anyway but I can see how its going to look.

All ive lived for these past years is to get Millstone back for myself and now Ive got it but for how long? They'll lock me up for sure and mebbe they wont even let me keep Millstone if I

live long enough to get out again. So fuck them
all. If I cant live here at least I can die here.
Fuck you all

'Poor old sod,' said Dalziel.

Whitby looked at him in surprise then nodded his
head and repeated, 'Aye, poor old sod. What do we
do now, sir?'

He was in Dalziel's hands. There'd been no thought
of contacting anybody else till he'd spoken to the Fat
Man.

Dragged from his bed, Dalziel's sleep-slurred voice
had said, 'This had better be bad, Jug.'

But when he heard how bad it was, the slur had
been replaced by a cold clarity.

'He's dead?'

'Definite.'

'And there's a note?'

'Aye. On the kitchen table under an empty whisky
bottle.'

'Bag the note, get out of the house, wait for me.'

He'd borrowed Pet Sheldon's car. Looking at his
face, she hadn't asked for an explanation. As he drove
out of the Avalon gate, he'd met the local newsagent's
van coming in with the morning papers. He'd stopped
him and helped himself.

One look at the front page of the *Mid-York News*
was enough. Without actually stating that a formal
charge had been made, Sammy Ruddlesdin was once
more giving the impression that it was safe to walk
the streets of Mid-Yorkshire again as DCI Pascoe, the
county's answer to Poirot, had got the titled perpetrator
(and his accomplice) under lock and key.

'Oh, Pete, Pete,' groaned Dalziel. 'I warned you.

Ignore their shit and eventually it'll drop off you. It's the buggers' praise you can never quite scrape away!'

The one good thing was that it was only the *Mid-York News* that had jumped the gun so dramatically and he didn't doubt that the other papers would be only too glad of a chance to make one of their own look an arsehole. So there was still plenty of time for Pascoe to regroup. Arresting the Denhams was fine. They had after all admitted a serious offence. But with just a little shuffling of the facts – and Pete was a very fine shuffler! – it should be easy to present their transfer to HQ as a subtle ploy to divert the press from Sandytown so that the local man on the spot could follow his instructions and bring the case to a satisfactory conclusion. Dan Trimble would be delighted. Case solved, full confession, perp dead, no trial. What could be more satisfactory?

'What do we do now?' he echoed Jug Whitby. 'You ring Mr Pascoe.'

'Me? I thought mebbe that you . . .'

'No. Your patch, Jug. Your local knowledge that brought you here. Any credit going should be thine. And Mr Pascoe's. You'll tell the press that you were here following Mr Pascoe's instructions, right? And it is right, isn't it? 'Cos he never told you to stop looking for Hen.'

'Aye, sir, but it was you . . .'

'I've not been here, Jug. I'm in bed fast asleep. I'm a convalescent invalid, remember?'

He rose from the step and stretched himself in the sunlight.

Pascoe would be up now, he didn't doubt, eager to get back to the Denhams, hoping – believing! – that, with a little more pressure, a little more cunning, he could get the answers that would make the headlines he had probably just read with his breakfast come true.

The news about Hen Hollis would come as a shock, then as a relief.

But it had better not come from Dalziel.

No way he could pass on the news without it sounding like a gloating *I told you so!*

'Which,' said the Fat Man to the unheeding sun, 'I bloody well did, too!'

Volume the Fifth

Miss Heywood, I astonish you. – You hardly know what to make of me. – I see by your looks you are not used to such quick measures

1

FROM: charley@whiffle.com
TO: cassie@natterjack.com
SUBJECT: farewell & festival!

Hi Cass!

My last mail from Sandytown! Like I told you after the
great anti-climax, I was ready to head straight back home
& immerse myself in the serene certainties of life at
Willingden Farm. Ordinary – run-of-the-ruined-mill – boring
– had never seemed more attractive. But Tom & Mary
were so pressing – Id lived through the dark days –
surely I wanted to see the dawn – that sort of thing – at
least that was Tom – Mary was more – of course you
want to get back to your family but I hope now we are
family too – sort of – at least thats how I think of you – &
Minnies really going to miss you – I know I am – but
please dont feel any pressure! –

Shes never said anything – but I think deep down in the
middle of the night Mary may have been having nightmares
that Tom was somehow mixed up in Lady Ds death – or
maybe it was her own dislike & distrust of the woman
making her feel guilty – & now the crisis is past – as often
happens – the strain begins to show!

How could I abandon her straightaway! So I said OK –
but Ive promised to be home for the Bank Holiday – if Im

not there at the Willingden Country Show on Monday to
see dad snapping up prizes for the Sexiest Heiffer – &
mum for the most scrumptious Victoria Sponge – Ill get
the gold medal for the Blackest Sheep of Family Heywood!

So Ive agreed to stay till today Saturday – for the
Grand Opening of Sandytowns first ever Festival of Health.
What better time & place for a wounded community to
start its healing – says Tom – I think hes practising his
opening speech on me! – but he may have a point.
Certainly Sandytowns showing remarkable resilience –
only 4 days since they found poor Hen & already the
locals have moved from shock! horror! to a kind of
knowing fatalism – the Hollises a doomed clan – not
marked for happiness – only Alan at the Hope & Anchor
seems to have escaped the curse – maybe his ma played
away! I even heard someone say – Hen always said he
were born at Millstone – & no bugger – not God in His
Heaven nor yon old cow at the Hall – were going to stop
him dieing there!

Ive made a lot of notes – might do a little paper some
time – *tragedy & the mass consciousness* – not snappy
enough? – OK – how about *pigs & needles & two yards
of rope!* Sorry. You can see Im doing it too – turning
tragedy into a topic.

Havent forgotten my thesis though. Combined a visit to
Claras sick bed with a surreptitious interview. Godly
Gordons alleged miracle cure is an even more popular
topic than Hens suicide – Tom can hardly refrain from
chortling with glee at his own cleverness in persuading
Gord to join his team of alternatives – naturally I didnt tell
him the only reason his precious healer had come to
Sandytown was cos hes got the hots for me!!!! Cant help
feeling flattered even tho theres no way I could fancy the
guy – tho I must admit I quite like him now. Anyway – he

seems to have got the message – theres been no sign of him for the past few days – I think Toms a bit worried he may not show for the festival opening – but I assured him Gord wouldnt let him down – not that kind of fellow.

Anyway – Clara is doing well – when it came down to it seems that its mainly broken bones & concussion – probably was from the start but Gords still getting all the credit locally! Could be moved now to an NHS specialist unit – but Ted Denham insists that she should stay at the Avalon – & the specialists should all come to her – his treat! Ted – as youd expect – has bounced right back from being pilloried in the *News* as no 1 suspect – rides into town on the Sexy Beast like Alexander the Great looking to be worshipped – which he is – everybody loves a rich young squire – who promises to be a lot more liberal with his money than dear old Daph! Hes promised Tom hell take her place in the Development Consortium – & fulfil all her undertakings – & more! The Festival of Health is of course Toms particular baby – but Teds first spectacular will come next week when Daphs funeral takes place. I dread to think what hes got planned for the wake! Havent seen much of Esther – but when I did the thaw begun at the hog-roast continued – maybe it wasnt me in particular she disliked – just life in Daphs large shadow. No word yet of the return of the Swiss toy boy. Maybe she thinks it wouldnt be decent to parade him till her aunts safe in the ground.

Back to Clara – not much useful there for the thesis – hoped she might have had a white tunnel experience – with Gord at the far end shouting – *go back!* – but all she remembers is some dream about a sweet shop – & not being able to get in! Something there for the Jungians maybe – must have a look when I get back to my books.

The cops have packed up & left the Hall. Bumped into

Novello before they went − or maybe she contrived to bump into me. She said − sorry − its the job. I said − yeah − mines the same − getting people to trust me − difference is − if I let them down − Ive failed −

Unforgiving or what!

Saw Andy Dalziel in the pub. He asked me how I felt about things. I said I was glad it was all over − wasnt he? He said being glad wasnt part of the job description. Not sure what he meant. Need to think about it. Hes on his way too − after the weekend. Says whatever else all the excitement did − its got him back on his feet & hes looking forward to being back on the job again in a few weeks. I said − Mr Pascoe will be pleased to hear that − & he said − you reckon? −

Funny thing about Mr Deal − whatever he says − no matter it sounds dead ordinary − it leaves you listening to the echoes.

Minnie has just come in to tell me its time for the off! Shes sitting on my bed staring at me accusingly. I think she takes me going home after the opening as a personal affront. Also I think shes got a whiff of whats going on between Uncle Sid & the bart. Not surprising − like Ive said before − if I was head of MI5 − Id get Min on the books straightaway! Happily she met George when he drove me back to Kyoto − & it was love at first sight! Shes decided if I wont be her sis-in-law by marrying Sid − shell do it the other way − by marrying George! Only compensation for me leaving her after the opening is that George is coming to pick me up!

Sids back in London − dont know if hell show today or not − be interesting to see what the future holds for the Odd Couple now that Teds stinking rich. Funny thing love. Poetry says it stays fixed even when everything around it changes. Not my observation. Its a creature of circumstance. All it needs is a handy pine tree & an even handier ex-best-mate – & there it goes! Still debating louse Liams penitent letter. Hope you & the mahogany hunk prove exceptions to the rule – & stay fixed – & eventually settle down in a nice little honeysuckle covered cottage in Willingden!

Got to go or Mins going to explode.

Next one from home!

Love

Charley xxx

Right, Mildred. This is the last time you and me are
going to speak. Always sad to say goodbye, but let's
face up to it, this thing between us has run its
course. Funny how things work out; first time I set
eyes on thee, I thought, no way you'll ever catch me
whispering sweet nothings into that thing's ear! Now
I'm feeling like I'm going to miss you.

That's why it's time to end it, of course. I've got to
admit I learned to enjoy it, but it's too bloody
dangerous to keep on with, as the vicar said to the
verger's wife as she pulled on his bell rope afore
morning service. There's stuff on here I don't want
any other bugger to hear – stuff I don't much want
to hear again myself!

So last time, last thoughts, last things.

All packed up and gone now, Pete and Wieldy and
the rest of the whole travelling circus. Wasn't till
they'd all gone that I realized how much I were
going to miss them. All this convalescing stuff's fine,
but I reckon if old Daph hadn't got herself topped
with everything that followed, and I hadn't got
myself involved like I did, then likely I'd have taken
another three weeks at least to get to where I am
now.

Cap took a bit of persuading when she came down

to see me on Thursday. Started reading the riot act when I said I'd handed in me notice and I was heading back home at the weekend. In the end I had to push her on the bed and show her how much better I was. I'm trying to think of Pet as a training session, getting me ready for the serious stuff again. Funny, ain't it? Me looking for ways of justifying what I know were a rotten thing to do by any standards. At least Pet can claim she did it out of love – though mebbe there was also a bit of payback for Fester letting himself be tempted by the thrill of the Bannerjee jump! Pet had to know about that. Nowt happens in these places that a good matron doesn't know about!

Any road, at least it gave me the confidence to get back to close contact with Cap. Must have been back to my old form too, 'cos when we'd done she asked, What's keeping you till Sunday? I told her I wanted to go to this Festival of Health opening ceremony and she wondered what the hell for? When I said I'd got to know a lot of the people involved and thought it 'ud be a nice time to say goodbye to them she gave me an old-fashioned look, so I had to take her mind off things again.

That at least convinced her my progress weren't just a flash in the pan and, like me and her animal rights activities, she knows when not to keep coming with the questions.

Truth is if she'd injected me with a truth drug, I'm not sure what answers she'd have got. It's all finished here. Isn't it? Pete's come through with his halo just slightly bent. He's played it exactly the way I forecast and now all he has to do is relax and take the applause. But nearly getting it wrong has really sharpened his already very sharp nose and he rang me to ask what I thought. Not that he said that's why he were ringing. Just to keep me in the picture, and hope I got back to work soon. But we both knew he were asking if I thought he'd got it sorted now.

What the fuck could I say? Mebbe if I'd been Irish I could have said I wouldn't have started off from here in the first place! Mebbe I should have said it's like when you're having a crap and you think you're done, but summat deep inside tells you to stay put 'cos there's more to come.

But what would have been the point? Loose ends? Never been on a case yet when there weren't loose ends. We're detectives, for Christ's sake! Servants of the State, not instruments of God. One thing I've learned in all these years is, dealing with human beings, you never know everything, not even when you know everything there is to know. So I said, you've done well, lad. No trial, no comeback! Relax and enjoy it!

Can't stop yourself thinking, but, as the minister said when he baptized twenty girl guides in the municipal swimming pool.

Thought I'd got meself under control till I went down to breakfast this morning and there was Franny Roote sitting chatting with some of the other inmates. He gave me a grin and a cheerful wave and I thought of picking up his wheelchair and hoying it off the terrace. Instead I waited till he came rolling up to me as I knew he would, and I asked him what he'd got to look so happy about.

He said, 'I don't know, Andy. But somehow this feels like one of those days when anything's possible. I'm sure you've had them, one of those days when you know the putts are going to drop, the conversion kicks are going to soar over the bar, the beer's going to be at just the right temperature, and round the next corner you'll bump into the girl of your dreams.'

He were right. I have had them. Those days when if you had any sense you'd raise every penny you could beg borrow or steal, and put it all on a horse you'd chosen by sticking a pin in a race card!

But this didn't feel like one of them, not for me any road.

I said, 'Hope you're right, lad.'

And off he went, doling out yon Third Thought crap like a farmer with a muck spreader.

Leaving me thinking, there's a loose end I'd love to tie up afore I leave here! Mebbe I'll get him to himself later on at the Festival of Health opening ceremony and have a real heart to heart. One or two others I'd like a last word with, even if it's only to say goodbye. They'll all be there at the Brereton Manor. Some I'll kiss, some I'll kick, likely there'll be a bit of booze going, I feel up to supping my share this time so I must be getting better! Then first thing tomorrow morning Cap's coming to collect me, and it's goodbye Sandytown!

One last thing is to clear all my recording from Mildred.

Lets take a look . . .

Fuck! Bet it's dead easy, but one thing cunning old Fester never told me was how to erase stuff. Got to be sure it's all gone afore I give it him back. Mebbe I'll just hang on to it then take it down to the rugby club one Saturday night and get the lads down there to record fifty choruses of 'The Indian Maid' over what I've said, then post it back to Fester!

Meanwhile Pet's coming to pick me up any moment. Don't want to risk losing this during the drunken orgies, so I'll pop it back in the bog cistern for safety. Young Charley's a whiz with electronics, I'll have a word with her, she'll likely know how to clear it.

Goodbye, Mildred. I've enjoyed it but we can't keep on meeting like this.

Goodbye!

3

FROM: charley@whiffle.com
TO: cassie@natterjack.com
SUBJECT: definitely the end! or maybe the beginning!!

Cass, I lied! Next time Id be writing from home – I said.
Should have remembered – you dont get away from Oz
till it lets you go! So still here – George downstairs
drinking tea with the Parkers – Min wrapped round his
legs! – while Im up here packing – he thinks! Too much
to get off my chest to you to think of that. So here goes.

   Everyone assembled for the opening ceremony of the
Festival of Health – & I mean everyone. Real buzz in the
air – funny that – death hasnt depressed Sandytown – its
brought it alive! The council freeloaders were all there
again – ready to start on the booze where theyd been cut
short at the hog-roast. The Denhams of course – Ess
looking v gorgeous & sexy in a – I think – Versace two
piece – could scratch her eyes out! – Ted in a linen suit
straight Out of Africa – every inch the benevolent Lord of
the Manor. Then there were the Parkers – Tom – energy
bursting out of him like a space rocket before lift off –
Mary – creamy Laura Ashley frock almost as pale as her
face – looking like an Avalon convie – the kids running
riot – Min asking me every two minutes when George was
arriving. Diana was here too – of course! Too busy to stop

& talk – acting as if she was a principal mover & actor – assuring me in passing that shed been on her feet the whole morning – despite the high price she knew she would pay for such exertions.

The nature of the occasion required a strong presence from the Avalon – principal among them Dr Feldenhammer in a white suit – looking ready to operate at the drop of a hat or a hernia – in his train Nurse Sheldon – suffering in the heat – but clinging close to her boss & interposing her ample frame between him & any pretty young thing that took his fancy with an admirable determination that made me wonder if maybe he hadnt just exchanged one strict keeper for another.

A thought has occurred – remember I was puzzled why Feldenhammers been so willing to throw his weight behind Toms support of alternative therapies? Simple answer – Sidney Parker! Min told him about seeing the doc & his Indian patient on the beach – & I bet Sid dropped a couple of large hints to get the doctor jumping aboard brother Toms hobby horse! Almost feel sorry for Feldenhammer – being blackmailed 3 ways for 1 offence!

Naturally all of Toms motley bunch of quacks were there too. I had a word with Miss Lee – looking more oriental than ever – even though its become clear in the past few days that her origins as Miss Doris Godley – late of Leeds & Tescos – far from being a well kept secret – was generally known – & disregarded as being of no importance! I asked her where her brother was – she said he was around somewhere – but I couldnt see him anywhere.

I thought – maybe hes avoiding me. I mean the pain of being in the presence of someone who inspires a deep but unrequitable passion must be intense. Made me feel a bit guilty – & a bit complacent too. I resolved if I saw him to try & put him at his ease. Being an object of desire has its responsibilities too − but youll know all about that!

Someone tapped me on my shoulder with a force that almost knocked me over. It was Andy Dalziel. I said − remind me not to get arrested by you! He grinned & said − best keep thy nose clean then lass! − Ill be back on the job soon −

I said − winding him up − & will you be re-opening the case? −

That got a reaction.

− why? − what do you mean? − very perturbed.

I said − I mean the case of Dr Feldenhammer & his dalliance with a patient − for all we know hes a serial interferer! −

He shook his great head & said − nay lass − bit of humanity eh? − us men are weak vessels − determined woman gets her hands on us − we are putty − & from what I hear − yon Indian lass were real determined −

− so − as usual − its the womans fault? −

− nay − he said − its a design fault − so blame the engineer − not the engine −

Interesting − seemed to come from the heart − but before I could dig further − Franny Roote came rolling up in his chair.

Andy said − Ive been looking for you Roote − whats kept you so long? −

& Franny replied − my ministering doesnt run to a timetable Andy − as youll find if you care to join your fellow patients next time I call at the Avalon −

− Ill not be there next time − said Andy − Im off home tomorrow − & theres a few things I need to get sorted afore I go − starting with thee! −

I thought this sounded promising − but before anything more could be said the Sandytown Brass Band − which had been playing a selection from the Shows – suddenly struck up the kind of fanfare you get when the Queen turns up somewhere – & as it died away over the loudspeakers a voice I recognized as Diana Parkers said – ladies & gentlemen – the opening ceremony will now commence – please give your attention to the man of the moment – Mr Tom Parker! –

There was a dais in front of the hotel – high enough for those on it to be visible to all of us crowded on the lawn. Tom advanced to the microphone – getting a rapturous round of applause. He held up his hands till the noise died away – then he said – this is a splendid & significant occasion – long anticipated – & marred only by the absence of one of its prime movers – who was a dear friend to me – as she was to everyone in Sandytown. Let us therefore observe a minutes silence in memory of one so tragically taken from us – Dear Daphne Denham –

You could have heard a feather drop – let alone a pin.

Then Tom marked the end of the silence by clapping his hands – & everyone joined in – producing an even bigger round of applause than the one that had greeted him – & all for Lady D. I felt the tears in my eyes – even Andy looked moved & poor Franny bowed his head to hide his expression.

Then Tom made his speech. Id feared he might get carried away – he can rattle on forever about the wonders of Sandytown as Ive tried to show you – but this was a masterpiece of concision – wise – witty – & to the point. Health was the basis of happiness – he said – Happiness was the outcome of health. Sandytown was devoted to offering both conditions to all who visited her.

A quick run though the attractions on offer – including of course the Avalon & all his team of alternatives – who would all be available for consultation in some ducky little

tents scattered around the grounds – then – with a cry of
– Be Healthy – Be Happy! – he declared the Festival
open.

While all this was happening – Franny had contrived to
put some distance between himself & Andy Dalziel – who
said – he can run – but he cant hide.

I said – whats so urgent that it cant wait – on a lovely
day like this? –

He said – how about the truth? –

I said – the truth about what? –

He said – dont disappoint me lass –

& I felt sick inside – because I wanted it all to be over
– & Id been telling myself that any doubts I had were daft
– I was a newly qualified psychologist not a copper – & if
the pros were happy then who the hell was I to carry on
worrying! Hows that for humility! But now big fat Andy
Dalziel was kicking me when I was down.

He moved off – then another finger tapped me on the
shoulder – by contrast with the Dalziel thud! not a tap at
all – a real tentative touch – like being brushed by a
falling leaf.

I guessed it was Gordon Godley – but when I turned
there was this young guy standing there – clean shaven –
hair cut short to his skull – smiling at me shyly.

It was the shy smile that gave him away.

I said – Jesus – is that really you – Gord?

He said – yes – sorry – I didnt mean to surprise you –

I said – no – yes – I mean I am surprised – but it
suits you – really it does –

He grinned like a schoolboy – & I found myself grinning back.

It really did suit him – I mean – he hadnt turned into
Brad or Leonardo – but he was OK – more than OK – he
was pretty neat!

I said – but why – then stopped myself cos I thought – you dont want to hear the answer. Then I found myself thinking – dont be silly – why not hear the answer? – no one has ever cut off their hair & beard for you before girl – probably never will again – enjoy it while you can! –

– Why did you do it? – I asked.

– I hoped – well I didnt really – not hoped – but I thought – if theres the faintest chance it would make a difference Id be crazy not to do it – but Im not expecting you to say straight off if it makes a difference – not till youve got used to it – I mean Im still getting used to it myself –

I think hed have gone on talking forever if I hadnt stopped him.

I said – its fine – & yeah I prefer it – but that doesnt mean anything except – I prefer it! –

– step in the right direction – he said – means I dont have to wear the wig & the false beard! –

Hed actually made a joke! Godly Gordon had a sense of humour! For me that was a bigger step than short back & sides – not that I was going to tell him that!

I said – I heard about you & Clara – up at the Avalon –

That got him all shy again – not boy-girl shy – but this-is-real-private-stuff shy.

He said – yeah – well – you know –

I said – no I dont actually – so how does it work –

Then he looked at me straight on – not a sign of shyness – & said dead serious – its the spirit moving through me – I dont know how – I dont even know which spirit – all I know is I dont use it – it uses me –

I wanted to ask more – but that would have meant another step – this one from me – towards the kind of closeness that might get him to open up –

Careful girl – I admonished myself.

I said – maybe Ill give you a call – if ever I have
toothache –

He said – yes – do – but I think of you anyway – I
mean I hold you in the light –

I said – sorry? – & he said – I mean – whatever my
gift can do to keep you from harm – you dont have to be
present for it to work – not always – if youre being held in
the light –

I said – oh – & is that the only way you think of me
then? –

Shouldnt have said it maybe – provocative! – & I felt
real guilty when I saw him go all red – & look away – &
start stuttering – no – Im sorry – but sometimes . . .

I cut in quick – hey – thats fine – really – a girl likes
to be in the dark sometimes – as well as in the light! –
look – shouldnt you be in your tent – curing lepers &
stuff? –

He said – oh yes I suppose – not sure where it is –
looking round like a Martian dropped on York race-course.
So I said – lets go find it then –

We set off side by side – arms occasionally brushing
against each other – sort of companiable – till we
reached a little tent with a tastefully designed shingle
reading – Gordon Godley – Healer – hanging by the
entrance flap. No queue though – I reckon most of the
guests were getting stuck into the booze & buffet –
appetite before ailment! – in fact there was only one
person by the tent – Franny Roote – & I reckon he was
still playing hide & seek with Andy Dalziel.

In fact – as we reached the tent – I saw Andy heading
our way. Maybe Fran saw him too – for suddenly he span
his chair round – & did a sort of wheelchair racing start!

Unfortunately he was right alongside a taut guy rope.
One of the wheels hit it – rose up – & next thing the

whole contraption went over − & poor Franny was sprawling at our feet!

Gord moved quickly. He stooped down − put both his arms round Frannys torso & pulled him up − while I righted the chair & manoeuvred it so he could sink into it.

But he didnt − he just clung tight to Gord − very tight indeed − I mean like they were doing the tango! I could see his face − Frannys I mean − filled with a sort of light − eyes shining − lips moving − but no words coming out.

They stood there − locked together − neither moving − like a statue of a pair of gay lovers.

Then Franny broke Gords grip − & pushed him away − finally letting go his own hold on Gord − till he stood there − all alone − unsupported − unaided.

Finally he took a short step forward − then another − then a third − & he threw his head back & screamed at the sky − I can walk! −

That got everyones attention I can tell you! Suddenly no one was thinking about stuffing their faces any more. The crowd at the buffet turned − dissolved & then reformed in a circle − with Franny & Gord at its centre.

Tom appeared − took in what was happening − his face filled with delight − if hed stage managed it things couldnt have turned out better! Andy Dalziel too got into the ring − looked Fran right in the face − hard to tell what he was thinking − but before he could say anything − who should come rushing forward but Ess Denham! Never heard her say a good word to − or about − Franny Roote − but now she grabbed hold of him like he was her long lost twin − & hit him with a hug that made his previous embrace of Gord look like a near miss!

What the hells going off here? − I asked myself.

Then Ess lowered Fran back into his chair − saying − dont overdo it.

People pressed close now – oohing & aahing & shooting questions & not listening to answers – & I saw Gord slip away into his tent.

I followed him – grabbed hold of his shoulder. He turned – & said – what? – I said – congratulations! He said – it wasnt me. I said – yes I know, the spirit working through you – He said – no – I dont know – Im not sure – & I said – oh stop being so negative! – do yourself a favour – be positive once in your life!

He looked straight at me – then he said – right! – I will be! –

& next thing I knew hed grabbed hold of me & plonked his lips on mine – like he was trying to gag me! –

My first reaction was – do I knee him or just push him off?

Then I thought – doesnt he realize hes the worst kisser in the universe? – & purely in a spirit of charity & education – I ran my tongue along his lips till his mouth opened – & I stuck my tongue in –

It was like igniting the blue touch paper on a firework – except there was no chance to retire! I could tell this was undiscovered country to him – the way he dived down my throat – & pulled me so close I felt my spine creak. When one of his hands slid down on to my buttock – the left one – I think – I managed to pull my head back & said – you think Ive got a boil on my bum needs healing or what? –

His hand jerked away like Id turned red hot.

I grabbed it & put it back.

– dont be shy – I said – or if you are – I can cure that – Perhaps Sis – I do have the nursing instinct after all.

Or maybe it was just I realized I was really having a good time!

Thought it would take a pick axe to prize us apart –

but all it took was a small figure bursting into the tent –
Minnie Parker of course.

She said – looking at Gord with some distrust – if you
marry him – will he be my brother-in-law when I marry
George? –

– Min – I said – whats with all this marrying? –
thats the way old books end. Nowadays on the other
hand . . .

I wasnt sure how to finish. I neednt have worried. Min
was quite up to the task.

– people just do sex – she said – but youll still be my
sister-in-law if I do sex with George – wont you? –

– Ill always be your friend Minnie – I said – now
bugger off! –

Cos I wanted to get back to educating Gord!

There you have it. Crazy huh? Me & the healer!
Nowhere for it to go of course – but somehow Im looking
forward to going nowhere with him!

What about Loathsome Liam & his fulsome apology –
you ask?

Well – I read through the letter a dozen times –
couldnt make up my mind – one minute it was forgive! –
next it was forget! – but no problem now. First thing I did
when I got back here was – tear it up! Why repeat an old
mistake when theres a whole world of new ones out there
just waiting to be made!

Cant wait for the Headbanger to meet Gord! Tonight
perhaps – or maybe tomorrow morning. Havent told
George yet – but hes just taking my bag home – me –
Im getting a lift in the famous sidecar – & its my intention
to return to Willingden by way of Willingdene – where I
look forward to putting Godly Gordons miraculous powers
to a strenuous & extended test!

But I shouldnt joke. After all – I did see what in another

age would be called a miracle today. I hope – for Frannys sake – it proves permanent.

& I suppose – in a way – me snogging Gord has to be some kind of miracle too – hasnt it? Or is that just overstating the totally unexpected?

Doesnt matter. Getting what you know you want is rarely a big deal. Plus theres usually some small print somewhere that we havent noticed.

Its when you get what was unimaginable – even in your daftest dreams – that you may find youve got an unconditional bargain!

Callous? Selfish? Certainly daft as a brush? I hear you say.

So whats new? Youve called me all of those – several times – ever since I was old enough to take notice of what you were saying!

For the time being the important thing is – Im happy. Like you – I hope. Your good works may get you to heaven – but I bet its the mahogany hunk that makes you glad to wake up every morning!

So sweet dreams sis. Come home safe to us some time soon. Bring the m.h. with you. Or if it all goes pear-shaped – well – never worry. Completely free of charge – Godly Gordon will cure your physical ills – & for a very reasonable fee your clever little sister will give you a one to one analysis session!

Love love love

Charley xxx

Volume the Sixth

*. . . There is something wrong here . . . But never mind . . .
It could not have happened, you know, in a better place. –
Good out of Evil – The very thing perhaps to be wished for.*

1

It was late afternoon when Andy Dalziel got back to the Avalon.

It had been a peculiarly unsatisfactory day. He had set out for the Grand Opening determined to resolve some of the questions still niggling away in his mind. But instead of answers, all he was coming back with was more questions. A lot of them centred on Franny Roote, but there'd been no chance to put them. The deliriously happy young man had been taken over by Lester Feldenhammer who, aided by Pet Sheldon, had probed and prodded at his legs, watched as he took a few still unsteady but increasingly confident steps, then invited him to attend at the Avalon for a comprehensive examination. After that he had sat down again in his wheelchair – talking to the crowds of people who came to congratulate or simply gawk – occasionally standing up as if to reassure himself he could still do it – & all the while smiling so broadly it would have taken a harder man than Andy Dalziel to try and wipe it off his face.

Maybe it was for the best, thought Dalziel. Maybe for once in my life I should let sleeping dogs lie.

But an old lion on the prowl doesn't give a toss about dogs, waking or sleeping. It's his nature to carry on hunting till he sinks his teeth in his natural prey!

His temper had not been improved when he decided

to call in at the Hope and Anchor on his way back to the Avalon. A perfect pint and a quiet chat with Alan Hollis, for whom he also had a few questions, seemed a good way to end his sojourn in Sandytown. But a notice in the window said the pub would not open on Saturday until 6 p.m., presumably to allow Hollis and his staff to go to the festival opening, though he could not recall seeing the landlord there.

So it was in a mood of some disgruntlement that Dalziel pushed open the door of his room.

Despite the fact that it was bright daylight still, the curtains were drawn.

He switched on the light.

The beams from the central bulb bounced back off the silver surface of Mildred, resting demurely on his pillow.

His mind threw up a possibility – some more than usually conscientious cleaner had looked in the lavatory cistern, spotted this intrusive object, removed it and left it on the bed for its owner to claim.

His mind threw this up and in the same mental gesture threw it away.

He went slowly forward and picked the recorder up.

He knew at once this wasn't his. The same make, the same model, meaning it was probably exactly the same in weight and shape. Yet one touch told him this wasn't Mildred. Man doesn't get to survive as long as he had without instantly being able to identify the woman he's touching.

He went quickly into the bathroom to confirm what he'd guessed, that Mildred was no longer there.

Then he sat down on the counterpane with the false Mildred and looked at it for a long moment.

Finally he let his thumb stray to the *play* button.

And pressed.

2

Good day to you, Andy.

Surprised to hear my voice?

Of course you are, but not perhaps as surprised as
a lesser mortal might have been. For it is your
capacity for taking a couple of long strides in a
direction you've no reason to be going in, plus of
course your sheer bloody tenacity of purpose, that
have made me decide to contact you like this.

I know you hate loose ends, you hate a story
unfinished, and so do I. So let me, like the all-seeing,
all-knowing author of an old novel stepping from
behind the scenery he or she has created and
addressing the reader direct, finish this one for you.
Nor is this a simple act of that over-inflated egotism
you have accused me of in the past. There is a strong
possibility, if left to your own devices, that you might
inflict considerable collateral damage travelling by
your normal elephantine route to the sunny uplands
of knowledge I am now going to open up for you –
damage to myself, I admit it, but also and more
importantly to Peter's career, to the lives of various
other people I have come to love, to the prospects
and reputation of dear little Sandytown which has
taken some hard knocks recently, and even perhaps
to yourself.

Let other pens dwell on guilt and misery. I quit such odious subjects as soon as I can, impatient to restore everybody, not greatly in fault themselves, to tolerable comfort. Myself included. This is not a confession. I have committed no crime, or at least none so serious as to be unforgivable by such a magnanimous judge as yourself.

Some brief autobiography first, to confirm or build on your speculation. I went to Europe determined to find a cure, and not much caring what form it came in. Ultimately, death is the cure of all diseases, is it not? I found a doctor as careless of his patients' lives as I was of my own. To him each death was a necessary step on his way to greater understanding. I will skip the months of pain and struggle which ensued. It is not your sympathy which I am trying to win. But if you are interested, I gave Peter some of the details, slightly confused since, of course, I could only leave him with the hope of my restoration, not its fact. Suffice it to say, I learned how to walk again. I would have been happy to heap praise and gratitude on Dr Meitler, my saviour, and demand that his ground-breaking techniques be universally acknowledged and developed. Alas, he was as reckless of his own well-being as he was of his patients', his laboratory was a fire-trap, and while I was still learning how to crawl out of my chair, the good doctor and all his research records went up in flames.

So I kept quiet. My motive at first was a kind of vanity. I wanted to reappear before those who knew me fully restored. I wanted to amaze them! But as the long months of recovering my strength passed, I began to see that there might be certain advantages to keeping the change to myself. Travel, for instance.

As I explained to you, it had become clear that, in the present climate, there was no way I would ever be able to visit America again. But if I could find another persona, another identity for my upright, perambulating self . . .

When I returned to the Davos Avalon, my thoughts were still confused, and I think I might have revealed everything to the head of the clinic, Dr Kling, with whom I'd developed an excellent relationship. But I found he had done an exchange with Lester Feldenhammer, so I kept quiet, and kept to my chair. Then two things happened. Firstly, and sadly, a young man I had become friendly with in my previous stay at the clinic, Emil Kunstli-Geiger, died. He had just been admitted when I first met him and there were hopes he might recover. But after some false starts, his condition had deteriorated and now the end was near. He was pleased to see me again and I gave him what comfort was in my power. Strangely it was talking to Emil then as much as my own experience that made me start taking the ideas of Third Thought seriously. But my first and second thoughts were always of life, and one day while getting something for him from a drawer in his room, I came across his passport and his driving licence. As I made the sad comparison between the way he'd looked then and the way he looked now, it struck me that there was a certain resemblance between us: shape of face, bone structure, that sort of thing.

A few days later he died. Before he passed away he thanked me for my care and urged me to take something to remember him by. I took his passport and driving licence.

A long wig and a fringe of wispy beard, and

suddenly I had another identity, though what I was going to do with it, I still wasn't sure.

Meanwhile my relationship with Lester had been developing. Here was a man I could talk to. We were not yet so intimate as to be on confidential terms, but when Daphne Denham and her entourage showed up last Christmas, I quickly assessed the situation. She was the predator, he was the prey! But I had little time to spare analysing Lester's problems. I knew I had one of my own.

Do you believe in love at first sight, Andy? When you first encountered your partner, Cap Marvell, did you know she was the one for you? I can tell from the way you talk about her how much she means to you – yes, as I'm sure you've worked out by now, I've listened to all your fascinating recordings – but there's no way of telling if it was a long slow burn or a sudden explosion.

With me and Esther Denham it was explosive. On my side it was like a message stamped on my soul with a white-hot iron – *this is the woman for you!* On hers, it was rather different. More, *oh Jesus, I don't believe this – can I really fancy a guy in a wheelchair? Get out of here now, you crazy bitch!*

I could see she was attracted, could tell how much this shocked her. I knew she was resolved once she got out of the room, she'd make sure she never saw me again. In fact she made an excuse almost immediately, said she needed to go to the loo. I boldly offered to show her where it was, a bit of behaviour which might have struck Lester and Daph as odd if he hadn't been in such a state of panic and she of lust!

We got to the bathroom, she opened the door and stepped inside, I pushed in behind her, she turned in anger which became amazement as I rose up out of my chair and kissed her.

There followed a moment of shock and resistance on her part, and on mine of terror that she was going to start screaming rape and bring the nurses running.

And then she started kissing me back, only stopping because she was laughing so much. It was, she said, so totally unexpected, so totally unimaginable, that it was comic!

I knew then I was right. She was the one for me. Except, of course, there was no way in Daphne's eyes that, in or out of my chair, I could be the one for her. And if Ess stuck two fingers up to Daph, it wasn't just her who'd get cut off without a penny, it was dear brother Ted.

Teddy is not, as you yourself have observed, the sharpest knife in the box. Ess has looked after him all her life. Family loyalties are, I believe, God's way of ensuring that even the most undeserving get a bit of unconditional love. If I wanted Esther, then Ted was part of the bargain.

We started meeting, or rather she and Emil started meeting, keeping well clear of the smart end of the resort where Daph was queening it up, and mucking down with the students at the Bengel-bar where I encountered George Heywood and the lovely Charley. Things got better every time we met and I knew by the end of her holiday that, however things panned out, I had to follow her home. And God, who's an old romantic at heart, wrote the perfect scenario!

Soon, despite all he did to try to extend his stay, it was time for Lester to return to Sandytown. By now we were best buddies and it seemed perfectly natural for me to head home to England with him, to the

Yorkshire that I knew so well, and to settle close to the Avalon and get involved with its work.

I cannot describe with what joy I made the journey – or with what reluctance Lester made his!

I got myself settled in my cottage. It was as secure as I could make it. Sometimes Ess would come and visit me there, riding on Ted's bike. Sometimes we would meet elsewhere at a distance and I would become Emil and we could manage whole weekends together. I was actually enjoying both my lives, but always I anticipated the day when I could be back on my own two feet permanently with Esther by my side.

That wasn't going to happen while Daph was alive, but I swear to you, Andy, that not once did I contemplate doing anything to get rid of her! The thing was, I came to like her, to enjoy watching her at play! And I became quite a favourite of hers. She saw I was close to Lester and she thought she was clever enough to wheedle things out of me about how he felt about her, and what was going on with Pet Sheldon! But I think she recognized a fellow spirit in me too, someone who is not perhaps too scrupulous when it comes to finding the quickest way to getting what they want!

So to the day of the hog-roast.

I was sitting in my chair, enjoying the champagne and watching the great storm bubbling up over the sea when Esther came up to me. I knew instantly something was wrong. In public she usually treated me as if I were a piece of furniture!

She was extremely agitated. Something dreadful had happened, she told me.

Teddy had killed Aunt Daphne!

I was, as you might say, gobsmacked. Esther told

me she'd been wandering round the grounds and by chance she'd stumbled across the body in some long grass beyond the hog-roast pit. I asked how she knew Ted was responsible. She showed me that fancy fake watch he wears and said she'd found it snagged on Daph's dress. Also, earlier that day, Daph had shown Ted a new will in which he was disinherited and they'd had a furious row.

Now you and I, Andy, sensible chaps with one eye always fixed steadily on the realities of life, might have reckoned that when someone has just written you out of their will, that is the last time you should choose to kill them!

Ted, alas, has rarely let reason cloud his behaviour, and neither Ess nor myself had the slightest problem to start with in accepting his guilt. Nor did his idiocy in leaving his watch at the scene of the crime strike us as anything but typical!

I asked where Ted was now. She said she didn't know, she couldn't find him. The storm was starting, everyone was heading for the house, so I said, 'Show me the body.'

She took me there. There was no sign of Ollie Hollis at the hog-roast, which struck me as odd. Seeing old Daphne lying there was truly upsetting. She had been so full of life, so vigorous for her age, such a dedicated goer! She didn't deserve to end up like this. I was furious with Ted, but for Esther's sake, I had to do my best to protect him.

Esther had removed the watch but God alone knew what other traces the idiot had left. I cast around for some way of obscuring them and also of misdirecting the investigation. It came to me in a flash what I had to do.

And so with Esther's help, I hauled the roasting cage off the barbecue pit, got the pig out of it and put poor Daphne in.

It really broke me up to heap this further indignity upon her. There were tears in my eyes and I have begged her spirit for forgiveness and understanding since. And, knowing as I do what she herself was capable of, I do not doubt I received it.

Esther was marvellous, doing everything I told her to. By the time we were done it was pouring down and we were both soaking and filthy and Ess had managed to burn her arm.

I told her to get back to the house, find something to change into, and get hold of Ted and do what she could to make sure he didn't do anything else stupid.

I meanwhile headed for the lowest bit of the lawn where it was turning really boggy, tipped my chair over and rolled around in the muck to provide a reason for my dishevelment. Then I lay there, trying to see into the future, and waiting patiently for the storm to abate.

After Pet Sheldon took charge of me, there was nothing for me to do but head for home and wait until Esther reported on further developments.

She came herself on the bike later that evening. What she told me was hard to take in. She'd found Ted getting dried off and changed in the house. He had denied any knowledge of Daph's death. He said he'd gone down to the beach with the kids. Sid had gone too. After a while, seeing that there was plenty of supervision, they'd slipped away to the old cave halfway up the cliff where they'd been banging away at each other till the storm started.

A lover isn't the best provider of an alibi, but as we

know it can be confirmed at least in part by Charley Heywood's testimony. (Oh yes, of course I've had a look at Charley's emails. Why not? If the brutal and licentious constabulary can pore and paw over them, why not I? And, though it was much harder, I even managed to slide beneath Ed Wield's defences and take a look at his interesting analysis of the witness statements. Perhaps happiness is making him careless!)

Myself, all I needed was Esther's assurance of Ted's innocence. No way he could deceive her about something like that.

Which left the interesting question – what had really happened?

And who was the clever bastard who had deposited Ted's watch on the body?

I would have loved to come clean with you and Peter from the start, but knowing how ready you are, Andy, to put me at the centre of all criminality, that would merely have set the investigation on a time-wasting false trail, and poor Peter had enough of those to follow already! No, I needed to stay free to pursue my own enquiries.

I worked out that Ollie Hollis's disappearance from the scene before the storm broke was perhaps significant. It occurred to me also to wonder why the hog-roast had been delayed. I'd noticed there was some evidence of recent repair to the winding gear. Ollie's handicraft? Perhaps. But it was well known that the actual creator of this complicated bit of machinery was Hen Hollis, persona non grata at the Hall since Hog's death, but the first person Ollie would turn to if he experienced any serious problem. So what if Hen had been there, doing a favour for one of the clan and delighting in enjoying Daph's booze and grub without her knowledge? Then she had stumbled across him . . .

I tried to hint at this possibility to Peter, but his mind was elsewhere. Ollie's death went some way to fitting in with my theory, but all it did for Peter was provide a possible culprit, caught apparently in flagrante with regard to one crime, and reported as being at loggerheads with the victim of the other.

With the enthusiastic support of ace reporter Ruddlesdin, Peter was trumpeted as the fastest gumshoe in the east the following morning, only to discover the bays had withered before even he was crowned. With friends like Ruddlesdin, Peter really needs friends like you and me, Andy!

Then followed all that weird business about the forged will and Clara Brereton. This brought Teddy right into the foreground. Silly ass! If he'd paid any heed to Esther, he would never have attempted to contact Clara. He is the worst kind of fool – the kind that thinks he is clever!

But at the same time as Clara's 'accident' was leading Peter down another false trail, Clara's involvement was stirring up some strange notions in me.

Wieldy was helpful here, feeding all the evidence and statements straight into his computer and thence straight into mine. As Esther got drawn into Peter's net, I knew that unless I could make some sense out of all this, I would have to come forward and confess to my part. Meanwhile, following the old principle that a good lie is best constructed on a solid basis of truth, it seemed sensible to prepare something to keep Peter happy when he started getting close to Esther's involvement. So we prepared a version which told the truth, except that it left me out.

Encouraged by the idiot Ruddlesdin, the media were already trumpeting another triumph for Peter. (Incidentally, doesn't it bother you, Andy, that locally at least the media seem so eager to cry, the king is dead, long live the king!) Of course I would never have let it reach the point where Peter laid formal charges, but I was hoping to find a way to test my hypothesis that Hen Hollis must be involved before I came forward and confessed my part in the drama.

And then the sad discovery at Millstone Farm was made.

Everything fell into place. Hen, Daph's sworn enemy, at the Hall without her knowledge or approval, had to be a prime suspect, didn't he? His guilt-inspired suicide in the house she'd ejected him from, the house where he'd first seen the light of day, was the perfect end to what would come to look like Peter's perfect investigation! It was also a result that cleared the Denhams and left me free to make my miraculous recovery (which I hope you've enjoyed!) and walk off with my beloved and now rather rich Esther into the golden sunset. I should have been as happy as Peter and the press at this conclusion to his labours.

But like you, Andy, I am both blessed and cursed with the kind of mind that cannot leave things alone.

I found myself recalling Pet Sheldon's description of her encounter with Daph by the stable not long before her death. She was angry, yes. But what struck Pet was that she was hurt, she was upset.

Making Daph angry wasn't difficult. Upsetting her was a lot harder.

Also I was troubled by the placing of Ted's watch

by the body. That was the act of a mind under control, not a mind spiralling into a panic that would rapidly lead to another murder followed by self-destruction.

And at a simple practical level, how would Hen have known he would find Ted's watch with his clothes in the room where he changed in the Hall?

But above and beyond all these doubts, reservations and queries, I had some special knowledge.

I have always been fascinated by the behaviour of my fellow human beings, their vanities, their hopes, their fears, their strengths, their weaknesses, above all their deceptions both of themselves and others. So in the months I have been living here in Sandytown I have taken careful note of what goes on about me. It is marvellous how eventually such notes of things apparently disconnected and of very little consequence may, so long as you do not try to force an issue or superimpose a pattern, come together to make a clear and often surprising picture.

Charley Heywood has an inkling of this and will, I suspect, become a very fine clinical psychologist. You too, dear Andy, are in your own way a painter of such pictures, at times almost an artist. As I say it is my suspicion you might already be sensing an outline that moves me to talk to you now.

What I had come to understand was that dear Daphne, a woman of strong appetites that the advancing years had done nothing to take the edge off, needed more than the odd encounter with a reluctant Lester to satisfy her needs. Once she had him chained up in the matrimonial bedroom, I do not doubt he would soon have been taught how to sing for his supper, but while the pursuit was on, she needed someone else to keep her in trim, someone vigorous enough to meet her high standards, and someone with very good reason to keep the liaison discreet.

She found him in Alan Hollis. He was in her employ. More, he was going to receive the reward of the freehold of the Hope and Anchor when she died. She could see him on a regular basis to 'go over the accounts'. The frequency of these meetings surprised no one who knew her attention to detail in matters of money. The living accommodation at the pub was used only by Hollis himself, and by lawyer Beard and his secretary when they came to town. (Your own feeling that Miss Gay might be worth talking to suggests that your mind was already drifting in this direction, Andy. Am I right?)

So she felt safe and secure in using Alan as her source of regular servicing. And had she continued to regard this as a simple mechanical transaction, perhaps all might have been well. Alas for her (and this is often the case with the wilful and self-centred personality) familiarity bred not contempt but something like affection.

She came to like and to trust Alan Hollis, and to believe her feelings were reciprocated.

Oh, Andy, there is a lesson here for you and for me. Never believe that those whom we use actually like us!

And now I must reach to the uttermost limits of hypothesis, based on such a flimsy ground of evidence and tragic hints that I can only justify it to myself by presenting it in the form of narrative fiction. Indulge me a while!

Daphne Denham, her soul in a state of considerable agitation after her confrontation with her deceitful nephew, looked out of her window and saw at his work the one man she knew could restore her inner harmony.

'Alan,' she called. 'Would you step inside a moment, please. There is a matter of accounting I need to discuss with you.'

Hollis obeyed, they went up to her room and a little while later she emerged, with the placid smile on her face of a woman whose entries have been double checked and whose books are in perfect balance.

For the next hour or so she moved serenely among her guests, receiving their compliments and gratitude with graceful condescension, till a rough encounter with the uncouth Mr Godley, a guest at her party only because he was protégé of her neighbour, Mr Parker, disturbed the even tenor of her ways. Seeking solitude to recover her equilibrium of spirit, she moved away from the main body of the party and found herself approaching the site of the actual hog-roast. Irritated already that her man, Ollie Hollis, had sent word of a delay in preparation caused by some defect in the machinery, she was further annoyed not to find him by the roasting cage, basting the revolving pig.

A sound, or a combination of sounds, caught her attention.

It came from the machine hut. It sounded like a champagne cork popping, accompanied by upraised voices and raucous laughter.

She approached, angry reproaches forming on her lips, an anger increased when she recognized one of the voices as that of her pet hate, Hen Hollis.

And then she stopped in her tracks as another

voice, even more familiar, rang in her ears. It was the voice of Alan Hollis, her servant, her server, and, so she foolishly believed, her friend.

What he was saying chilled the blood in her veins.

'Aye, fill us up, Hen, it's been hard graft today. And the hardest bit of all was tupping Her Ladyship! By God she's a handful – nay, she's a barrowful! It's like being in bed with a prize porker. And that's just what she sounds like when she comes, tha knows, like one of her own pigs when you slit its throat. Whee whee whee, it squeals, and that's the noise Daph makes too. Whee whee whee – oo, don't stop, Alan – whee whee wheee!'

Lady Denham turned and rushed away, not stopping till she reached the stables. Here, to her beloved old horse, Ginger, she poured out her heart. For the time being anger had been drowned by hurt, that this man to whom she had given herself with abandon, this man whom she had trusted and even liked, this man who had been the beneficiary of her generosity in life and who would be an even greater beneficiary on her death, this man had betrayed her, had mocked her, had bandied her name around in the company of his low relations, had given her arch enemy, Hen Hollis, a weapon to mock her with . . . How could she bear the pain? she asked dear patient Ginger. How could she bear the shame?

There was a noise behind her. She turned to see another object of her hate approaching, Nurse Sheldon, her rival for the affections of Dr Feldenhammer. What had she heard? Had she said anything to the horse that Sheldon could use against her?

The creature was daring to look sympathetic, to ask

*if she was all right! This was not to be borne! She
dashed the tears from her eyes and set out to put the
creature in her place. A few moments later she had
reduced her to a quivering wreck capable of nothing
more than the futile gesture of hurling a glass of wine.*

*Fortified by this triumph, Lady Denham felt just
anger coursing through her veins to replace those
weakling emotions of hurt and distress. These Hollises
would find out who they were dealing with!*

*Back she went to the hog-roast hut. Silence fell as
she stood in the entrance. Behind her the sky grew
lurid as the storm approached, a sheet of distant
lightning etched her against its fleeting brightness.*

*'Ollie Hollis,' she cried, 'you can start looking for
a new job tomorrow morning. Hen Hollis, you are
trespassing on my land. If you are not gone in five
minutes, I will set the dogs on you. And as for you,
Alan Hollis, I am giving you notice to quit the Hope
and Anchor. And when you go, take a long look
back, for by then I shall have removed your name
from my will and the Hope and Anchor will be as far
out of your reach as loyalty and decency clearly are
from your soul!'*

*As she finished, thunder rolled through the air. She
turned and walked away, triumphant, confident that
nothing that Hollis could say could be anything more
than a gnat's bite to the reputation of Lady Daphne
Denham.*

*Then she felt a hand on her shoulder. She turned.
It was Alan Hollis. His once longed-for touch was
now anathema to her. She slapped his face. To her
shock and horror he struck her back. She fell,
cracking her head against a stone. But worse was to
come. For the second time that day she felt the weight*

of his body upon her. Once more she was squealing like a stuck pig, but this time the resemblance went further than mere sound. For his hands were round her throat, and she was truly dying.

I think that probably gets as near the truth as any fiction does, Andy. I reckon Ollie would panic and take off; Hen, after his initial delight that his old enemy is dead, would probably begin to consider the consequences as they might affect him, but cool-headed Alan would get him to drag Daphne into the long grass, then tell him to make himself scarce, there was no reason anyone should ever know he'd been there.

Now Alan himself heads back to the Hall. The storm is getting nearer and people are getting agitated. He sees Clara and tells her what's happened. Why would he do that? you ask. Because, my dear Watson, another little bit of local knowledge I have acquired through keeping my sharp blue eyes skinned, is that dear calm and collected Clara has been following auntie's example and sampling Alan's wares herself! She it was, I suspect, who came up with the clever idea of putting Ted in the frame. I mean, he was the most obvious suspect, and she happened to know where he'd left his clothes and his watch when he changed to go swimming. So while Alan takes charge of relocating the booze into the house, she slips off, breaks the clasp of the watch and snags it on Daph's dress. Then she returns, and she and Alan give each other an alibi for all the significant period.

Later that evening, Ollie fetches up at the pub, still in a state. His asthma is so bad he heads off to Miss Lee's for relief. It is clear to Alan that Ollie

cannot be relied on. Sooner or later he's going to
come clean about what happened. When Hen shows
up a little later, Alan first of all makes it clear that in
the eyes of the law they will be equally guilty. OK,
Hen may get a lighter sentence because he didn't
actually strangle Daphne, but he'll still be going to
jail. And, here's the clincher, Alan probably assures
him that he will not be able to inherit Millstone
Farm. (Interesting legal point that, as it was by
Hog's will, not Daphne's, that it reverted to Hen, but
I don't suppose he was in a state of mind to debate
such niceties!)

He then tells him where he'll find Ollie. To be fair,
perhaps all he meant was for Hen to try and talk
some sense into him, but when it turned out that
Hen had gone over the top and stuck a needle right
through the poor sod's spine, that must have seemed
like a sign from whatever God he worships that
everything was going his way!

Now the only weak link remaining is Hen. Easily
dealt with. Alan knows where he'll be, and that night
he heads out to Millstone with a bottle of scotch.

Could be Hen had already done the deed, but I
doubt it. Whatever, by the time Alan leaves, Hen is
dangling from a rope in the stairwell, there's a
suicide note on the kitchen table, and at a single
stroke Alan has got rid of the one remaining witness
and provided the police with a self-confessed
murderer.

As it turns out, this has another benefit. With Ted
no longer a suspect, there is nothing to prevent him
coming into his rightful estate. Clara had already
tried one trick to get at Ted's huge inheritance – by
threatening to publish the second will. Of course

that's been no use since everyone got to know it was a fake. But she has another card up her sleeve now. Did she fall or was she pushed? Well, I've no idea. Either's possible, knowing Ted. Whichever it was, the threat that Clara might suddenly get her memory back is going to be very useful.

But not to worry, Andy. I'll make sure that Ted pays nothing till she publicly recalls that it was an accident. I think that will be worth a few thou, don't you? And really, Clara deserves a supplement to her meagre inheritance, I think. To Daph in most things she was a very good and faithful servant.

Of course, the big question to such a devotee of justice as yourself is what to do about cunning old, ruthless old Alan Hollis.

Rest easy, Andy. There are some forms of justice best left in the hands of God. Why not leave it to Him to summon Alan to the great central court in the sky where, I do not doubt that, as He dispenses his justice, attending on his right side will be dear old Daphne Denham and on his right revolting old Hen Hollis. How apt it would be if the Lord arranged things so that Alan's comeuppance could be traced, however indirectly, to Daphne herself?

Well, nothing is impossible, Andy. Who should know that better than I?

So there we are. Of course it's going to be hard to prove any of this, and what would be the point? What I say is mostly speculation, Peter's got his result and all you'll do if you try to stir things up is make either him or yourself look an awful ass.

I suppose you could educe this little statement of mine in evidence of *something*. Would it be admissible? I don't know, but, if so, then that would mean that everything you yourself have committed to Mildred (love the name, by the way) would be equally admissible, if anyone had a copy and a reason for publishing it. Our private thoughts can be so embarrassing, not to mention the revelation of all those little corners we've cut, those little pleasures we've enjoyed. I must say I'm surprised at you, Andy, choosing to hide Mildred in the cistern! The indignity to her person apart, nowadays we have all been so educated in criminality by television that it's the first place anyone would look!

But no need to worry about her. She is quite safe. No worries about me either. Restored to rude health by a miracle (and it was a miracle, Andy; with only the timing a little displaced) I shall not readily forget that I owe God a life. I have my literary work, I have my Third Thought mission, I have the woman I love by my side – what possible threat can I pose to the world in general or yourself in particular? Like Scrooge I am a converted sinner. My name will probably descend to future generations as a synonym for benevolence and magnanimity!

So there we are, Andy. Tell Peter I shall drop in on him soon, to let dear Rosie see for herself that I am still the same *upright* young man I always was!

Will our paths cross again?

Of course they will, in this life or the next.

So let me end not with a definitive goodbye, but with a hopeful aufwiedersehen!

By the way, to delete, you just press the small D symbol on the bottom left of the control pad. Then if you want to delete everything press it again.

Be clever, dear Andy, and let who will be good!

Slainte!

3

Andy Dalziel walked clockwise three times round the room then three times widdershins.

This had no superstitious significance, it was simply a reflection of the maelstrom of warring emotions raging around his mind.

Rage indeed was there, rage that the sly serpent Roote had managed to wriggle into his head and leave his slimy trail across the innermost recesses. Fear was there too, fear of what might be the outcome of this invasion. Mildred had been a mistake. From the beginning of time, man had been taught the lesson that confiding your most intimate thoughts to a woman was a recipe for disaster, but still he never learnt!

Yet also there was a sense of self-congratulatory pleasure at having his vague suspicions confirmed. About Roote, about Alan Hollis, about the whole damned business!

Allied with this, however, was guilt. Guilt that he hadn't spoken out. But how could he have done? he defended himself. With Peter Pascoe in charge, everything Dalziel said had rung in his own ears like the smartass commentary of a know-it-all spectator on the touchline. But there was more to it than that, he had to admit. He had repressed his suspicions because he liked Alan Hollis, liked him for his excellent beer and his welcoming manner. What had he called him? The prince of landlords!

Put not your trust in princes!

And there was resentment. Resentment at having this moment of decision thrust upon him just when it felt like he was going to be able to walk away from Sandytown, close that book, put it on the shelf and never open it again. He'd even managed to get his head round the alleged miracle of Roote's cure. It had entertained him to think that now the manipulative bastard was going to be able to shack up openly with Esther Denham. She was very bright and very mixed up, a combination which, with luck, might prove enough to give the doting Roote a taste of his own medicine! Also – a much bigger plus – the 'miracle cure' had acted as the spark to ignite the sexual atmosphere he'd felt surrounding Charley and the healer from the start. Every story should end with at least one couple walking off into the sunset, and it had warmed his cockles to see that ill-matched pair finally getting together.

How the revelation of the truth about everything would affect them, he wasn't sure. Probably not at all. They were young, they were resilient. But there were others who would suffer. He guessed that Cap would forgive his one-off with Pet, but it would mark the end of the unspoken absolute trust he felt existed between them. What would old Fester make of the news that Pet loved him so much she was willing to open her legs to another man on his behalf? Maybe he would remember his own sessions with the Indian Maid. Or maybe he would exercise the ancient right of men to require better behaviour of their women than they could manage themselves.

He was assuming of course that, if he did ignore Roote's advice and stir things up, the scrote would somehow put Mildred on public display.

Of course he would! Why wouldn't he?

What was certain was that a reopening of the case so soon after its apparently satisfactory conclusion was going to make Peter Pascoe look a bit silly, to say the least. Roote, with his own Pascoe brother/father fixation, clearly thought this was the clinching argument for doing nothing.

But why the hell had the toe-rag left his stupid message at all?

What was all that crap about some kinds of justice should be left to God? Was he really beginning to believe that Third Thought rubbish he spouted? The old Roote would surely have known that an Andy Dalziel with vague suspicions might just decide to hold his peace, but giving him certainties could only have one outcome.

He stopped walking. His mind was clear. Only one thing mattered. Daph Denham, that splendid monster of a woman, with more life in her as she approached seventy than most people had at seventeen, was lying dead. And the bastard who killed her was home and free.

No matter what the consequences, Detective Superintendent Andrew Dalziel, Head of Mid-Yorkshire CID, couldn't leave that one to God.

He looked at his watch. Just coming up to six. Hollis would be preparing to open the Hope and Anchor.

The wise thing would be to ring Pete Pascoe and lay it all before him. But Dalziel was finally acknowledging that he didn't have the build or the technique for tip-toeing around his deputy's supposed sensitivities. Any road, to do so was bloody patronizing! Pete was a big boy now, he could look after himself.

And more weighty than any other argument was the burning desire he felt in himself to see Hollis's face when he realized the game was up.

Alan Hollis was his to bring down, no matter what else he brought to ruin with him.

He left his room and went down to Pet Sheldon's office.

She was sitting behind her desk.

'Like to borrow your car again, luv,' he said. 'Last time, eh?'

She sighed and tossed him the keys. She was a grand lass, too good for old Fester, he reckoned. He would miss her.

'Thanks,' he said.

As he turned away she said, 'Oh Andy, someone left this for you. Going-away present, maybe.'

She tossed him a jiffy bag with his name on it.

'More likely a letter bomb,' he said.

He put it on the passenger seat unopened as he drove down the hill into Sandytown.

It was still a minute or two off six as he approached the pub. He saw the front door was still unopened as he turned into the car park. But the rear entrance he'd used on his last visit was ajar.

He was making his way towards it when he heard a woman scream.

He broke into a run. He was out of breath after the first couple of strides, reminding him that the famous curative powers of Sandytown still had a lot of work to do, but he had enough momentum to take him through the doorway and across the kitchen, till he came to a harsh-breathing halt at the head of the cellar steps.

He looked down and saw that God had got there before him.

The single bare bulb cast sharp-edged black shadows over a scene Caravaggio could have painted.

Jenny the barmaid was kneeling among a chaos of beer kegs and splintered wood. Buried beneath it, staring up at her with unseeing eyes, lay Alan Hollis.

Hearing Dalziel's feet on the stairs, Jenny looked round. Her face showed natural shock but she was a strong-nerved Yorkshire lass. One scream, then she'd descended to check out the state of her employer when lots of women would have run outside for help.

'He's gone,' she said, tears welling up in her eyes. 'That old cow did for him in the end. He'd been going on at her for months about getting the cellar sorted, but she were too mean to cough up. And now it's done for him.'

That was no doubt how many in Sandytown would see it, thought Dalziel as he studied the collapsed keg rack. What had gone first wasn't immediately clear, one of the old shelves or one of the supporting props. But once movement started, it would have been as unstoppable as an avalanche.

Others, perhaps, would not blame Daphne, or at least only name her as an instrument of fate. The Hollises were a doomed race, everyone knew that. Even when destiny seemed to give them a break, it never lasted long.

'Nay, lass,' he said as he helped Jenny back up the stairs. 'Let's not rush to blame anyone. It were an act of God.'

Or of his agent, Roote, he thought.

As he summoned Sergeant Whitby and the emergency services, his mind ran and re-ran the implications of what had happened. The case was certainly altered. In every sense.

Could Roote really be responsible for what had happened in the cellar?

Of course he bloody could!

And that would put his recorded message in quite a different light. Now it made sense as a warning not to act precipitately, to sit back and give God a chance. More than a warning. An instruction backed by a threat.

Dalziel didn't like threats. If he'd been the kind of man to concern himself over such things, he might have felt complacent that he'd decided to ignore it in the name of justice. Instead he was asking himself whether that same justice required that he off-loaded on to Pascoe everything he knew or suspected. It wasn't a pleasant prospect, in fact it would be unkind, disruptive and almost certainly ultimately non-productive.

In fact, would he be contemplating it at all if he didn't resent so much the threat that Roote was holding over his head in the shape of Mildred? To ignore a threat for the sake of justice was one thing, to ignore it simply because it really pissed you off was just plain daft!

The debate was still raging in his mind an hour later when he finally left the Hope and Anchor to the emergency services and climbed into Pet's car to return to the Avalon. The weather was on the turn. The bright warm day that had blessed the opening of the Festival of Health was now fading memory, a rising wind was hurrying shreds of cloud along the darkening sky and spattering the windscreen with the first drops of rain.

It was, after all, a Bank Holiday weekend.

As he put the key in the ignition, he noticed the jiffy bag on the passenger seat.

He thought, if it really is a letter bomb, mebbe I

can go back to being a poor old convalescent cop again, only this time, I'll definitely check in at the Cedars!

He picked it up and tore it open.

Out of it slid Mildred.

There was an unsigned note.

Andy, as I told you, I removed Mildred for safe-keeping. Do try to take better care of her in future, and all your womenfolk. Safe journey home!

Dalziel sank back in his seat. A strange feeling was welling up inside him. He resisted it for a moment, then gave in. It was admiration for Franny Roote! You had to give it to the bastard, using the threat of a threat to give pause, but knowing that the reality of the threat might ultimately be counter-productive. Young Charley Heywood could do a lot worse than go to Roote for tutorials!

He started the car, drove out of the car park and turned up the hill to North Cliff.

Suddenly the problem of whether Roote had anything to do with the death of Alan Hollis had ceased to be a problem.

If I'd got to the pub and found him working down in that cellar, I might have pulled the whole bloody issue down on top of him myself! thought Dalziel.

So let it go! The buck stops with the man at the top, and that's me!

As for Franny Roote, let the clever bugger win this battle. There was a whole lifetime ahead to sort out the war!

He wound down the window. Suddenly the cold wild weather seemed his proper element to be revelled in, not shut out.

'Watch out, you scrotes!' he bellowed out of the open window. 'Dalziel's back!'

A blast of wind with half the North Sea on its back blew his words back into the car.

He wound up the window hastily.

He didn't give a toss what Tom Parker said, any fool knew there was nowt like a cold sea breeze for giving a man a nasty cold!

Ahead of him as he crossed the town boundary at the foot of South Cliff, the wind caught at a colourful banner stretched across the road, tossed it high, snapped a cord, and twisted it into an unreadable plait. It didn't matter. He'd read it on the way down.

Welcome to Sandytown, Home of the Healthy Holiday!

'Sod that,' said Andy Dalziel. 'If that's what healthy holidays do for you, I think I'll take up smoking again!'

On Beulah Height

Reginald Hill

They moved everyone out of Dendale that long hot summer fifteen years ago. They needed a new reservoir and an old community seemed a cheap price to pay. They even dug up the dead and moved them too.

But four inhabitants of the valley they couldn't move, for no one knew where they were. Three little girls had gone missing, and the prime suspect in their disappearance, Benny Lightfoot.

This was Andy Dalziel's worst case and now fifteen years on he looks set to relive it. It's another long hot summer. A child goes missing in the next valley, and old fears resurface as someone sprays the deadly message on the walls of Danby: BENNY'S BACK!

Music and myth mingle as the Mid-Yorkshire team delve into their pasts and into their own reserves of experience and endurance in search of answers which threaten to bring more pain than they resolve.

'All Reginald Hill's novels are brilliantly written, but he has excelled himself here: and has, too, put together an intricate narrative with the complex ingenuity of a watch-maker' T. J. BINYON, *Evening Standard*

ISBN: 0 00 649000 X

Arms and the Women

Reginald Hill

When Ellie Pascoe finds herself under threat, the men in her life assume it's because she's married to a cop. But while they trawl after shoals of red herrings, Ellie is blasted off course with a motley crew of women on a voyage of discovery whose perils make Scylla and Charybdis look like a pair of Barbie dolls.

Irish arms, Colombian drugs, and men who will stop at nothing, create a tidal wave which threatens to sweep her away. She heads out of town in search of haven, but instead finds herself at the very edge of the storm in a remote clifftop house undermined by the sea where she must reach deep down into her reserves to find the strength to survive.

'Luminously written, thrilling in the best old-fashioned sense of the word'   *Daily Mail*

ISBN: 0 00 651287 9

Good Morning, Midnight

Reginald Hill

Like father like son…

But heredity seems to have gone a gene too far when Pal Maciver's suicide in a locked room exactly mirrors that of his father ten years earlier.

In each case, accusing fingers point towards Pal's step-mother, the beautiful enigmatic Kay Kafka. But she turns out to have a formidable champion in Mid-Yorkshire's own super-heavyweight, Detective Superintendent Andrew Dalziel.

Gradually, it becomes clear that the fall-out from Pal's suicide spreads far beyond Yorkshire. To London, to America. Even to Iraq. But the emotional epicentre is firmly placed here in Mid-Yorkshire, where Pascoe comes to learn that for some people the heart, too, is a locked room – and in there, it is always midnight.

'Unfolds compellingly and displays all his familiar intelligence and wit. *Good Morning, Midnight* shows Hill on top form'
Sunday Times

'The writing is brilliant, witty and erudite…as enjoyable as anything Reginald Hill has ever produced'
Evening Standard

'Literate without being pedantic, humorous without undercutting suspense, Hill's book will keep you reading far beyond the midnight hour'
Sunday Express

ISBN 0 00 712343 4

The Stranger House

Reginald Hill

They came to The Stranger House. And death followed close behind.

For over 500 years, the Stranger House has stood in the village of Illthwaite, offering refuge to all manner of travellers. People like Sam Flood, a brilliant young Australian mathematician. And Miguel Madero, a Spanish historian who sees ghosts.

Sam is an experienced young woman, Miguel a 26-year-old virgin. But both want to dig up bits of the past that some people would rather keep buried.

As they uncover intertwining tales of murder, betrayal and love, they must put aside their differences in order to uncover the dark mysteries at the heart of this ancient place...

'Grim, gory, fascinating, enraging and entertaining'
Independent

'A mystery novel but far more than that. It's gripping... Hill is wonderful' *The Times*

'You're enthralled by the cunning of the plotting... great'
Observer

ISBN-13: 978-0-00-719483-4